THE ENDEAVOUR OF ELSIE MACKAY

THE ENDEAVOUR OF ELSIE MACKAY

FLORA JOHNSTON

Allison & Busby Limited
11 Wardour Mews
London W1F 8AN
allisonandbusby.com

First published in Great Britain by Allison & Busby in 2025.

First Edition

ISBN 978-0-7490-3137-4

Typeset in 11/15.5 pt Adobe Garamond Pro by Allison & Busby Ltd.

By choosing this product, you help take care of the world's forests.
Learn more: www.fsc.org.

Printed and bound in the UK using 100% Renewable Electricity at
CPI Group (UK) Ltd, Croydon, CR0 4YY

In memory of Elsie Mackay.

And dedicated to Jane, Catriona and Sandy, who also heard her story from the original storyteller.

13th March, 1928

Afterwards, even those who were present couldn't be sure what had taken place in the eerie grey morning light.

'There were two of them in flying suits. You couldn't make out who they were.'

'No, there were definitely three. One was much smaller; that would be her.'

'Ah, but I saw the woman driven away by a chauffeur in that flashy monogrammed car. I'll swear she didn't get in the plane.'

'They're only going to Dublin anyway. They've been ordered to move the machine to Baldonnel Airfield.'

'Don't be a fool. Did you see the weight of that aeroplane? Could barely get off the ground. She's loaded for a much longer journey than Ireland.'

'That's because they're headed for India; the captain's chasing the long-distance air record.'

'There's a fortune on offer for the first aviator to fly west across the Atlantic and reach Philadelphia. If anyone can do it he can.'

'Not in weather like this.'

'It will be the woman's fault. Women have no business in aeroplanes.'

'I tell you, I saw her drive away in the car. She's a financial backer, that's all.'

'More money than sense, then.'

'If she is on that plane she'll be the first woman to fly the Atlantic. And good luck to her I say.'

They slipped out of their Grantham hotel in darkness, unobserved. The cars took different routes, for one had an important detour to make. Snow had fallen heavily all week, adding to the ethereal atmosphere as the first light of morning spread over the still, silent airfield. Bundled in their flying suits, the pilots – two or three – wheeled *Endeavour* from her hangar. Sleek black and gold against the white snow, she was a thing of beauty right enough. Her gold-painted wings had reflected the sun's brilliant glory on hour after hour of test flight over Lincolnshire; now they glowed with quiet, steady warmth, softening the monochrome chill.

Those few people who knew what was going on huddled together, going over charts, their breath rising in clouds up into the air that would soon carry all their dreams. Such long months of planning, such careful weeks of preparation, such difficult days of frustration when it had seemed all their efforts might come to nothing.

It was now or never.

Flight fever was everywhere in 1928. Barely a week went by without another hopeful record attempt. Cinema newsreels showed smiling adventurers taking to the skies; newspapers printed column after column about the lives and families and dreams of these modern pioneers, glorying in each rare triumph, picking apart each all-too-common disaster. Trailblazers or reckless fools? No one could quite decide.

There were no cameras at Cranwell today. No newspaper men, no sponsors, no families brimful of pride and fear. It was all so low-key, so *unlikely* in this weather, that most of those present believed the machine was simply being moved to its new location in Ireland. Any greater purpose was shrouded in secrecy as thick as that blanket of snow.

But for those who cared to notice, there was a tension in the air. A sense of significance in those final tightly clasped handshakes. They climbed into the machine, and out, and in again, until no one was quite sure whether two or three remained on board as she throbbed into life and slowly began to churn up the snow-covered runway.

It was said to be the longest runway in the country and *Endeavour* made full use of it, trundling along at first, faster and faster and faster, straining every strut and bolt as she gathered speed, tossing up a blizzard behind her. Far away, so very far away, nearly a mile along that runway she rose slowly, sweetly into the air and soared towards those heavy, snow-laden clouds. The group of mechanics waited as the roar faded, as she disappeared westwards, then stamped their numb feet and hurried towards the shed, eager for the warmth of the brazier and a much-needed cup of tea.

Endeavour circled, dipped a wing and was gone, carrying the mysterious aviators westwards to their destiny.

Now or never.

PART 4

April 1917

~~~

April to August 1917

I have been long of opinion that . . . . of . . . and that for years . . . .

PART ONE
Ambition

.∾ᦣᦉᦣ∾.

April to August 1927

I have been long of opinion that, instead of the tardy conveyance
of ships and chariots, man might use the swifter migration of
wings, that the fields of air are open to knowledge, and that only
ignorance and idleness need crawl upon the ground.

The History of Rasselas, Prince of Abissinia, Samuel Johnson, 1759

Chapter One

In the steamy warmth of the Garnethill kitchen, Alison could hear the low hum of voices that meant her son-in-law Rob was with a patient in his little consulting room. She glanced at the clock on the mantelpiece above the gleaming black range. Stella would be home with the children soon, and their return was always boisterous. She'd have to intercept them and usher them quickly into the kitchen.

She pushed aside the P&O brochure that had been spread open before her on the table and turned to place the kettle on the range to heat. Stretching up, she checked that the washing on the pulley was dry, then removed the items, folding them and laying them on the kitchen bed for now. They'd have to be cleared from there before the boys went to bed, mind you. Bread and jam, a pot of tea, and she was just collecting the crock of butter from the little scullery off the kitchen when she heard a door opening and a woman's voice followed by Rob's tones. Good, his patient was leaving. They could have their tea in peace, and maybe he would even manage to join them.

She laid the butter on the table, but just as she did so she heard the outer door bang and footsteps running through the close. Too late! Most of Rob's patients were indulgent of his small family but he did have the odd crusty customer who wouldn't take kindly to being barged aside by Duncan and Jacky. Alison hurried into the shadowy hallway, ready to scoop up her grandsons. Amid a flurry of noise and movement she was aware of Stella's delighted exclamation, of a woman in fur coat and chic hat, an embrace and an urging to stay for tea, before Duncan barrelled into her and threw his arms around her waist with all his five-year-old energy. 'Gran, Gran, Gran, we saw the monkey man, we saw the monkey man.'

And then the visitor was gone and Rob retreated to his consulting room, promising the boys he would join them in a few minutes. Stella hung up her coat and hat and sent the boys to wash their hands as she fetched beakers for their milk. Alison poured the tea, and both women sat down at the table. 'That was Elsie, wasn't it?' Alison asked.

'It was. She's had trouble with a persistent sore throat and their own doctor has been no use so I suggested she see Rob next time she was in Glasgow.' The boys reappeared and for a moment or two Stella was busy settling them with their bread and jam. Then she glanced across at her mother. 'She's exactly the sort of contact Rob needs, you know. She might help him find some wealthier patients.'

Alison was silent. She had heard her daughter on this topic before. It was hard not to, sharing a house as they did here in Garnethill, on the north-western edge of the city centre. It had seemed perfect when they moved in together soon after Jacky's birth, pooling their resources to afford a property with a much-prized private bathroom and enough space for them all. It was on the ground floor of the tenement building, ideal both for Rob's patients and for Stella manoeuvring the heavy pram. The children slept in the closet bed in the kitchen, and Alison had her own room with enough space for the few items of furniture she had saved from their family home in Thurso. The other small room was fitted out for Rob's consultations. This left only the parlour, but as in many Glasgow tenements another double bed was hidden in the wall there, behind painted wooden shutters, and that would do for Rob and Stella. 'We mostly live in the kitchen anyway,' Stella had laughed, 'and when we do want to use the parlour we close the shutters and no one even knows the bed is there.'

Rob had trained as a surgeon before the war, but the toll of those years at the front had left him with unsteady hands, occasional blinding headaches and an impatience with the establishment. He had thrown himself into helping recovering soldiers and sailors at the Princess Louise hospital for amputees at Erskine, but when his work there came to an end he decided to set up a private medical practice in Garnethill. Stella polished the plate he had screwed into the doorway, rubbing her cloth carefully over the letters Dr R. CAMPBELL M.B. Ch.B., and saw her hope and pride reflecting back at her in its blurry brass surface.

Three years later, however, Alison watched as her daughter became increasingly discontented. Garnethill hadn't provided the influx of wealthy patients she had hoped for, and Stella was now beginning to speak about moving further out of the city into one of the new bungalows being built in leafy villages like Bearsden.

'The boys will need a room of their own one day,' she reminded Rob at regular intervals. 'It would be nice to have *both* a parlour and a bedroom, don't you think? That's not such an unreasonable thing to wish for.'

Alison would have moved out to give the young family more space, but Stella didn't want that either, relying on her help with the children and the housework. It would be interesting to see how they all got on if Alison took up her sister's suggestion of a few weeks at sea!

Rob entered the room, pulling her back into the moment. 'Tea?

Yes thanks, I'm gasping.' He dropped down beside his sons, who had long since finished eating and were playing with toy cars on the floor. Alison watched him as Stella buttered him a scone. He looked peaky again, she decided, as he ruffled Duncan's fair hair and took his place at the table. Those dark shadows under his eyes usually meant the headaches he had endured since the war were bothering him. But he carried on, just as they all did, and if his patients noticed the slight shake in his hands or the strain in his voice, they were reassured by the warmth and empathy in his manner.

'How did you get on with Elsie?' Stella asked as she passed him his tea.

'Fine.'

'Fine? Is that all?'

'Stella, I can't discuss a patient's business, even if she is your friend. *Especially* if she is your friend, in fact.'

'Don't be absurd, I'm not looking for medical details. What I mean is – was she happy? Do you think she will see you again?'

Rob passed his hand over his eyes. 'How should I know? I always aim to leave my patients happy.'

'Oh, don't be so stuffy. Will she recommend you to her friends? You do need to find some wealthier patients, you know.'

Here she goes again. Alison felt the familiar surge of irritation and clattered the children's dishes together, taking them through to the scullery. Really, Stella was being impossible at the moment, but it would only make matters worse if she were to wade into the discussion herself, as she was tempted to do. As she ran the plates under the tap, Alison thought again about the elegant woman in the fur coat and smart hat. The Honourable Miss Elsie Mackay. She wondered how much the friendship had to do with Stella's current discontent – but on the other hand, she had to acknowledge that her daughter, worn down by the monotony of housekeeping and child-raising as many young women were, was rarely as full of life and sparkle as when she spent time with Elsie.

The strangest coincidence had brought them back together. Stella had often spoken of meeting Elsie in those far-off days in Paris in 1919, back when she was a typist with the peace conference and Elsie was a rising film star using the pseudonym Poppy Wyndham, darling of the newspapers because of her beauty, her charm and the romantic story of her elopement and disinheritance. Alison herself remembered seeing Poppy Wyndham in several pictures, including *A Son of David* where she played alongside Ronald Colman. Stella had treasured the crumpled card the actress had given her, and repeated her words: *I feel sure we shall meet again.* And five years later they had.

By that time Poppy Wyndham was no more. Elsie's marriage was over and she had returned to her maiden name and the forgiving embrace of her father, who just happened to be one of the richest and most powerful men in British industry. James Mackay, Viscount Inchcape, was chairman of P&O, the biggest shipping company in the world, and divided his time between a grand townhouse in fashionable London and the seclusion of Glenapp Castle in Ayrshire.

Elsie turned her back on acting and found a new passion for interior design, taking responsibility for the creation and maintenance of the living quarters across her father's extensive fleet. She had been in Glasgow for the launch of one of these ships on the Clyde when she and Stella encountered one another again. Alison was in Aberdeen with her sister Maggie, but remembered the letter she had received from her daughter.

I would never have gone out at all if I'd realised the crowds were so thick and the day so hot, but I thought it would amuse Duncan to see the ship being launched. As it was he had a tantrum and I had to carry him, and my morning sickness was worse than ever. I really thought I would faint, and I fought through the crowds to the side of the road where I had to sit down on the kerb or I'd have collapsed. Well, wasn't this sleek silver Rolls-Royce driving past just at that time. The woman inside ordered her chauffeur to stop and jumped out to see if I was all right. She took us into her car – that cheered Duncan up – and once her chauffeur had dropped her beside her father she ordered him to drive us home. I knew who she was, of course, but she didn't recognise me so I didn't say anything. Later in the day she called round to see how we were, so I explained then and invited her in for a cup of tea!

From that day an unlikely but, as far as Alison could see, genuine friendship had flourished between them. Every few months when Elsie was in Glasgow, Stella left the children with her mother and met her friend for a stroll in the botanics or tea in the Willow Tea Rooms in Sauchiehall Street, while magnificent presents arrived for the boys at Christmas and on their birthdays.

With tea finished, the boys ran outside to play in the back green with the other children from the surrounding tenements. That was another gripe of Stella's; she wanted to be able to open her back door and let her children out into their own private garden. Alison came back to the table, where Rob and Stella had both lit up cigarettes and Rob was reading the newspaper. Stella picked up the discarded P&O brochure and looked at the colourful picture on the front of elegantly dressed men and women playing tennis on a ship's deck in front of two gleaming funnels. 'What's this?'

'Maggie sent it to me. She has suggested we take a pleasure cruise in September.'

'Goodness! Will you?'

'I think I might. It's a while since we had a holiday together.'

Stella turned the pages. 'Looks lovely. Is it this one?'

'The *Ranchi* – to the Mediterranean.'

'How funny. I believe that's one of Elsie's ships.' She looked up. 'Can you afford it?'

Alison tried not to sound defensive. 'I can. We don't need a *cabin-de-luxe*. You know I've been careful with the Thurso money, and it was always my plan to use some of it to travel. And besides, it will give you young ones some time without me under your feet.'

'What, to go dancing?' Stella threw a glance at her husband but his face remained buried in his newspaper. 'Hardly. And besides, I certainly don't feel young any more. Not at thirty-two.'

The grand old age of thirty-two. Perhaps it wasn't Alison who needed a holiday, perhaps it was Stella. 'Will you manage a holiday this year?' she asked. 'Rob?'

Rob looked up. 'What's that? A holiday? Oh, I dare say we'll take the boys to Rothesay for a week or two. What do you think, Stella?'

'We always go to Rothesay. Last year we went during Glasgow Fair and the steamers were packed and the guesthouses so busy, it was hard to keep track of the boys on the beach. I'd like to go somewhere different. If we wait until August it will be quieter and perhaps Corran would join us. It's a few years since she's done that.'

Corran, Alison's eldest daughter, far away in Oxford with her books and her secrets.

'That's a good idea,' Alison said. 'And I have another one. If I do decide to take this cruise in September, how about the two of you take off for a few days yourselves before that and I look after the boys?'

'Would you really? I mean, would you manage on your own?'

I managed to raise four of you with a husband away at sea and I already do the lion's share of housework in this place. Not that you notice. 'I'm sure I'll manage, dear, and if not I can ask Luisa to come over and help.'

19

'Well, if you're sure – that would be rather nice, wouldn't it, Rob? We could go to a hotel.'

Rob looked dubious. 'I'm not sure we can afford that.'

'We'll just have to afford it.'

Perhaps wisely, Rob said nothing. Instead he folded up his newspaper and got to his feet. 'I promised to take some books over to Alex for young Danny Aitken – you know, the lad whose father I helped a few weeks ago. Do either of you want to join me?'

'You go,' Stella said to her mother. 'I'll stay with the boys and put them to bed. I've walked far enough today and my feet are killing me.'

Alison hesitated. It might be good for Stella and Rob to have an hour or two together; on the other hand, the mood Stella was in they would probably just bicker. She herself had been busy in the house all day and would welcome both the walk and the chance to see her son and daughter-in-law Alex and Luisa. 'Thank you. I'd love to come.'

As she crossed the hallway to her bedroom to get ready, Alison marvelled again that she could visit Alex, her eldest son – her only surviving son – whenever she wanted. He had gone to sea as a boy of sixteen, and she had become accustomed to a relationship of long absences and occasional stilted letters (*The grub is not too bad. China is hot. In Gibraltar and the Rock is fine*), broken by precious spells of leave. But four years ago Alex had shocked them all, returning from a spell in the Mediterranean with a young Italian bride, Luisa. He continued in the navy at first, but Luisa was desperately unhappy without him. Alison had deep misgivings when her sea-loving son resigned from the navy and found himself work with the great shipbuilding firm of Alexander Stephen and Co. at Linthouse, overseeing the sea worthiness and sea trials of the vast liners and cargo vessels that they launched into the waters of the Clyde. How could Alex, with saltwater coursing through his veins, possibly relinquish a life of wide horizons and exotic ports for the crowded streets and noisy factories of Scotland's biggest city? And yet, despite his mother's scepticism, he did. 'I've had enough of that life,' he told her. 'I'm ready to settle down with a home and a family now.'

As Alison pulled on her gloves she reflected that although the longed-for family had not yet arrived, Alex and Luisa appeared to be happy, with the rich cloak of their good-humoured love protecting them from the challenges of their mixed marriage. Luisa's English, already serviceable, had improved greatly and she had many friends among the vibrant Italian community in Glasgow. Alison was very fond of her daughter-in-law, and it was with pleasurable anticipation that she walked down the hill into the city centre beside Rob to catch a tram out to Partick, where Alex and Luisa lived in a lovely two-bedroomed tenement, always beautifully kept.

The city was at last emerging from the gloom of winter, and hazy low sunlight glinted between tall buildings, softening their black sootiness. The sharp April wind blew the smoke and the odours through the streets, even if it didn't quite disperse them. Alison had grown up on the shores of Loch Linnhe and then lived her married life in Thurso, breathing fresh sea air. Glasgow was full of people like her. As she walked through the city she liked to identify the different accents: Highland voices, Gaelic voices, Galloway voices, and that's before you listened to the Irishwoman leaning out the window and calling for her bairns or the Italian couple chatting away behind the counter in their own language. All these people from their own vast landscapes, thrown together in these narrow closes and trying to survive in the smog.

She missed the open skies and she missed her garden, but Glasgow had some fine green spaces and she had her family about her. Still, perhaps it was time for a break. She had slipped the P&O brochure into her bag to show to Alex and Luisa. Would she go?

She rather thought she would.

Chapter Two

Glasgow

Rob offered his arm to his mother-in-law as they stepped down from the tram and made their way along Dumbarton Road. There were people all around them: workers hurrying home after a shift; clusters of lads hanging about on street corners; a young couple furtively embracing in the shadows of a close. As a rowdy group of men spilt out of the pub on the corner, the smell of beer drifted through the swinging doors, calling to his thirst. Maybe Alex would offer him a whisky.

Alex and Luisa lived on the second floor, and as they climbed the stairs Alison remarked on the sparkling cleanliness of the stair with its attractive wally tiles. 'See how her doorhandle and letterbox shine too.'

Rob wasn't sure if her praise implied a criticism of Stella's housekeeping, but chose to ignore this as they knocked on the door. Silence was often the best policy when caught between his wife and mother-in-law. A shadow appeared briefly behind the stained-glass oval window, before Luisa opened the door with an exclamation. '*Benvenuti*! Come in, come in. There is tea. Come.'

Tea!

Rob followed Luisa through to the parlour, where they were soon seated with cups of tea and some sort of sweetbread that Luisa explained she had obtained from Fazzi's, the newly opened shop selling all sorts of Italian foodstuffs. 'It is heaven!'

'Alex liked a piece of clootie dumpling when he was a lad,' Alison said, eyeing the sweetbread suspiciously. 'I can't imagine that's changed.'

Alex grinned at his mother from his seat by the fire, his long legs stretched out in front of him, his face brown and weathered from his years at sea. 'Why should it be one or the other?' he asked. Then he turned to Rob. 'Got those books? Thank you, Danny will be pleased. He'd just begun algebra at school before he had to leave to work in the yard. His headmaster wanted him to stay on but there was no question of that; he's the eldest boy in a long family and they need his wages. But Danny's determined to keep learning at night classes, so I said I'd see if I could find him some books.'

'I've my old school algebra here and a geometry book too. Does he have a goal in mind?'

'I asked him that. His headmaster thought he was bright enough for the Tech, but the lad knows that's not possible. He has his eye on a move into the drawing offices. He has a neat hand and a sharp mind, but he lacks the training.'

Rob nodded, thinking back to the evening a few weeks earlier when he and Alex had been walking home after a drink together and had come across a distraught young Danny Aitken, whom Alex knew from the shipyard. His father, Geordie, had had an accident at the yard that day and had taken a turn for the worse in the evening. To complicate matters, his mother was in labour with child number seven. They had followed him to the crowded room-and-kitchen where Rob had been able to reduce the father's

23

fever while a local woman helped the mother. 'How is his father?' he asked Alex now.

'Back to work, thanks to you.' Alex hesitated. 'There's something I want to ask you about that, actually. Fancy a pint?'

I thought you'd never ask!

'Rob and I are popping out for a quick one. All right, my love?'

Luisa was showing her mother-in-law an embroidered cushion that she had just completed. She looked up with a smile. 'You boys have fun, but don't be too long.'

Rob watched the tender kiss between Alex and Luisa, and thought of the prickly atmosphere that often pervaded his own house these days. Stella was always tired, that was the trouble. It was easy for Luisa with no small children to care for, although of course he would never say that out loud. Still, how good to get out for a couple of hours and share a drink with his brother-in-law.

The pub was packed, and they found themselves a space at the corner of the bar, deep conversation and laughter swirling around them. Rob breathed in the smell of beer mixed with cigarette smoke that had tantalised him earlier, and felt himself relax. 'What was it you wanted to ask me?'

Alex lit up and slid an overflowing ashtray between them. 'I have a proposition for you. From Mr Fred Stephen, you know, the director of the shipyard.'

'Oh aye? What could anything at your shipyard have to do with me?' He sipped his beer, savouring the taste, the feel of the cool liquid sliding down his throat.

'I mentioned what happened that night with Geordie Aitken to Fred Stephen, and how he's back working because of you. They're a grand employer, you know, they like to do right by their men. They have all sorts of welfare schemes: a canteen, evening classes and the like. Turns out Mr Stephen's been thinking for some time about how to improve medical care for the workers. We've an ambulance room for immediate treatment of men who suffer an accident at work, but there are other conditions that prevent a chap doing his job properly and may lead to him being dismissed, but that if they were caught sooner might be treatable. Mr Stephen would like to hold a clinic on site in the shipyard one day a week where workers with medical complaints can see a doctor, subject to permission from the foreman. Would you be interested? Your pay would come direct from Stephen's, who would collect subs from the men. I think it's a grand scheme!'

Alex's enthusiasm was infectious but Rob hesitated. He knew just what Stella would think of this idea – yet another distraction to pull him away from the wealthy patients she was so desperate to cultivate. 'I'd need to know a bit more,' he said. 'Salary, provision of medicines and the like.'

'Of course. I'll set up a meeting for you with Mr Stephen if you're interested. Do say you'll do it, Rob. You're just the right man.' He paused. 'The workers at the yard – they're good chaps, but it's not everyone who could get alongside them. But I know you will. You went through the war with lads just like them.'

And that was it. He felt the hairs on his arms prickle. The war. That was the reason he missed his work at the Princess Louise hospital so much; that was the reason he found it hard to relate to the cossetted patients who now came his way. Those years he had spent as medical officer to his regiment, eating, drinking and sleeping among them, treating their physical ailments and listening to their troubles, following them into battle and doing his hopeless, inadequate best to deal with whatever came their way. The war had left its mark on him, trembling hands and blinding headaches only the more obvious consequences, but there was an honesty in his relationships with those men that he had found nowhere else other than in his days playing rugby. And that was a whole different story.

He drained his glass and signalled to the barman for another. 'It's tempting,' he said. 'I'm not sure Stella will like the idea, though. On the other hand, I can present it to her as regular income, if the pay is good enough.'

'I can't imagine money being a problem.'

'How's the shipyard order book looking?'

'We laid down the hull of a magnificent new P&O passenger liner just last week,' said Alex, who seemed to have found some sort of land-based fulfilment in the fashioning of the ships in which he had once sailed the seas. 'There was a boom after the war as owners replaced vessels they'd lost. That could never last, and there have been some lean years since. But our yard has the expertise to produce the latest technology and so Lord Inchcape, the chairman of P&O, came to us. This will be the first British passenger liner fitted with turbo-electric machinery, and she'll go like a dream when she's launched.'

They finished their drinks and returned to the house, where Rob excused himself to use the bathroom. Like themselves, Alex and Luisa had their own private bathroom rather than the shared toilets on each floor that many of the older tenement buildings still had. Even this little room had daffodils on the windowsill and a delicate lace curtain to screen the tiny window from surrounding buildings, no doubt made by Luisa. Coming back through, he found the other three poring over the P&O brochure and discussing Alison's proposed cruise.

'What ports will you visit?'

'Quite a number in Spain and southern France, but we also stop in Naples.'

'*Napoli!*' Luisa's deep brown eyes sparkled with delight. '*Bellissimo!* I shall write to my father and he will meet you and show you our beautiful city. And my little brother Giovanni you shall come to know too. Oh, if only I could come with you.'

'It will be interesting to hear what Luisa's father has to say,' Alex said soberly. 'We know he can't write freely in his letters.'

The excitement left Luisa's eyes. 'Indeed. The new laws in Italy mean he is no longer free to write what he thinks, whether in his letters to his daughter or in his newspaper. I hope he is not a fool to become involved in politics, but I fear he may. And yet, other friends tell me that life is much better since Mussolini came to power: the streets are clean, there is far less crime and even the trains run on time.'

'If that's true it's a miracle. Do you remember, Luisa, that day I was supposed to rejoin the ship in La Spezia and my train didn't appear?'

'You thought you would be put on trial for not returning but I found a shopkeeper with a load of wine to transport in a trailer and you travelled among the barrels.'

'Aye, and one of them had a slow but satisfying leak! I was in danger of being put on a charge of drunkenness rather than absence by the time I got there!' They all laughed, and Alex held out his hand for the brochure. He flicked through, interested not in the destinations but in the ships. 'The passenger liner is the future of shipbuilding. Cargo and freight are slow these days, but there are ever more people keen to sail on these luxury ships.'

The conversation continued and Rob leant back in his chair. Working at a shipyard? He had never imagined it. Alex and Luisa lived just a stone's throw from the river, along which stretched a metal forest of cranes, engine sheds and workshops, the vital organs of this city. Every detail that went into the creation of the 'Clyde-built' ships, long the envy of the world, could be found along this riverside, from the drawing offices where designs were perfected to the squads of riveters who joined the vast iron plates together, the engine and boiler shops, the carpenters, turners, polishers and plumbers. The thundering, beating heart of Glasgow, so very far removed from the genteel streets where he and his family lived, and even further from the life to which Stella aspired. He remembered his visit to the Aitkens' room-and-kitchen, a family of nine living out their lives in a tiny space. And they were lucky ones with regular wages coming in. Medical care was needed in the shipyard, and if he had the opportunity to provide it to men like those he had worked alongside in wartime, he would be glad to say yes.

Alison was on her feet, and it was time to return home to Stella and the children. 'Alex and I will walk with you to the tram stop,' Luisa said. 'We like to stretch our bodies for bed.'

'Stretch our *legs*. *Before* bed,' Alex said with a wide grin. 'We tend not to talk about the rest of what we stretch! Especially in front of our parents.' He winked at Rob, who smirked.

Alison shook her head. 'You young ones act as if yours was the first generation to discover sex.'

'Mother!'

'Well, really, Alex. Where exactly do you think you came from if that was the case?' She pulled on her hat and stalked out into the hallway, leaving her son wrong-footed.

Rob grinned at Alex and followed her out, calling 'I'll let you know about the yard,' as he left.

Chapter Three

London and Paris

Elsie gave a quick wave to the gatekeeper and leant back against the soft cushioned leather as her silver Rolls-Royce slowly exited Tilbury Docks. She preferred to drive herself home from work but today she was not returning home to Seamore Place but instead travelling south-east to Croydon, where she would board the Imperial Airways service to join her parents in Paris for a few days.

She hadn't planned to come into the docks this morning, but had woken in the night with the horrible realisation that she had completely overlooked one tourist class corridor on her inspection of the newly returned *Cathay*. She could have telephoned the office to ask someone to carry out the work for her, but preferred to check everything herself. It was a habit she had absorbed from her father. And so there was an early start – nothing unusual there – a rigorous examination of the overlooked rooms with subsequent report left for Miss Taylor to type up and pass on to the maintenance team, and a hurried journey across country to the airfield.

As with driving, she would rather fly herself than be a passenger, but the Imperial Airways service was wonderfully convenient and on the whole reliable. It was one thing to jump in her de Havilland biplane and fly north to Glenapp Castle, landing in the field they kept cut short for the purpose, and quite another to obtain permission to fly into Paris – particularly today. Elsie had picked up *The Times* from the breakfast table as she left the house, and now she turned the pages to see if there was anything about the American man's flight. Her attention was caught by their own advert for P&O pleasure cruises on the *Ranchi*, and she scanned the page for the competition: Canadian Pacific, White Star Line, and there was Cunard with her grand liners *Aquitania* and *Berengaria*. A page of dreams. Still, none of them had anything remotely approaching the marvel that would be the newest P&O liner, whose hull had been laid down on the Clyde just last month and whose elegant apartments and luxurious facilities, existing so far only inside Elsie's head, would surpass anything yet seen in the ocean liner market.

But today aeroplanes rather than ships were on Elsie's mind as she turned the pages. A friend had telephoned her last night to tell her that another attempt to win the Orteig Prize for the first non-stop flight between New York and Paris was underway. Yes, here it was, his name was Captain Charles Lindbergh and he had taken off from Long Island yesterday morning in his monoplane *Spirit of St Louis*. His machine had been spotted a couple of times heading for Newfoundland, but right now he was somewhere out there in the vast emptiness over the Atlantic Ocean. Elsie had once crossed the Atlantic by magnificent liner and knew what it was to stand at the rail and see nothing but sea and sky as far as the eye could reach, with more stars than one could imagine scattered over the night sky, but that couldn't begin to compare with the isolation, and yes, the splendour, of a tiny monoplane striving across that wide, wild expanse. If he was still in the air at all, that was. Many before him had tried and failed, and even now the search was underway for the wreckage and bodies of two Frenchmen, Nungesser and Coli, who had been lost in the same enterprise just a couple of weeks earlier.

Elsie folded the newspaper and held it tight between her hands, so tightly that her knuckles were white. She didn't know this young American, had never heard of him until the last day or two, but dear God let him make it. Surely soon someone would make it. The technology was there and the rewards for the future of aviation would be immeasurable. How fortuitous that if this flight were successful she would by some chance be in Paris at the very time he touched down at Le Bourget Aerodrome. She slipped her fingers into her bag where she kept her rosary and felt the beads. Chance or design? As her chauffeur pulled into the airfield at Croydon and she stepped out of the car into the soft warm May air, she found herself scanning the skies although she knew he would not fly near here. Up there – somewhere – in the only place where it was still possible to be free. Her mouth was dry as she crossed the grass towards the aircraft that would carry her to Paris, thinking not of her own flight but of the young man even now engaged in the supreme battle with his human weakness and all that the elements would throw at him. Godspeed!

She settled herself in one of the wicker chairs laid out along the aeroplane. There were about twenty of them flying today. She looked to the front to see if it was the pilot with the eyepatch – rather extraordinary when you came to think of it – but it was not. Elsie always watched take-off with great concentration, more aware than her fellow passengers of all that could go wrong at the critical moment. And then they were gaining speed and there was a lurch as the miracle happened and they left land behind, committing themselves to the air currents that, if given due respect, would carry them with infinite grace.

* * *

'There's no better way to travel,' she said to her father later that evening, as they returned after dinner to the luxurious suite in the Hotel Majestic on the avenue Kléber, which her parents had taken for the month of May. Her mother, easily tired after her long illness, had retired to bed, and Elsie and her father stood by the magnificent window, looking down on revellers below. Car horns were hooting and people were cheering, as they celebrated the landing of the *Spirit of St Louis* at Le Bourget. Charles Lindbergh had succeeded! The flight from New York to Paris had been completed in just over thirty-three hours. The world had become a little smaller, a little more connected, in this triumph of human endeavour.

James Lyle Mackay, Lord Inchcape, shook his white head dismissively and stepped over to the sideboard where he poured two glasses of port. He handed one to his daughter and sat down, while Elsie remained by the window. 'It's all very well for an adventurer like that young man, but it will be a long time before sensible Mr and Mrs British Public entrust their lives to some flimsy steel tube dressed up with canvas. You know I won't set foot in one of those things, and most sane people think like me.'

'That's where a day like today makes such a difference,' Elsie argued, coming to sit opposite him and leaning forward in her eagerness. 'Lindbergh has shown that it *can* be done. Think what that means for commerce, for diplomacy, for administering the colonies. As a company, this is the perfect time for us to embrace the new technology of air travel. After all, you've always been keen to adopt other new ideas that have made our ships faster and more efficient and safer.'

'Safer. That's the thing. The safety record of P&O across our cargo and passenger fleet is second to none, and that's why people sail with us. I won't have our good name tarnished by being mixed up with such a daredevil and downright dangerous enterprise as your commercial air service notion. Every day I read of another air crash in the newspapers. I won't have it, Elsie, and frankly I don't know why I allow you to continue to fly that plane of yours.'

She shook her head in exasperation but said no more, instead crossing back to look out of the window again. She had probably been foolish to reopen the conversation at all – as if the old man had ever been known to change his mind – but she had been intoxicated by her sheer delight at Lindbergh's success and had hoped that he might see that on this day another enormous obstacle to human progress had been overcome. What opportunity that offered to P&O, and how desperately she wanted to be part of it. But her father was implacably opposed to air travel. While she had at various times taken her brother and sisters up in her biplane, he had absolutely refused every attempt to persuade him. He had spent his life in thrall to the ebb and flow of the tide, born in the east-coast town of Arbroath and first accompanying his own father on an overseas voyage at the age of eight. Four years later his father had drowned in the Atlantic Ocean, lost in a shipwreck, but still young James had been drawn to the sea. Hard work and commitment had taken him far in the service of the Empire and he now ran a vast fleet of ships crossing the globe, and was never happier than when out on the waves on his own beloved yacht.

Looking down on the crowds, Elsie reflected that her first foray into flying had taken place when she was estranged from her father, in those foolish days when she had been married to Dennis and pursuing an acting career as Poppy Wyndham. Dennis had gained his own pilot's licence during the war and encouraged her, always astute to publicity opportunities. She cringed when she remembered the magazine shots that still sometimes appeared, showing her applying her make-up in the cockpit like some foolish flapper. But in the painful months when her world fragmented into jagged shards and she knew she had to escape from Dennis and this self-made prison, the thought of flying had kept her going: that sense of elation as she soared into the air, far, far above the ant-like people below, escaping their petty concerns and rivalries. When she was reconciled with her father – and her fortune – she wasted no time in engaging Britain's leading aviator Sir Alan Cobham to continue her tuition, soon becoming the first Scottish woman to gain her flying certificate.

Relieved that the whole Poppy and Dennis Wyndham episode was over, Lord Inchcape grudgingly accepted her passion for flight, although she sometimes wondered if his willingness to welcome her, a woman, into the firm as a full employee was in part an attempt to distract her from her aeroplane. Five years later, he surely knew that was something he could never do. She had gained immense respect among the flying community, being invited onto the advisory committee of pilots to the Air League and becoming a member of the council of the Scottish branch. But these accolades notwithstanding, her father refused to consider air travel as anything more than a hobby for the richest and brightest young things.

Turning away from the window, Elsie thought how maddening it was that with all his business acumen and enterprise he was unable to recognise the symbolic power of Lindbergh's flight. It might take a few years but air travel would one day overtake the sea as the main means of transport, both passenger and freight, and she meant to be part of it. She looked across at him, dozing off in his armchair, and felt a tug of fondness. She loved him dearly. Everyone said how alike they were and she knew that many of her character traits came directly from him: ambition, fearlessness, capacity for work and a certain stubbornness. But he was an old man now – seventy-five – and although he held the reins of his business empire as tightly as ever, he was also planning for succession by bringing her brother, Kenneth, and brother-in-law Alexander into the running of the company. If only she had been a boy! She embraced her responsibility for the interior design and upkeep of the fleet, but how much more she could have done if she had been allowed into the boardroom.

Instead one day Kenneth would be in charge.

Elsie was more hopeful she could persuade *him* to do anything she liked.

The hysteria in Paris over Charles Lindbergh's successful flight showed no sign of abating in the coming days. Elsie slipped into a picture theatre to watch newsreels of his arrival at Le Bourget, where crowds had overrun the airfield and stripped souvenirs from the *Spirit of St Louis*, while Lindbergh himself was hustled away to safety. As she left the picture house and strolled along the banks of the Seine, she noticed that the stalls were already selling Lindbergh souvenirs. She stopped and bought a small brooch that caught her eye, a cheap silver thing in the shape of the aeroplane with the words *Spirit of St Louis* stamped on it. She was sure her father noticed it at dinner that evening, but he said nothing.

The newspapers reported on a flurry of receptions and meetings with French dignitaries, and plans for a tour of Europe before Lindbergh's return to America. Reading *The Times* among the palm trees in the hotel lounge, one item in particular caught Elsie's eye. Lindbergh would fly to England in a few days, landing at Croydon Aerodrome. She folded up the newspaper.

It was time to leave Paris.

Chapter Four

Glasgow

Three-year-old Jacky's favourite thing was to feed the ducks.

Stella handed him a bag of crumbs, warned him to step back from the edge, and settled down on a nearby bench. She loved the park at this time of year, when the green on the trees was still so fresh and the early summer sunshine held the promise of better days to come after a long, dark winter. She fished in her handbag and brought out the letter that had arrived that morning from Corran in Oxford, and which she had saved to read until now. What would her older sister think of her suggestion of a family holiday together in August? You never knew with Corran.

Corran's letter was full of life in Oxford, where she was a classics lecturer in St Hilda's College. She wrote about exam season and plans for May Week celebrations, about the lilac in the college gardens and about a meeting with a mutual friend. She was looking forward to the long summer holiday but as vague as ever about her plans.

I should manage to join you for a week or so in August, though. I'm longing to see Duncan and Jacky again. They won't be such little boys now.

Stella glanced across at her dreamy younger son, who was crouched on the wet ground, engrossed in the activity of the ducks. Jacky was named after his uncle, Stella's beloved brother Jack, whose cruel slaughter somewhere near Arras remained a gaping hole in the heart of their family. Jacky bore his name but was the image of Rob, his father. It was Duncan, her fair-haired older son, whose every quicksilver movement bore the imprint of the wee boy his uncle had once been. She sometimes caught her mother standing over the two boys asleep in their bed in the kitchen, just gazing. Jacky usually slept curled up in a tight ball facing the wall, thumb in his mouth, probably because his older brother always sprawled as he slept, arms and legs outstretched, taking far more than his share of the space. Stella watched as Alison reached out a hand and tenderly stroked aside the blonde hair falling over Duncan's face. 'It's strange to me that no one else looks at Duncan and sees five-year-old Jack.'

Stella tucked the letter away and stood up, calling to Jacky and taking him by the hand. 'Time to collect Duncan from school. Daddy will be home soon.' Rob was out doing house calls this afternoon. Tomorrow he would go to the shipyard to meet this Mr Stephen. Stella had shrugged when told of Alex's proposal. It would be regular work, even if it wasn't quite what they had in mind on moving to Garnethill. She knew Rob missed his work with the men at the Princess Louise hospital, knew too that he struggled to hide his frustration at the trivial concerns of some of his private patients. Maybe one day a week at the shipyard would be good for him.

Her mother thought she was too impatient with Rob, but there was so much her mother didn't see. The whisky bottle that lived permanently in their bottom drawer, for example. Stella measured Rob's frame of mind by how quickly the bottle was emptied and replaced. Any time she challenged him about it, he brushed her off.

It was the war, of course. Always the war. It was the reason for everything. When he tossed and turned and screamed in his sleep, she would have brought him as much whisky as he liked if she thought for a moment it would help his distress. Sometimes Duncan peered round the door, his hair tousled and his eyes huge in his wee face. 'Is Daddy dreaming about the soldiers again?'

So yes, she wanted Rob to be happy, to be fulfilled. As she met Duncan outside the school and watched the two boys run ahead to their close, she reflected that she just wished someone wanted that for her too. The boys encountered a closed door. Of course, Mother was out, spending the day with her church committee ladies. That was where her mother seemed to find fulfilment, through charity work. She had tried to involve Stella – and goodness knows there were plenty of desperate causes to help with in the Glasgow slums – but something in Stella rebelled at the complacency of these well-meaning middle-class church ladies.

She went inside and set about making a snack for the children. She knew how fortunate she was – look at poor Luisa, longing for a baby of her own – but she couldn't help but hanker after the life she had once known. The life when she had been an independent person, respected for her knowledge and her qualifications, a young woman with a career. That woman had lived in Paris, working as a typist firstly at the peace conference after the war, and then at the British Embassy. An opportunity had even come up to serve with the League of Nations, but it would have meant a move to Switzerland. It came along just at the time she fell in love with Rob, and she was faced with a stark choice: marriage or career?

Unlike Corran, who had her own history with Rob, she chose marriage.

She didn't regret it – she loved Rob and her children dearly – but in the long days filled with the chatter of the boys and the endless round of household chores, her mind would drift back to those months in Paris and she wondered where on earth that independent woman had gone. She missed the work, and even more she missed the fun she had had with her friend Lily, the light-hearted laughter and confidential chats they had shared in their room high in the eaves of the Hôtel Majestic. Now Lily travelled the world as a diplomatic wife, writing unsatisfying letters full of tennis and bridge parties. Maybe that was why Stella's friendship with Elsie had come to mean so much to her. Elsie didn't see her as Rob's wife, as the boys' mother; she saw her as Stella, the woman she had first met in Paris, and that helped her hold on to her sense of self.

Rob had his patients.

Corran had her books.

Elsie had her ships.

Stella looked out of the kitchen window onto the washing blowing in the back green, and wondered if she too would ever have anything more.

Children released from school were pouring out of the back closes to gather there, and soon her own two joined them. Stella made herself a cup of tea and stood by the window, half dreaming of that different time and half watching her boys. A taller child tried to bring some order to the chaos of boys and girls freed from the constraints of a day at their desks. Two armies were formed, and now the young recruits began to march.

Stella shivered.

Boys have always played at soldiers, she told herself. *It doesn't mean a thing.*

But still, her heart was cold as she watched Duncan eagerly seize a stick and sprint to the washhouse, crouching down and aiming his weapon round the corner. Jacky and one or two of the other smaller ones, too little to be of interest to the commanding officers, had at least wandered off to play their own game at the side. Stella had reacted this same way the other day when Duncan proudly marched up and down the close, showing his parents the military drill he learnt in school. Rob had laughed and applauded but Stella had turned away. 'He's *five*, Rob. Why on earth is the school teaching five-year-olds to be soldiers? Haven't we learnt a thing?'

'Drill keeps them fit.'

'Gymnastics would keep them fit!'

She turned away from the window. Rob and her mother would be home soon and there wasn't a thing ready for tea. It was silly of her to worry. Duncan and Jacky were a new generation, one that thank God would never face the horrors that her own generation had endured.

But was that true?

Her work in Paris had all been about forging a new and lasting peace. If that was to prosper, then surely the same work must take place here among the schools and the closes and the back greens, just as much as in the corridors of power. She glanced back outside and saw to her relief that the organised battle had quickly descended into chaos. Someone had found a half-deflated football and both sides were haring after it as fast as they could. She felt the tension ease out of her.

The war was over for good.

Chapter Five

Glasgow

When Rob had agreed to come and see round the shipyard, he hadn't considered the noise.

On his first day Mr Stephen gave him a tour of the whole sprawling complex on the south bank of the Clyde, and within fifteen minutes Rob was convinced he would have to decline the offer. Fred Stephen led him first into the engineering works, a vast brick and iron shed. Light poured in from the glass ceiling that soared above them, as magnificent as a medieval cathedral, but the cacophony that reverberated all around him was closer to bedlam than sacred praise, while furnaces glowed with the fires of hell. He could feel himself sweating, but it was the noise that affected him most, and the familiar hammer began to pound in his own head almost immediately.

'See – we have these ambulance barrows in every shed,' Mr Stephen bellowed above the clamour, indicating a wooden trolley with a red cross painted on the side. 'Accidents are part of shipyard life, but this way we can navigate tight corners and get the casualty to help as soon as possible.'

Rob nodded. It seemed to him that there were hazards and potential for injury everywhere he looked, but as the man said it was an accepted part of industrial life. Mr Stephen led him through the shed to the opposite entrance, and he gulped fresh air gratefully as they emerged. His companion laughed. 'Takes a bit of getting used to. We'll look at the joiners' shop next. That's quieter.'

As they entered the joiners' shop, the smell of sawdust took Rob back to the converted stable block at the Princess Louise hospital where the men worked so hard to produce wooden limbs. He breathed it in gratefully and looked around. The noise of the machinery still set his teeth on edge, but he steadied himself and made an effort to focus not on his surroundings but on the men and boys hard at work all around him. They were the reason he was here. He turned to Fred Stephen, about to speak, but just at that moment a young lad hurrying past dropped the tool he was carrying onto the hard flagstone floor, and Rob flinched at the almighty crash. The glance Mr Stephen gave him this time was more analytical. When they emerged outside, he asked, 'The trenches, was it?'

'Aye,' said Rob shortly, balling his fists to keep his hands from trembling.

'Well, don't worry, you'll be based in the main office. That way the men can come to you from any part of the yard. Of course, if you're on site when there's an incident we'll call on you, but it's really more routine medical help I want to offer, ailments that might otherwise lead to absence and dismissal. Let's take a quick walk down to the wharf. That's the heart of Stephen's.'

Rob followed him over cobbled pathways and between buildings towards the great river. Smoke belched from a chimney above them and hung in the damp air. A train rattled by, the clanking and screeching just another echo of the horrors of the past. But as they emerged between two sheds onto the quayside, he stopped and took a breath. This was something completely different.

He was familiar with the sight of large ships being constructed all along the banks of the River Clyde, but to stand beneath the cranes and timber framework and grasp that the enormous shape above him was the emerging hull of a passenger liner was astonishing. Even the clamour as sheets of iron were riveted together, as men perching precariously on platforms bellowed to one another, as pulleys creaked and wooden beams clattered, was less overpowering out here under the arch of the grey Glasgow sky than it had been inside that iron and brick temple. 'Hull 519,' Stephen said proudly.

'We're building her for P&O. She'll be the largest passenger liner we've ever constructed, and will run on turbo-electric engines. She's a modern-day marvel.'

So here she was: the ship that Alex had spoken about with such enthusiasm. Now Rob was being drawn into her story too. She was simply swarming with men, each going about his task apparently independently, and Rob couldn't help but be impressed by the sheer scale of the enterprise. The post-war boom was long since over and opportunities for many workers had grown worse rather than better since last year's General Strike, but across the yard Stephen's must surely be providing valuable employment for hundreds or even thousands of men. Generations of the same family worked alongside one another, like Geordie Aitken and his son Danny, with whole communities dependent on one yard. He said as much to Fred Stephen as they made their way back to the purpose-built red-brick office building that also housed departments like the drawing office and print rooms.

'Thousands of men, and even some women,' Stephen said, as he opened the door to a long boardroom. 'We have women tracers for example, and some of the fitting-out work like French polishing and upholstery involves women too. Let's take a seat in here while we talk things over.'

The contrast with the bustling, noisy shipyard just outside the tall windows was profound. In the boardroom all was elegance and luxury. Thick carpets hushed even the sound of his footsteps. A long polished wooden table ran the length of the room, and a coal fire blazed brightly beneath an elaborate mantelpiece. Portraits of earlier generations of Stephens hung on the brocaded walls, looking down with pride on glass-cased models of the ships they had brought from original concept to ocean wave. Fred Stephen poured an inch of whisky into two glasses and handed one to Rob.

'Welcome on board.'

Rob took the drink and gulped it down. Fire met and consumed cold fear. 'I can start next week.'

Chapter Six

London

The *Spirit of St Louis* followed the snaking line of the Thames through the heart of London as far as Blackfriars Bridge before turning south. Streets below were packed with cheering Londoners waving the Stars and Stripes in Lindbergh's honour. Elsie had already driven to Croydon Aerodrome and made her way to the front of the enclosure, near the official welcoming party. She could see Mr Houghton, the American ambassador, and Sir Samuel Hoare, the Secretary of State for Air, who was an acquaintance of her father's. The police held back eager crowds, and enterprising onlookers had scaled every available shed roof and water tower. All eyes were on the skies, and a hum of excitement spread through the crowd as the white plane came into view. Elsie gazed in awe. To think this machine had flown all the way across the Atlantic Ocean! She fingered the cheap little brooch on her lapel, the souvenir she had bought in Paris, and fixed her gaze on the *Spirit of St Louis*.

So intent was she on the plane that she was slow to notice the chaos unfolding around her. As Lindbergh swooped gracefully down, what looked like tens of thousands of people broke through the fencing and streamed over the airfield, causing him to thrust upwards again while some on the ground screamed and others cheered. Officials on foot and in motor cars hurried to drive the crowds back and clear a space, while Lindbergh circled above. Elsie held her breath as he came in a second time. This time he managed to land, but no sooner had the machine come to a halt in front of her than the crowds pushed through once again, engulfing the official welcoming party and the *Spirit of St Louis*.

And my father thinks there's no popular enthusiasm for flight.

Lindbergh remained in his cockpit until officials were able to clear a space, secured by a rope, around the aeroplane. She watched as he removed his helmet and goggles and was ushered into a car, which very slowly edged its way through euphoric crowds to the traffic office, while some of the ground crew came forward and wheeled the monoplane into a hangar for safekeeping.

Elsie had come with the intention of speaking personally to the young pilot but she could see now that any such hope was futile. Still, there was no point in her trying to even reach her car, never mind drive away, while such dense crowds remained. They showed no sign of moving, chanting his name and even singing a song about Lucky Lindy that seemed to be everywhere just a week after he had completed his flight. And then another roar from the expectant crowd as, still dressed in his leather flying coat, Lindbergh emerged from the traffic office and swung himself up the ladder onto the control tower. He spoke briefly into a megaphone but Elsie couldn't hear a word above the noise of the crowd. All she knew was that this young man had achieved what many believed to be impossible, and she must find a way to speak with him while he was in London, whatever it took.

* * *

In the end it was straightforward. When she finally made it home to Seamore Place, she found an invitation awaiting her to a dinner at the Savoy Hotel on Tuesday evening in honour of Charles Lindbergh, hosted by the Royal Aero Club, the Royal Aeronautical Society, the Air League of the British Empire and the Society of British Aircraft Constructors. Elsie placed the invitation beside a row of others on the hall mantelpiece with a thrill of anticipation. Everyone who was anyone in the world of British aviation would be there, and instead of the usual frivolous society gossip, all the conversation would be of aeroplanes, of Lindbergh's flight and of the possibilities and challenges for air travel that lay ahead. Here at last was her opportunity to meet the American pilot for herself! She turned and made her way up the elegant staircase to change, humming the catchy refrain of "Lucky Lindy!"

'I'll be down at seven for dinner.'

Her eldest sister, Margaret, regularly expressed concern at Elsie living in London with only the servants for company whenever their parents were overseas or in Glenapp. 'Come and stay with us. You may come and go as you please,' she said with an attempt at graciousness. But Elsie loved her time alone in the quiet, graceful mansion house. When she had returned to the family fold after fleeing her marriage, her parents hadn't quite known what to do with her. Her mother embarked on an exhausting series of engagements, hosting elaborate dances in her honour here at Seamore Place and parading Elsie at one society event after another. While Elsie was grateful for this very public display of parental acceptance that eased her return, she eventually took her father aside.

'I'll go mad without something to do. Mother thinks I should find another husband, and that's why she's displaying me like an eighteen-year-old deb. But I'm not eighteen, I'm nearly thirty, and I'm quite sure I will never marry again. Can't I work for you?'

Five years later, the top floor of Seamore Place contained Elsie's office, where she developed her ideas for ship interiors and kept detailed files on each vessel's itinerary and maintenance schedule. She enjoyed her work, although she longed to be more involved in the strategic side of her father's business. He would sometimes summon her to his study and ask her advice about some matter or another, but because she was a woman there was no question of inviting her into the boardroom. Interiors were far more suitable.

Still, she was grateful for her employment and her office, and it was here that she kept all the paperwork relating to her other passion: aviation. Her files contained not only the documentation of her own flight training and the purchase and maintenance of her biplane but numerous newspaper cuttings about the burgeoning aviation industry. The society columns still loved to report on the appearance of the glamorous Miss Elsie Mackay at countless society dinners and grand functions, as she increasingly took the place of her ailing mother at her father's side. She smiled through it all, knowing that she could soon return to her office with its grand view over the London rooftops and pick up her inky pen.

Elsie spent the next two days rehearsing in her head all the questions she wanted to ask Charles Lindbergh, and chose her outfit with care. 'This pink silk scarf, do you think, Nancy?'

Nancy, who had grown up in Ballantrae near Glenapp Castle, had been Elsie's maid since her return to the bosom of the family. She looked critically at the scarf Elsie was holding. 'I would choose the ivory one, Miss Elsie. Your little badge stands out much better against it.'

'You're right, of course.' Elsie pinned her Royal Aero Club badge to the scarf and waited as Nancy made some final adjustments to her wavy dark bob. As she stood up she picked up the other brooch, the one in the shape of Lindbergh's plane, and pinned it to the collar of her dress. 'Tonight I shall meet the man I envy most in all the world! Wish me luck.'

There was nothing terribly distinctive about the dinner itself: ruby-red wine in crystal glasses glinting in the light of chandeliers and the clamour of five hundred voices all intent on being heard. Elsie was relieved to be seated by her old friend and fellow aviator Tony Joynson-Wreford, whom she had known since the war.

'Rather a fuss this, isn't it?' Tony said, gesturing round the crowded tables with an arm that came perilously close to knocking over Elsie's glass. 'It's an achievement, but after all Alcock and Brown got there first, all those years ago, just after the war. That's Arthur Whitten Brown over there – I wonder what he makes of all this palaver.'

'I think it's wonderful,' Elsie said as Tony drained his glass and looked round for a waiter to refill it.

'The fame and fortune the lad has made for himself are wonderful, that's for sure. He's set for life. But if there's all this acclaim for flying with the wind, what rewards await the first person to fly in the opposite direction?'

'Do you really think there's a plane or a pilot strong enough to fly in the face of those winds?'

Tony winked at her. 'You're looking at him.'

'Really? Are you serious? Do you have a plan? What does Olive say?'

'Olive doesn't speak to me much at the moment, far too busy being sick in the mornings. Yes, we do have a plan but it's all a bit hush-hush for now. Have you ever met All-Weather Mac – Captain Robert McIntosh? He's one of the Imperial Airways pilots. He has a backer who has offered him a splendid machine and he's asked me to join him. We plan to fly from Baldonnel Airfield later this year. The first men ever to fly the Atlantic east to west won't be

Yankees, they'll be Brits, and then, my dear, your friend Tony will be a very wealthy man indeed.'

East to west. The hardest route of all. Elsie was fascinated but there was no opportunity to discuss Tony's plans further as Lord Thomson, chairman of the Royal Aero Club, had risen to his feet to give the first speech. Even this formal part of the evening was far more interesting to Elsie than these occasions usually were, and she listened intently as Charles Lindbergh stood to reply and told the story of his flight in his soft, shy American tones. He emphasised that rigorous planning rather than luck had ensured his success, and spoke of seeing only the light of one solitary ship on his entire crossing until the sailing boats near the Irish coast came into view. 'We have no secret to hide so far as my flight is concerned,' he concluded. 'Everything about it is open to every country, and if there is anything concerning the flight or the plane that I can explain I shall be very glad to do so.'

Tony excused himself as soon as the meal ended, and Elsie looked around. There were people she knew everywhere, from Air Vice-Marshal Sefton Brancker to Sir Philip Sassoon, the Under-Secretary of State for Air. She had no desire to be snared into conversation with any of them. Her eyes moved past them to another familiar figure, and her heart leapt. Sir Alan Cobham, Britain's leading pilot, had taught her to fly, and the man he was talking to was Charles Lindbergh himself.

Her first thought was how young the American looked close up. She knew he was only twenty-five but somehow, seeing him beside Alan Cobham, who was in his mid-thirties like herself, this tall, slim American looked little more than a boy. *There is no shadow of grief on his face*, she thought. The medals on his chest – like the shiny Air Force Cross pinned there by the King at Buckingham Palace this morning – were symbols of great achievement but not of war. When men like Alan and Tony took to the skies, they still heard the echo of German guns, were still haunted by plummeting, burning wreckage that contained their friends. Perhaps it was his freedom from that shadow that had enabled Charles Lindbergh to do what so many older and more experienced men had failed to do. As she drew near, Sir Alan broke away from his conversation and turned to greet her. 'Lindbergh, may I present the Honourable Miss Elsie Mackay? Miss Mackay is herself a very skilled aviatrix. I had the pleasure of teaching her to fly, and I've rarely had a student with such aptitude, nor such courage.'

'Pleased to meet you,' Lindbergh said, shaking her hand. 'We have some fine lady pilots in America too.'

His grip was cool and firm, and she thought of those slender hands wrestling with the controls, steering the machine, dipping low over the waves and high above the clouds as they battled the winds. The light of one solitary ship in all that expanse. She took a quick breath, determined not to gush. The questions she had been rehearsing all week had flown from her mind. She realised Lindbergh was looking at her brooch and blushed. What on earth had possessed her to wear it? But Alan came to her rescue. 'We've been discussing the commercial potential of air travel, something which I know is of interest to you.'

'Indeed,' she said eagerly. 'I was out at Croydon on Sunday, and could hardly believe the crowds. There is so much popular enthusiasm. Do you think commercial air travel will take off now in America?'

'My country is so vast it's a sure thing,' Lindbergh said. 'When I return to the States they want me to do a tour to raise the profile.'

'And how will you return?'

'By sea. Flying into those headwinds is a whole different ball game. I flew the *Spirit of St Louis* to Gosport yesterday and your people have promised to see her safely transported across the Atlantic. I'll catch a ship at Cherbourg.'

'The east to west crossing will be the next one everyone wants to achieve,' Sir Alan said.

'Will you try?' Lindbergh asked.

'No, that's not for me. I'm working on a scheme for Africa at the moment. I plan to fly round the whole continent, landing only in British territories, in order to show those who still need convincing that aviation will bring new life to our Empire.'

Elsie thought of Tony's plans but they were not hers to share. And besides, she wanted to think about them some more for herself. Then Charles Lindbergh excused himself. 'My evening is not over. I promised to attend the Derby Ball at the Royal Albert Hall this evening, so I guess I must take my leave of you all.'

Elsie soon followed, her mind whirling with all she had heard and seen. At home she refused a drink and climbed the stairs, but did not stop at her first-floor bedroom. Instead she climbed on, up to the top floor and into her office, where she looked around at the bookcases, the desk, the filing cabinets, the drawing board. As befitted someone working in interior design, it was both tasteful and practical. A comfortable armchair and side table sat to one side, but she walked to the window and pushed it open, letting the warm June air flood the room. Elsie leant out into the night. In one direction she could see the vast expanse of darkness that was Hyde Park, the sky above studded with stars, while if she looked the other way all was streetlights, rooftops and the nighttime world of London. She loved to stand here and look out over the skyline and down to the streets below, the closest she could come to soaring in her little machine while her feet were still planted firmly on the ground. Everything she had heard tonight – from Tony, from Alan, from Lindbergh himself – made her even more sure that the time was right to launch a commercial airline.

But could she ever convince her father?

She looked towards the darkness of Hyde Park. Just imagine

the stir it would cause if *someone*, returning from a record-breaking exploit, were to land their aeroplane right there in the heart of London. Tony wanted fame and fortune. Elsie had no need of either, but she knew the value of good publicity. That would make her father pay attention. But what record-breaking exploit?

Tony planned to cross the vast expanse of the Atlantic in the far harder westwards direction. The idea gleamed before her as the pinnacle of human endeavour. She was wise enough to know that neither her own flying experience nor her little plane were up to that task, but how she would love to join Tony in his enterprise. It was no use, though. His plans were so far advanced that there was unlikely to be room for her. What's more, her father would never allow it, and she knew from long experience that with his contacts, determination and ruthlessness he was perfectly capable of stopping her. It was a foolish dream, that was all. All she could hope to do was to support and encourage Tony in his efforts and develop her airline ideas out of the popular acclaim he was bound to receive, should he succeed.

She closed the door behind her and descended the stairs, feeling a little as though the clouds had blotted out those sparkling stars. She entered her bedroom and decided not to ring for Nancy but to get herself ready for bed. She was on her monthlies, and as she went along the corridor to the bathroom she thought as she often did what a nuisance it was to be a woman.

A woman.

She stopped.

No woman *has ever flown the Atlantic in either direction.*

Now there is a record that Tony can never achieve.

She remembered what Charles Lindbergh had said about planning. With the right planning and the right team, was there any reason she couldn't make the first flight across the Atlantic by a woman? Once Tony had succeeded she might approach him, and see if he would join her on the venture. But it would be her aeroplane, specially chosen for the gruelling flight, and she would be at the controls.

She looked in the mirror and thought again about that awful staged photo of her applying her face powder in the cockpit. This time she would present a very different picture to the world.

Elsie Mackay, first woman to fly the Atlantic and pioneering founder of Britain's first self-funded commercial airline.

She had a new dream.

Chapter Seven

Glasgow

'No, you have it. Honestly, I couldn't.'

'You've hardly eaten a thing.'

'I'm not hungry.'

Stella sipped her tea as Elsie took the final scone. The legendary Willow Tea Rooms weren't quite the same under new management, but she still loved to come here. It was only a ten-minute walk from home but today was one of those Glasgow summer days when the rain simply teemed down and she was wet and bedraggled. Still, the moment she stepped into the cool, sophisticated space designed by Charles Rennie Mackintosh, all sensuous lines and white elegance with vibrant bursts of colour, she felt its graceful magnificence soothing her spirits. These meetings with Elsie were a precious gift, sparkling amid the grey monotony of her days. Even if today she didn't really feel like eating afternoon tea.

Elsie enthused about the ambience of the tea room. 'How I would love to decorate the new liner completely in the Mackintosh style! It's not possible of course. Many of our guests prefer traditional decoration, but one of the best things about this new ship is that there's enough space to offer variety. Those who wish to sit in a Jacobean library may do so, while the younger generation will enjoy the latest salon like this.'

'How is it coming along?'

'Oh, splendidly. I was over at the shipyard yesterday and the squads are well at work on the hull. Of course, it will be simply ages until she looks anything like a ship to you and me, but it's essential I have the interior plans agreed and materials ordered in time for the fit-out next year.' She put her fingertips together and leant forward, her dark eyes shining. 'What do you think of a swimming pool?'

'A swimming pool?' Stella didn't quite understand, and in any case was fighting to hold back a second wave of the nausea that had prevented her accepting the scone.

'On the ship. Wouldn't it be the height of luxury – a full-sized heated swimming pool for the first-class passengers? Some still baulk at the idea, the weight of the water, the effect of the waves and whatnot, but the White Star Line has proved it is possible. I'm determined our new P&O liner will be the first of the fleet with her own swimming pool, and my idea is to model the design on ancient Roman baths. People will flock to book on her.'

Stella took a mouthful of tea in the hope it would settle her stomach. 'My mother and aunt are booked on a P&O pleasure cruise in September, on board the *Ranchi*. Is that one of yours?'

'The *Ranchi* was one of my first! She's a lovely ship. She does the Bombay mail run for part of the year, but she spends a few months cruising too. I had such fun designing her interior. I think the writing and card room is my favourite. It's a marvellous, calm bright space. Your mother will have a splendid time.'

'I'm sure she will.' Stella glanced at the rain streaming down the window. 'Who wouldn't want to escape this weather for the

Mediterranean? I swear it's rained every single day since Duncan's school holidays began. If it's like this when we're away too, I'll scream.'

'You spend your holidays in Rothesay, is that right?'

'Oh no, didn't I tell you? We're not going to Rothesay this year. I suppose it's my fault – I had a hankering for something different. Rob has a patient whose sister takes in holidaymakers in a house near the harbour in a little town in the south-west called Portpatrick. We can get there by train and it will make a change, as long as this weather improves.' She remembered how Rob had come home so pleased with himself, having arranged the holiday in Portpatrick, clearly expecting her to be delighted too. She was glad not to be going back to Rothesay, but it was hard to summon particular enthusiasm when they were simply swapping one chilly coastal boarding house for another. But Elsie reached out and caught her hand.

'My dear, Portpatrick is just along the road from Glenapp. You must come for the day! We're there for most of August and September. My father is sure to have arranged a string of shooting parties but we'll find a day that works. When do you go?'

'Mother, Luisa and I take the children down on Monday, and Rob and Alex will join us next weekend,' Stella said slowly, as her brain tried to process this staggering news, which promised to change the whole complexion of their holiday. 'My sister, Corran, will come for a week too.'

Elsie dug in her handbag and pulled out a little notebook and pen. 'Do you know the address? Put it in here. I'll write to you there and suggest a date. You simply must come.'

The rain still streamed down the window beside them but a shaft of light was struggling through, transforming the drops of water into sparkling diamonds. Glenapp! She would leave the boys with her mother and Luisa and spend a whole day with

Elsie in luxury at Glenapp, the mythical fairy-tale castle. Stella scribbled down the address in Portpatrick. 'I'll have to see how it fits with the rest of the family.'

'Of course. Bring them all too. I'm sure your little boys will love it. There are woodlands for adventures and even a path onto our own private beach. We'll have a picnic.' Elsie slipped the notebook back into her bag and checked her gold wristwatch. 'But now I must be going. I promised my father I'd be back for dinner this evening.' She looked around and almost immediately the waitress was at their side. Stella watched, saying nothing, as Elsie settled the account. On the first few occasions they had met for tea, Stella had tried to pay her way, but Elsie always rebuffed her and she no longer argued or even felt guilty about it. Elsie was an heiress and a wealthy woman in her own right; Stella and Rob needed every penny they earned if they were ever to move to that bungalow.

The gleaming silver Rolls-Royce was parked directly outside, surrounded by a swarm of small boys. As soon as the two women emerged from the tea room, Elsie's chauffeur stepped forward with a large umbrella to protect them from the rain. Stella treasured these little insights into a life of luxury that friendship with Elsie brought her. 'I can walk home,' she said, but Elsie dismissed this. Stella slid in beside her, breathing in the soft smell of leather and reflecting how much more pleasant this was than a trail up the hill in the rain. Particularly today. She had known for three or four weeks now that she must be expecting another baby, and she was still queasy most of the day. She wasn't quite sure how she felt about it. She and Rob had always said they wanted three children, so it was as well to get on with it – but at the same time another baby would just pull her even further down into the same monotonous existence. She had told Rob last week, and things had certainly been a bit better between them since then. There was something special about these days when only the two of them knew about the new life growing within her. The whisky bottle had remained untouched, as far as she could see, and his kiss when he left for the shipyard that morning had been particularly tender. But on Monday she would leave him alone for the week. Would the bottle move from the drawer to the kitchen table when he had the house to himself?

She pulled her mind back to Elsie's invitation, which glowed before her, a pearl amid the wet sand of this summer holiday. Three weeks in Portpatrick suddenly seemed a much brighter prospect, and she thanked the happy chance that had brought this particular boarding house to Rob's attention.

Glenapp!

Chapter Eight

Glenapp Castle

In the end the trip to Glenapp Castle became a full family day out. They piled onto the train at Portpatrick, heading for Stranraer, where Elsie had promised someone would meet them.

Alison glanced across the carriage at Stella, who was looking out of the window. She knew her daughter would have preferred to come alone and wander round manicured gardens arm in arm with Elsie, but the written invitation was quite clearly for all of them, and the rest of the family had pounced on it eagerly. Alison herself remained to be convinced that any of this was a good idea, but a family outing was at least better than Stella disappearing off by herself.

Alex had been unexpectedly enthusiastic. 'I've met Lord Inchcape briefly at the shipyard, and I've heard all about Miss Mackay; she's responsible for the interior of many of the ships. Not just the liners, the cargo ships too. Some of the sea captains I've met are none too impressed with her designs, mind you. Silk cushions and fancy footstools don't sit too well with the old salts who hanker after the days of bare boards and eating off a sea chest!' He laughed. 'Of course I'll come. I wonder where Lord Inchcape keeps his yacht? I'd love to get a glimpse.'

Luisa was enchanted by the idea of visiting a real Scottish castle and the two boys rushed to fetch their wooden swords, desperate to play at being knights. Only Corran was ambivalent, but when she realised everyone else would be going, she shrugged. 'I might as well come along.'

Corran had strolled back into their world on Monday after a mammoth train journey down from Caithness. She was the only member of the family who still returned regularly to the northern shores where they had grown up, happy enough to go there alone. At least Alison thought she was alone, although sometimes she wondered. Corran kept her distance, and not just in terms of location. She spent her term times in her rooms in St Hilda's College, Oxford, but what she did with her holidays was more of a mystery. No one had mastered the evasive answer and contained smile quite like Alison's elder daughter.

But now the train was pulling into Stranraer station and it was time to get off, making sure nothing and no one was left behind. Rob scooped up Jacky while Alison took Duncan by the hand. And there was Elsie coming towards them, as elegantly dressed as ever in a chic blue hat and jacket over a cream linen dress. She strode up to Stella and caught both her hands. 'It's such fun you're here. Come – I've brought the Rolls. It will be a wee bit tight but I'm driving, which saves us one passenger.'

The Rolls.

'Two of you come up front beside me and the rest can squeeze in the back.'

The boys were nearly beside themselves with excitement by this time and Alison was amused to see that Alex wasn't far behind. He followed Elsie round to the driver's side. 'This is the new Phantom, is it not? How does she drive?'

'Splendidly. You'll see. It's all down to the engine: overhead valves rather than side valves in the previous model.' She smiled. 'I'll ask my chauffeur to give you a look under the bonnet later on if you like?'

'Would you really?'

Luisa screwed up her face. 'So dirty.'

'Nothing some hot water won't cure,' laughed Elsie. 'Now come on, who's sitting up front?'

Alison and Stella climbed into the front beside Elsie, while the two men, Luisa and Corran squeezed into the back and took the children on their knees. Elsie drove them north, away from the coastline at Stranraer and into a sloping glen that was lush green with trees and rhododendron bushes. She pointed out various landmarks as they drove. 'Much of this glen is part of my father's estate,' she said. 'See the church there? That's Glenapp Church. It's a dear little place, mostly used by the family and estate workers. It has a lovely atmosphere, so peaceful and prayerful.'

'Has your family always lived here?' Alison asked, glancing across at the little stone church overlooking the valley.

Elsie negotiated a sharp bend before she answered. 'Goodness no. I moved about a great deal as a child: born in India, convent boarding school in Belgium, homes in London and Aberdeenshire. My father bought Glenapp during the war, and we're happier here than we have been anywhere else. We have carried out a great deal of work on the house and the gardens. My mother has not been well of late and the air here is much better for her than in London. We build most of our ships in Glasgow and Newcastle, so it's fairly convenient for those too.'

She turned off the main road and pulled up at a large set of gates. A man stepped smartly out of the lodge house, opened the gates and touched his cap. Elsie gave him a wave and carried on. Alison looked for the castle, but still the driveway wound round between high trees, while a steep gorge dropped away to one side. A green haven surrounded them and the outside world already felt far distant. Eventually as they passed a large monkey puzzle tree and drove between another set of gates, the castle appeared before them. Elsie pulled up in the courtyard right in front of the entrance doorway. Alison made to climb out, then realised that Elsie was waiting for staff members to approach. The car doors were opened from the outside. 'Welcome to Glenapp, ma'am. Please step this way.'

The formal greeting took her aback and as she climbed down she realised that everyone else had fallen silent too. Only the children were not overawed, as Duncan tried to poke Jacky with his sword behind his father's back. Alison looked up at the castle. A turret and a square tower with battlements made it every inch the fairy tale that Luisa had longed for. Ivy grew over the central part, while the newer stone on either wing spoke of recent building work. It was graceful and beautiful certainly, but could it really be a home?

Elsie opened her arms in welcome. 'Come in and have a cup of tea and meet my parents. Later we'll explore the gardens and head down to the shore. I'm pleased you have such a glorious day for your visit. There's a sweet little beach hut that is just perfect for a picnic lunch.' She led them through the grand doorway into an entrance hall.

Alison paused and looked around. This was smaller and more intimate-feeling than she had perhaps imagined. Above the doorway was a stained-glass coat of arms bearing the words *MANU FORTE*, which she had already noticed on the door of the Rolls-Royce. Elsie led them up a short flight of stairs and into the drawing room, which stretched from the front of the castle to a large window to the rear looking out over the gardens and the sea beyond. 'Come, see our view!' she said, walking towards that window, but Alison stopped in dismay. This room was filled with ornaments worth goodness knows how much, and beautifully upholstered furnishings that had surely never seen a child's sticky fingers. The boys simply couldn't be let loose in here. She looked round. Rob had Jacky grasped tightly by the hand, while Stella had an equally firm hold of Duncan. Rob grinned at her then turned towards Elsie.

'If you'll excuse me, I might just take these lads outside for a run around. They've been travelling all morning and it will do them good.'

'A first-rate idea,' came a deep voice from behind them. Alison watched as Elsie's parents entered the room. Lady Inchcape was pale and slender, leaning on her white-haired husband's arm. He led her to the seat nearest the fire that blazed despite the summer weather and then turned his attention back to Rob and the children, his eyes twinkling. 'One of the servants will show you where the outside toys are. My grandchildren come here often and their toys are at your disposal. Though I'm not sure you need them, eh lads, with those fine swords your father is holding behind his back?'

Rob ushered the boys from the room and Lord Inchcape stood, straight-backed and observant, until everyone had been introduced and seated. Alison watched him with interest. So this was the powerful baron who ran much of British shipping across the globe. The sea had played an enormous part in her own life, from her earliest days growing up on a west-coast sea loch to those years in Thurso with a sailor for a husband, and then Alex's naval career. Even now that she had relocated to Glasgow, a strange twist of fate saw her family still involved in shipping, first with the shipyard and now with this unexpected link to Elsie Mackay and the Inchcapes.

As a maid served the tea, Alex and Lord Inchcape were already involved in a detailed discussion about sea trials on the measured mile near Wemyss Bay, which made little sense to anyone else. Lady Inchcape turned to Alison. 'Elsie tells me you plan to take a pleasure cruise on one of our ships, Mrs Rutherford?'

'Yes, my sister and I are very much looking forward to visiting the Mediterranean on the *Ranchi* next month.'

'You'll have a wonderful time,' Elsie said. 'I do believe the *Ranchi* is my favourite of the ships I've worked on so far. She has the most marvellous ventilation system leading into the cabins so that passengers are never too hot or too cold. And Captain Kennedy, who skippers her, is by far my favourite captain.'

'A grand fellow, Kennedy,' Lord Inchcape said, moving seamlessly between conversations. 'Mrs Rutherford, we would be delighted if you could come for dinner after your voyage and tell us all about it. It's useful to get a fresh perspective, isn't it, Elsie? This whole business of pleasure cruising has taken off since the war and it's important to know where we can improve.'

'I should love to take a cruise one day.' Stella said. 'Do you often travel on the ships yourself? It must be rather splendid to draw the curtains, for example, and know that you chose the fabric.'

Elsie shook her head. 'I've no plans to be on board over the next few months. I'm terribly busy with our new ship under construction in Glasgow, and we do a lot of entertaining here at Glenapp in August and September. Once that's over, Mother and I plan to go to Freiburg for the whole of October, don't we, Mother? We've heard of a splendid sanatorium with a rest cure, which we hope will be just the thing for her. It's so damp here by that time of year.'

Lord Inchcape finished his tea and laid down his cup. 'And now I regret I must leave you for my study. A mountain of correspondence awaits me, as usual.'

'We shall go out and explore the gardens,' Elsie said. 'I've arranged a picnic lunch down on the shore.'

Lady Inchcape smiled graciously. 'Mrs Rutherford, you would be welcome to remain here and take luncheon in the dining room if you prefer.'

'Oh no!' Alison said, horrified, and then modified her tones, afraid of sounding rude. 'I have promised to help with my young grandsons, you see.' Then she hesitated and said truthfully, 'I miss my garden now that we live in Glasgow. It will be such a pleasure to spend time in yours.'

Lady Inchcape nodded politely, but Alison was aware of her daughters laughing at her. As if she would turn down a tramp in the grounds and a picnic on the beach in favour of a refined dining-room luncheon with Lord and Lady Inchcape. The gathering broke up then, and Elsie led them back outside into the soft summer air. They followed a path round the side of the castle to a grand balustraded terrace where they paused, looking down over beautiful formal gardens and beyond them to the sea. Here the dramatic volcanic plug of Ailsa Craig caught the eye, and even from this distance Alison thought she could make out gannets diving around it.

'West over the Atlantic. Next stop America,' came Elsie's voice from behind. She sounded wistful for a moment, then stepped forward briskly. 'Come, let's go down these steps, find Rob and the boys, and head towards the shore.'

It was a long walk but Alison loved every moment, breathing in the scent of freshly cut grass and the heady fragrance of rosebushes. She found herself side by side with Corran and slipped an arm through hers. They hadn't managed a good chat yet since Corran returned to them, all crammed in the boarding house as they were.

At first they discussed Alison's cruise. Corran, who had once spent a summer working in the British School of Archaeology in Rome, was full of enthusiasm. 'You must go to Pompeii when you visit Naples.'

'Yes, we hope to, but we also want to meet Luisa's father and brother.'

Alex and Luisa were walking a little way ahead of them, hand in hand. Corran gestured towards them. 'Very lovey-dovey, aren't they? I never imagined Alex would end up with a child like her. She bolts like a startled horse every time I come near. Perhaps it's because I tried my rusty Italian on her.'

'She's hardly a child, Corran, she's twenty-seven.'

'Ten years younger than he is.'

Alison glanced at her. Was Corran jealous of Luisa? Corran and Alex had been close as children, but that was a long time ago. 'Luisa is good for Alex,' Alison said. 'You need to get to know her better, that's all. It will be interesting to meet Signor Rossi and hear what he has to say. It's difficult for Luisa and Alex to get a clear picture of the political situation through letters.'

'Fine, but don't miss out on Pompeii, because I know you will find it fascinating.'

They walked on, and just as Alison was beginning to wonder if the path would never end and if luncheon in the dining room might not have been a good idea after all, they emerged through trees onto the shore. The 'sweet little beach hut' turned out to be an elegant painted wooden pavilion complete with verandah overlooking the sea. An array of food and drink that made the boys whoop with excitement awaited them on a long table. Tired and hungry, they all helped themselves from the tiny sandwiches, pies and slices of smoked salmon, jugs of lemonade and bottles of champagne.

'This is a bit different from the soggy sandwiches laced with extra sand we had on our childhood picnics,' Alex said, heaping food onto a plate and sitting down on the verandah steps.

'Do you remember that time we had a picnic at Dunnet Head and you managed to drop Father's entire flask of coffee in the sea?' laughed Corran. 'He was not pleased.'

Alison happened to be watching Stella as Corran spoke, and saw the shadow pass over her face. Poor Stella. Alison knew that the easy bond between Corran and Alex this holiday reminded Stella daily of what she had lost. The savagery of Jack's death had not only ripped through her future, it had cast a dark shadow over her childhood memories. But then Stella turned to answer an excited question from one of her sons, and Alison watched as Rob came up behind her and put his arms around her. There was a tenderness in the gesture that Alison thought she hadn't seen for some time. Perhaps this holiday away from Glasgow would be good for Stella and Rob.

More tired that she cared to admit, she was happy to sit in her deckchair in the warm sunshine and watch her family enjoy the afternoon. The boys were playing with a ball on the sand with Rob and Elsie, while Stella had wandered over the rocks with Luisa. Alex and Corran sat, dark head and fair head close together as they had so often been throughout childhood, deep in conversation. But Alison noticed that for all he was listening to his sister, Alex's eyes constantly strayed towards Luisa. When she and Stella turned and walked back, something about Luisa's strained demeanour caught his attention. He got to his feet and put his arm round his wife, steering her away from the others. At that moment Jacky ran up to his mother, catching her by the hand and dragging her over to join in the game. Elsie came back to the pavilion, pouring herself a drink and flopping down beside Alison and Corran.

'It's so lovely to have you all here. I rarely come down to the shore on my own but it's a special place, don't you think?'

Alison looked at her. There was no doubt she was as attractive as the newspapers said, with her dark hair, sparkling eyes and creamy face, flushed just now after running around with the boys. She had the poise and elegance that came with her upbringing, and a confidence about her every movement. Her fame and her wealth had led Alison to dismiss her as a charming socialite whose life of ease had been handed to her on a plate. But watching Elsie now, she could acknowledge there was more to her. There was a strength of character and determination in her features, and a warmth about her welcome that felt entirely genuine. Despite herself, Alison was drawn to the younger woman. Perhaps her friendship with Stella might be a good thing after all.

Elsie was asking Corran about Oxford, and the challenges of being a woman working in classics. 'How do you cope with the condescension of all those male professors?'

Corran leant back and adjusted her hair, which she still wore unfashionably long. 'Many of the men do look down on us, but of course I teach in a women's college. A female cocoon within a man's world, if you like.'

'And are your students permitted to graduate?'

'The girls I teach can graduate. Oxford has awarded degrees to women since 1920. At Cambridge, where I studied myself, it's still the case that women sit the exams but are denied a degree. I was placed first in my year but was given nothing to show for it. It's a scandal that even now, in 1927, there is such discrimination. I don't think I could bring myself to teach there for that reason.'

Elsie nodded. 'I like your female cocoon notion. I think I inhabit something similar.'

'In what way?'

'I'm sure you can imagine just how male-dominated the world of shipbuilding is. Whether it's the "bowler hats" in the boardrooms or the "bunnets" in the yards and workshops, there are men simply everywhere. And then I wander through and give them all a shock. I'm fortunate, of course, that my father employed me – but even he will only permit my official involvement in interior design. Fabrics and finishes are suitable for a woman; engines and business decisions rather less so.'

Alison could see a spark of interest and recognition in Corran's eyes. 'Maddening, isn't it? All my life I've fought against this idea that the female brain is somehow more limited than the male. I can't imagine environments more disparate than your shipyard and my university, yet still the same old attitudes prevail.'

The game on the beach was breaking up and Rob, Stella and the children came to join them. Rob poured himself some more champagne while Stella organised lemonade for the boys. Alex and Luisa were still down at the edge of the sea, hand in hand. Alison saw Stella watching them. 'Everything all right?' she asked.

Stella sat down beside her mother. 'I think so.' She took a slow breath, and in a quiet voice said, 'I just told Luisa that Rob and I are expecting another baby. I wanted her to know first.'

'I see.' Another baby! Alison tried to gather her thoughts. 'Well, that's lovely, of course. Do you feel well? When will the baby arrive?'

'Not until early next year. February I think. But I rather dreaded telling Luisa. I know she does long for a child of her own.'

'It was kind of you to tell her separately.' Alison looked towards the pair at the shore, who were now making their way back up the beach. The wind that whipped across the waves was soft, but dark clouds had gathered on the horizon. Elsie suggested they should return to the house. It was a fairly long walk, and the rain might not be far away.

Alison got to her feet and moved over to the table, tidying the remains of the picnic even as her mind whirled with the implications of Stella's news. 'Are there some hampers we can use to carry this back?'

'Oh, we'll just pile it all into the beach hut. The servants will come back for it later.'

Rob tipped some more champagne into his glass. 'Shame to leave it.' he said with a grin. They gathered their possessions and began the walk back up the path, the two boys running ahead. Alison watched Rob slip an arm around Stella. She had sensed a new tenderness between them. If this baby brought them closer again, that would be a very good thing. On the other hand, her daughter often seemed weighed down with family life and caring for the two boys. How would she cope with the strain and exhaustion of a new baby? She would need a great deal of help. As she slipped her cardigan back on and began the walk up the path towards the castle, Alison was more glad than ever to have booked the cruise with her sister. A holiday ahead of this new arrival might be just what she needed.

Chapter Nine

Glenapp Castle

Although the sky had darkened, the rain stayed away as they made their way back through the gardens. Stella found herself walking beside Corran, and repeated her news for her older sister's benefit. Corran stopped and hugged her.

'That's marvellous! I wonder if it will be another little boy. Is Rob aiming for a whole rugby team perhaps?'

'Oh no, we always wanted three. This will be our last,' Stella said quickly, blushing slightly. Huge families were largely a thing of the past among the middle classes, suggesting that most people she knew used contraception, as she and Rob did, but no one ever alluded to it. She felt awkward mentioning it even obliquely to her maiden sister of all people. Corran surely had very little knowledge of such things, living her cloistered life in her female college. Stella could hardly remember her ever mentioning any male friends other than occasionally that Labour MP she had got to know in France at the end of the war. She decided to probe gently and to move the conversation on at the same time. 'I read an article the other day that mentioned that friend of yours who became an MP. Do you still hear from him?'

'Rarely. I imagine he's very busy with parliamentary business and constituency affairs.' Corran's tone didn't invite further discussion and it was no surprise when she in turn came up with a diversion. 'Look at that door in the wall there. I wonder where it leads?' She turned to look for Elsie. 'Is that a kitchen garden?'

'Yes, and our hothouses. They're quite magnificent. Would you like to take a look?' Elsie pushed the door open, revealing a lush walled haven beyond.

Stella peered through. She could see carefully cultivated beds of fruit and vegetables with grand glasshouses running along one wall. Far too much potential for damage. She shook her head. 'I'll take the boys back up to the lawn for a final run around while the rest of you look in there.'

It had been a long day in the fresh air and Jacky's little legs were tired. She hoisted him up on her hip for the final climb to the terrace, where the two boys seemed happy playing a makeshift game of hopscotch on the slabs. Stella sat down on a wrought-iron chair and breathed in the soft air and that spectacular view over the water with Ailsa Craig standing tall against the ominous mass of thick dark clouds. Even as she remembered Elsie's wistful tone that morning – *west over the Atlantic* – her friend pulled out the seat beside her and sat down, breathless. Almost at once a servant was beside them, unasked, bearing a tray with two tall glasses of lemonade.

'I thought you were in the kitchen garden.'

'Sillers, the head gardener, is there and it's the joy of his heart to show visitors round – especially one as interested and knowledgeable as your mother. I would just be in the way.'

'This has been a marvellous day,' Stella said, sipping her lemonade. 'It was so kind of you to invite us.'

'It's been lovely to get to know your family.'

Stella laughed. 'Do you know, at first I was a bit cross that you'd invited everyone. I rather wanted to come by myself. But actually, it's been such fun for Duncan and Jacky and I'm glad you've met everyone else too.'

'Father has a partridge shooting party arriving this evening, all MPs I believe, and I will have to play the lady hostess as Mother is sure to retire to bed. I can't tell you what a breath of fresh air a day with your family has been. I've had grand conversations with Alex about the shipyards, with Corran about Oxford and with your mother about her forthcoming trip.'

'I'm glad. I'm not sure Mother really approved of our friendship before today. She thought my head was being turned by your luxurious lifestyle.'

She laughed as she said it but a cloud seemed to shadow Elsie's bright face. 'And was it?'

Stella was puzzled. 'No, of course not – at least not in the way she thinks, that I might envy your wealth. Oh, I hope one day Rob and I can have a bigger house, one with rooms for us all and a back door that opens onto our own garden. Especially now that we have a new baby coming.' She smiled across at Elsie and accepted her warm congratulations, but then returned to her subject. 'Money is not the problem.'

'Then what is?'

Stella rested her chin on her hands and stared out to Ailsa Craig. Aware of a slight tremor in her voice, she said, 'I think – I want to be *seen*. I want to exist.' She swallowed. She had never put this into words before. 'I look at Corran and those girls she's educating at university and I think – really, what is the point? What is the point of giving women an education, a career, if they just have to give it all up on marriage? When I was in Paris I worked on some of the most important issues in the world. And then I was offered the chance to move to the League of Nations, but that was just when Rob asked me to marry him so of course I turned it down.'

'And do you regret it?'

'No – no! How could I? I love Rob, and I love Duncan and Jacky. But it does seem hard, that I have to give up every single other aspect of myself in order to have them.'

They were both quiet for a moment, watching the two boys play. The game had descended into an argument, and Jacky as usual was coming off worst. He came running over to his mother, who pulled him up onto her knee and wiped his runny nose with her hanky. She looked over his dark head to Elsie. 'Look at me now! From the glamour of Paris to living out my days in a Glasgow tenement and facing another six months of feeling like a whale.'

'You have a husband who loves you, and whom you love,' Elsie said quietly. 'That counts for a lot.'

There was something jagged in her tone. Elsie had never said much about the end of her marriage to Dennis, but it must have been painful, even if she had managed to avoid a messy divorce with her father instead using his influence to secure an annulment. 'I know,' Stella said carefully. 'And I'm lucky to have the children – I just need to look at Luisa to be aware of that. Does it make me wicked still to long for more?'

'Not wicked, no.'

'I think Mother was afraid I was envious of your beautiful clothes, your grand home, your silver Rolls-Royce, but I really am not. If I envy you anything, it's the fact you get up every day and go to work and you have a purpose. You are seen.'

Stella heard the words piling out of her mouth, a whine as childish as Jacky's, but was unable to stop them – and somewhere, deep down, she didn't want to stop them. Somewhere in the midst of that torrent of self-pity was, she knew, the skelf that had dug deep and was poisoning the rest.

'I suppose each of us wants what lies just out of reach,' Elsie said. Her chin rested on her hand as she gazed out to sea. 'After I escaped my marriage I thought I was free – and then it looked as if my parents were going to put me in a gilded cage here and display me to a whole new set of bidders. Fortunately my father understood, and let me join the business. But still I want more.'

'Such as?'

'I long for my father to include me in the business beyond interior design, and I long for him to take my plans for aviation seriously. But that's a step too far for him.'

'What plans?'

Elsie leant forward. 'Oh, so many! Principally I would like P&O to set up an aviation branch. A commercial airline poised to take advantage of the advances in technology that will make air travel the transport of the future.' Her hands went to her lapel, where Stella had already noticed a small silver brooch shaped like an aeroplane, and she unpinned it. 'This is the *Spirit of St Louis* – the machine Charles Lindbergh used for his record-breaking flight. One day I would like to do something similar.'

'Really?'

'It may be a foolish dream. But it's important to have dreams, don't you think?'

Jacky wriggled down and Stella let him go. 'I suppose that's what I'm saying. I don't think I have any dreams left.'

'I don't believe that for a moment. The children are the main part of your life for now, but it won't always be that way.' Elsie pushed the brooch across the table to her. 'Take this. Keep it as a symbol of all the adventures that lie ahead, for both of us.'

'Elsie, I can't!'

'Of course you can. Don't worry about the value – it's a cheap trinket, they sell them ten a penny. But it means a lot to me as a reminder to hold on to my dreams, and I want you to take it to help you do that too.'

Stella lifted the little brooch and pinned it to her dress, unexpectedly moved. 'Thank you, I will.'

They were silent for a moment, looking out to sea as the first raindrops began to fall. They could hear voices drawing closer. Elsie caught her hand urgently. 'It's hard for me to find true friends, Stella. Everyone wants to be with me because I'm rich. That's why I was afraid when your mother said your head had been turned. To have a friend like you, who loves me for who I am and not for my wealth or the invitations and favours I can obtain, it means the world.'

Stella squeezed her hand. 'To me too.'

And then the rest were back and they stood up to join them. Time to catch the train. They walked round the side of the castle just as a car arrived through the main gates. Lord Inchcape and the staff were already at the entrance, awaiting the newcomers. 'Ah, here you are at last, my dear. Our guests are arriving.'

'I just need to take my friends back to the station, Father, and then I will be there.'

'Surely Lochrie can do that?'

Alison stepped forward. 'Of course he can. We've taken up so much of your time already, Elsie dear, and your father needs you now.'

Lord Inchcape shook Alison's hand. 'Thank you, Mrs Rutherford. I hope you've enjoyed your day with us. Don't forget, we want to see you back here for dinner as soon as you return from your cruise. Here . . .' He slipped a card into her hand. 'Contact me any time. Any help I can offer, I will happily oblige.'

For a moment or two there was confusion. Men dressed in tweed piled out of the newly arrived car, full of hearty greetings, as their shotguns were unloaded. Elsie grimaced quickly to Stella as she climbed into the back of the car, Jacky nearly asleep on her shoulder. She turned her head as they pulled away and saw one of the men leaning very close to Elsie, a proprietorial arm wrapped around her waist.

A gilded cage.

PART TWO
Horizons

September to November 1927

There is a tide in the affairs of men,
Which, taken at the flood, leads on to fortune;
Omitted, all the voyage of their life
Is bound in shallows and in miseries.

Julius Caesar, Act 4, Scene 3, William Shakespeare

Chapter Ten

Glasgow to London

'But Mother – are you sure?'

'Of course I'm sure. I am vexed for poor Maggie, though; to break her leg this week of all weeks.'

'But travelling alone for three weeks . . . Won't you be lonely?'

Alison turned from adding the required luggage label to her suitcase and faced her daughter who was leaning against the door frame. 'I shall hardly be alone on a ship of several hundred passengers, Stella. I'm perfectly capable of making conversation with strangers. Besides, I believe there is quite a fashion among a certain type of widowed lady to take a pleasure cruise. I shall be quite content.'

'Widowed gentlemen too, surely. Perhaps you'll come back with a sweetheart.'

'No need to be foolish, dear. Now, where is my scarf? Thank you. My cab will be here shortly so I'll take my suitcase out onto the step. Let's just say goodbye now.' She hugged her daughter. 'I'll send the boys a postcard from every port. Look after yourself.'

'You too. We have your itinerary so we're going to pin a map up in the kitchen and follow your travels every day. It will do wonders for their geography.' Stella kissed her mother on the cheek. 'What an adventure! Poor Aunt Maggie must be mad with frustration. I wish I could come in her place.'

'We both know that's not possible,' Alison said as she opened the door. 'The agent thinks he will get most of Maggie's fare back so she can use it for another holiday sometime. But it was senseless me cancelling too when everything's in place. And here's the cab – goodbye, my dear!'

Twenty-four hours and several hundred miles later, Alison waited until the cabin door closed behind her steward then lowered herself into the wicker chair. It was bliss to get off her feet and sit, just for a while, in silence. She could feel the slight movement of the ship and the low vibration of the engines. She looked around. They had chosen an inner cabin to keep the price down and she had feared it might be gloomy, but with electric lighting and bright décor the room was light and comfortable. The rugs on the floor added a colourful touch even to this simple cabin, and the two 'berths' looked reassuringly like real beds, with brass bedstands, positioned against two adjacent walls to give a decent amount of floorspace. A notice on the wall explained how to adjust the heating and ventilation system, and Alison smiled as she remembered Elsie's enthusiasm for it that day in Glenapp. This cabin was far more comfortable than the poky hotel room she had endured in London last night. No wonder she was weary, after the long journey down from Glasgow the day before and then barely sleeping a wink on that awful excuse for a mattress, but now she was here. Her home for the next three weeks.

She reached into her handbag for her hairbrush. The cabin they had chosen might not have its own bath or lavatory but there was a neat washstand and mirror in one corner. She walked over to check the glass and her reflection gazed back at her, weary and travelworn. Never mind, nothing a splash of water and a dab of face powder wouldn't help. She opened the wardrobe, neatly incorporated into the wall, in which her steward had already hung her clothes. No doubt there would be all sorts of finery on display in the coming days. Stella and Luisa had tried to persuade her to buy some new outfits for the cruise but she had refused to spend money on anything she wouldn't also wear back home. 'No one will pay the slightest bit of attention to Maggie and me,' she had said.

Well, events were already working out rather differently than she imagined.

There was no Maggie, for one thing, and rather than slipping inconspicuously into a table in the background, she was to dine at the captain's table this evening. There was no requirement to dress formally on the first evening but still, she felt she must take a little more care than might otherwise have been the case.

She had arrived at the P&O passenger berth at Tilbury Docks earlier that day, fatigued and plagued by second thoughts. Even her first glimpse of the *Ranchi* along the quayside, bedecked with colourful flags, failed to lift her spirits. All around her crowds of people rushed about with purpose. As she passed through the ticket office she was inspected, interrogated and directed by countless officials, and yet she still wasn't quite sure where to go next. Doubts assailed her. What kind of fool was she, a woman in her sixties, to imagine she could possibly do this on her own? The moment she'd heard Maggie couldn't make it she should have contacted the travel agent about a refund. The very idea of a jaunt across the Mediterranean was surely a wicked waste of her savings anyway – a quiet few days at the spa hotel in Strathpeffer would be far more fitting! But no, she had chosen to plough on regardless, and now, assuming she wasn't confined to her cabin with seasickness for the entire trip, she would either find herself completely alone and without conversation for three whole weeks or – and even less appealing – lumped in with all the widows of a certain age and required to chat endlessly about garden fetes and the royal family. *Alison, you were a fool to come.* She heaved her suitcase up with two hands and glared at the woman dressed in furs – who wears furs on a warm day in September? – who minced in front of her, issuing plaintive instructions to the porter pushing her teetering tower of luggage on a trolley towards the gangway.

'There you are!'

Someone caught hold of her arm amid the seething crowds. 'I've been looking for you everywhere. They said you'd checked in but you weren't yet on board. Are you waiting for your sister? Let me find someone to help with your suitcase.'

Alison turned and found herself facing Elsie, trim and sparkling as ever in a smart grey felt outfit, her arms wide in her characteristic gesture of welcome. As she explained Maggie's misfortune, her luggage was whisked away and Elsie took her arm, steering her up the gangway. 'Are you joining this cruise after all?' Alison asked, bewildered.

'Oh no. I was at the docks today anyway, and I realised you would be leaving on board the *Ranchi*. I thought I'd come to wave you off. How terribly unlucky for your sister. Are you travelling alone then? Good for you!' Elsie glanced at her watch. 'We must make sure you are well looked after, particularly now that you are on your own. There's just time for me to show you round. Come along!'

Alison found herself guided through a maze of corridors as Elsie opened doors and pointed out different rooms. 'That's the main dining saloon in there, and this is the drawing room – it has some lovely cosy little nooks and crannies. This music saloon can also double as a ballroom. The *Ranchi* has a first-rate orchestra.

Ah, now there's a piece of luck – here's Captain Kennedy. Hello, Captain, come and meet a friend of mine!'

'Miss Mackay, what a pleasure. I didn't expect to see you on board today.'

'No, and I'll be leaving just as soon as 'visitors ashore' is called. But may I introduce Mrs Alison Rutherford, who is boarding today. Her sister who was her fellow traveller has had an unfortunate accident and so Mrs Rutherford is making the trip alone. I assured her you would look after her.'

Alison wanted to clarify that she didn't need any looking after, thank you, but it was hard to do so without being rude and anyway, the captain's accent as he welcomed her on board chased other thoughts away. 'Oh, you're from Glasgow!' she exclaimed without meaning to.

'It's always a pleasure to meet a fellow Scot. Would you do me the honour of joining me for dinner at my table this evening, Mrs Rutherford?'

'The best of our officers are always Scots, and Captain Kennedy is the very best,' Elsie laughed. 'Now I only have a few moments but we must see about your cabin. Do you have a suite? A *cabin-de-luxe*?'

'We booked a two-berth inner cabin.'

Elsie frowned and looked to the captain. 'Is the ship full or is there any possibility of an upgrade for Mrs Rutherford?'

The last few moments had been so bewildering that Alison felt she had hardly uttered a sensible word, but at this she grabbed hold of her scattered thoughts and her self-respect. 'I'm perfectly happy with the cabin I have chosen and paid for,' she said firmly. 'No, really. I don't want any favours.'

She saw a flash of humour in the captain's vivid blue eyes. 'Of course, Mrs Rutherford. I wouldn't dream of it. I could however perhaps ensure that no one else is allocated the bed your sister was to be in. Would that be permitted – or would it count as a favour?'

He was mocking her. Alison drew herself up but at that moment a loud voice was heard calling for all visitors to return to shore. 'Oh heavens, I must be going and I haven't nearly shown you everything I wanted to!' Elsie cried. 'Let's find you a good space on deck for the departure. Be seeing you, Captain, have a good voyage!' She set off almost at a run, and hustled Alison up a couple of steep flights of stairs. Then they were on deck, pressed against the rail alongside many others. A steward handed Alison a bright pink ball of paper ribbon, even as Elsie kissed her. 'Have a super holiday and if you need anything, get the captain to wire me at Glenapp. I'll be there most of the time you're away.' Then she was gone, and Alison followed the example of those around her and tossed the coloured ball to the crowd waiting on shore, holding tight to one end as she did so. The men on the dock freed the ropes and chains, and soon the great liner was held to shore only by a fairy web of pink, green and mauve streamers. Alison caught sight of Elsie at the front of the crowd, waving madly, and waved back. As the *Ranchi* gently slipped away from the quayside to begin her progress towards the mouth of the River Thames, Alison breathed out a long sigh and smiled.

As she emerged onto deck after a splendid dinner, Alison breathed in the cool, salty air and reflected that she was somehow always drawn back to the sea, from the shore of Loch Linnhe, where her father had been the ferryman between Corran and Ardgour, to the wild Pentland Firth. She missed the sea in Glasgow, but take a walk anywhere near the Clyde and great iron Leviathans of destroyers, liners and cargo ships dominated the skyline, providing not only work and prosperity for the city but a tantalising glimpse of different worlds to those who chose to dream. The captain had nodded at that and told her how as a wide-eyed twelve-year-old who had never been further than Govan, he had stepped on board one of those cargo ships to begin his apprenticeship as an indentured seaman. The tide had washed right up that river and swept him from the tenements, and he never looked back.

She had enjoyed her conversation with him over dinner. She had spoken about Thurso and he had told her of his empty house in Helensburgh, closed up since the death of his wife. They'd chatted about the voyage ahead and she'd shared her plans to meet up with Luisa's father in Naples. All this as stewards brought plentiful food and wine while the grand dining saloon, so beautifully designed by Elsie, hummed with conversation and laughter.

When the meal was over he offered to escort her to the drawing room before returning to the bridge, but she preferred to go out on deck for a while. And so he had departed, promising to come back and join her later if possible, and here she was, leaning over the rail and breathing in the salty darkness of the south-east English coast.

She tugged her wrap around her shoulders. How ridiculous all her earlier fears now seemed. She watched the lights of smaller fishing vessels bobbing in the darkness and thought how extraordinary it was that no one – *no one* – knew exactly where she was or what she was doing at this precise moment. Her children, her grandchildren, her sister, her friends from the church and her charities . . . she had three whole weeks in which she need please no one but herself. She was shocked by how much the thought thrilled her.

It would take them three days to reach Lisbon, their first destination, and before that they must cross the Bay of Biscay. 'It's set fair,' Captain Kennedy had told her. 'We shouldn't have any problems.' But Alison realised that even seasickness wouldn't worry her, not with this new and liberating concept of being entirely without responsibility. If she wanted to lie in bed and suffer, no one would be affected. Had that ever been the case in her life before? Even if Maggie had been here, she reflected a little guiltily, she would have felt the need to soldier on. But as it was, this sense of freedom was utterly intoxicating and she laughed aloud in the darkness with glee.

A door behind her opened and she turned, wondering if it might be the captain come to find her, but a noisy group of young people tumbled out, laughing and singing. She watched as they passed her without seeing her – the invisibility that comes with age suited her just fine sometimes – and took up a position a little further along the rail, fooling around. But the spell of the moment was broken, and she became aware for the first time of the coolness of the air around her, and of just how tired she was. It had been a long two days and her cabin was a welcome prospect. She stepped back inside and made her way slowly downstairs.

Slowly?

She wasn't really taking her time in case the captain returned, was she?

Annoyed at herself, she sped up and soon found her cabin. Her steward had turned down the bed and left the lamps on with a soft and welcome glow. She really could get used to this! She gave herself a wry smile in the mirror, remembering Stella's throwaway comment about a sweetheart. She had not the slightest desire for another man in her life, but she couldn't deny it had been an enjoyable experience to have the captain pay attention to her, listen carefully to her and laugh with her. Of course, he had been asked by Elsie – who was after all his employer – to welcome her on this first evening. 'Tomorrow you slip back among the ranks of the unnoticed,' she murmured to herself as she began to unpin her hair.

It really was a delightful prospect.

Chapter Eleven

Oxfordshire

Corran reached the end of the lane without meeting a soul. The first tinge of yellow was beginning to show on some of the leaves that hung completely still in the damp mist, and her boots were splashed with wet mud. She pushed open the rickety gate and walked down an overgrown path to the door. No light glowed from the window; she was first as usual. The key should be where they always left it under a broken stone near the corner of the cottage. Yes, there it was. She unlocked the door and stepped into the tiny hallway, breathing in the familiar chilly dampness. To her left was the kitchen and she walked through and laid the bag of provisions she had brought on the table in the centre, crouching down to light the stove. She might have a long wait, but she could boil some water for a cup of tea. Once that was underway she crossed to the living room. She had left the fireplace set last time she was here, so as long as the wood was not too damp she should get some heat into the room before too long. She reached out to light the kindling with hands that trembled slightly. This part – the anticipation – was always the worst.

She wasn't quite clear who owned this cottage but no one ever appeared to use it other than themselves. Their visits were sporadic; they had last snatched a few days here before she travelled north to Scotland for her summer holiday. This time they would spend a weekend together before she cleaned up her boots and took the train back to Oxford, arriving on Sunday afternoon in plenty of time for dinner. Her colleagues and students knew she occasionally stayed with a friend in the country, and no one thought anything of it. She occasionally caught her older colleague Katherine Jones, whose rooms were adjacent to her own, watching her thoughtfully, but really, what was there to notice? Spinster Miss Rutherford, dry and dusty classics tutor, nearly forty now and like Katherine herself one of that generation of 'surplus women' left behind by the war – there couldn't possibly be anything interesting about her private life.

Keeping secrets had become second nature to Corran.

It was harder for Arthur, of course. Ever since he had been elected Labour MP for his Manchester constituency at the 1922 General Election, his life had come under a fair degree of scrutiny. They kept to strict rules, rarely meeting anywhere other than at this cottage, which Arthur had arranged through some friend. No other communication in between times. They used postcards of France – a nod to where they had first met, working for the army education scheme towards the end of the war – with a simple code to confirm the dates on which they could both be here. Weeks went by without contact, punctuated by these short, intense, stolen days hidden away in the cottage at the end of the lane.

Corran decanted some hot water into a cracked basin and carried it through to the icy bedroom, which had no heat source at all, then made her tea and took it into the sitting room. She perched on the edge of the worn sofa, leaning towards the fire. It wasn't yet warm enough to remove her coat. She had brought both novel and newspaper but couldn't relax enough to read. Sometimes she wondered what a normal relationship would feel like. Her relationship with Arthur was like the bathwater spurting from the college pipes: either scalding hot or icy cold. Week followed week in the lilac-scented haze of the college walls when she barely thought of him at all. She taught her students and read her books and wrote at her desk overlooking the garden or strolled by the river, and she was content. She was content. But then a postcard would appear in her pigeonhole, she would cross the days out on her calendar, the train would carry her to the deserted single platform station, and finally she would find herself sitting here, perched on the edge of the sofa, every fibre of her body hungry and desperate for him to walk through that door. A coiled spring.

It was their own fault. From early on in their affair, when she had startled herself by realising how easy it was to shed her maidenly reserve, they had begun each reunion by falling into bed together. No demure cup of tea, no easy chat to catch up on each other's lives. That would come later. As soon as Arthur walked through that door she knew they would be in each other's arms, shedding their clothes for all the cottage was freezing, as needy as opium addicts starved for weeks of their drug. So no, she didn't miss him during those weeks when she couldn't see him, but now that pleasure was imminent she sat gripped by tension, her whole body aroused with anticipation.

She laid down the cup and saucer and walked to the window, pushing aside the grimy net curtain that screened them from the outside world. No sign of him coming down the lane. He never knew which train he would catch when he came straight from the Houses of Parliament, like today. He would arrive stinking of cigar smoke from long committee meetings, his scar prominent against the pallor of his face, his eyes heavy and his shoulders drooping.

It was a far cry from those brief glory days when Labour had actually been in government, albeit minority, and he had worked with John Wheatley to deliver much-needed new housing across the country. That was Arthur's proudest achievement, but how quickly things had changed. Last time she had seen him, in July, he had been in despair at legislation the Conservative government had just brought in to limit trade union power in response to last year's General Strike. 'And many of my Labour colleagues don't even oppose it.'

There was a movement in the lane. The window had steamed up a little as heat began to emerge from the fire, so she dragged her sleeve across it. Yes, here he was, walking unevenly with his old injury just as he had done that first time she'd seen him on the platform at Dieppe. She knew now how it felt to run her fingers down the dreadful scars beneath his shirt that marred his white skin all down one side, the legacy of the exploding shell on the Somme that had ended his war. He was drawing closer; he raised an arm in greeting. She moved to the door and held it open. He walked through, laying down his bag right there in the tiny hallway. She closed the door and turned the key, locking it firmly before turning towards him and opening her arms. They were together and they were safe.

When their lust was sated and their slippery bodies had begun to cool once more in the chilly air of the bedroom, they were at last ready to move into the rest of their weekend together. Corran hugged the thin blanket round herself and watched him dress, then slipped out of bed, her body tingling with cold and with the aftermath of passion, and removed her contraceptive sponge, cleaning up using the water she had laid out earlier. Soon they were in the kitchen, and as she pulled out a chair and sat down, he lifted eggs from the basket and began to make an omelette.

Corran had spent much of her life in institutions where her food was made for her and Arthur was by far the better cook. She adored the intimacy of these moments. It was as if they had to get the sex out of the way first, and now she could enjoy just being here with him, watching the flex of his wrist as he whisked the eggs, the deftness of his long fingers as he chopped the onion, the half smile on his face as he told her a funny story from his day. She dug in the basket and pulled out some cider, pouring two glasses for them. It was another nod to the beginning of their friendship in a cabin hidden deep in a forest in northern France, a cabin that they often said eerily foreshadowed this little English cottage.

As he served the omelette and pushed her plate across the table to her, Corran realised how hungry she was. Was there anything better than this – freshly cooked food and two whole days with the man she loved? 'Delicious.'

They ate their supper and decided against going outside for a walk in the fading light, instead going through to the little sitting room where Arthur built up the fire once more while Corran put Beethoven on the gramophone. 'How's the novel coming along?' he asked as she returned to sit beside him on the sofa, tucking her legs up under her and leaning her head on his shoulder.

She looked into the crackling flames. Arthur was the only person in the world who knew that when she sat scribbling at her desk she was probably not working on Latin translations or lectures on Greek architecture but on a detective novel set amid the ancient ruins of Rome with a lady archaeologist as its protagonist. 'It's finished. I've just sent it off to a few publishers,' she admitted.

'Don't suppose you'll let me read it?'

'No. If they like it I'll know it's worthwhile and you may read it, but if no one wants to publish it then I'll burn it unseen.'

'It's bound to be worthwhile,' he said, stroking her hair behind her ear. 'If Miss Sayers can do it then so can you! I'm sure you're far cleverer than she is.'

'I'm clever at ancient languages and mythology and even at crosswords, but that doesn't mean I'll be clever at creating characters other people want to read about.'

Arthur stretched out his legs. 'When you write your next one you should set it in the House of Commons. I could give you a whole host of evil characters to kill off.'

'That would be a bit of a giveaway, don't you think?' she said, tilting her head to smile up at him. 'People might wonder where I got all that insider information.'

Arthur groaned. 'Oh, if only we could —'

She reached up and put her fingers over his mouth. 'Sssh. Don't spoil it. You know we said we wouldn't. Not ever.'

It was true. This silence was the cost of continuing to see each other. Years ago, when they had realised they couldn't bear to let each other go, they had agreed never to discuss the possibility of being together openly, never to dwell on what simply couldn't be.

It simply couldn't be because Arthur was already married.

He had told Corran in those early days in France that his marriage to Mary was a dreadful mistake. They were not the only couple to be swept into hasty decisions by the emotion of a young sweetheart heading off to war. By the time they realised their incompatibility there was nothing to do but live with it. There was no wealthy father in the background, as for the Honourable Elsie Mackay, who could arrange a convenient annulment and make it all go away. For Arthur and Mary, the only possibility would have been an unpleasant and scandalous divorce, which neither of them wanted and which in any case became impossible once Arthur decided to pursue a parliamentary career. Instead he found solace with Corran, his love. He assured her that Mary wasn't in the least bit interested in whom he spent time with as long as he was discreet, and he inferred, if not quite stating aloud, that she too had other relationships.

With a fulfilling career and no desire to marry, Corran found it easy enough to accept Arthur's home life and his sham marriage. Then came the sticky moment four years ago when he confessed that Mary was pregnant. Perhaps it had been naïve of her to imagine that husband and wife no longer shared a marriage bed, but the hurt and bewilderment of that day stayed with her. She wanted to end it then, arguing that his new role as a father changed everything, but he pleaded with her. When the next postcard arrived in her pigeonhole, she wrestled with herself but in the end was drawn back to the tiny cottage and all it contained. The rarely mentioned existence of young Ronald remained as a hard knot in Corran's stomach, but at least Mary produced no more children. The months passed and the years passed, and the rhythm of college terms and idyllic escapes to the cottage continued.

Only they had to be careful. Every moment of every day they had to be careful. For theirs was a relationship that, if it ever became known, would detonate an explosion violent enough to destroy both their careers.

Two days later Corran waited until Arthur was safely away on his train and then locked up the cottage and returned to the railway platform. On the short journey back to Oxford she gazed out at fields slipping by, every moment of the last forty-eight hours a smouldering fire within her. Its glow would sustain her through the chilly weeks ahead, as the nights lengthened and ice formed on the inside of her college window.

The train pulled into the station and she opened her compartment door, walked along the corridor and stepped down onto the platform. As she did so she heard someone calling her name and turned. Her colleague Katherine was striding along the platform towards her, tying her headscarf as she walked.

'Corran! I thought it was you. How funny, I must have been in the next carriage. Have you had a nice weekend?'

'Very pleasant, thank you.'

Katherine slipped an arm through hers. 'I've been in London visiting my brother. Did you get on at Paddington too?'

'No, I joined the train en route.' She hesitated. 'The friends I stay with live in the countryside.'

'Splendid.' As they left the station and walked through Oxford towards the college, Katherine spoke about the play she had seen in London the night before and Corran shook off her disquiet. It was natural enough that they would both return on the same train, just in time for tea, and Katherine showed no further interest in her weekend, talking instead about the forthcoming week. As they passed together through the gate of St Hilda's, nodding to the porter, Corran felt the routines and rituals of college life reach out and claim her once more.

Until next time.

Chapter Twelve

Nice

More than a week into her cruise, Alison felt completely at ease. She had got to know the ship, finding her own favourite corners, and had made casual friendships with some fellow travellers while quietly maintaining her independence. At Lisbon, Gibraltar and Palma she had gladly joined excursions on offer and had been interested in all she had seen, but she was even happier sitting on deck with her knitting or novel on her lap, looking out to sea.

This evening they would arrive in Monaco where the ship would stay for two nights. She was scanning through a list of sightseeing excursions when a shadow fell across her. She looked up to see Captain Kennedy. She had dined at his table on two more occasions and had walked with him on deck now and then; now he had sought her out.

'Not taking part in the deck quoits competition, Mrs Rutherford?'

She glanced along the deck in the direction of shouts of laughter and enthusiastic applause. 'I rather fear I would disgrace myself if I were to try! I never was much good at sports. A brisk walk is more my idea of exercise.'

'In that case, would you like to accompany me around the deck?' he asked, extending his arm.

She wished he wouldn't stand and watch her as she tried to get up from the deckchair because really, there was no elegant way of doing that, and his outstretched hand simply made her feel more awkward. She lurched towards him then smoothed down her frock and took his arm. 'Thank you.'

'Do you mind if I smoke?' he asked, taking out his pipe.

'Not at all.'

'We'll arrive in Monaco harbour in time for dinner,' he said once he had lit up. 'Do you have plans for our time here?'

'I expect I shall explore Monaco independently. I prefer wandering around these towns and harbours at my own pace. And I'd rather like to see Nice, so I'll join an excursion for that.'

'Actually, that's why I sought you out. I shall travel to Nice myself tomorrow morning by motor car. I've an appointment with one of our agents there. It shouldn't take long but it's a matter I prefer to deal with personally. I wonder, if you don't have other plans, would you care to accompany me? My business won't take long and then we could perhaps have lunch together and take a look at Nice. It's a beautiful town.'

Alison glanced up at him, sharp for any hint of duty, but could see only genuine warmth in his blue eyes. 'I'd love to if it's not an inconvenience to you.'

'You would be doing me a favour. I don't often get the chance of some leisure time on a voyage, and if I went alone I'm sure I would just turn around and come straight back once my business was done. This way we both have an enjoyable day.'

A red ball bounced across the deck right into their path, bringing their promenade to a halt. Captain Kennedy kicked it gently back towards its owner, a small boy of similar age to Duncan. A young woman in a nanny's uniform snatched it up and apologised, her cheeks burning as she realised her charge had sent his ball rolling into the path of the ship's captain.

'It must be hard to keep children entertained on a voyage,' Alison said. 'I have two grandsons around that age and they're constantly on the go.'

'I have three granddaughters. One of the girls has a real affinity with the sea, but it's hard to know what she can do with it. If she'd been born a boy she would follow me into P&O.'

Long ago in far-off Thurso, Stella had longed, like Alex, to go to sea. It had not been possible because she was a girl. 'Why don't you speak to Elsie – I mean Miss Mackay,' Alison said. 'I'm sure she would take an interest in a young woman looking for a career in the shipping line.'

Captain Kennedy laughed. 'She's just seven at the moment so it's a bit soon, but it's a good thought. I'll bear it in mind. Although what her mother, my daughter, would say I hate to think. She has no time for the sea. I stay with them when I'm on shore leave, and young Janet can't get enough stories of the ocean wave.' He stopped. They had reached the door that led to the bridge. 'But now I must leave you. Thank you so much for agreeing to accompany me tomorrow, Mrs Rutherford. Shall I meet you in the drawing room at 9.30?'

'That sounds ideal. I'm looking forward to it,' she said and watched him depart. This voyage continued to be full of surprises.

The drive from Monaco to Nice was every bit as spectacular as her guidebook promised. She had expected him to drive but one of the stewards took the wheel as they sat together in the back. 'I can steer a ship but rather shamefully I've never learnt to drive a motor car. I spend so much time at sea, there's little need.' He insisted she sat on the left to get the full glory of the views as the road climbed and curved and dropped along the rugged coastline. Tiny red-roofed villages, elegant modern mansions and breathtakingly beautiful harbours sat against an improbably deep azure sea. For the most part Alison drank it in silently, occasionally bracing herself to avoid being flung against him as the driver navigated a particularly sharp bend.

'It's such an extraordinary colour of blue,' she said, as they passed Villefranche-sur-Mer and followed the coast round. 'I think I imagined the Mediterranean would be like Argyll and the islands, you know, those white sands and stunning blue-green seas. But this is a very different shade of blue. It's almost as if a child had chosen blue from a paintbox – the simplest and bluest of blues.'

They arrived in Nice where Captain Kennedy suggested leaving her in the salon of a good hotel for morning tea while he conducted his business, but Alison was having none of it. 'I believe there's a flower market; I should like to see that.'

She spent a happy hour wandering amid the flowers and fragrances of Cours Saleya and losing herself in the narrow streets of the old town before a glance at her wristwatch told her it was time to make her way to the Hotel Negresco on the promenade des Anglais, where they had arranged to meet for lunch. The midday sunshine was strong and the breeze rising from the sea was disconcertingly warm for someone from Scotland. The waves crashed powerfully onto the pebble beach as she hurried along the promenade among fashionable couples out for a stroll. She could see the grand dome of the Negresco ahead of her, but before she reached it she saw Captain Kennedy coming towards her. How hot he must be in his naval uniform! He stopped and held out his hands as though to prevent her walking any further.

'Is something wrong? Was there a problem with your meeting?'

His face was grave but he shook his head. 'My meeting was fine. I trust your morning has been enjoyable too. Regrettably it seems there has been a terrible tragedy close to the Negresco and things are in a state of upheaval there. It might be more pleasant to find somewhere else for our lunch.'

'What kind of tragedy?'

He shook his head. 'Let's wait until we're seated and we can talk properly.'

Alison glanced backwards towards the grand hotel. There did seem to be a flurry of people outside. Then she hurried along beside Captain Kennedy, finding she had to walk quickly to keep up with his long stride. He seemed distracted, but led her through an archway into streets she recognised, where she had been wandering just a short time earlier. They stopped at a pavement café opposite the opera building. 'It's a bit simpler but do you think this would do? I've eaten here before and the food is good.'

'It's far more to my taste,' Alison said honestly, glancing at the tables with their cheerful yellow tablecloths. 'I'm not really one for fine dining – with the exception of the *Ranchi*, of course!'

He laughed and pulled out the chair for her. Soon they were seated with a carafe of wine between them, and he told her what had been happening along at the Negresco.

'An appalling tragedy took place last night. You'll be aware of the dancer Isadora Duncan?'

'Of course.' American Miss Duncan was a familiar figure from newspapers and magazines. Her uninhibited and imaginative dance career had won her international fame, but censure and scandal followed both her professional and private life wherever she went. If she thought about her at all, Alison rather admired her, as she admired any woman who refused to be constrained by society's expectations.

'Miss Duncan was trying out a new automobile last night, driving along the promenade close to the Negresco, when the end of her scarf was caught by the wind and became tangled in the spokes of the wheel. By all accounts it dragged her from the car, her neck broken.'

Alison's hand flew to her mouth. 'Oh, how dreadful. Such a beautiful, free-spirited woman. What a terrible way to die.'

'Indeed. There are still some policemen along at the hotel this morning, and whole crowds of ghoulish onlookers. I thought we would have a more pleasant lunch elsewhere. I hope you don't mind.'

'Not at all,' Alison said, although somewhere at the back of her mind she heard the old familiar echo of decisions being made for her. She picked up the menu and tried to focus on that rather than on the mental image of a beautiful, free-spirited woman dragged from her motor car by the fine fabric she had carelessly slung round her neck a few moments earlier. She smiled across at Captain Kennedy. 'This is perfect. I think I'll try the mussels. What will you have?'

The meal was delicious and conversation flowed freely between them. They found themselves talking about Glasgow, the city they had in common. 'I'm seldom there nowadays,' Captain Kennedy said. 'I returned occasionally as a young man while my parents were still living, but each time I felt less connected to the city. Now I spend most of my shore leave with my married daughter in England but I don't belong there either. The sea does that to you. It's hard to put down roots in water.'

'Glasgow fascinates me. It feels like a city trying to work itself out. Maybe that's because I'm an outsider myself.'

'I expect you're far less of an outsider now than I am, and I was born in Glasgow.'

'That's my point,' Alison said, finishing her wine and refusing a top-up. 'I'm an incomer, but Glasgow is a city made up of as many incomers as people like yourself who were born there. I think that makes for a different character of city and I like it. I like getting on the subway and listening to the voices and trying to work out whether they come from the north or the east or from Ireland or further afield. One hears the Glaswegian in their voices, and I don't just mean accents. It's as if their old lives are laced through with a sharp taste of Glasgow hardship and humour. My daughter-in-law, Luisa, she has many Italian friends in Glasgow, and it's fascinating to watch how they hold their two cultures together. The children who grow up here create a new sort of identity, a kind of Scottish Italianness or Italian Scottishness that is neither one nor the other but something unique in its own right. All of that, it seems to me, seeps into the tenements and the shops and the factories that make up Glasgow, creating a very individual kind of city.' She stopped. 'Sorry, Captain Kennedy, I'm talking too much.'

'Please – would you call me Matthew?'

Her mouth was dry, and she thought she might have that other glass of wine after all. She must be spending too much time alone to be babbling on like that! Yet there was something about him that made him very easy to talk to. 'Of course. And my name is Alison,' she said, looking at his vivid blue eyes, his sun-weathered face, his dark hair liberally threaded with silver.

'Thank you, Alison. Please don't apologise. What you describe makes me think of a ship's crew, which I suppose is the 'city' I know best. We have a real mix of races and types on board, from the newly minted officer cadets straight from Dartmouth to the lascars, without whom nothing would get done. You'll have noticed them.'

She had, although there was little interaction between the

passengers and the Indian crew members who were busy around the ship. She supposed it was natural, given P&O's strong links with the British Empire in India, that they would employ a good number of Indian crewmen. The *Ranchi* spent much of her year on the Bombay mail route. She said so to Matthew, who nodded. 'That's true, but also many Indians came over to serve with our forces in the war,' he said. 'Afterwards some chose to stay and work on ships sailing out of British ports, although that did cause tension as there are people who believed the lascars should be dismissed in favour of British veterans.'

'That's hardly fair if they came here to fight for the Empire.'

'Indeed.'

They finished the meal and Captain Kennedy – Matthew – insisted on paying. 'You are here as my guest today.' As they left the café and walked back to the promenade, he lit his pipe and asked what she would like to do next. 'We could climb up to the castle for the tremendous view, although it is quite a hike. Or we could wander round the harbour.'

'Perhaps the harbour, but first I must buy a postcard. I've promised my two grandsons, Duncan and Jacky, that I'll send one from every place I visit.' And then, from some place she really didn't expect, came the words, 'Jacky is named for his uncle, my younger boy, Jack. He was killed near Arras.'

The pause after her words was filled only by the sound of the waves washing the pebble shore, and it lasted so long that she knew what must be coming.

'I had a son. William. He went down on the *Invincible*.' Another long pause but she could tell he wasn't finished. 'I was away at sea and his mother struggled under the weight of grief. By the time I came home she was dead too.'

And there it was again. Nearly a decade after the end of the war, and life had slowly rebuilt itself to such an unimaginable extent that one could take a voyage on a luxurious vessel for no purpose other than sheer pleasure. But beneath the smooth ripple of the sparkling waters lurked hideous dark depths from which the sea monster of grief might burst forth at any moment, tears cascading from its gnarled back.

Jack.

William.

She slipped her arm into his and as they stood together in the warm air, looking out over the glorious picture-postcard view of the bay, they saw instead the ravaged wastelands of Flanders, the churning, blazing waters of Jutland.

The inexpressible comfort of someone else who knew.

Chapter Thirteen

Glasgow

'That sounds like the post, Jacky. Run and get it, will you, love?'

Stella unpacked a parcel of mutton and some vegetables from her shopping bag along with the newspaper. Rob was with a patient in the consulting room and would eat with them before heading out on house calls in the afternoon. Tomorrow was a shipyard day, when he would come home smelling of beer and cigarette smoke, full of stories of the men he had met. Meanwhile Stella was trying to get to grips with the extra housework and childcare responsibilities that came her way in her mother's absence. She was into the fourth month of her pregnancy now and had more energy again, but she missed the chance to sit down between chores and have a good blether over a cup of tea. Instead she found herself breaking up the monotony of the long hours with only quiet, dreamy Jacky for company by reading the newspaper in more detail than she would previously have done. She had taken to buying it while out for the messages in the morning, rather than leaving Rob to bring it in later. It was a window onto the world beyond the four walls of her kitchen.

Jacky ran back into the kitchen. Not so silent or dreamy now! He was jumping with excitement as he thrust a picture postcard into her hand. She crouched down to look at it with him. Gibraltar Rock. She showed him where his name was written beside Duncan's – *Masters Duncan and Jacky Campbell* – and read out his gran's message, then let him feast on the image on the front as she poured him a glass of milk. Only then did she pick up the other item he had discarded, and her heart leapt as she recognised Elsie's writing. She would get the stew started, and then sit down with a cup of tea, a cigarette and the pleasure of Elsie's letter. The newspaper could wait.

Even the writing paper Elsie used was thick and luxurious, embossed with the words *Glenapp Castle* and that now-familiar coat of arms. The feel of it under her fingertips filled her with extraordinary pleasure.

My dear Stella,

Just a quick note to tell you that I saw your mother off at Tilbury last week. What a shame your aunt couldn't go! Still, your mother seemed happy enough. I introduced her to Captain Kennedy and the last time I saw her she was waving enthusiastically among colourful streamers and flags as the Ranchi eased away from the quay. What an adventure!

Stella pushed down the surge of envy that threated to rise up inside her. It was good of Elsie to see her mother off. What a difference that day in August had made. Before that, Alison had been openly sceptical about Stella's friendship with Elsie but now the whole family had embraced her. Why, Mother even had an invitation from Lord Inchcape himself to report back on her voyage!

I am writing to you at my desk in Glenapp, overlooking the terrace where we drank lemonade. It's one of those autumn days where there's a startling clarity to the light. I look out on Ailsa Craig and the ocean beyond and almost fancy I can see all the way to the eastern seaboard of America.

Jacky was tugging at her skirt so Stella laid the letter down to fetch him some paper and crayons, wondering as she often did if he might have inherited some of his uncle Jack's artistic talent. True, his scribbles looked no different to any other child's, but he never seemed happier than with crayon in hand.

Talking of adventure, I wonder if you have read about the flight of Captain Hamilton, Colonel Minchin and Princess Anne of Löwenstein-Wertheim-Freudenberg? They set off over a week ago to attempt the journey westwards across the Atlantic, but nothing has been heard of them since. I look out of my window and wonder – are they out there somewhere above that ocean? But of course, I know they must be dead.

A knock at the door interrupted the sound of Elsie's voice in her head. Stella was tempted to ignore it, but with Rob busy in the consulting room she had better see who it was. She laid down the letter, walked through to the hallway and opened the door.

'Good morning, Mrs Campbell. Is your mother in?'

The lady in the close was swaddled in coat and hat as if it were the middle of winter. Stella vaguely recognised her. 'I'm sorry, she's away on holiday at the moment.'

'Is she? Now that's a nuisance. You'll be missing her, I'm sure. I've seen you in church with your wee boys. Quite a handful, aren't they?'

Stella swallowed. Nosy besom. 'Oh, they're not so bad,' she

said as evenly as possible. 'But I'm afraid Mother won't be back for a couple of weeks. Can I help at all?'

'Not really, dear, but perhaps I could leave something for you to give to her.'

'Of course. Won't you come in and have a cup of tea, Mrs . . .'

'Mrs Baker. No, I won't trouble you, lass. If I could just leave these leaflets for her, that would be grand. She will know what to do with them.'

Stella took the bundle and closed the door behind the visitor, mightily relieved that her dutiful offer of hospitality had been turned down. Anxious to get back to Elsie's letter, she hurried through and dropped the leaflets on the table. She glanced at Jacky, who was still occupied with his crayons, then sat down, topped up her tea and picked up the letter once more.

I know her a little, the Princess. Knew her, I suppose I should say. She was older than me but we attended some of the same social events, and we shared a passion for aviation. She was an Englishwoman but strangely proud of her German title, the legacy of a very brief marriage to a German prince before the war. Most others would have dropped it but that's Anne for you: never one to bow to convention! She was a brave, brave woman, and what makes me angry is that every single newspaper report I've seen depicts her as a silly old frump with more money than sense while the men, Captain Hamilton and Colonel Minchin, are tragic heroes. She financed their effort, and went with them as a passenger in order to become the first woman to 'fly the sea'. Instead I fear she has become the first woman to die in the attempt.

Stella remembered Elsie's words as they sat in the warm afternoon air, watching the dark clouds gather out to sea. *One day I would like to do something similar. It may be a foolish dream.* The brooch Elsie had given her was pinned to her coat, a talisman of both their hopes. But the death of this princess was surely a reminder to Elsie of just how dangerous some dreams could be.

Meanwhile that awful American Charles Levine is the truly irresponsible one, flying from Paris to England with no authorisation and barely the first idea how to handle an aeroplane. I see he's signed up Captain Hinchliffe to attempt the east–west crossing. Did I tell you my friend Tony is preparing to do the same thing? I do hope he gets there ahead of Levine and Hinchliffe, but I have heard that Hinchliffe is one of the best. The race is on!

The names Elsie mentioned meant little to Stella. Her friend was so caught up in all this aviation fever, which to Stella was a distant world, as unreal and dreamlike as the pictures in which Elsie had once acted. She skimmed those paragraphs when reading the newspaper, drawn more to accounts of international affairs and devouring anything at all about the League of Nations, which drew her back to her time in Paris. She turned the page and saw that the letter was almost at an end.

Mother and I are off to Freiburg in Germany on 27 September and I don't expect to be back for a month at least, maybe two. It will be dreadfully dull and I'm not looking forward to it in the slightest, but we all hope it will be good for Mother's health. She couldn't possibly go alone and Father is too busy with work, so of course it falls on the unmarried daughter to play chaperone. Could we meet at the Willow Tea Rooms before I go? Write to me at Glenapp with a date. Please give my love to everyone and my best love to the little boys.

Your dear friend, Elsie

Stella longed to say yes to Elsie's suggestion, but would it be possible with Mother away? She could almost feel the sensuous, soothing atmosphere of the Willow Tea Rooms and the sparkle of conversation with Elsie that would, for a few hours at least, lift her out of her own little world. She had had nothing but drudgery since Mother left for her holiday. She had to make it happen somehow. Perhaps Luisa would help? She turned to glance down at Jacky and gave an exclamation. He was lying face down on the floor at her feet, crayon in hand. The paper lay untouched beside him and he had instead scribbled all over both sides of the postcard, obscuring both the picture and her mother's writing. She yanked him up, snatched the postcard away and smacked him. 'What a mess! That's naughty. Poor Duncan hasn't seen it yet!' she scolded, annoyed with herself for not noticing.

Jacky wailed and reached for the postcard but she put it up high and ignored him, turning instead to stir the stew. It had stuck to the pot. Of course. She could hear Rob ushering a patient out in the hallway. He appeared in the kitchen doorway.

'Can't you keep him quiet when I've a patient in the house?'

She stood with her back to him, stirring the stew ever more fiercely. She heard him walk into the room and pick up his son. 'Any tea in the pot?'

Tears were pricking her eyes and the walls were closing in once more. She slipped a hand into the pocket of her pinny where she had thrust Elsie's letter and felt the smooth, cool paper, with its whispers of flight over the Atlantic, of flag-bedecked ocean liners, of Willow Tea Rooms. She turned round. 'Give it here. I'll freshen it.'

Rob sat down and reached out a hand towards the bundle of leaflets she had discarded. 'What's this?'

'I've no idea. Some friend of Mother's handed them in for her.' Stella busied herself around the kitchen, making more tea and readying plates for their stew. Rob had lit a cigarette and was reading one of the leaflets. He frowned.

'Is Alison somehow involved in this?'

'In what?' Stella poured his tea and took the leaflet he proffered. The heading proclaimed WOMEN'S WELFARE CLINIC and it gave opening hours for an address in Govan. She read the paragraph underneath. 'Mary Barbour – she's the rent strikes woman, isn't she?'

'The very same. She's a councillor now.'

'I've heard Mother speak about her. She's doing marvellous things for women and children.'

'Hmm. You know what this really is?'

'Birth control?'

'Exactly. The Labour Party has blocked child welfare clinics from giving contraceptive advice, so Mary Barbour has set up a specialist clinic in Govan. I had no idea your mother was involved.' Rob frowned. 'I'm not sure that's very wise.'

'Why on earth?'

'It's a controversial topic.'

'Since when did that stop Mother!' Stella laughed as she dished up the stew. 'But seriously, Rob, surely this is a good thing? I know the newspapers are full of letters from people who believe that providing young women with sensible information will cause the collapse of society, but you can't possibly think like that?'

'Perhaps not,' Rob said. 'But are formal clinics the way to go? Modern methods of birth control are all very well, but they take a level of competence to administer correctly and many of these people can't even read.'

Stella stared at him. 'Then surely clinics are even more important! Can't you hear how hypocritical you are being?'

He pushed the bundle of leaflets aside. 'I'm not particularly comfortable with it,' he said. 'And it's not really appropriate conversation for the table, is it? Especially with Jacky here.'

'As if he understands a word!' she scoffed. But mention of Jacky took her mind back to the morning's events. 'We've had a postcard from Mother and a letter from Elsie. Let me show you – though you may struggle to make sense of the postcard!'

Chapter Fourteen

Naples

Somehow it was the final week of her cruise already, and the one she was looking forward to most, with two days in Naples. Today Alison hoped to meet Signor Rossi, and tomorrow she would join a coach excursion to Pompeii and Vesuvius. She dressed carefully, choosing a thin green dress and a wide-brimmed straw hat to protect herself from the sun.

As the passengers lined up to get into the little tender boats that would take them ashore, they gazed at the slopes of Vesuvius overlooking the bay with its wisps of smoke drifting from the crater on top. 'What a thrill!' declared one Englishwoman with whom Alison had formed a casual friendship. 'This is the whole reason I chose to come. I've wanted to see Pompeii ever since our governess told us about it when I was still in the schoolroom. Will you join the excursion?'

'Not today,' Alison said, clutching the arm of a crew member as she inelegantly scrambled into the boat. 'Thank you.' She sat down and looked around her, drinking in the beauty of the view and the thrill of knowing this was where Luisa had grown up. 'I'm keen to see Pompeii too – I have a daughter who is a classics scholar and she has visited – but today I have another appointment in Naples.'

'Oh yes, you have family here, don't you? How very exotic, I must say. I do look forward to hearing all about it at dinner, my dear. If we make it back and are not all lost in a volcanic eruption!' She giggled and Alison smiled politely, her eyes on the shore.

The sailors rowed them the short distance ashore and soon she was standing on the bustling quayside. Heat engulfed her, carrying with it familiar harbour smells of fish and fumes. Her fellow passengers filed off, following a young Italian man who held high a placard: Official P&O excursion. As soon as it became clear that she was not accompanying them, she found herself accosted by three or four other Italians who urged her to hire them for an individual sightseeing tour. She shook her head firmly and walked away, ignoring the cries of '*Signora!*' that followed her. In her handbag, which she gripped close to her side, was a piece of paper with Signor Rossi's address. Luisa had written to her father telling him when the ship would dock, but no other communication had been possible so she was prepared to set off and find his house alone. She had studied a map before leaving the ship and had a fair idea of which direction to take. However, it was with a huge sense of relief that she heard her own name among the clamour. 'Mrs Rutherford?'

The man approaching her was tall and smartly dressed in linen jacket and trousers. He was younger than she was – perhaps in his early fifties. His hair and skin were darker than Luisa's but she saw an echo of her daughter-in-law in his warm smile. 'Signor Rossi,' she said, clasping his outstretched hand. 'I am very pleased to see you.'

'*Benvenuti a Napoli!*' He kissed her hand and the hopeful

guides melted away, looking for custom elsewhere. 'I am happy to meet the mother of Alex at last. Come, it is not far.' He led her along narrow streets that curved away from the harbour, and she looked about her with delight at the painted houses, the wooden shutters, the stalls and the shops. A large charcoal drawing on the wall of one house caught her eye and she recognised Benito Mussolini and smiled – she couldn't quite imagine people in Glasgow decorating their homes with portraits of Prime Minister Baldwin! The temperature between the tall buildings was even higher than it had been on the quayside and she was glad she had worn a thin dress, feeling sweat trickle down her armpits already. After ten or fifteen minutes they stopped outside a yellow-plastered building. A beautifully polished stairway led up to the first floor. They entered the pleasant coolness of his apartment, and soon stood in a spacious room with tall windows opening onto a balcony, which to her surprise overlooked the Bay of Naples. She had thought they were walking away from the shore but must have curved back round towards it. The room was elegantly furnished, and the embroidered cushions and lace table covers reminded Alison immediately of those in Luisa and Alex's home in Glasgow. One wall was lined with bookcases and a door stood open into a small office space with desk, typewriter and an untidy heap of papers. But it was that magnificent view that drew the eye, and Alison said so. Signor Rossi looked pleased as he led her onto the balcony. 'Later in the day it will be too hot, but it is pleasant here now. I shall make some coffee while you enjoy the view. Then later I show you our city.'

As she waited, Alison leant over the balustrade and looked towards the bay. How thrilling it was to see the *Ranchi* out there, anchored some distance away. She could hear conversation and music drifting from the open windows of neighbouring apartments, but voices came from behind her too. She turned at the sound of footsteps. Signor Rossi carried a tray with gleaming silver coffeepot and two small cups, which he laid on the table. His every movement had a fluid elegance about it. He was followed onto the balcony by a teenage boy. Where there had been a whisper of likeness to Luisa in her father's face, this youngster could be nobody but her younger brother. The same golden-brown hair, the same wide-set eyes, the same strong cheekbones. He greeted her politely, but his eyes did not meet hers. Used to the awkwardness of teenage boys, Alison smiled. 'It's lovely to meet you, Giovanni. You are very like your sister to look at. I'm afraid I don't speak Italian.'

'Giovanni has learnt English in school although he would do better if he applied himself more.'

'You are not in school today? Is it a holiday?'

Giovanni shook his head and glanced at his father.

'He broke his arm fooling around. He is much better now – school next week, *sì*? – but he has missed a few weeks.' He spoke to the boy in Italian and then turned back to Alison as Giovanni gave her a clumsy salute of farewell and ducked back into the house. 'In the meantime he must make himself useful. Now he will deliver some letters to the newspaper offices for me.'

Alison sat down as Signor Rossi poured the coffee. She inhaled its delicious aroma. 'You make even better coffee than your daughter, Signor Rossi.'

He laughed. 'That cannot be true. But please, call me Niccolo. My dear Luisa. She is well and happy?'

'Very well.' She hesitated. 'She is happy in Glasgow, although she misses you and her sunny homeland. I know she and Alex would like a baby, but there is plenty of time.'

'*Sì, sì. Se Dio lo vuole.*'

Alison felt in her handbag. 'She wrote you a letter.'

Niccolo took it and slipped it into his jacket pocket. 'A good thought. I should also like to write a letter to Luisa *mia* and give it to you. May I do so?'

'Why, of course.'

'*Buono*.' He hesitated, and dropped his voice until she could scarcely hear it. 'There are things I cannot say in letters I send in the ordinary way. Our beloved country has changed.'

'Changed?'

He shook his head and made a tiny gesture, enough for her to realise that he did not want to say any more outside on the balcony. Uneasy, Alison sipped her coffee. She remembered the conversation between Alex and Luisa back in Glasgow, and of course she had read about Mussolini and his *fascisti* in the British newspapers, which were generally full of praise for the way Il Duce had at last brought some order to the chaos existing in Italy since the war. Law must be imposed first and freedom could come later. She had noticed some young men dressed in black shirts and tasselled hats on the way from the harbour to the apartment, but they had been relaxed and smiling and seemed no more threatening than Glasgow policemen.

They finished their coffee with polite conversation about the destinations Alison had visited on her cruise before Niccolo ushered her back inside and suggested they visit the fortress. In that beautiful drawing room, Alison hesitated. 'Don't you want to write your letter?'

'If you permit, I shall do so this evening and bring it to the ship tomorrow. When does the *Ranchi* sail?'

'Very late tomorrow evening.'

'*Buono*. I should like to take time to consider what to say. I do not wish to alarm Luisa, but there are important things I must say for Giovanni's sake. I need her help.'

'I don't understand.'

'No.' There was a sadness in his expression. Sunlight streaked across the tiled floor between them, but for the first time Alison felt a chill. 'You are here on holiday, to see the fortress and Pompeii, not to hear about the troubles of our land. The many tourists who come these days on the ships, they have no interest in that.'

'Surely I'm more than a tourist!' she exclaimed. 'In Glasgow, I treat Luisa as my daughter just as much as Stella. If there is something difficult you need to say to her, don't you think I should know too? After all, I will be the one who gives her the letter.'

He looked at her for a moment and then nodded his head and gestured to the fine brocade sofa. He closed the balcony doors before returning and sitting on the seat opposite, his elbows on his knees, leaning towards her. 'I fear for Giovanni,' he said.

'Why?'

'We have only each other. You know our story: we thought Luisa would be our only child but when she was eleven Giovanni was born and my wife died. In the years that followed I worked at the newspaper and it was hard but we managed. Then Luisa met Alex and moved to Scotland and only Giovanni remains here, to have his mind poisoned in school by the teachings of the *fascisti*. He comes home singing their anthem 'Giovinezza', he writes essays about how the world powers cheated Italy out of her rightful reward after the war, he has a picture of Il Duce on his bedroom wall. On Saturdays he dresses in his black shirt and marches with the Balilla, like all other boys his age.'

'And that's why you fear for him?'

'Not only that. The government suspect I am a supporter of the antifascists. I am no longer permitted to publish freely in the newspaper but there are other ways to get the word out in print. It is better that you don't know. Giovanni – he does not know what I do, but he knows what I believe and that may be enough.'

'Surely your own son wouldn't betray you!'

He smiled sadly. 'You do not know the power of the enemy. They mould and shape and turn children against their parents. But whether or not Giovanni betrays me, if I keep doing what I am doing – and how can I stop? – then sooner or later they come for me. What will happen to my precious boy then? And so I write to Luisa. I have decided Giovanni must live in Scotland with her.'

Alison stared at him, trying to absorb what he had just said. The last sentence was so momentous that she pushed it aside for now and unpicked his earlier words. It sounded very much as if Luisa's father was an underground journalist, working for a government-approved newspaper as a front but writing, or at least printing, resistance pieces at the same time. 'What will happen to you if they come for you?'

He folded his hands tightly together, and only the incessant tapping of his smart leather shoe told of turmoil beneath his composure. 'It is better not to think. There have been many murders, Matteotti only the most prominent. Others from our movement have been exiled to Ustica, an island off the coast of Sicily. Either way, how can I be a father to Giovanni? And without me – or even with me – the *fascisti* will control him.'

There was something incongruous about listening to his disturbing words in the gentle, refined atmosphere of this beautiful room. Alison pictured Alex and Luisa and tried to imagine a teenage boy crashing into the harmony of their tenement home. 'What does Giovanni think of this?'

'He adores his sister. He cried for weeks when she left. She was the nearest thing to a mother that he knew. But I have not yet said anything. He would not want to leave; already he is influenced by those who teach that the duty of all sons of Italy is to become soldiers and fight for Italian military glory. Also, it is very difficult to get travel documents and permission to leave the country. But a child will be permitted to visit his much-loved sister for a short holiday. Luisa must write a letter suggesting it.'

'Only you don't mean him to come back.'

'No, I don't mean him to come back.' The shadow over his face showed just how much that thought cost him. 'Not until this evil has been defeated, which will not be soon.'

'If Giovanni is not in Scotland legally it could be difficult for Alex and Luisa. He can't just stay, you know. There are rules and procedures.'

He stretched his arms out in appeal. 'Yours is a country with laws and justice and compassion. They will not turn away a child in need. Anyway, he cannot stay here. I must try.'

For the rest of the day, Niccolo showed Alison around landmarks of Naples, but although they did not mention that astonishing conversation again, it weighed heavily on her mind. She tried to enjoy the colourful market stalls and to listen her host's stories of the historic fortress and other buildings around the city, but shadows in narrow streets felt sinister now and she found herself anxious to return to the safety of the ship. Back at the apartment she tried to engage Giovanni in conversation but could get only a few words out of him. Once again she tried and failed to imagine this surly teenager as part of their family's Glasgow life. It would affect not just Alex and Luisa, but Stella, Rob and the children too. The notion was preposterous, and she must tell Signor Rossi so. As her host prepared to take her back to the ship, he left the room briefly and she heard raised Italian voices from another room, followed by the slamming of a door. He re-entered the room with a weary smile. 'Come, I take you to the harbour now.'

He escorted her back to the ship in plenty of time for dinner, resolutely deflecting any reference to their earlier conversation. Only when he left her at the gangway did he say, 'Tomorrow I bring the letter for Luisa.'

This was her moment. She should tell him now that the very idea of the boy coming to live in Glasgow was absurd. But she couldn't quite find the words. 'What was Giovanni upset about earlier?' she asked instead.

He sighed. 'Arguments, always the arguments. There is a weekend camp for Balilla and I forbid Giovanni to attend. His broken arm means the leaders will not object, but he and I both know he is well enough – only I refuse to let him go. Now he is angry and has gone out with the friends who are bad for him.'

Alison shook his hand and made her way slowly down to her cabin, deep anxiety weighing upon her. Giovanni would not take kindly to his father's idea for his future, that much was clear. How on earth would Alex and Luisa cope with this angry young Italian? What if he refused to stay and ran off back to Italy? If he did stay, would it be possible for him to attend school in Glasgow? He was fifteen and untrained for any trade, so what else could he do? She only had the vaguest idea of the legal requirements for settling in Britain, but she knew that since the war it had become harder for those classed as aliens to be granted permission to stay, never mind to work. And of course, all this meant leaving Signor Rossi alone in Italy to continue his subterfuge. How could she tell Luisa that her beloved father risked imprisonment or even murder?

Perhaps Niccolo was exaggerating. Surely if things were as bad as he said the British newspapers would be full of it. The Italian community that Luisa was so much a part of in Glasgow, they must know what was going on, yet any vague impressions she had picked up of Mussolini had been positive.

But then she thought of the bleak expression on Niccolo's face, and she knew that he spoke the truth.

Chapter Fifteen

Glasgow

Rob had been working at the shipyard for a week or two when he encountered Danny Aitken again. The boy was waiting for him when he stepped off the ferry after crossing the Clyde. 'Carry your bag, Doctor?'

'Thank you but I'm sure I can manage. It's not heavy,' he said, amused. 'What brings you here, Danny?'

'Och, I was up early this morning and I wanted out the house, it's that full of weans. I like to watch the ferry.' He matched his stride to Rob's amid the stream of men making their way from riverside to shipyard gates.

'Remind me what you're doing now.'

'I've been taken on in the drawing office,' Danny said, his voice full of pride. 'I just fetch and carry, like, but the boss says if I pass my night classes he might take me on as an apprentice draughtsman next year.'

'That's marvellous, Danny. You make sure you keep working hard and if I can help in any way let me know.'

'You've helped already, Doctor. I could never afford all they books.' They reached the gates and Danny touched his cap. 'See you later, Doc.' He hurried off, and Rob made his way more slowly towards the room set aside for him in the red-brick main offices. A succession of men would come to see him through the day, usually shuffling and shamefaced, unsure if they should really be there. He treated ailments from burns to boils, from abscesses to fractures. Nearly every man he spoke to had a persistent hacking cough, but they wouldn't come to him about that unless they were coughing up more blood than phlegm. Each man had to tell his foreman the reason for his visit in order to gain permission to see 'Doc', as he became known, but despite this Rob knew the symptoms a man presented with were often not the whole story. He had learnt that back in the war. The man who told his foreman he needed to see the doctor about a sprained ankle might eventually confess to a burning sensation on urinating, while another ostensibly there about an infected cut was actually taking the chance to ask advice about his wee boy's fever.

After that first morning, Rob often found Danny waiting to meet him by the quayside or hanging about the gates to walk back with him at the end of the day. Alex thought it was hilarious – *what have you got that I haven't?* – but Rob quite enjoyed his brief chats with the lad. And he knew the answer to Alex's question. It was the legacy of years of coming alongside frightened young men, whether in the trenches or at the Princess Louise, and winning their trust. Like Archie, the rugby-daft boy he'd helped with his two new legs. Archie still wrote to him occasionally from Inverness, where he worked in a lawyer's office and was doing well. Archie was very different from Danny – he was well educated and came from a comfortable background – but there was a vulnerability about both young men that something in Rob couldn't help but respond to.

He soon learnt that Danny spent as little time as possible at home in the Govan room-and-kitchen with his parents, grandad and many siblings. On the second day they walked together, Rob asked after the wee brother who had been born on the evening he first met the family. Danny's thin face turned scarlet. 'He's died.'

Rob could have kicked himself for not having considered this possibility. It's not as if he wasn't hugely aware of the desperate infant mortality rates among the overcrowded Glasgow slums. 'I'm sorry to hear that.'

Danny looked up at him then, a fierce light blazing in his brown eyes. 'He only lived a few weeks. Didnae have a chance really, he was that wee when he was born and the hoose that cauld and damp. But Ma's in the family way again.'

Rob remembered the tiny, birdlike woman whose only concern that evening, despite her own labour pains, had been for her man's health. Clearly her man had recovered. But Danny preferred recounting to Rob what he had learnt in his evening classes each day. 'When I go home I tell our Chrissie, and she has a go at the sums too,' he said. 'She left the school even earlier than I did though she's smarter than me. She's in service but she wants a shop job. Only now she's winchin' Murdo Craig fae the engine shed, so she'll likely get married afore long.'

Between Danny's chatter and the long line of men he saw each day, Rob's hours in the shipyard flew by – so very much faster, he reflected, than his house calls in the West End. About a month into his time at the yard he was crouched down, carefully draining pus from an older man's infected foot, when there came the sound of someone running along the corridor and hammering on the door. A boy, even younger than Danny, fell into the room.

'You're needed at the quayside, Doctor. A man's fallen frae the hull.'

Rob grabbed his bag, abandoning his patient, and raced along the corridor, shouting to the clerkess to call for an ambulance as he followed the messenger outside. As they ran through the yard he was aware of people watching him, a blur of faces and a murmur of rumours. The boy led him right to the dock where Hull 519 was under construction. 'Up this ladder and doon the other side,' his guide instructed him. 'We need to get right inside, ken.'

Rob halted, breathless from his sprint. He'd been fit once, able to run the length of a rugby field at full speed. Not now! He looked up at the wooden scaffolding. 'Up there?'

'Aye, follow me.' The boy took his bag and scurried up the ladder, onto a platform, disappearing through an opening into the darkness of the hull. Rob gripped the ladder and pulled himself up to the platform. His mouth was dry. He turned around, and began to climb backwards down the ladder, descending into the darkness of the huge metal cavern.

And then froze as noise exploded in his head.

He had been here before.

Beneath him, he was conscious of white faces grouped around the base of the ladder, gazing anxiously up at him, but all around him came the resounding clamour of great iron plates being riveted together. Was he descending into a ship, a dugout, an enemy trench? He could scarcely tell. He clung there, hands gripping the ladder tightly, unable to move up or down until a frantic voice came from below.

'Doc! Down here! Hurry!'

The desperate shout broke through his paralysis and he forced himself on down the ladder to the rough wooden boards on which the unfortunate man had come to rest. Rob dropped to his knees beside him and stretched out a hand gently, familiar actions steadying his nerves. The man was unconscious but breathing.

Blood seeped from a gash in his head and the angle at which his crumpled body lay made Rob think that his back was probably broken. Internal bleeding too, most likely. He looked up. 'How far did he fall?'

The nearest man pointed up to a platform running along the inside of the hull. 'From there. He was climbing the ladder between the second and third levels when the ladder slipped and he fell all the way.'

Rob followed the man's shaking finger with his eyes, but made no comment. Instead, 'What's his name?'

'Blake. Jimmy Blake. I'm his overseer. He's a guid worker.' He bit his lip. 'Will he be all right?'

Rob didn't answer but opened his bag and began to wipe the blood from the man's face. He could staunch the bleeding but there was no sense in moving him until the ambulance arrived. Although whether he would survive being transferred to hospital was doubtful. 'Jimmy, can you hear me? You've had a fall, Jimmy, but you're doing grand and help is on its way. We'll get you out of here just as soon as we can.'

Dear God, the words were even the same. The lies.

His attention was all for the injured man, but he became aware of raised voices behind and glanced round. A young lad, just fourteen or fifteen, had pushed his way forward. Two men tried to hold him back but he struggled free and came closer, then Rob watched in horror as he crumpled to his knees with a howl of anguish that echoed round and round the metal hull.

When Rob finally arrived at the riverside to get the ferry back across the Clyde from Linthouse to Whiteinch, he found Alex waiting for him. Darkness was falling, and the lights of the shipyards reflected on the river. They were packed in beside workers making their way home, and much of the talk was of Jimmy Blake.

Rob stared out at the water and said nothing, but a pulse beat angrily in his forehead.

'Want a quick one?' Alex asked him as they disembarked. He nodded and they made their way to their usual bar where they each ordered a 'hauf an' a hauf'— a half pint of beer with a whisky on the side. Rob knocked back his whisky and immediately demanded another.

'How is he?' Alex asked.

'They took him to the Western Infirmary. Broken back. I doubt he'll survive the night.'

'Christ, man, I'm sorry.'

Rob stared at the sticky varnished surface of the bar, seeing again the events of the afternoon, hearing a teenage boy's tormented cry. 'Did you know his lad works in the yard too? He heard about it, came running over. Why the hell no one stopped him I don't know. No boy should see his father like that.'

'Ah, that's bad. But at least if the boy's in work they'll still have a wage coming in. And Stephens will see them all right.'

'Will they?' Rob asked fiercely, lifting his head. 'Will they really? What's that, then, blood money?'

'Hell, man, what do you mean?'

Rob waved to the barman for another drink. 'It's not good enough, Alex. Jimmy Blake didn't need to fall. If someone had secured that ladder properly it would never have happened. It was the same last week, you remember, when that young lad in the steelworkers' shed burnt his hands. Could he not have had gloves on? It seems to me the foremen are gey casual with the safety of their men.'

'Now that's not true at all, and it won't do any good if you go around spreading rumours,' Alex said, glancing round the pub where plenty of familiar faces from the yard were sharing an after-work pint. 'Stephen's has a good safety record, all things considered, but it's a shipyard no' a bloody nursery. Every man that comes to work here knows the risks. It was the very same when I was at sea.'

'And that makes it all right, does it?' Rob shook his head. 'In the weeks I've been there I've seen so many avoidable dangers. These men put up with risks because they've no choice. Where else will they find work?'

'Well, perhaps Stella's right and you should keep to looking after your wealthy West End patients!'

Rob looked his brother-in-law in the eye. 'Really, Alex? Is that what you think? Is it only wealthy West End clients who deserve good care? I know there are risks in a shipyard – but is it such a bad thing to want to make things better and safer for the men where we can?'

'Of course not.' Alex drained his own glass and shook his head at the offer of another. 'But at least be careful how you go about things.' He glanced round the pub again, noisy with the banter of men released for a few hours from the incessant hard graft of their lives. 'There are a fair few Reds here in the yard, and all it takes is a spark like yours to light a blaze of industrial unrest. That won't do the men or their wives and bairns at home any good.'

'I'll be careful,' Rob promised. 'But Fred Stephen seems a decent chap. I'll have a chat with him about some measures that could be introduced without causing a stir.' He paused. 'I have a friend, an old rugby teammate. John MacCallum. He spoke out during the war while the rest of us pretended the big questions were nothing to do with us. Afterwards I promised myself I'd never stay silent again. These men's lives are too valuable to be lost for the sake of an insecure ladder.'

Alex glowered, but said no more. Instead he picked up his hat. 'I'd best be getting back. Coming?'

Rob shook his head. 'I'll stay a wee bit longer.'

'I'll see you next week, then.' He hesitated. 'Don't go taking it to heart, though, eh? It's good you were there to help.'

'Aye.'

He waited until his brother-in-law had gone, then ordered another drink. And maybe another, before easing himself off the stool. He really had better get home to Stella. Usually he took the tram, but he fancied the walk tonight. Clear his head. It was dark now, a fine night, and the gas lamps glowed in the night air. By the time he had walked back into town and up the hill towards home, he could hardly feel the effects of his earlier drinks. No harm to call in at the local for a final swift one. It had been a long day. And then, realising that tea would be over and the boys off to bed, he stopped at Alfonso's for a fish supper. That way he wouldn't have to bother Stella for some food. Considerate really.

And all the while, the scream of a teenage boy ripped through his mind.

He fumbled with his door key but eventually got the door open. Stella said they never locked their front door when she was a child in Thurso. Country lass. Not like him: he'd grown up in Edinburgh and moved all the way to Glasgow. East to west. Fine city. Built on the shipyards.

Fuck the shipyards.

He opened the kitchen door but she wasn't there. Must have gone off to bed already. He walked over to where his sons lay asleep in the boxbed. As usual, Duncan lay sprawled out like a starfish, while Jacky was curled in a wee ball. He reached out a hand, laid it gently on the rumpled cover. Was there anything so precious as a small child asleep? *His* boys to nurture and provide for, and another on the way. But oh, the way Jimmy Blake's son had been broken by the sight of his father's crumpled form. He felt the tears well up in his eyes. Tea. He needed a cup of tea.

The range was barely warm. No matter, he would light it

again. He started moving around the kitchen, quietly he thought, but then the door opened and Stella stood before him in her nightdress. 'Shh! What are you clattering about for? You'll wake them!'

'Ach, I'm no' making a sound.'

'You made sound enough to waken me!' She stared at him, and something inside him withered at the scorn in her eyes. 'You're drunk, Rob. You stink of beer and cigs.'

''s been a long day.'

'Made longer by a few hours in the pub!' He came towards her but she moved away. 'Go to bed.'

Her flannel nightdress revealed the curve of her belly usually hidden beneath layers of clothing. Suddenly all he wanted was to lie down in the comfort of her arms and stroke their unborn child. He followed her into the hallway and then stopped. 'Where are you going?'

'I'll sleep in Mother's room tonight. Let you sleep it off.' He could hear the ice in her voice and watched, sadly, as she closed the door of Alison's room behind her. Oh well. His head was swimming now and he knew he needed to lie down. He walked through to the parlour where the bed shutters were open and the covers crumpled. He could still see the indentation where she had been lying. He stripped off and pulled on his pyjamas, sliding into bed, grateful for the faint warmth she had left behind. Sleep.

But there was to be little sleep for Rob or any of them that night. Perhaps it was no surprise that the nightmares would return after such a hellish day. He was climbing down a ladder, not into a ship's hull but a shell hole, foul and rancid, with body parts floating in the water below and the sound of a boy's scream ringing all around. There was the boy, fighting to escape the grasp of men holding him, men dressed in German uniform who were forcing his head down into that filthy water while Rob watched on, helpless, clinging to the ladder and screaming for them to stop. And the boy was calling for his daddy.

Daddy!

Stop!

Daddy!

'Daddy, wake up!'

Fingers were poking at his eyes, trying to prise out his eyeballs, and he lashed out. This time the high-pitched shriek woke him. Dear God, it was Duncan, his wee Duncan, and he was sitting on the floor with tears streaming down his face and a hand pressed to his rapidly swelling cheek.

'Duncan, shit, I'm so sorry. I hit you. I didn't mean it.' Rob struggled from the bed, sleep and drunkenness rapidly receding, but before he could reach Duncan, Stella was there, scooping him up in her arms.

'There, there, my wee lamb, you're fine. Daddy didn't mean to hurt you. He had one of his bad dreams and hit you by mistake. Silly Daddy, eh? We'll put a cold cloth on it and tuck you back in bed. Come on, my love.' She carried the boy from the room. Rob looked after them, but knew he wouldn't be welcome. His legs wouldn't hold him up for long anyway. But there was no way he could sleep again, not now. The parlour was freezing so he pulled a blanket from the bed, sat down on the sofa and wrapped it round himself. Huddled into himself and stared at nothing.

Resisting the bottom drawer.

Eventually the door opened again and Stella walked in. Avenging angel? She was carrying a beaker so perhaps not.

'I brought you some hot milk.'

She sat down beside him and he took it, sipping it gingerly in case it made him feel sick. 'How's Duncan?'

'Asleep. He knows you have nightmares so he accepts that's

what happened. He'll be proud of his shiner in the morning.' She paused. 'What brought it on?'

He swallowed more milk then told her about Jimmy Blake. 'I know I shouldn't have gone drinking but it brought it all back, and I was so damn angry at the attitude that says some men's lives matter less than others.'

She clasped his hand. 'I'm sure you did all you could.'

'No. There's more I can do. There must be. I'm going to do everything I can to get better safety measures introduced to the yard.' He laid down the mug and put his hand to his head. 'God, my head hurts.'

'Time to go back to bed.'

But if he returned to bed, would the ghosts accompany him? He looked at her. 'Are you . . . ?'

She smiled, and his heart turned over. 'I'll join you,' she said. 'Can't have you waking the boys a second time.'

Rob extinguished the candle and climbed into bed. He felt her slip in behind him, and then the warmth of her body pressed against hers, one arm cradling him. He breathed in the soft feel and fragrance of her.

Maybe he would sleep tonight after all.

Chapter Sixteen

Naples

When Alison said farewell to Niccolo Rossi and returned to her cabin, she had little appetite for dinner in the gleaming dining saloon and even less for endless chatter about the excursion to Pompeii. She would ask her steward to bring her something simple: a sandwich, perhaps, or some soup. He did so, but brought something else too: a note from Matthew inviting her to join him for a drink in the cocktail bar after dinner.

It would mean changing after all, but Alison found she was relieved. She longed to talk this over with someone, and Matthew was the only person on the ship she trusted well enough to confide in. She ate her sandwich and changed into a grey silk dress that she liked especially, then made her way up to the cocktail bar. 'I'm meeting the captain,' she said to the waiter who approached her.

Soon afterwards Matthew pulled out the chair opposite her. 'Have you ordered?' he asked, lifting the cocktail menu.

'I waited for you. Besides, I'm not too sure where to start when it comes to cocktails.'

He laughed. 'A gin sling, perhaps? Or a sidecar if you prefer cognac? I'm rather intending a large Scotch for myself.'

'I think I'll just have an orange juice. The kind of day I've had, I could do with a clear head.'

He ordered their drinks and then looked at her with concern. 'A hot and tiring day?'

'Worse than that.' She proceeded to outline her conversation with Niccolo. 'He will give me a letter tomorrow for Luisa saying everything he can't put in his usual letters, including the fact that he fears for his life and wants her to invite her brother for a holiday. Only his intention is that the boy should stay in Scotland until the situation in Italy has settled down, whenever that may be.' She took a sip of her orange juice. 'I wonder if he's exaggerating? I haven't read anything in the British newspapers to suggest that a decent educated man like Signor Rossi could be in danger.'

'Does he seem unstable? Prone to exaggeration?'

'I only met him today, but I wouldn't say so. And his daughter is an intelligent young woman.'

'If he really is involved in some sort of underground resistance or subversive propaganda then it wouldn't surprise me if he were in genuine danger. Sailing from port to port as we do, we hear a great deal. There has been trade in information at harbours since men first took to the sea. It's no secret that since the attempts on Il Duce's life, the Italian government has passed laws outlawing all opposition. With the church and the King on his side, Mussolini has complete power. There are ugly stories circulating of what the secret police do to those who undermine him. Many opponents have already fled the country and others have been imprisoned in remote islands.'

'Then Luisa's father is in danger.'

'I'm afraid so.'

Alison took a deep breath as she felt her familiar home

landscape shifting. There was only one thing she could do. She lifted her head and looked at Matthew. 'That's that, then. When I get back to Scotland I must do what I can to arrange for the boy to join us. It's the least I can do for his sister and his brave father. But it's not quite the outcome I imagined from my holiday!'

As she spoke, a steward approached their table and hovered, waiting to be acknowledged. Matthew sighed at the interruption, no doubt imagining some message from the bridge was about to pull him away. 'Yes, Jones?'

'Excuse me, sir, madam, but an Italian gentleman wishes to come on board and speak with Mrs Rutherford. Most agitated he is.'

Alison and Matthew looked at each other.

'It can only be Signor Rossi.'

Matthew got to his feet. 'Come, let's meet him together. Jones, I will escort Mrs Rutherford to my study. Bring the gentleman there.'

If she had not been so distracted, Alison would have loved her first sight of the captain's wood-panelled cabin, complete with thick carpet, comfortable green leather chairs and nautical charts and instruments. It smelt faintly and not unpleasantly of the pipe smoke she already associated with him. A closed door she guessed led to his sleeping quarters. 'Miss Mackay did me proud,' he observed as he pulled out a chair for her and then, unasked, poured three glasses of whisky from a decanter on the side. Soon there came a knock on the door, and Niccolo was ushered in. The grave, slightly weary, elegant Italian of earlier was gone, replaced by a deeply distressed man who stood before her with hands outstretched.

'Alison, forgive me. I need your help. May I speak with you privately?'

'Whatever is the matter? You can say what you like in front of Captain Kennedy here.'

'Captain . . . ?'

Matthew took a step forward. 'I am the captain of the *Ranchi*.'

Niccolo looked between them, eyes wild, then shook his head. 'Then there is no use.'

'Please, Niccolo.' Alison laid a hand on his arm. 'Please, sit down and tell us what has happened. Is it Giovanni? I have told Captain Kennedy what you told me earlier.'

For a moment it looked as though Luisa's father would flee from the room like a startled hound, but then he dropped into a seat at the table and buried his face in his hands. Alison and Matthew sat down. The Italian lifted his head and looked directly at her. 'I came here to ask you to hide Giovanni on this ship tomorrow and take him to his sister right away. But with the captain here, you cannot. All is lost.'

'But why?' she asked. 'What has changed? Have they come for you?'

Niccolo shook his head. 'Not for me, no. Not yet. But Giovanni must leave this country before it destroys him.'

'What has happened to your son, Signor Rossi?' Captain Kennedy asked.

'Happened to him? What has he done, you might rather ask. I should beat him until he weeps, but I dare not. And he weeps already. He weeps. I just want him to be safe.' His voice broke.

There was a wooden clock on the wall, which chose that moment to chime an unexpected four times. 'A ship's clock,' Matthew muttered. 'It marks the watches of the night.'

Alison ignored him. 'Tell us,' she said to Niccolo.

He took a breath, composing himself. 'You know Giovanni was angry this afternoon. He met up with some older boys. He is impressed by them. He follows them. He is a silly little boy. I hear a disturbance in the street outside but I think nothing of it. Such things happen regularly these days. Then Giovanni comes home, and he is frightened. Blood on his clothes and, how you say, bruises on his face. He is so frightened, he tells me all. These older boys attack a man from our neighbourhood they believe is communist. The beating is too much. Giovanni thinks the man is dead.'

'Did Giovanni kill him?' Alison whispered, her eyes never leaving Niccolo's stricken face.

'No – no! Giovanni, he is a child, just fifteen. He had no idea things would go so bad. When he realised, he tried to stop the other boys and they turned on him, said he is traitor like his father. They hit him and knock him down and he falls on top of the other man and has his blood all over him. He escaped and ran home.' Niccolo looked up. 'He is no longer safe. This will be told to police and they will not allow him to leave, even to visit his sister. I must get him away at once.'

'You want to save him from the police?'

His laugh was harsh. 'The police applaud the boys for doing their filthy work for them! Communists, socialists, liberals, Jews – none have a place in our new Italy.' He looked directly at Captain Kennedy. 'Please, sir, will you help my son?'

Captain Kennedy picked up a pen and drummed it on the table for a while. Then he shook his head. 'I'm sorry for you, sir, but it's just not possible. I cannot take a passenger whose name is not on the manifest and who does not have the appropriate travel documents. I would be breaking all sorts of laws.'

Signor Rossi gave a broken cry. 'Then my boy is lost, and I too.'

Alison gazed between them in horror. This was Luisa's father, Luisa's brother. How could she continue her voyage, sailing away on her luxurious ship, and return home to tell her daughter-in-law that

137

she had abandoned them to danger? There had to be something she could do. Perhaps she should offer to stay in Naples. She might be able to argue with the authorities – they wouldn't hurt her, surely, as a British woman. But then a better idea came to her and she turned to Matthew. 'Do you remember the day we met, when I came on board?'

'Of course.'

'Do you remember what Elsie said? If I needed anything, to wire her at Glenapp? Matthew, we must contact Elsie. If anyone can help, she can.'

'But her father is Lord Inchcape, the chairman of this whole fleet,' Matthew protested.

'Precisely. Lord Inchcape is one of the most powerful men in the country. Surely he can get Giovanni out of Italy. Please, Matthew, help me contact Elsie. I understand you can't make the request, but if you can arrange for me to talk to her, everything else will be on my head. Please, Matthew. He's just a boy. Like Jack. Like William.'

He stiffened at the mention of his son and she thought she had gone too far, but then he nodded. 'Very well. Come with me to the wireless room and we'll see what we can do.'

It all took a terribly long time. Niccolo returned to his apartment to check on Giovanni while Alison and Matthew promised to let him know the outcome of their attempts. By morning, Alison had been able to contact Elsie, who was hugely sympathetic, and agreed to consult her father. There was nothing else to be done until they heard back, so Matthew persuaded her to take the excursion to Pompeii as planned. 'It will take your mind off things,' he said. 'I will be here for whatever occurs.'

She knew she would find it hard to focus on the excursion but she was never likely to be here again, so reluctantly she agreed.

The trip took her to the crater edge and around the ruins, and she found herself reflecting on lost civilisations, the fragility of humanity and even of dictators. Which of course led her back to Mussolini, and to Giovanni and his father. What if the police came for them today after the disturbance last night? Were they already too late? She bought a postcard for the little boys, one for Corran and another for Luisa. *Your homeland is beautiful*, she wrote on the back.

And deadly.

Arriving back at the harbour, her mouth was dry and her skin was clammy. As she dismounted from the coach she saw men in black shirts, the *fascisti*, standing at the water's edge. Had they been there earlier? Were they waiting for her? She felt their eyes on her as she passed, waiting for a shout or a hand on her arm. This must be what it was like for people like Niccolo Rossi, living in fear all the time. She could barely make herself climb the gangway at walking pace, longing to push past the other travellers to the front of the queue and go in search of Captain Kennedy. But there was no need. He was waiting to meet her, and drew her to one side. 'It's all arranged.'

'What do you mean?'

He glanced around. There were too many people so he led her to his cabin and closed the door. She stood with her back to it, facing him, like a prisoner awaiting the judgement of the court.

'Lord Inchcape has agreed that we may bring Giovanni home to England on the *Ranchi*. He has an appointment with the Home Secretary tomorrow to make arrangements for his alien papers to be produced, enabling him to stay at least temporarily. He remembered you, Luisa and Alex from the summer and said he was glad to be of assistance.'

Until that moment, Alison hadn't really registered the strain she was under, but all at once her legs felt weak and she leant back against the door. 'Matthew, that's wonderful. Where is he? Is he on board?'

Matthew guided her to a seat. 'Given the – irregular – nature of what we are proposing and what may need to be arranged in the way of paperwork, Giovanni's presence on the *Ranchi* will be kept secret. No record will appear in our documentation at Lord Inchcape's express instruction.' Something about the way he said this made Alison realise that it went against the grain for him to have something so disorderly happen on his ship. 'His father will bring him on board after dark this evening, shortly before we sail. Only a few trusted crew members will know of his presence.' He cleared his throat. 'I'm afraid it means he must sleep in the spare bed in your cabin, and he must remain there at all times throughout the voyage. As you do not have an en-suite cabin we'll provide a chamberpot for him and see that it's emptied.'

Alison stared at him. 'He's not going to like that. He's a fifteen-year-old boy and I'm old enough to be his grandmother.'

It was perhaps embarrassment that made Matthew's tone sharp. 'He may not like it but he'll have to put up with it – as, I'm afraid, must you. There are no free cabins and although I considered swapping you to a better-equipped cabin, that would cause more of a stir. If only you had booked a cabin-de-luxe in the first place!'

This was so ridiculous that Alison laughed aloud, despite the gravity of the whole matter. 'I hardly anticipated this situation would arise! Oh well, what will be will be, and I really am grateful to you for intervening in this way.'

His eyes softened slightly and he nodded. 'As you said, he's just a boy. Now go and enjoy your dinner, for I suspect you may not enjoy the rest of your cruise in quite the way you had hoped.'

As they sailed into Tilbury Docks, Alison reflected that Matthew had spoken truly. The contrast could not have been greater between the first two weeks of her cruise, all finery and fun, gentle flirtation and freedom from responsibility, and this final week. The little cabin that had been her own private haven now had the distinct, half-forgotten, sweaty aroma of teenage boy. From the moment his father pushed him on board under cover of darkness and turned away with a bleakness that pierced Alison's heart, Giovanni had barely spoken a word. He accepted his confinement, picked at his meals, and toileted and changed behind the curtain they had rigged up. Alison swung between spending as little time in the cabin as possible to give the poor boy privacy, and being terrified to leave him alone in case he tried to escape. Her attempts to engage him in conversation, or to interest him in the life ahead in Glasgow, got her nowhere, and she largely left him to his silence. She took her meals in the saloon as usual, strolled on the deck and read her book, but the views had lost their charm and her fellow passengers found her silent and distracted. Captain Kennedy moreover was quite definitely avoiding her. And so she found herself standing on deck on the final grey morning as they crossed the Channel, wondering just what awaited them in England. No one had explained how they were meant to get an extra passenger, entirely without documentation, ashore without anyone noticing.

A note was pressed into her hand by her own steward, who was of necessity one of the few people in on the secret.

Wait in your cabin until everyone else has disembarked. Someone will come for you.

It was signed *MK*. She slipped it into her bag with a tug of sadness. There had been the beginnings of a friendship with Matthew, but everything that had happened in Naples had well and truly tossed that overboard. She had drawn him into a potentially illegal situation, and lost his regard as a result. Perhaps it was just as well, she was returning to life in Glasgow with a whole new challenging dimension in the form of this sullen boy. She took one last look at the grey sea around her and descended to join him. She told him what the note said but, listless as ever, he gave the slightest shrug.

They waited, and waited, and waited. They felt the creak and groan of the ship being tied up and all around them they could hear sounds of people disembarking, of luggage being moved along corridors, commands shouted, bursts of laughter, farewells given. Gradually it grew quieter. Surely it would be safe to leave now? What if they were forgotten? How long should she wait before reminding anyone of her presence? If only she had a porthole to see the outside world. Could it hurt to open her door just a touch? She looked across at Giovanni. He was lying on his bed, eyes shut, but she was sure he wasn't asleep. And then, after an eternity, came a knock on the door.

'Come in.'

It opened, and Matthew stepped into the room.

'Matthew! What on earth is going on? We've been waiting hours. Surely —' She stopped as Matthew stepped aside. Two women stood there. One, as she had rather expected, was Elsie, eyes dancing with excitement. But beside her to Alison's astonishment was Luisa. Her face was pale and dark shadows under her eyes spoke of a long uncomfortable journey and a week of anxiety. Alison had imagined taking Giovanni across to Alex and Luisa's home and explaining the situation, she hadn't realised the Inchcapes would bring Luisa here to meet the ship. Luisa didn't even glance at her mother-in-law but hurried over to Giovanni, whose eyes were still closed.

'Gio!'

There was a new stillness about him. A rigidity.

'*Gio, sono io. Luisa.*'

Slowly, slowly he opened his eyes. He eased himself up into a sitting position. She reached out, grabbed his shoulder and gave him a little shake. 'Gio!' Her voice broke as she pulled him to her. 'Gio!' Her arms were around him now holding him tight, and the noise the boy gave was somewhere between a cry and a laugh before he began to sob.

Alison, Matthew and Elsie looked at one another and with silent agreement stepped into the corridor. Alison brushed tears from her eyes and thought she saw Matthew do the same. Elsie was bouncing on her toes. 'Father has arranged all the documentation and we've booked you onto the sleeper train to Glasgow. Luisa and Giovanni will have one compartment and Alison, you will have another. I offered to take you to Glenapp for a couple of days but Luisa thinks it better for Giovanni to settle into his new home straight away.'

Thank goodness for that! Just one more night away from home, and her own compartment would be luxury after the last dreadful week. 'Are you coming north on the train too?' she asked Elsie.

'Oh no, I'm going to fly,' Elsie said casually. 'I thought it might be quite fun for Giovanni to be my passenger, but Luisa felt the train was a better idea.'

'Indeed!'

The cabin door opened and they all turned around. Brother and sister stood there, so alike as to be uncanny, Luisa's arm around Giovanni's shoulder. The boy looked at the two women. 'Thank you, Mrs Rutherford, Miss Mackay,' he said, clearly under instruction from his sister. His voice was so subdued that Alison's heart ached for him. She smiled.

'It's all right, Giovanni. Luisa will have told you we're going by train to Glasgow now, where you will stay with her. There will be more family to meet, but we can take our time about that.'

Giovanni turned to the captain to thank him too, and as he

did so Luisa threw her arms around her mother-in-law. 'How can I ever, ever thank you?'

'You don't need to.'

'And my father?' Her voice was anxious. Alison pictured again Signor Rossi walking down the gangway, his head bowed to mask his tears.

'He's a brave man. We must pray for him. He is pleased that Giovanni is safe with you.' She paused. 'What does Alex say?'

'Alex is happy to welcome Gio into our home. He remembers him as a little boy when we first met in Napoli. But how dreadful that my country should have become such a place that children are forced to flee. Perhaps my father will escape one day too.'

'Perhaps.' But Alison was fairly sure the man she had met in Naples had no intention of running away. They followed Elsie, Matthew and Giovanni along eerily empty corridors.

The captain stopped at the gangway. 'Here I must leave you.'

'I can't thank you enough,' Alison said to him. He took her hand but rather than shaking it and letting go, he held it tight. Aware of Elsie and Luisa looking on with interest, Alison felt her cheeks colour.

'I'm on board for another six weeks but then I have a spell of leave. May I contact you? We could meet for lunch in Glasgow, perhaps take a walk. I could show you where I grew up. If it would interest you, that is.'

Her cruise had not gone at all as she had planned, and indeed this last week had been ruined completely, for all she was glad to rescue Giovanni. But Captain Matthew Kennedy was watching her now with a crease of worry on his forehead and doubt in those blue eyes. She smiled, and felt the warmth of a pavement café in Nice flow through her bones once more.

'It would interest me very much.'

Chapter Seventeen

Freiburg

The October days edged by in the sanatorium on the outskirts of Freiburg, and Elsie found herself with little to do but read, walk and think. She scoured the newspapers each day, eaten up with frustration that while she was stuck here in Germany, almost every other aviator seemed to be engaged in the tremendous tussle to make record-breaking flights. A letter from Tony gave the desperately disappointing news that the old war injury to his knee had flared up during test flights and he was unable to participate in the Atlantic crossing. The attempt had gone ahead with a replacement pilot, but they had been forced to turn back due to the weather. *So the prize is still there for some lucky beggar,* Tony wrote. *Sadly it won't be me.*

Elsie cut out all the articles she could find about flight and stored them in her writing case. Each day she expected to read that the records that interested her most had fallen, but one attempt after another came to nothing. Even the American millionaire Charles Levine had abandoned his scheme to fly west across the Atlantic for now; he and his pilot, the one-eyed flying ace

Captain Hinchliffe, instead set off for India and a long-distance endurance record. They didn't get very far, firstly grounded by mechanical failure in Vienna and then taking a pleasure trip to Rome for an audience with Mussolini, who was known to be keen on aviation. Elsie read the fawning article with a slightly sick feeling as she thought of the scared and sullen boy she had met on board the *Ranchi* just a couple of weeks earlier, forced to flee his homeland for fear of Il Duce's secret police.

Worst of all was the newly qualified American aviatrix Ruth Elder, who wanted to be the first woman to fly the sea. A knot formed in Elsie's stomach when she read that Ruth and her co-pilot had set off from New York to Paris in their monoplane *American Girl*. When she read a few days later of the failure of the flight and the miraculous rescue of the pair by a passing tanker, she chose not to examine her reaction too closely. She was pleased that the American girl hadn't drowned, and if she was also pleased that she hadn't succeeded in her attempt, that was natural enough, wasn't it?

The weeks passed and her pile of cuttings grew. She sat with her mother on the verandah, breathing in clean mountain air and the scent of fir trees, or walked alone in the forests with the crunch of pine needles beneath her feet. It was almost unbelievable, but both records remained untouched. No woman had yet flown the Atlantic in either direction, and no man or woman on earth had succeeded in crossing from east to west. It was unlikely now, with winter approaching, that there would be further attempts before next year.

When the thought had first crossed her mind back in May she had relinquished it with reluctance, sure that others would get there first. But here they had reached almost the end of 1927, and the prize was still there, just out of reach. Even Tony had pulled out.

It was waiting for her.

She longed to be in London where she could speak to the right people and establish once and for all whether there was any possibility of her dream becoming reality, but instead she was stuck here in Germany, helpless. And then her father wrote, proposing to join them for a week at the end of October. This was her opportunity! She wrote hastily to Tony, arranging to meet him, but not telling him why. If her scheme were to have any chance of success, absolute secrecy was key. But first, she must explain to her father that she was going back to London. Soon after he arrived, she took him for a walk in the beautiful grounds.

'I had hoped we could have a week here together, all three of us,' he said, frowning.

'I know, but I really must return to London, Father, even briefly,' she said, slipping her arm through his. 'There are some matters to follow up with the new ship, and I need to see my dressmaker if I'm to have anything decent to wear for Christmas this year. I've been away from London for such a long time. If I can take a few days while you are here with Mother it will help awfully.'

He laughed. 'Mustn't stand between a woman and her dressmaker!' He squeezed her arm. 'You're a good daughter, Elsie. I know there are things you would rather be doing than taking care of your mother here, but it's worth it – I can see a change in her already. Why, there's even colour in her cheeks! Another month will make a big difference. Then we'll whisk her up to Glenapp for December as usual, and hopefully she will be fit for our voyage to Egypt in January.'

'Egypt?'

'Didn't I mention it? We sail on the *Razmak* early in the new year and will stay in Egypt until Easter. It's all arranged. It will do wonders for your mother's health.'

Elsie stared at him. 'When you say "we". . . ' she said slowly.

'Well, of course you must come too. I will be working a good deal of the time and your mother needs companionship.'

There was a wooden rail beside the path, and Elsie stopped and leant on it, looking out over the valley. The scent of burning wood and leaves drifted across to them. Egypt! By the time she returned after Easter it would be too late; the records would be broken. Her chance would be gone for ever. Just moments ago she had had such plans, and now those plans were in danger of flaring and disappearing as quickly as pine needles in the gardener's bonfire.

No. She wouldn't allow it.

She took a deep breath. 'Father, I can't. I simply can't. I'm behind with my work on the new ship as it is, with all this time away from my desk. That's the real reason I'm so keen to get back to London this week – as if I ever cared all that much about my frocks! I can't possibly trot off to Egypt for three whole months.'

'Not even if your mother needs you?'

'You said yourself she is much better. I know you won't ask my sisters – they have their husbands and children, and somehow that seems to absolve them from any other responsibility! But couldn't we engage a companion? Just this once?'

He turned towards her and put a hand under her chin, tilting it up so that she was looking right into his eyes. She shivered. It was a gesture she remembered vividly from childhood, when he summoned her to his study to be reprimanded. For a moment her nerve nearly went – but she wasn't a child now. Keeping her voice calm and steady, she said, 'This new ship is the pride of our fleet. You said so yourself. You are the one who asked me to do this work, and you have always taught me that if a job is worth doing it's worth doing well. How can I do that if I'm never at my desk?'

She knew she had won the battle when she saw admiration

overcome disappointment in his eyes. 'I will miss you,' he said, dropping his hand.

'I know, Father dear. I'll miss you too. Perhaps the work will be done in time for me to come out and join you before you leave Egypt, but I can't give up a whole three months and still do this job to the level the company deserves.'

He nodded. 'You're right, my dear. When I took you on I said I would hold you to the same high standard I hold all my employees. That means I applaud you putting your work ahead of pleasure, even if your mother and I must do without your company.'

He took her arm and they continued on up the path between tall pine trees, Elsie's heart thudding. She hadn't lied to him exactly, but she had embarked upon a course that meant she couldn't be completely honest with him again until the whole thing was over. She knew only too well the power and influence her father held – influence that had managed to annul her marriage, for example, or obtain documents for young Giovanni that masked the true story of his arrival. Lord Inchcape would be able to put a stop to her schemes in an instant if he had the slightest suspicion of them.

But then another thought dawned on her, something that had almost passed her by amid the consternation that she might be whisked off to Egypt at just the wrong time.

Her parents were still going to Egypt. Her father would be far away across the world when she put the final, critical details in place. She would never have a better opportunity.

The stars were aligning in her favour after all.

Back in London she welcomed Tony round for drinks at Seamore Place, swearing him to secrecy. When he understood her proposal he gave a whoop and drained his glass. 'By Jove, you're serious, aren't you?'

'Never more so.'

He reached for her father's port decanter and poured himself some more. 'Well, if anyone can do it, you can. Lord, how I wish I could come with you. What a team we'd make, you and I taking on the sky, but it can't be. I gave it my damnedest, but the old knee won't take it. The man or woman who does achieve this has to be at the peak of physical fitness as well as mental sharpness. Don't overlook that, Elsie: get some medical advice. But your de Havilland will never make it, you know.'

'I'm not a fool, Tony. My wee biplane can barely make it to Glenapp in a gale! That's why I wanted to consult you. I need a co-pilot, someone with experience who will share their knowledge with me, and I need a new machine that can cope with the Atlantic conditions. I have more than enough money to fund it, you know that. There is one other requirement. The entire enterprise must take place in complete secrecy, starting with this conversation and not ending until the flight is underway and can't be called back. Otherwise my father will get wind of it and he'll stop my funds or lock me up or something.'

Tony frowned, looking serious for once. 'Wouldn't it be better to tell him? It's a big risk, Elsie. You might not come back.'

'Don't be so melodramatic. I fully intend to come back,' she said briskly. 'The attempts that have taken place already – including your friends, I might add – I've studied them all, and I understand why they were unsuccessful. With proper planning and funding and the right weather, there is no reason to fail. Nothing will be left to chance. I'm going to fly the Atlantic westwards, and I'm going to open my own commercial airline on the back of doing so. What I need from you is a recommendation of the right person to assist me.'

'Very well, if you're sure. The man you need is Hinch.'

'Hinch?'

'Ray Hinchliffe. The one-eyed pilot. He's the very best.'

'I thought he worked for Levine?'

Tony snorted. 'Not any more. Seems no one can work with Levine for long! Hinch was mortified when Levine's ground crew behaved so outrageously at RAF Cranwell that they were thrown off the base – the very base where Hinch himself had served as an instructor during the war. And then when Levine wanted to take his mistress along as a passenger on the Atlantic flight, I believe Hinch just had enough. He's gone back to his old job with Imperial Airways, though. You might have to buy him out.'

'That wouldn't be a problem,' Elsie said, getting to her feet and walking to the window. She eased the shutters open and looked down on the square, eerily lit by gas lamps in the late October fog. There was no one about. She turned to face Tony. 'I don't want to state the obvious – but a one-eyed pilot? Is that a good idea?'

'You wouldn't think so, would you, but with Hinch it doesn't make a damn bit of difference,' Tony said, his voice full of admiration and even a little bit of hero worship. 'He sits in the traditional co-pilot's seat to have better vision, and it doesn't hold him back one bit. He lost his eye in the war. He was known as a bit of a daredevil then – but he's one of the finest, most experienced aviators in the whole Empire. He's the man for you, Elsie.'

She came back to sit down but found she couldn't stay still and was soon back on her feet. 'Will he be interested?' she asked, pacing back and forth across the room.

'I'd say so. Now that the deal with Levine has fallen through he'll look for another opportunity. He wants that record as much as anyone. He's got everything going for him except the funds to do it himself. Word is he's short on cash, and he has a wife and child to support.' Tony hesitated. 'There's only one thing I can think of that might count against you, and it's this. You're a woman.'

Elsie swung round. 'What, is he some kind of woman-hater? Or doesn't he believe that a woman can handle an aeroplane?'

'I don't think it's that – he's always seemed a decent sort of chap – but when he had his falling-out with Levine over his mistress he said women had no place in aviation. That might just have been the circumstances, though. Mabel Boll was a trophy hunter wanting to come along as a passenger for the glory.'

'Well, I have no intention of being a passenger,' Elsie retorted. 'My co-pilot must accept that I will play a full and equal part in our venture. That's why I want someone who will share their aviation knowledge with me as we train for the flight.'

Tony drained his glass and got to his feet. 'It might not be a problem. Let me talk to Hinch. I'll lay out your proposal, and I'll tell him what a fine aviatrix you are too. If he's interested the next thing will be for us all to get together – say over lunch on Thursday? At The Ritz?'

'That sounds splendid. I do hope he agrees.' She paused. 'I may bring my bank manager along so that we can thrash out the money side of things. We need to move quickly as I must return to Germany in a few days. You will stress the need for discretion, Tony?'

'That won't be a problem with Hinch. The man's not one for idle gossip.' He kissed her. 'Until Thursday – and to the skies!'

Chapter Eighteen

Glasgow

Jimmy Blake died.

Rob had his desired meeting with Fred Stephen, who agreed to tighten up on safety in various areas. 'We can't delay the schedule, though. You do understand that? Stephen's only won this contract on the basis of efficient delivery. The men won't thank you if you jeopardise their employment.'

The threat was there on the table between them, but there was enough common ground for Rob to feel that some progress was made. And soon something else occurred that distracted him, at least superficially, from the traumatic events of a few weeks earlier. When Danny came to meet him one morning, Rob could tell there was something on his mind. More than once he thought the boy was about to come out with it, but then he turned away. He was waiting at the gates on the way home, but lacked his usual free-flowing conversation. After a few attempts to draw him out of himself, Rob stopped. 'Spit it out, Danny.'

The lad's thin face coloured. 'Dunno what you mean.'

'There's something you want to say to me, isn't there? Is it about the yard? Blake?'

'Naw.'

'At home, then? Is something wrong?' He drew Danny down to sit on the wall that ran along the pavement at this point. As he placed a hand on his shoulder he could feel the boy's bones protruding through his threadbare jacket. 'Come on, Danny. Is it a medical thing?'

'Sort of. But no' for me.'

Well, that was not unusual. The shipyard workers knew they were privileged to have easy access to a doctor and often took the chance to seek advice on behalf of their families. 'Who, then?'

'It's Chrissie, my sister. She made me promise I would ask you . . .' He pulled the bunnet from his head and twisted it between his hands, distressed, scuffing his toe on the ground.

'How old is your sister?'

'Seventeen. There's Chrissie then there's me and then there's all the weans. I'm fifteen, see.'

He was so skinny and undernourished that he looked about twelve. 'So what did Chrissie want you to ask me?'

Silence.

'Danny, if you don't tell me now I'll board the ferry and your chance will be gone. What will Chrissie say when you go home this evening?'

Danny took a deep breath then, and the words tumbled out of him faster than a pipe of waste water gushing into the Clyde. 'Murdo Craig asked Chrissie to marry him. They'll have their ain hoose – just a single end but there's only the two o' them. There's eight o' us at hame.'

'Go on.'

'Aye, so Chrissie wants to wed her man but she disnae – she disnae – ach, Doctor, ye ken what oor ma's life has been. Chrissie

154

disnae want that. And I dinnae want it for her either.'

With a growing sense of dismay, Rob realised where this was heading. 'What did she want you to ask me?'

Poor Danny was scarlet now. 'There's things the posh folks use, but we dinnae ken much about them. All Ma says to her is to get aff at Paisley, but if that's what *she* does it hasnae worked, has it?'

To get aff at Paisley – the local expression for premature withdrawal. Rob stared at Danny, who, now that the telling was done, looked ready to bolt. He wasn't quite sure whether to laugh or to send the boy away with a flea in his ear. All right, this wasn't a formal consultation, but he hadn't for a moment imagined his involvement in the shipyard would include giving advice on birth control to a seventeen-year-old girl, and he knew his employers would frown on it. It was a hot topic in the newspapers, with many religious and political figures declaring that such information encouraged moral laxity. Then he looked at the thin, frightened, embarrassed face of the boy beside him and realised just how desperate Danny and Chrissie must be, to have come up with such an idea. If Rob were to report him he would be in all sorts of trouble, even risking his precious position in the drawing office. These youngsters had grown up witnessing their mother worn out by giving birth to child after child, and had no doubt battled themselves to keep their younger siblings alive. Now Chrissie, a young woman just awakening to sexual feelings, was terrified of all that her longed-for escape from the family home might involve. It would surely do no harm to direct her towards the work of Marie Stopes.

'There's a book I could recommend.'

'Chrissie's no' much of a reader, Doc.'

'No, of course.' Then Rob remembered his conversation with Stella a few weeks ago. The drama at the yard had completely put it out of his head, but Mary Barbour's clinic advertised on those leaflets was right here in Govan. He could never raise such an awkward topic with his mother-in-law, but he could perhaps ask Stella if the leaflets were still in the house. Although even passing one on was beyond his remit.

'Danny, it's for your mother to help your sister with these things, not a doctor. I might be able to get hold of some information, but no promises.'

That was enough for Danny. Relieved the awkward conversation was over, he grinned, far more like his old self, and jumped to his feet. 'Cheers, Doc!' he said, and sprinted off towards home.

Back at their tenement, Rob found that Stella and Alison had spent the afternoon with Luisa. Stella had returned in time to meet Duncan from school while Alison had stayed over in Partick for tea.

'How's Giovanni getting on?' he asked, whirling Duncan round the kitchen. It was a month now since Alison had returned from her cruise bringing an unexpected addition to the family.

'Hard to say. Careful, Rob! Now Jacky wants a turn.'

'And he shall have one!' He spun Jacky too then laughed and shooed the boys away. 'Go and play until tea.' He pulled out a chair. 'You were saying.'

'In some ways he's settled well. His English is not bad and he accepts that he must live in Glasgow for now. Luisa is overjoyed to have him. But he hates school, and there's hardly a day he comes home without having been in a fight. He can handle himself well enough, mind you, generally comes out on top. Mother thinks they should give up on school and get him a trade but Luisa is determined he should continue his education as he would have done in Italy.'

'And her father?'

Stella shook her head. 'Not a word. No reply to their letters. He's simply disappeared.'

'At least your mother got the lad out.'

'Yes.' A heavy silence hung between them, then Stella jumped up. 'I nearly forgot! A card came from Corran. You won't believe what she's going to do next. Here, take a look!'

Rob took the postcard, read the brief note on the back and laughed out loud. 'An authoress! Well, well, well. Published early in the new year, she says. How very like Corran. She always did do the unexpected. Quite an achievement!'

He caught a flash in Stella's eye and realised he had said the wrong thing. Stella no doubt was thinking that she too would like to do the unexpected, only she was trapped in this life of domesticity that she sometimes seemed to resent so much. He glanced across at the two boys, who were fully engaged on sailing their bed across the high seas. To divert her attention, he told her about his conversation with Danny.

'It's not something I can help with myself,' he finished.

Stella came and sat down beside him, stretching her legs out in front of her with a groan. Her ankles had begun to swell these last couple of weeks, something that had bothered her through her last two pregnancies as well. 'Why not?'

'I'm a doctor, Stella. This is hardly a medical matter. The boy had a cheek, all things considered, coming to me.'

'I imagine he couldn't think of anyone else to go to. Just think about that poor girl and all she's seen at home. It's so hard for young women to get sensible information. You can give her one of Mother's leaflets for the clinic in Govan.'

'Yes, I wondered about that. But you know, it's not really any of my business. I'm there to treat the shipyard workers for medical conditions. My employers won't want me promoting Mary Barbour's clinic, and it's important I keep them on side just now, particularly with the new safety ideas.'

The children's voices were becoming fraught. Stella called across a warning then turned back to her husband. 'You're such a hypocrite about this, Rob! You support the boy going to night school but won't give the girl advice that might better her future?'

'It's not the same thing at all!'

'Fine.' She got to her feet and clattered the cups together. 'Duncan, stop that at once! Give me the address and I'll see to it.'

Rob laughed. 'Don't be ridiculous. You can't go marching in there talking about birth control to a woman you've never met. I thought you hated it when your mother's church committee ladies did that kind of thing?'

'I do, but don't you see that's the point? This clinic was started by Mary Barbour. She's a Govan housewife herself, and they know she stands with and for working people because of the stance she took against rent increases when the men were away at war. My only role is to push a leaflet through a door. This poor girl has asked for help, and she has as much right to choose the size of her family as we do. Give me her address. What harm can it do?'

Chapter Nineteen

London

The three men rose from the table in the richly gilded dining room of The Ritz when Elsie approached. Tony grinned at her like a schoolboy embarking on a madcap escapade, but Elsie's agent, Rogers, whom she had telephoned the night before, looked frankly terrified. She hoped he had the nerve for the job, but there was no option other than to let him into the secret as he controlled access to her bank accounts. Her gaze swept past him and she looked carefully at the man who just might become her partner in the greatest endeavour of her life. Tall and thin, he was probably in his late thirties, a similar age to her. The patch covering his left eye drew her attention, while the cool blue gaze of his other eye revealed that he was assessing her just as carefully as she was assessing him. Well, good. She instinctively knew that today was no day for the charm and flattery that as a former screen actress and society hostess she was perfectly capable of utilising.

'Let's get down to business,' she said when their soup had arrived, and was glad her voice didn't betray her nerves. 'Thank you for agreeing to meet me, Captain Hinchliffe.'

His reply was little more than a grunt but he was listening. Tony leant forward eagerly and Rogers stared at the tablecloth.

'I am seeking a partner in an enterprise to fly westwards across the Atlantic. Now that we have reached the winter months without anyone achieving this goal, I believe there is a window to put plans in place for a flight early next year that will be both the first east-to-west crossing and the first flight over the Atlantic by a woman in either direction. You have been recommended to me as the best pilot to approach, and I have the funds to make it worth your while.'

That much she had rehearsed, speaking to her reflection in the mirror before she left Seamore Place. Captain Hinchliffe took a drink from the ruby-red wine in his glass before replying. 'I was engaged on a similar scheme earlier this year that turned out to be a spectacular waste of my time. Why should your proposal be any different, Miss Mackay?'

'Because I know what I'm talking about. Tony here will vouch for my skill as a pilot, and I'm sure you know I'm a member of the council of the Air League. I'm not naïve enough to think I can do this alone, which is why I want to partner with a more experienced pilot who can advise me on conditions I've not yet encountered, but I'm more than confident of my ability to fly. I'm no frivolous glory hunter.'

'No? Why do you want to do this, then? For the fame and the money, I suppose.'

Elsie laughed. 'Oh no, Captain Hinchliffe, I have more than enough fame already and the money will all be yours.' She paused, sensing that her next words mattered a great deal. 'Why do I want to do it? Because I'm convinced this is the moment. Those who have tried and failed – I've studied their efforts and I believe we can learn from where they went wrong. We all saw the impact that Charles Lindbergh's achievement had; a successful flight in the other direction will cause an even greater sensation. It will prove to the world that aviation really is the travel of the future. On the back of that enthusiasm, I propose to establish an independently successful British commercial airline that does not rely on government subsidy. At one level it's a straightforward business initiative.'

He was listening closely. 'And?'

'And?'

'You said 'at one level'. That suggests another level too.'

She hesitated, trying to find the right words, and sensing that honesty here mattered more than anything else, including the financial incentive. After all, if they were to take this on together, they would get to know each other very well indeed. 'The 'other level' you mention is the call of the skies, which I hear day after day. Don't you, Captain Hinchliffe? How lucky we are to be alive at such a time as this! That call I hear – it's the call to the human spirit to take on and conquer the elements; it's the call to the pioneer to embrace new technology, to balance risk, planning and effort, to prove what we can achieve. I believe it's the same impulse that took Scott and Amundsen to the Antarctic, and which may one day take mankind to the moon. I want to be part of it – and I believe you do too.'

She was sure she could see a glimmer of appreciation in his eye, but he was not yet ready to be convinced. As for Rogers, the sheer horror on his face was almost comical. Elsie did her best to ignore him. 'Fine words,' Hinchliffe said, as the waiter removed their soup plates and brought the next course. 'But does a woman like you really appreciate the danger and difficulty, I wonder? There's a reason this hasn't been achieved before. To fly nearly three thousand miles into prevailing winds, with no possible landing place should anything go wrong. A slight miscalculation and the flight will go off course and eventually run out of fuel, plunging into oblivion. Then there's the fatigue and exhaustion involved in flying for so many hours, much of it blind, through storms and ice and fog. Are you physically and mentally strong enough to deal with that, Miss Mackay? It's a bit different from any flight you've undertaken before, I'll warrant.'

'It is,' she said steadily. 'I imagine you haven't flown in such conditions either, or not for such a length of time. After all, your endurance flight to India didn't make it beyond Austria – is that not right? Yet I have approached you because I believe you have the spirit and the strength to take it on, and with proper planning and the right machine we can manage this together.'

Hinchliffe was silent for a moment and Elsie concentrated on her salmon, giving him space to think. Rogers had forgotten to eat and stared at her open-mouthed, but Tony winked across at her. She frowned at him, trying silently to prevent him making one of his jovial comments that might spoil the charged atmosphere. Eventually Hinchliffe spoke. 'Some damned good pilots have already taken this on and failed. I knew Fred Minchin.'

'And I knew Princess Anne, who financed him and died with him.'

They held each other's gaze for a moment, the cold sea closing over the wreckage of their friends' machine, and then he said, 'Tell me your terms.'

Hope fluttered within her but she spoke calmly. 'Your first task will be to hunt down and purchase the best possible machine for our flight, here in Britain or in America if necessary. All expenses paid, of course. I will pay you a wage of £80 a month thereafter, and should we succeed, all prize money will be yours to keep. You will then have the opportunity to be fully involved in my commercial airline from the outset in whatever capacity you wish – pilot or management.'

He stared at her. Having been primed by Tony that Hinchliffe had financial worries, she had made sure the terms were generous. She knew too about his family. 'You have a wife and child, I believe?'

'Joan is four. My wife, Emilie, is expecting another baby soon.'

'As reassurance for them, although I have absolute confidence we will succeed, I will insure your life for £10,000. That way you know that should anything go wrong, your family's future is secure.'

She knew he wanted to do it. She could see it in his eyes and in the way his leg had started jiggling against the table. 'Attention to detail,' he said. 'That's what Levine didn't have, but it's the most important thing. Which engine is best equipped for such a gruelling journey? What fuel load do we need, and how do we best transport it? What have the weather patterns been in previous months and years, and what is the best route to combat them? Can we avoid the Newfoundland fogbanks, or if not, how do we navigate them? How will we deal with the risk of ice forming on the wings? There are a hundred and one things to go into before we can set off.'

'That's why I want to work with a man of your experience and knowledge,' she said. 'But to be clear, I will be fully part of the planning process, and I will be fully part of the flight itself.'

He nodded slowly. 'I shall want to see you fly before I agree.'

'I think a test flight together seems a sensible next step, to ensure we each have confidence in the other,' she said smartly.

He laughed, and the atmosphere changed at once, becoming almost jubilant. 'Very well. Where do you keep your current machine? Good. Let's meet at the airfield tomorrow and we'll take that test flight.'

'Thank you.' She hesitated. 'Tony did tell you my other condition? The need for absolute secrecy? My father has contacts everywhere, and he mustn't know that we are planning this or he will prevent it. He wouldn't hesitate to destroy you, you know.'

'You can rely on my discretion.'

The agent cleared his throat. 'If I may . . . it might be a sensible p-precaution to ensure the funds you intend to use are not accessible to L-Lord Inchcape.' Even as he spoke the words he looked horrified, as if he could scarcely believe his own treachery.

'What would you suggest?'

'If you have a trustworthy friend we could begin transferring money into their account now, while there is no suspicion. Then if a time comes in the future that L-Lord Inchcape seeks to s-stop your funds, the money due to Captain Hinchliffe will not be affected.'

The poor man looked close to tears and Elsie reached out and gave him a reassuring pat on the arm. 'Thank you, Mr Rogers, I'm immensely indebted to you. I know I can have absolute confidence in you. We'll talk some more.' She rose to her feet and extended her hand to her new partner. 'Captain Hinchliffe, I can't tell you how much this means to me. It has been a real pleasure to meet you, and I very much look forward to working with you. Our endeavour begins tomorrow.'

Chapter Twenty

Glasgow

Stella glanced up at the window and blew a kiss to Jacky, who was perched on a chair beside Luisa, waving with all his might. He would be fine; he loved playing with his aunt Luisa although he'd been disappointed that Gio was out at school. Duncan and Jacky adored their new big cousin, who seemed to have endless patience for games of football with the wee boys.

She wouldn't be long, just the length of time it took to cross to Govan and push a leaflet through Chrissie Aitken's door. Rob had remained stubbornly insistent that he couldn't hand out leaflets for the clinic as part of his role at the shipyard – not even informally to Danny – so Stella, just as stubborn, had insisted on taking some herself. Besides, she was glad of a distraction today.

Because today, 8th November 1927, marked ten years since Jack had been killed.

The knowledge of the anniversary had been there ahead of them these last few days, looming, unspoken, but this morning dawned as ordinary as any other. Mother offered to take Duncan to school on her way to meet a friend, no doubt seeking the same sort of distraction as Stella. Her drawn face suggested she hadn't slept much, but breakfast with the boys was as chaotic as usual and any lingering melancholy was lost in the usual fluster of trying to get Duncan out on time, Mother warning him that he would get the belt if he was late. Stella also absorbed herself in preparations for the day. It was only now, having left Jacky with Luisa and walked across Dumbarton Road towards the river, that she allowed the memories to steal in. She had been at Edinburgh University when the news came, living in Masson Hall, the women's residence. She had returned from lectures on that grey, dreich November day to find the kindly warden waiting for her, and had known at once.

Just as she had known four weeks earlier, when she hugged her broken brother farewell in a shabby London boarding house, that she would likely never see him again.

The overwhelming waves of grief had receded, but the sharpness of this sorrow would never, ever ease. That was one reason she and Rob belonged together, no matter how imperfect things might sometimes be. They carried one another through this pain. She watched her children playing and the injustice of the fact that they had been robbed of their uncle rose up within her. How he would have adored them! He might well have had children of his own by now. Instead, with Alex and Luisa apparently unable to conceive and Corran determinedly single, Duncan and Jacky looked unlikely ever to have cousins of their own.

No wonder they had taken to Giovanni so completely.

As she approached the quay she made an effort to focus her mind back on her day. *War is something which nobody but madmen and fools would ever engage in*, she had read in her newspaper yesterday. The words of Labour leader and former Prime Minister Ramsay MacDonald. How true, and thank God her children were growing up in better times, with the League of

Nations working for international peace. There was nothing to be gained by reliving the horror; what she wanted to do today was to remember all that had been good about Jack. Tonight Alex and Luisa would come round and they would all drink a toast to his memory, sharing stories. In the meantime it was good to have a task to undertake. She had been deliberately vague about where she was going when she left Jacky with Luisa. Her sister-in-law's Catholic church was among the most vocal opponents of Mary Barbour's clinic, never mind the complex emotions tied up with Luisa's longing for a child of her own.

She boarded the ferry to Govan at Pointhouse, and felt a lightening of her spirits in the crisp, cold air. She touched the *Spirit of St Louis* brooch on her lapel. It was good to be here, unencumbered by child or even by bags of messages. She was conscious of receiving some scrutiny as a woman alone – and moreover a woman who was quite clearly expecting a child – but held her head high with assurance and no one bothered her.

After disembarking she paused, unfamiliar with the south side of the river. She knew that the Aitken family lived in a close on the opposite side of Govan Road from the shipyards, just beyond Govan Cross. It wasn't far, but as she walked along the wide road she felt her confidence ebbing away. The bustling street was busy with shops and street sellers, with men standing on street corners and women pushing prams and dragging children along. All very familiar and yet somehow very different. She had deliberately left her fur hanging in the hallway at home, but even her shabbier coat seemed both warm and well cut in comparison with much of what she saw around her. In fact, what struck her was the number of children and women dressed only in jerseys or shawls even on this chilly day. As she turned off Govan Road into the narrow streets between two tenements, her unease increased. Children kicking a can with their bare feet – *why were they not in school?* –

broke off from their game to watch her. She looked up and down the street and identified the close entrance that she needed and then baulked. Two women with aprons over their dresses stood in the doorway, arms folded, watching her.

Stella very nearly turned and fled. But no. All she was doing was passing on information, and she looked forward to telling Rob about it triumphantly later. She was doing no harm; these women would step aside and let her through.

They didn't.

'Think you're a wee bit lost, hen.'

Stella swallowed. 'I don't think so. I'm looking for Chrissie Aitken's house.'

'Oh aye? What for?'

'I – have something for her.' She tried again to moisten her dry mouth. 'I think she lives on this stair. Could I get past please?'

She was aware of a cluster of children behind her, watching. One of them called out, 'Are you fae the poorhoose?'

'No – no! I'm just – a friend.'

At this the smaller, scrawnier woman snorted. 'What like is Chrissie Aitken doin' wi' posh friends like you?'

'Well, I'm not a friend as such, I just have something for her.' Stella lost her head. 'Could you give her this please?'

She thrust the leaflet into the woman's hand and turned away, face burning. She had barely taken two steps however when the woman bellowed, 'What in the name of all that is holy is this? Hey you – Mrs Posh Knickers. What are you giving this filth to wee Chrissie for, eh? Her and her Murdo are no' even wed yet. You sayin' she's a whore or something?'

Stella turned. 'No – of course not!' She tried to steady her voice. 'It's not filth,' she said quietly. 'It gives details of the new Women's Welfare and Advisory Clinic, that's all. I thought Chrissie might appreciate it.'

'Might *appreciate* it, might she? Well, I'll tell you what I would *appreciate*. I would *appreciate* if you bugger right back across the river and keep your middle class neb awa fae oor young lassies. Think we havenae heard aboot this? It's a capitalist plot to suppress the working classes, so it is, to stop us havin' bairns cause you think we're no' guid enough. Eugenics, that's what they call it.' She screwed up the leaflet into a ball and tossed it into the street where the children pounced on it. 'My Bert, he says the government wants to stop folks like us havin' bairns so they can get out of their obligations to provide us with decent housing and decent wages to feed a family.' The woman stepped towards her and Stella backed away in alarm. 'Go on – get out of here.'

Stella stumbled a little as she turned, the whoops and the cheers of the children ringing in her ears. When something struck her back she knew it was the screwed-up leaflet fired after her. Her cheeks were burning and tears stung her eyes. Rob had been right. She should have considered how it looked, her marching in with her leaflets, dressed in her fine clothes. She had always hated that kind of thing from the church ladies and here she had fallen into the same trap. She heard footsteps running behind her – they were chasing her now! She quickened her own pace, but then a voice called out, 'Stop! Please stop!'

It was a young woman. She stopped and turned around, and a girl of perhaps seventeen or eighteen came running up to her. 'Chrissie?' she guessed.

Chrissie nodded, coughing dreadfully as she caught her breath. 'You were looking for me.'

'I'm Stella Campbell. My husband is the doctor at the shipyard.' Stella looked at her. The girl was thin, with straw-coloured hair tied up and a brown shawl around her shoulders. She was not pretty exactly, but her wide green eyes and strong cheekbones were striking, drawing a second glance. 'I'm sorry if I caused you any trouble back there, Chrissie.'

Chrissie shook her head. 'It's just Aggie and I can handle her. Besides, I move out next week when I marry Murdo.' There was pride in her voice. 'I cannae wait.' Then she glanced behind her. 'I'm sorry they were rude to you.'

'Och, it was my own fault. I should have seen how it would look. But my husband said your brother asked some questions, and I happened to have leaflets for Mrs Barbour's clinic.' She hesitated. 'I have another in my handbag. Would you like it?'

Chrissie's cheeks coloured but there was a determined light in her eyes. 'Aye.'

Stella opened her bag and handed over a little pile of leaflets. 'Here – take a few. You might know other people who would be glad of one.' *Your mother for instance*, she thought, but decided not to say.

'Thank you, Mrs Campbell.' The girl glanced back towards the street again. 'I'd better be going. I'm meant to mind the weans while Ma's at the shop.'

Stella nodded and watched her go. As the girl hurried away she called after her, 'Good luck, Chrissie!' Chrissie looked back, a long strand of her yellow hair blowing in the wind, grinned and waved.

Back on the ferry, Stella was glad of the breeze on the water, which gradually cooled her burning cheeks. She breathed deeply and felt a stirring of triumph. Thank goodness Chrissie had seen her from the window and come running after her. Would the young woman summon the courage to go along to the clinic? Perhaps, perhaps not, but at least the choice was now her own.

Stella stepped onto the familiar comfort of dry land on the north side of the river and began the weary haul back up to Luisa's house. She tired more easily now and her swollen ankles ached. She and Rob had agreed that this child would be their last; imagine how it would feel to go on producing baby after baby, not because you wanted to but because the only reliable alternative was to turn away from your loved one's embrace?

Yes, she had made a fool of herself, but on this day when Jack felt so close to her she was able to smile, thinking how he would have laughed at her. She would collect Jacky and head home, in time to make some of the sugary tablet that the boys loved so much and which had been Jack's favourite.

They would eat it this evening as they remembered him.

PART THREE
New Year

December 1927 to January 1928

A guid new year to ane an' a'
An' mony may ye see

Traditional Scottish ballad

Chapter Twenty-One

Glasgow

Corran paused before a display case full of amulets and pulled out her notebook. Her heroine, Lydia, had solved her first case in Rome, but Corran was already sketching out a new mystery for her that would take place among the pyramids. These treasures in the Egyptian gallery in Kelvingrove Museum were exactly what she needed.

It was something of a relief, too, to escape the constant clamour of family life and lose herself among the objects. Corran loved this magnificent red sandstone building that housed Glasgow's museum and art gallery. Luisa had shown signs of wanting to accompany her, but was quickly dissuaded when she mentioned carrying out research for her next novel. Her family didn't quite know what to make of her unexpected new venture – after all, the first book was not yet published – and accepted that she needed to be alone. She stepped out of Alex and Luisa's close into the bitterly cold Glasgow air, wrapping her fingers tightly around a small parcel deep in her pocket.

She had travelled up to Glasgow on Christmas Eve, emerging

from the station in the late afternoon to find the lights of the department stores on Argyle Street and Sauchiehall Street ablaze as shoppers hurried to and fro, laden with parcels and seeking last-minute gifts. As she pushed her way through, she reflected how Christmas had grown in appeal and importance during her lifetime. When they had been children in Thurso there would have been a book or a toy and some of her mother's tablet on Christmas morning, but beyond that the day continued as normal. The main celebrations were saved for the turn of the year. Now the people of Scotland seemed to have embraced the festivities that had long been popular further south. Arriving at Alex and Luisa's home, where she met Giovanni for the first time and tried out her rusty Italian, Corran found her sister-in-law elbow-deep in preparations for a Christmas Eve feast to be enjoyed before she and Giovanni went out to midnight Mass. 'Will you join us?'

Corran was taken aback. She rarely gave much thought to the religious aspect of Alex's mixed marriage, but of course Giovanni and Luisa were both Catholic, while Alex had been raised in the presbyterian Church of Scotland – although she was fairly sure it meant little to him on a personal level. She wondered how their different denominations played out in a city like Glasgow, where religious identity carried so much significance. 'Thank you, but I'm tired from the journey and will be in bed long before then.'

Alex winked at her. 'Christmas Day's a Sunday so Mother and the others will likely go to the kirk as usual. You could always join them.'

Here in the museum, Corran smiled to herself. She and Alex had proved themselves the heathens of the family, attending neither mass nor kirk over Christmas. The whole family had come together at Rob and Stella's in the afternoon for a meal.

She had enjoyed her nephews' wide-eyed excitement at the array of food on offer, and had gladly been swaddled within the layers of festive family life, but now she found herself needing an escape. She stood among the Egyptian artefacts and looked towards the door. Would he come?

It was the kind of risk they rarely took in England, but here in Glasgow they felt much safer. Three weeks ago, in the damp cocoon of the cottage, they had been delighted to discover they would both be in Glasgow over Christmas. It was too good an opportunity to miss. Arthur's wife and child would spend Christmas in New York with Mary's sister who had emigrated there a couple of years earlier. Not included in the invitation, Arthur would stay with his own sister, Cath, and her family in Glasgow. Coiled together in bed in the musty cottage, they had made a tentative arrangement to meet here amid the Egyptian artefacts two days after Christmas, acknowledging that either one of them might be unable to get away. But here she was, and yes, coming through the doorway now, here he was too. Arthur.

She was obscured by a display case and could watch him unseen. His red hair was thinning, and his uneven walk seemed more halting. He scanned the room, trying to look casual, yet she suspected the hands in the pockets of his overcoat were clenched. She quickly looked round. Only one other visitor was present, a young man who was engrossed in the long description attached to a display of Egyptian grave goods. She stepped forward, warmth spreading through her at the obvious relief and pleasure on his face. 'You made it.'

They risked a chaste kiss – a greeting between old friends – before she felt in her pocket. 'I brought your Christmas present.'

He took the package from her outstretched hand. 'Shall I open it now?'

'If you like.'

'I do like.' He pulled away tissue paper to reveal a small silver photo frame containing a country scene. He smiled. 'Where we walk.'

'Exactly. I really wanted a snapshot of the cottage but thought it unwise. The view is the next best thing.'

'I shall keep it on my desk.' He slipped it inside his pocket. 'I have something for you too,' he began, but before he could bring it out the man at the other side of the room sneezed and Corran glanced across. He buried his face in his handkerchief, but just before he did she had the feeling he was watching them. Idle curiosity, no doubt, but still. She gave a tiny shake of her head and walked towards the door, Arthur following. In the grand central hall she paused, glancing to the steps that led up to the upper gallery, but there were too many people about. 'Let's walk over to the park.'

They strolled along a path between carefully manicured hedges, keeping a sedate distance apart. Arthur handed Corran his gift, which turned out to contain the latest Upton Sinclair novel, *Oil!*. 'You'll enjoy it,' he said. 'It exposes the greed of the oilmen of California, but it's entertaining too.'

How splendid it was to walk beside him like this, in a way they never could in Oxford or London, even if she had to resist the desire to link her arm through his. 'How was your Christmas?'

'Rather quiet actually.'

There was something odd in his tone. She glanced up at him. 'How's that? I thought your sister had a full household?'

'Indeed she does. But unfortunately they have scarlet fever in the house so I checked into a small hotel instead.'

'Arthur! Did you spend Christmas alone?'

'Not quite. I shared my Christmas luncheon with two spinster sisters who reside permanently at the hotel.'

Spinster – how she loathed that word. She pushed the thought aside. 'That's dreadful. I'm surprised you didn't return home to Manchester.'

He stopped and drew her down onto a bench that was set back a little way among the trees. 'Why would I do that, Corran?' he asked. 'I had arranged to meet you today. I wouldn't have missed this for the world.'

She bit her lip. It was so frustrating, this need to duck and dive and hide for the sake of a precious hour here or there. It wasn't even as if his wife wanted to be with him! She hated to think of him alone in a dreary boarding house while she had been enjoying laughter and warmth and family time. Just imagine if he had been there too, among them all, unwrapping presents, complimenting her mother on the Christmas pudding, lying stretched out on the floor to play with the boys' new train set as Alex had done. Instead, after a lonely Christmas here in Glasgow he would return to a cold, empty house in Manchester. 'When will you go south?' she asked.

'I haven't decided. It rather depends on you. I've nothing to return for – Mary and Ronald are away until the end of next week. If we can meet again I'll stay in Glasgow for a few more days.'

She shook her head. 'I would love to but unfortunately we are going away. We—' She stopped. A glimmer of an idea occurred to her. Was it possible? Why not? Her family were already aware of the previous connection between them in Dieppe. Could she invite Arthur to join them? 'That is – unless you come with us.'

'Come with you – what do you mean?'

Corran could barely get her words out fast enough to explain. 'My sister, Stella, has a friend who has a castle. Yes, really. It's hidden away in the woods in Ayrshire. She's invited us for Hogmanay – Stella and Rob, Alex and Luisa and myself. There will be no one else there except Stella's friend and her elderly parents. We travel down on Friday and come back on Tuesday. Why don't you come too?'

'What would your family think?'

'I'll say I bumped into you unexpectedly today and asked you along because illness at your sister's place leaves you alone for Hogmanay. Scottish hospitality demands no less! Alex and Stella know we were friends in Dieppe. It's the most natural thing in the world. Oh, do come, Arthur!'

His green eyes were clouded with doubt. 'It's such a risk.'

'There's no risk at all!' she exclaimed. 'Don't you see? Even if someone you know hears about it, there's a perfectly reasonable explanation.'

'Won't your sister's friend mind?'

'Not at all. You'll have heard of her. She's Elsie Mackay – you know, Lord Inchcape's daughter.'

Arthur drew back. 'The arch capitalist! Oh no, Corran, I don't think so.'

'Why not?' She glanced around. A couple of families were walking by, and a man was hurrying along the path towards the gate – the same man she had seen in the museum, if she wasn't mistaken. He glanced their way then was gone. She took Arthur's hand briefly. 'Can't you see what an opportunity this is? Don't let politics stand in the way.' She paused. 'We have spent one other New Year together – do you remember?'

'Of course. December 1918. Peace had not long been declared and you and I had just come back from Luneray. You were angry with me because I taught the soldiers about communism.'

Angry? Corran shook her head. 'I was confused. Things were changing quickly. But I remember that Hogmanay, how I taught you all to sing "Auld Lang Syne" properly, and the chief passed round his whisky.' *And I was falling in love with you although I didn't know it.*

178

'You wore a red dress.'

'What?'

'That New Year in Dieppe. You wore a dark red dress. I can picture it yet.'

'That old thing! I wore it all through the war.' She felt unexpected tears prick at her eyes. 'Nine years ago. They were simpler times in many ways. Do come, Arthur. Please.'

He looked out across the park, frowning deeply, then he turned towards her and smiled, the smile that made her heart flip over. 'All right, Miss Rutherford, if you insist. I would love to come.'

Chapter Twenty-Two

Glasgow

On the same day, Alison met up with Matthew just as eagerly as her daughter met Arthur. This might only be their second rendezvous since their time on the *Ranchi* in September, but they had exchanged long letters in the intervening months. Last week, now on shore leave, he had written to tell her he had an appointment with his lawyer in Glasgow. Perhaps they could meet for a cup of tea afterwards? Alison selected her favourite tweed skirt with a thrill of anticipation and said farewell to Stella and Rob, who seemed to find the whole situation highly amusing. 'Behave yourself!' Stella laughed.

My goodness, the young can be patronising.

They had arranged to meet in George Square. Alison was early, and held her winter coat close around herself as she sat down on a bench to wait. What a contrast to the days she had spent with Matthew in Nice just a few months ago! She shuffled her feet in an attempt to deter some pigeons from coming too close, then felt a stir of pleasure as she saw him across the square, looking round. He raised his hand in a wave and came towards her, his long black overcoat swinging with his purposeful step. How funny to see him dressed not in naval uniform but in civilian clothes. He tipped his hat to her as he drew close, and though his clothes might be different his smile was just the same.

He sat down beside her and brushed her cheek with a kiss. At first they were content to catch up on the most immediate news. He told her about Christmas with his daughter and grandchildren; she told him about their own festivities.

'How's Giovanni?' he asked. He always asked that in his letters too.

'He's doing well, all things considered. He doesn't enjoy school – I suspect he has a hard time there – so he's glad to be on holiday and helping in an Italian café nearby. But we're all desperately worried about Signor Rossi.'

'Still no news?'

'Not a whisper.'

Matthew shook his head. 'I've asked our agent in Italy to make enquiries, but nothing has come back. My ship won't return to Naples for another few months yet, but when we do I'll see if I can discover anything.' He took her hand. 'But it's cold today. Where shall I take you for that cup of tea? The Willow Tea Rooms? The Station Hotel?'

Alison hesitated. 'Those would be lovely,' she said. 'But I had another idea. I mentioned that Gio is working in a café in Partick during the school holidays. It's a tram trip away, but how would you like to go there for your cup of tea?'

'That's a grand idea!' he said. 'It's just across the water from my old stomping ground too so perhaps we could take a quick look around.'

Plans made, they stood up and set off for the tram stop. Matthew looked around him as they walked. 'I spent my childhood years in Govan yet would you believe I never once came into Glasgow city centre,' he said. 'Govan was its own community in those days. We had no cause to come this way.'

In Dumbarton Road, Alison led him to the Italian café and pushed the heavy door. Signora Simone stood behind the counter with her son, Paolo, an array of sweetie jars and colourful bottles reflecting in the mirror behind her. She ushered Alison and Matthew into a booth near the window while speaking over her shoulder in rapid Italian to her son, who disappeared through a door behind the counter. 'Giovanni is in the kitchen,' she said. 'I take your order and he bring.'

They ordered a pot of tea and Matthew decided to sample the freshly made ice cream despite the chill of the day. Alison glanced around. The café was fairly quiet, but two women were enjoying a cup of tea and a blether in the next booth, and an elderly man sat alone with his newspaper at the counter. The booths were elegant, made of carved wood and mirrored glass, with a marble-effect table between the benches. Soon Giovanni appeared bearing a tray, which he laid on the table before sliding into the seat beside Matthew and giving them a shy smile.

He was so like his elder sister to look at, with wavy dark golden hair and wide eyes. 'You remember Captain Kennedy, Gio? He was on the *Ranchi*.'

'Good to see you again, son,' Matthew said, shaking his hand. 'You look a bit less peely-wally than you did at the end of that journey!' His eyes softened. 'I'm gey sorry to hear about your father, though. He's a brave man.'

'Thank you,' Giovanni said, staring at the tabletop and picking at a ragged fingernail.

'We still hope for good news,' Alison said.

The boy shook his head. 'He would have been in touch if he could. Something bad has happened to him.'

'Luisa says there are many reasons he might not be in touch.

Someone could be hiding him, for instance, and he wouldn't want to put them in danger.'

Gio lifted his head then, his dark eyes fierce. 'Luisa wants to believe that. But I know these people. They have hurt him and I am to blame.'

Alison stretched her hand out and covered his, noticing grazing on his knuckles. 'That's not true, Gio.'

'He was fine until I was in trouble.' His voice trembled a little, and she was reminded that he was still only fifteen. Just a boy.

'Your father was involved in very dangerous affairs long before you knew anything about it, and he knew the risks he was taking. What mattered to him was making sure you were safe. But if anything has happened to him – and we hope to God it has not – it's the fault of Mussolini and his Blackshirts. No one else.'

She could see Giovanni was unconvinced and decided to change the subject. There was a dark bruise on his cheekbone as well as those grazed knuckles and she reached out and touched it gently. 'Fighting again?' she asked, in a mock severe voice.

He ducked away. 'Boxing,' he said, with a hint of pride. 'I go to the boxing club three times a week. It keeps me fit.'

'And means you can handle yourself,' Matthew said, nodding. 'I remember what the closes of Glasgow are like, son, and it can't be easy for you as a foreigner, aye?'

Gio shrugged. 'I'm all right. They are stupid boys with stupid rhymes, that's all. And Paolo is my friend. He grew up here – his parents moved here when he was a baby – so he knows all about being an Italian in Glasgow.'

'Luisa tells me you don't plan to go with them to Glenapp at Hogmanay but will stay with Paolo and his family instead?'

'That's right. They ask me to work here; I am good worker. The customers, they like me.' He hesitated, and glanced at Alison with a spark of defiance in his eyes. 'Soon I leave school and work here every day.'

Alison smiled, not rising to the challenge, but Matthew glanced round the café. 'This is a fine place, but is it really the life you want? What about the sea? There's always a good career waiting for bright lads on the ships. I could help with that.'

'Oh no!' The horror on Giovanni's face made Alison laugh out loud. 'Nothing would be worse. That journey was the most terrible experience of my life.'

The bell above the door tinkled and an older lady walked in, holding the hand of a small child who was jumping up and down with excitement. Giovanni got to his feet. 'Here are customers. I must go.' He shook hands again with Matthew and smiled at Alison. 'Thank you for coming. I shall tell Luisa.' Then he stepped towards the newcomer with a little bow and led her to a booth with a flash of his charming smile.

'Poor boy,' Alison said, finishing her tea. 'What a burden he carries. But he's happy here with the Simones. Luisa should take comfort in that. Now, let's have a stroll down by the river before you go back for your train.'

They made their way between the tenements on the other side of Dumbarton Road towards the river. Matthew slipped his arm through hers, and she thought how good it felt to walk together. Soon the houses disappeared, and shipyards and docks stretched before them. Access to the wharves was restricted in many places but they made their way to the ferry crossing point. There was no holiday here; the clamour from the shipyards resounded as loudly as ever, and they stood for a while and watched a cargo ship being unloaded a little way along the quay. Matthew pointed out various landmarks across the river to Alison, who told him about the family's connections to Stephen's shipyard.

'If I hadn't gone to sea I'd likely have worked there myself or else in Fairfield,' Matthew said. 'It was the sea or the shipyards for us lads when we left the school.' He turned and looked west to the curve in the Clyde. 'Then, much later, I settled with Eleanor and the children in Helensburgh, further along the river.'

'I've never been to Helensburgh.'

'Oh, you must! It's a bonny train journey.' He glanced at his watch. 'Sadly there's no time today, but I'll be back in January, before my shore leave ends. I'll check on the house before I return to sea. You could accompany me, if you would like? We could make a day of it.'

It was lightly said, but when she glanced at him there was a tenderness in his expression that made her heart beat unaccountably quickly. She took a breath and steadied herself. 'Let's do that.'

Chapter Twenty-Three

Glenapp Castle

'There you are.' Lord Inchcape laid aside his newspaper and rose to his feet as his daughter entered the room. 'I thought I had missed you.'

'Good morning, Father,' Elsie said as she sat down at the long, polished table. There were just the two of them at breakfast now that her sister and brother and their families had returned to their own homes after the Christmas celebrations. Mother always breakfasted in bed. 'Isn't it quiet without the others?'

'Blessed peace.'

'You don't mean a word of it,' she teased, thinking of the day before when she had opened the door of the understairs cupboard to find him squashed in there beside two giggling grandchildren as they played sardines. He laughed.

'Perhaps I don't. It is grand to have some young life about the place, especially at Christmas. But your mother needs rest. It's only two weeks now until we set off for Egypt. We must be sure she is well enough for the journey. I hope your friends won't disturb her.'

'We'll be quiet as mice,' Elsie promised, digging into the boiled egg that a servant placed in front of her. 'There aren't many of us – just my friend Stella and some of her family, but no children. I rather hoped young Giovanni would come with Alex and Luisa – you remember the boy we brought back from Italy? Stella writes that he will spend the weekend with friends. At least that sounds as if he has settled well in Glasgow.'

'Do you think they will get here all right?'

Elsie glanced through the window that overlooked the terrace to the sea beyond. 'It's only a light covering so far, and not much more forecast until tomorrow. The snow is far worse down south for once. The trains here are running fine, and the Rolls will handle the road to Stranraer without much difficulty.'

'Well, be careful if you drive to meet them yourself, which I imagine you will.' He replaced his cup, brushed the crumbs from his napkin and got to his feet. 'If you'll excuse me, I've some correspondence to see to. Pop in briefly after breakfast, would you?'

Elsie watched as he left the room. His passion for his work was as strong as ever, and after a week of disruption he was glad to get back to his desk. All through her childhood it had been the same: holidays and festivities were to her father little more than a frivolous interruption to the real business of life. She understood that. She was looking forward to the arrival of her friends and some pleasant fun as they brought in 1928 – but, just like her father, she would be glad when this holiday period was over and she could get back to the real work of preparation.

For there was much to be done.

She stretched across the table for the newspaper he had discarded. There would be no word of Mrs Grayson, of course there would not – all hope was surely lost – and yet she turned the pages, scanning quickly, just in case.

There. A tiny paragraph towards the back.

Everything that could be done by searchers of the sea and sky in their efforts to find the missing aeroplane Dawn has been done, and the search is about to be abandoned.

In black and white. *Abandoned.*

Whatever had possessed the woman to embark on her Atlantic attempt so late in the year? Elsie poured some coffee from the silver pot into her favourite green coffee cup, then got to her feet, carrying it over to the window. Ailsa Craig stood firm as ever against the grey ocean waves. It was the question all the newspapers were asking, but Elsie knew exactly what had possessed her. The longing to succeed, the desire to be first. The dream that burnt in Elsie's own heart.

She had been dismayed to read that Frances Grayson, niece of former President Woodrow Wilson no less, had set off in *Dawn* from New York on 23rd December. Was Elsie's ambition of being the first woman to fly over the Atlantic to be thwarted? But Mrs Grayson's flight had ended almost before it began, not even reaching its first intended destination of Newfoundland. She and her crew were presumed lost in the waters off Nova Scotia somewhere. Another failed attempt.

Elsie held her coffee cup and saucer in hands that were not quite steady. Last week she had travelled down to London to represent her parents at the funeral of Lord Lawrence of Kingsgate, railway chairman. While there, she had met with Captain Hinchliffe, who had returned from New York the day before on board the Cunard liner *Berengaria*. Hinchliffe produced paperwork and pushed it across the table. On top lay a photograph of an aeroplane. 'Stinson Detroiter SM-1. She's perfect for our purposes.'

Elsie looked at the photograph and felt the hairs on her arms prickle. 'Tell me more.'

'I met with Bill Mara of Stinson and went through every last detail with him. The original model was a biplane but she's been redesigned as a monoplane, and that's what we'll use. The age of the biplane is past, Bill says. She has the same Wright Whirlwind engine as Lindbergh's *Spirit of St Louis*, and is by far the best machine out there. Bill was proud that Scenic Airways have chosen the Detroiter for their Grand Canyon sightseeing trips, but perhaps more relevant for our purposes, Eddie Stinson won the Ford Air Tour in a Detroiter SM-1 just this year.'

'Eddie Stinson.' Elsie looked up. 'Something to do with Katherine Stinson, right? She was a real pioneer of female flight in America.'

'That's right, same family. I believe Eddie's her brother.'

How appropriate. Elsie looked back at the photograph. 'Will she handle the Atlantic?'

Hinchliffe cleared his throat. 'When I mentioned the Atlantic, Bill nearly showed me the door. You know how it is, there have been so many failures lately and he doesn't want his company associated with bad publicity. I had to tell him our plan was to make an overland trip to India. He was full of enthusiasm for that idea.' He shuffled the papers on the table between them to reveal a technical drawing of the monoplane. 'It strikes me that mentioning India could be a useful diversion when the time comes, if needed. Anyway, she has a large cabin – designed to carry six passengers – so we can adapt that to have plenty of space for fuel. Enclosed cockpit for comfort.'

'Dual controls?'

He held her gaze across the table and she knew they understood each other perfectly. 'Of course.'

They parted soon afterwards, Elsie to return to Scotland and

Hinchliffe to Purley and new baby Pamela, who had been born during his absence in the States. The purchase was made, and arrangements were now underway for the Stinson Detroiter to be shipped to England in January for construction at Brooklands Aerodrome.

Elsie looked out at the bleak, wintry sea that – many miles away – had claimed yet another victim in these last few days. Was the shiver that ran through her one of fear or excitement? She wasn't quite sure. All she knew for certain was that she had now set in motion the greatest endeavour of her life. If she could only keep it secret from her father, it would not be stopped until it reached its final conclusion – whatever that might be.

A few hours later she pushed such thoughts to the back of her mind and welcomed her Hogmanay guests to Glenapp. In the end the chauffeur drove through sleet showers to collect them, and Elsie stood in the entrance hall, arms open wide. 'Come out of the cold! You must be frozen!'

The blazing fire in the drawing room brought warmth and light to the chilled travellers, even as hail rattled against the window outside. Rob pulled out a chair for Stella and Elsie watched as she eased herself into it. 'How long to go?'

'About six weeks or so. Jacky came early, though, so you never know.' She shifted position, trying to get comfortable. 'I plan to have the time of my life this weekend, as it will likely be my last outing before I'm swamped by nappies and sleepless nights again. Who knows when I'll next resurface.'

Just then the maid appeared with a pot of tea and a laden cake stand, which she placed on the low table. As she thanked her, Elsie glanced quickly at Luisa, whose longing for her own baby was known to them all, but she was smiling. She remembered the last time she had seen Luisa, down in Tilbury Docks, strained and anxious. 'How is Giovanni?' she asked, picturing the sullen, bewildered boy who had stepped out of that cabin into the corridor.

'He is well, thank you. We are very grateful for all you and your father did for him. He improves his English and works hard.'

Beside her on the sofa, Alex gave a snort. 'His English is improving, I'll grant you that, but I'm not so sure about the hard work.' He turned to Elsie. 'Luisa wants Gio to be a good student, but the boy's not interested.'

'What does he want to do?'

'He's made friends with an Italian family who run an ice cream café. That's where he is this weekend. They have asked Gio to work for them and nothing would please him more.'

'Our father is a journalist,' Luisa said, her dark eyes stormy. 'He wants more for his son than to be an ice cream seller. I do not know where Papa is, but one day we will find him again. When he returns he must have a son to be proud of.'

'When Gio returns to Italy he can pick up his education again, but while he's in Scotland and speaking a language not his own, it's too much to ask. I'm sure your father would want the boy to be happy.'

The red-haired man who had entered at Corran's side was listening to all this with interest. Stella had telephoned from Rob's consulting room the day before to ask if Corran could bring along an old friend from the war who would otherwise be on his own for Hogmanay. Accustomed to house parties with ever-changing guest lists, Elsie had welcomed him without a second thought. Now, as the stranger leant forward and asked Luisa a question about her father, she took a second glance. Had she seen him before somewhere?

Alex held his wife's hand. 'We don't know what has happened

to Luisa's father,' he said sombrely. 'After the incident in Naples and Gio's disappearance, we believe the authorities became suspicious of Niccolo's undercover activities. If anything serious had happened to him – if he had been imprisoned or worse – then surely we would have heard. It seems more likely that he managed to escape before being arrested.'

'That is my daily prayer,' Luisa said quietly.

'It's a damned disgrace how this Tory government cosies up to Mussolini,' Corran's friend said. 'He has outlawed all opposition and all representation of the working man, and yet Foreign Secretary Chamberlain strolls around with him in the Italian sunshine as if he is Britain's closest ally! No doubt he would like the fascists to take hold here too.'

'The circumstances are very different, sir.' Elsie looked up at the sound of her father's voice. He stood in the doorway, a piece of paper in his hand. 'Italy has been in turmoil since the war and the peace conference, and was in dire need of firm government. Stability is essential for the international peace we all want to preserve. My men in the Mediterranean tell me there's a wonderful difference in transport and administration. No doubt there are some ruffians among Mussolini's men who have taken things too far, as in the case of our dear friends here, but how can you have democracy unless you first establish order?' He stalked over and held out a hand to the man whose words had provoked his comments. 'Callaghan, I believe?'

'Indeed, sir. Pleased to meet you,' Arthur said, rising to his feet.

Elsie glanced between them. That was why their extra guest was familiar. Corran's old wartime friend was none other than Arthur Callaghan, the Labour MP. This could get interesting – Elsie knew just how scathing her father was about socialism. But Lord Inchcape had already turned away from the newcomer and was moving round the party, greeting Rob and Stella, Corran, Alex and Luisa as old friends. He turned to Elsie. 'I brought something to show you, my dear.'

She glanced at the thin slip of paper and felt the familiar tremor of fear that everyone who had lived through the war experienced at the sight of a telegram. He sought to reassure her. 'Nothing to worry about, rather the opposite. It's from the King of Afghanistan, no less. You'll remember he and his wife have been travelling from Bombay to Port Said on the *Rajputana*. The King has very graciously wired to thank us. Here: "*The Queen and myself will always remember the voyage as one of the most pleasant experiences in our lives.*" Rather a feather in your cap, wouldn't you say?' He waved aside the offer of a cup of tea. 'No, my dear, I am on my way to your mother. I'll leave you young ones for now. The King of Afghanistan, eh? In 1928, when we launch our new liner, we shall welcome ever more influential guests to experience the pleasures of your interiors.'

His mention of the ambitious latest liner was seized upon by Alex and Rob, who knew her construction first-hand. Alex was full of enthusiasm for the all-electric engines, while Rob spoke more quietly about the safety measures he had discussed with the shipyard owners.

'When will the ship be ready?' asked Corran.

'She'll be launched for fitting out next year.'

'And that's when you become involved, Elsie?'

'Oh no,' Elsie said. 'My designs are largely complete. By the time she's ready for fit-out, everything that can be prepared in advance must be in place.'

'Tell them about the swimming pool,' said Stella, leaning forward to help herself to another piece of cake.

'It will be a first for P&O, but we've included a full-sized swimming pool for first-class passengers.' She turned to Corran with a smile. 'I must give you a tour one day. The design for the swimming pool is inspired by the baths of ancient Rome.'

'Sounds like Corran's detective story!'

'Hey, Corran, perhaps you should set your next mystery on one of Elsie's ships.'

Elsie sat back, listening to their laughter, and heard again her father's words. He was right: praise from the King of Afghanistan *was* a feather in her cap, and she loved to hear the pride in his voice. But oh, if only he could be as encouraging and supportive of the dreams that lay far closer to her heart.

That was impossible, of course, but in a few months' time, when she had returned in triumph, the world of aviation at her feet, would he be proud of her or would he cut her off for ever?

Only time would tell.

Chapter Twenty-Four

Glenapp Castle

The next day was Hogmanay, the very last day of 1927.

They would dine later than usual, then play games and perhaps dance to the gramophone until midnight approached. Stella brushed her glossy dark hair and applied her lipstick, then tossed it down on the dressing table. 'I don't know why I bother trying to look attractive when I'm so puffy and sweaty all the time.'

Rob was at the other side of the room fixing his bow tie. 'You look beautiful,' he said automatically, without so much as a glance in her direction. As he slipped on his jacket he removed his hipflask from the pocket and took a mouthful. He held it out to her. 'Want some?'

She shook her head. 'My heartburn's been awful for the last day or two. I can't think of anything worse than whisky.' She watched him in the mirror, trying to work out how much he had already drunk. She knew from the bottle in the bottom drawer at home that he had tried to cut back since that awful night when he had got so drunk and lashed out at Duncan, but an evening like this would be a challenge.

Not that Duncan had minded. He had been proud of his black eye, telling everyone at school that he got it in a fight with a much bigger boy. She wondered how Duncan and Jacky were getting on. Alison had been happy to stay in Glasgow with the boys, urging her daughter and son-in-law to go and enjoy themselves. Stella wondered how much that had to do with her new friend Matthew Kennedy, although she knew that tonight Alison planned to bring in the New Year with neighbours. Jacky would fall asleep but Duncan was determined to stay awake. She wondered if he would manage. Probably. Her older son had a stubbornness about him that didn't easily give in.

She stood up and turned, looking round the blue and cream bedroom that was theirs for these few nights. It was tastefully furnished, and the quality of everything from the bedding to the towels to the paintings on the wall was exquisite. And the size! She laughed aloud.

'What's funny?'

'I'm just thinking of our closet bed off the parlour at home and comparing it with this.'

'There's no comparison, is there? But then, you didn't marry a shipping magnate.'

'And you didn't marry a society belle with her own career.' Stella picked up her silk wrap and slung it round her shoulders. 'Although that's not quite true. I did have my own career when you married me, I just had to give it up.'

'Do we have to do this again tonight, Stella? Can't we just enjoy the evening?'

For a moment the success of their New Year hung by a thread, thin as gossamer, then her tension and her sadness escaped in a sigh. 'You're right. I do want to make the most of these days without the boys and before the baby comes. But when Lord Inchcape spoke yesterday about the Italians and the peace conference, I couldn't help but think – I was *there*! I sat in on those sessions, I typed up what Orlando and Sonnino said! And now look at me. I read about world events and I might as well be reading one of the boys' fairy stories, it's all so far removed from my life.'

Rob walked over and took her hands. 'You're still the same beautiful, intelligent woman you were then.'

She looked at her reflection in the mirror. 'Am I, though? It feels as if marriage and children have consumed everything else I ever was. I'm not sure what's left.'

She knew she sometimes exasperated Rob with her harking back but she couldn't help it. It was all right for him, he had added a rich layer of family life onto the person he was before. She had been required to lay that person down, and no one seemed to understand what that had cost her.

'It's just the stage we're at,' he said. 'Soon baby number three will be born and our family will be complete. Before you know it our children will be at school. There will be plenty of time for you to do other things then.'

'And I mean to,' she said. 'Where's that aeroplane brooch Elsie gave me? I'll wear it tonight. It will make her smile.' She pinned on the brooch, picked up her bag and made for the door.

'Do you think she's happy?'

'Who?'

'Elsie.'

Stella stared at him in bewilderment. 'Of course she is. What on earth do you mean?'

'Don't you think there's a tension about her that wasn't there in the summer? I wondered if she had said anything to you, given how close you are.'

'We haven't had a chance to speak alone.' Stella opened the door. 'I'm sure you're imagining things. Let's go down.'

* * *

Hidden in the shadows, Corran watched Rob and Stella leave their room and walk arm in arm to the top of the staircase. Stella wore a deep blue evening dress with an extra panel of material sewn into it by Luisa's expert hand, and looked elegant despite her pregnancy. Corran glanced down at her own frock. She never bothered much about clothes and had been bringing this dress out on formal occasions for years. She had declined Luisa's offer to embellish it with lace for the Hogmanay party. 'If it's good enough for Oxford, it's good enough for Glenapp.'

That wasn't true. Her college buildings might be glorious in their beauty but they were sparse in comfort, very different from the luxurious, no-expense-spared atmosphere of this castle. She looked again and confirmed that Rob and Stella were out of sight. She knocked on the door in front of her and, not waiting for a reply, slipped in.

The room was empty.

Arthur's jacket was slung over the back of a chair so he hadn't gone downstairs. Perhaps he was using the bathroom further along the corridor. She would wait. She wandered over to the window, where he hadn't closed his curtains yet. She peered into the darkness, sleet streaming down the glass, then pulled the thick brocade curtains, shutting out that wild, cold night. To her left was a desk covered with papers. During the afternoon most of them had taken advantage of the short hours of daylight and a break in the weather to get some bracing air, but Arthur had mumbled that he had work to do. And right enough the top piece of paper was headed *Socialist Revival*, with a scrawled list of points beneath. She felt slightly guilty. Arthur was uncomfortable as a guest of wealth and privilege, and had only come to please her. An envelope in his writing was addressed to his good friend James Maxton, Clydeside MP, who was chairman of the left-wing Independent Labour Party. Stella knew from long conversations in the cottage that Arthur, Maxton and their ILP colleagues were increasingly dissatisfied with Ramsay MacDonald and the parliamentary Labour Party to which they were affiliated, believing that they had compromised their socialism in the hope of regaining power.

What could be taking him so long? At the other side of the room was a comfortable-looking chair and low table on which sat the book he was reading. She crossed over and sat down, idly flicking through the pages as she waited. It was full of impenetrable economic theory. Did he ever read for pleasure? She still hadn't shown him her novel, insisting that he should wait to read it in its final, published form. That was just a few weeks away now, and she wasn't too sure how she felt about it.

As she replaced the book, something slipped from between the pages. A photograph that he was using as a page marker. She picked it up and felt an iciness steal into her heart. It was a family group: an elegant woman seated on a garden chair, a child on her knee and a man – Arthur – standing beside them with his arm on her shoulder. It was not the sight of Mary that disturbed Corran – she regularly saw photographs in the newspaper of the pair of them at some function or another. No, her eyes were drawn to the small boy who was looking up at his father and laughing with such complete joy that she could almost hear his giggles escaping from the snapshot in time. As for Arthur, she thought she knew and loved his every expression, yet there was something in his eyes as he looked down at his son that she had never seen before.

Such intimacy between father and son.

The door handle turned and she slipped the photograph back randomly between the pages, rising to her feet as Arthur entered the room.

'Where on earth have you been? We were supposed to be downstairs fifteen minutes ago.'

He stopped, startled, and then closed the door behind him with a smile. 'Corran, love.'

She folded her arms. 'You're not even changed, Arthur! Where have you been?'

'I had calls to make. Elsie arranged for me to use the telephone in the library.'

'Telephone calls? On Hogmanay? To whom?'

'Does it matter?'

'It does rather,' she said, hating her waspish tone even as she spoke. 'I thought we would have some time together but I've hardly seen you. You've been working all afternoon. I came along to your room to snatch a few minutes alone before dinner, but you weren't here.'

He sighed. 'I received a message to call a party colleague.'

She stared at him. 'A message? How can that be? No one knows you're here.'

'That's what I thought. It rather seems they do.'

'But how?'

He shrugged. 'It's the way of things, Corran. No one trusts anyone in parliamentary life. They are always watching.'

'But then – do they know about us?' A note of panic creeping into her voice. All they had been so careful to hide. All she stood to lose.

'There's nothing to worry about.'

'That's not what I asked you!'

'Corran, you can trust me. We'll be late for dinner. We can talk more tomorrow.'

She stared at him, then balled her fists and turned away. 'Well, you'd better dress, then.'

'You're right.' He opened the wardrobe where one of the servants had hung his clothes. 'Would you believe Elsie offered me a valet to help me dress? It's absurd. What is it about rich people that they lose the ability to do up their own buttons and tie their own shoelaces?'

Normally she would have agreed with him but her feelings were in turmoil. She sat down again and felt her eyes being drawn to the book containing the photograph. Looking away, she focused instead on Arthur, watching as he changed, her eyes on those familiar scars. He pulled on his trousers and, sensing her gaze, smiled the smile that always made her heart flip over. He came towards her, his chest still bare. He put his arms around her and she closed her eyes, breathing in the scent of him, feeling the warmth of his puckered skin against her cheek. 'I'm sorry,' he murmured into her hair. 'Let's get through this awful party tonight and we'll have a good walk tomorrow, just the two of us.'

Everything within her was churned up and stormy, but as ever desire won. She stood up and embraced him. As they kissed his hands slipped to the buttons at the back of her dress, and she let him undo them, knowing exactly where it would lead. Her lipstick was already smudged and now her hair would be messed up. Her dress would be crumpled. Her stockings would likely snag.

She didn't care.

Downstairs in the drawing room, the others had gathered for drinks. 'I can't think where Corran is but it's hardly a surprise. She's been running late all her life,' Stella told Elsie.

'I'm sure she'll be down in time for dinner,' Alex said. 'What about Arthur? Has anyone seen him since lunchtime?'

'He may still be in the library,' Elsie said. 'He asked if he could send a telegram to his wife and child.'

'In New York?' her father asked sharply.

Elsie nodded. 'He offered to pay, but I told him not to bother.'

'He's a socialist, they have a knack for spending other people's money.'

'Don't be ridiculous, James, the man is a guest here,' Lady Inchcape said, placing a hand on her husband's arm. 'Of course he must contact his family on Hogmanay. I wonder why he didn't go with them?'

'Pressure of work is what he said to me,' Alex said. 'Not that I've spoken much with him. Quiet fellow, but he and Corran worked together during the war. We all know that bonds forged in those circumstances endure a long time.'

Stella glanced at him and saw nothing unusual in his expression. She had her own suspicions about her sister's relationship with Arthur but kept them to herself. Alex and Corran were close, but her brother wasn't particularly perceptive. Not like Rob, whose doctor's eyes often saw below the surface. She remembered his unexpected comment about Elsie earlier and looked across at their hostess, who was deep in conversation with Luisa. There was no sign of any tension. Elsie was radiant in shimmering dusky pink silk, and as she waved her arm expressively the diamond bracelet around her wrist glinted in the light of the chandelier. Stella joined them.

'We're discussing Italy,' Elsie said. 'I do love it so. Our Mediterranean cruises this year will call at Livorno and Naples, as well as Cagliari in Sardinia. I asked Luisa what tours she would suggest from Naples. It's good to have local recommendations and to offer something a little different from the other shipping lines.'

Luisa held up her hands. 'The places I know and love are simple. They would not appeal to your passengers.' She shook her head. 'Il Duce welcomes tourists but he will not show them the true Italy, the one that has destroyed my family.'

'My dear, I am so sorry. That was thoughtless of me. You must be worried sick.'

Luisa lifted her chin, and Stella thought how lovely she looked, with her long curls the colour of dark honey falling against the deep crimson of a dress that was both simpler and yet more striking than Elsie's expensive gown. 'My father is strong. I am sure he has escaped and will make his way to safety. Then he will contact me.' She slipped her hand into the little bag at her side and pulled out her rosary beads, fingering them carefully. 'Every day I pray for him.' She crossed herself, and to Stella's astonishment Elsie did the same.

'May God protect him.'

'I didn't know you were a Catholic!'

Elsie smiled. 'Didn't you? I went to convent school in Belgium, although I admit it didn't mean so much to me then. I do attend the presbyterian kirk at Glenapp alongside my parents and the estate families. Remind me to take you there before you leave. It's such a sweet building, I love it. But my Catholic faith means a great deal to me and I often visit St Andrew's Cathedral in Glasgow. I always take my rosary with me when I fly.' She turned back to Luisa. 'I shall also pray for your father every day, my dear.'

Stella looked between them with a strange sense of being the outsider. She attended church regularly with her mother, the children and sometimes Rob, and the beliefs she had been taught as a child were laced through her life, but she would never speak about prayer with her friend or her sister-in-law. Her faith was a private matter, in what she thought of as the Scottish way. She had been inclined to see Luisa's Catholicism as a superstition, but there was a strength and meaning in the way she and Elsie spoke that made her pause. Then the door opened and she looked round to see Corran enter the room with Arthur a step or two behind. Stella glanced at her sister. Her eyes were bright and her cheeks a little flushed but she seemed quite composed as she approached Elsie's parents to apologise for their late arrival. Elsie moved away to welcome them. Stella turned back to Luisa, who was gazing out of the window with a forlorn expression. Stella doubted she had even noticed Corran's arrival and slipped an arm through hers. 'What's Gio doing this evening?'

Luisa's face brightened a little at the mention of her brother. 'He is with the Simone family. Gio loves to spend time with them, especially with Paolo, who is a little older than him, and Sofia, who is a little younger. I am glad he has made friends his own age.'

At that moment the butler appeared and ushered them through to the dining room, which sparkled and shone as candlelight reflected on the glass and silverware. 'Ah, but will there be black bun?' Alex's voice murmured behind her. Stella turned round and was met with that grin of Alex's that still recalled Jack to her even after all this time.

Ah, Jack.

Maybe it was the effect of the turn of the year, but he seemed close to her tonight, somehow. The brother she had loved so dearly and missed so deeply. Rob's wartime demons might manifest themselves more vividly, but her own had never left her. She took her seat with a shiver. Rob noticed.

'All right?'

'Jack.' It was all she needed to say, and as he covered her hand with his, his warmth and reassurance transferred itself to her. They might often argue and grow impatient with each other these days, but he understood her pain and that was such a comfort.

It was what had brought them together, after all.

Chapter Twenty-Five

Glenapp Castle

Lord and Lady Inchcape retired after dinner. Elsie was relieved. Her father and Arthur had bickered on and off throughout the meal, mainly about the Trades Disputes Act, which had been introduced after the General Strike to curb the power of the trade unions. Stella joined in briefly when the conversation moved on to international affairs, speaking in favour of disarmament, which Lord Inchcape dismissed as a fool's dream. 'The Germans won't accept it and quite frankly I don't blame them. Any government that votes to reduce its armed forces betrays its own people.'

Lady Inchcape put a stop to the conversation at this point, but tensions simmered on below the surface and Elsie was glad to bid her parents good night after the meal. She knew her father loved nothing better than a robust debate, but the rest of them didn't want to see out the old year in the throes of a circular argument that could have no end.

The thick velvet curtains were drawn tightly against the howling gale that rattled the windows, a staccato accompaniment to the jazz music playing on the gramophone. Warm lamplight illuminated their charades, their laughter and their stories, but as the minutes ticked on towards midnight there came a change in the atmosphere, a stillness charged with significance. Elsie looked towards Rob. 'Would you help me refill everyone's glass? The servants stay downstairs for their own celebration now.'

Rob obliged. Soon, they all had a drink in hand. Elsie glanced at the black marble clock that ticked on the mantelpiece. There were still a few minutes to go until 1928. Impulsively she said, 'There's a game we always used to play on Hogmanay. We stand in a circle and go round, and each of us says what we hope for in the new year. It can be profound or silly but it must be true. Come on, everyone, up on your feet. Rob, you go first.'

'That's easy,' he said as they all stood up, glasses in hand. 'The safe arrival of a healthy baby in a few weeks' time.' He looked to his left. 'Stella?'

'The same, of course.'

'Not allowed,' Elsie said. 'You mustn't say the same as someone else.'

Stella narrowed her eyes a little, and Elsie watched as she fingered that little aeroplane brooch. 'I'm not sure, then. It's hard to see beyond the arrival of the baby, but I hope I can find a way to do something useful and rewarding with my time.'

'Having a baby is useful and rewarding, surely,' said Alex, who was next in line. Elsie glanced between him and Luisa. Perhaps this game had not been such a good idea after all! What would she say when her own turn came?

'Anyway, that's mine,' said Stella, shrugging her shoulders. 'What's yours, Alex?'

'For my part I'll be happy to see the completion and safe launch of Hull 519.'

'Does the ship not have a name?' Arthur asked.

'It's always a closely guarded secret until launch day. I heard

206

rumours of *Taj Mahal* but I've no idea if that's true.' He looked at Elsie, eyebrows raised.

'Even if I knew, I couldn't possibly say. Luisa, you next.'

'The return of my father, of course.'

There was a silence. 'We all wish for that,' Corran said quietly. 'My hope is much less significant, but I do hope my book doesn't receive too many dreadful reviews.'

'That's hardly likely!' Elsie laughed. 'We're all dying to read it. Arthur, what about you?' She braced herself for a political monologue, but he surprised her.

'If Manchester City rejoin the First Division this year, I'll be the happiest man in England.'

As they all laughed, the clock give a little whirring noise that Elsie knew well. She held up her hand. 'Hush! It's nearly midnight!'

The chimes sounded out, light and high, echoed by deeper notes from the grandfather clock in the hall. Elsie clasped her glass tightly as those twelve notes sent previous years cascading through her mind: childhood years in India; the war years when their London mansion became a convalescent home; parties with the bright young things during her years with Dennis, and now back here with her family in Glenapp. Would this year bring the fulfilment of her dream? She looked round her friends and saw how Stella leant against Rob, her hand stroking her belly; how tears glittered in Luisa's eyes; how Corran and Arthur clasped hands when they thought no one was watching. The chimes came to an end and she raised her glass. 'Happy New Year!'

'A good new year!'

Glasses chinked, and it was time for the familiar manoeuvres as they all went around the circle wishing one another a very happy new year. Rob approached her.

'You didn't share your hope for 1928.'

It was said lightly but there was a keenness in his grey gaze. She laughed. 'I've nothing special to say.'

As gentle as to be almost imperceptible, he drew her a few paces away from the circle. He leant towards her, his hand still resting on her waist. 'Is that true? I have wondered.'

'Wondered what?' She could feel her cheeks burning. She glanced round and saw that Stella was watching them, a puzzled frown on her face. She stepped aside quickly and raised her voice. 'It's time for "Auld Lang Syne", and we need a first foot. Alex, you're too fair and Arthur is ginger! Rob, it will have to be you. You'll find what you need in the entrance hall. Meanwhile we'll be ready. I'll play.' She watched, making sure that Rob left the room, and then strode over to the grand piano near the window, trying to suppress the uneasy feeling that had arisen with his words and his touch.

Soon Rob was back among them bearing the piece of coal and bottle of whisky that had awaited him in the hallway. Elsie played the first line of "Auld Lang Syne". They all joined in, and when they reached the final verse, another deep voice joined them too. As they finished, Lord Inchcape crossed the room, dressed in a long, richly embroidered dressing gown. 'I was still awake so I thought I'd come and wish "a guid new year to ane an' a",' he said. Elsie got to her feet and he took her in his arms.

'My dear girl, may 1928 be your happiest year yet.'

Chapter Twenty-Six

Glenapp Castle

In the small hours of the morning, Elsie made a decision.

She rose early and after breakfast took up a position in the drawing room where she could see the others arriving downstairs. When Rob had finished his breakfast, she intercepted him. 'May I ask you something?'

'Of course.'

'I wondered if we might take a walk. It's dry at the moment.'

'I'll pop upstairs and get a warm jumper and see if Stella would like to join us. She was still asleep when I got up. Yesterday evening really took it out of her.'

Elsie hesitated. 'It was more as a doctor that I wanted to speak to you. If you don't mind, that is.'

He looked at her sharply. 'I'll be back in a minute,' was all he said, leaving the room. Elsie walked over to the window and looked out at the terrace below. Was she doing the right thing? So few people knew of her proposed flight: Captain Hinchliffe, of course, and Tony, and Rogers, her agent. Her wealthy friend Sophie, in whose bank account she was storing funds, knew a little but not the full story. She hadn't intended to tell Rob when she invited them all for Hogmanay, but something about his perceptive concern last night had made her waver. She had been unable to sleep. Never before had the turn of the year held such significance! In 1928 surely someone would conquer the east–west route – would she be the one? Lying in bed, tossing restlessly, she suddenly recalled Tony's words: *The man or woman who does achieve this has to be at the peak of physical fitness as well as mental sharpness. Don't overlook that, Elsie; get some medical advice.* She couldn't consult their family doctor, who would go straight to her father, and she couldn't risk speaking to a stranger who might sell her story to the newspapers. That left Rob. But would he tell Stella? Would he try to stop her? Would he understand?

He reappeared in the drawing room wearing a thick knitted sweater and they made their way to the cloakroom off the entrance hall. 'Wellingtons, I think,' Elsie said. 'Would you like to borrow some? The gardens will be muddy after all that sleet and rain.'

Outside the sky was heavy and the wind whipped through the bare trees, hustling Rob and Elsie round the side of the castle. 'I don't think we'll have long before the next shower,' she said. They crossed the terrace and descended the slippery steps into the formal garden in silence. Rob was clearly waiting for her to speak, and Elsie couldn't quite find the words to begin. She was discovering how terribly hard it is to articulate a secret that you have held close to your heart for so long. Eventually she stopped and drew him into a bower. Water dripped from the canopy above them and underfoot was slimy and treacherous, but it gave an illusion of privacy – for all there was no one about – which might help her to open up.

'What's troubling you, Elsie?'

His grey eyes were full of compassion. She looked away, setting her face towards the sea and the incoming storm.

'What I tell you must be completely confidential.'

'I never divulge what my patients tell me, whether I know them personally or not.'

'It's not what you think. I want to ask your advice – your *medical* advice – about a flight.'

'A flight?' His quiet, professional manner vanished into bewilderment.

'Yes.' She took a deep breath. 'If someone were to undertake a long flight, thirty-six hours say, what physical preparations would it be wise to make? What nutrition would be most beneficial? How could a person best train their body to stay awake for such a long time? Is there any advice you can offer as a doctor? Theoretically, that is.'

He looked right into her eyes, and she could see him working it out. 'Thirty-six hours, you say?'

'Potentially.'

'Can I start with some advice not as a doctor but as a friend?'

'No.'

'Very well.' He placed the tips of his long fingers together as he considered her question. 'The body will be placed under enormous strain, so it's important that the theoretical person undertaking this theoretical flight is already in prime condition to withstand that strain. Careful preparation is critical. I'd recommend a rigorous programme of exercise, endurance, running, that kind of thing. A healthy diet with plenty of milk, fruit and red meat. As for nutrition during the flight itself, flasks of coffee as a stimulant, and food that can be prepared in advance. Nourishing sandwiches would seem sensible, and perhaps some soup. Beyond that I would need to give it some more thought.' He stopped and looked straight at her. 'Tell me you're not considering the Atlantic crossing, Elsie?'

'I am.'

'Then as both your friend and your doctor I advise you most strongly not to attempt it. You must have seen the latest reports about Woodrow Wilson's niece. Yet another casualty of that damned crossing. Why on earth would you even contemplate it?'

'Rob, I'm not asking you to understand. I'm asking for some practical help.'

'How can I help you with something that is practically signing your death warrant?'

She felt a flicker of anger surge within her at his lack of faith. 'I wouldn't even consider this if I were not completely confident that it is achievable. Look at Lindbergh! I have the best plane, the best co-pilot, and our flight will be meticulously planned in every single detail.' She took a deep breath. 'I am going to be the first person to fly the Atlantic westwards, and the first woman to fly the Atlantic in either direction.'

Saying it aloud calmed her, somehow.

'You're speaking as if this is more than an idea; as if your plans are already in place.'

The first raindrops were beginning to blow into the arbour from that leaden sky. She folded her arms tightly. 'That's because they are. I've recruited the best pilot out there, Captain Ray Hinchliffe, and he has been over to America and chosen a machine for us. It's being shipped across as we speak. Once it's assembled and adapted for our needs we will spend some weeks in training and then, at the earliest possible opportunity, we will set off.'

'What does your father say?'

'He doesn't know.' She caught hold of Rob's arm. 'You absolutely mustn't breathe a word, Rob. Not to him, not to Stella, not to anyone. Remember, you promised.'

'That was when I thought you were talking about your health!' he protested. 'To tell you the truth, I thought you were going to tell me you'd found a lump or something. Elsie, this is different.'

'It's exactly the same and you promised. If you breathe a word I will never forgive you. Never.'

He looked at her for a moment or two and then sighed. 'All right, I won't say anything. But I can't pretend I like it.'

'I'm not asking you to like it. I'm asking you to give me professional advice. I'll pay a consultation fee, but it's more discreet here than in Glasgow. Would you think about it seriously, please? Would you perhaps write down an exercise regime and a diet for me for the next few weeks – let's say for two months – and anything else you can think of that might help during the flight itself? I really am concerned about how to stay awake.'

'There were techniques we used to teach the men on sentry duty during the war,' he said. 'All right. I can do that. If you're going anyway, no matter what I say, I suppose I must do what I can to ensure you are well prepared.'

The rain was heavier now. She could see the worry on his face, but there was something else there too in those grey eyes. A glint of understanding, of admiration even. He reached out and pulled her into a tight hug. Her face rested against the cold damp of his coat, but there was warmth and comfort in his strong arms, and she was so very glad she had told him.

'You're a remarkable woman, Elsie Mackay,' he said quietly into her hair. 'I'll help you all I can.'

Upstairs in her bedroom, Stella could not pull herself away from the window.

She had woken to the sound of the door closing quietly. Rob going down for breakfast, so she thought. She lay in bed, luxuriating in the comfort of sheets that had never been mended, and revelling in the knowledge that no small feet would come running through, no hands would tug at her, wanting her to come and see. But the baby was pressing on her bladder – some things are the same wherever you are – and she knew she wouldn't get back to sleep again. Time to get up. She eased herself into a sitting position, taking her time. All through her pregnancy she had felt queasy in the mornings and it was grand to have the luxury of being able to go slowly. Eventually she got to her feet, picked up a robe from the chair and slipped it on. The room was still in darkness, so before walking along the corridor to the bathroom she crossed to the window, pulling back the heavy thick curtains to let in some light and see what kind of day it was.

A dreich day, was the answer. She stood looking out at the monochrome garden with wild grey sea beyond. One more day to enjoy the roaring fires of Glenapp before returning by train to Glasgow tomorrow. She would be ready to go home. This was the longest she had ever been away from Duncan and Jacky, and Mother must need a break by now. Just then a movement caught her eye on the terrace below. The two figures were well wrapped against the foul weather, but were unmistakeably Rob and Elsie. They wore wellington boots – where in the world had he got those? – and so were surely setting out for a walk. A bit unexpected, but perhaps they had decided to get some fresh air during a gap between showers. The clouds out to sea suggested the next storm was not far off.

Rob and Elsie disappeared from view as they descended the stone steps, then reappeared again, walking along the central path on the tier below. She would dress and go down for breakfast, by which time they would probably have returned from their walk. Stella was about to turn away and answer the increasing need to empty her bladder when she saw Elsie take hold of Rob's arm and draw him into a secluded alcove. It struck her as a strange and almost secretive movement, and for the moment her bathroom needs were forgotten as she watched. If it had been summer she would have been unable to see them for leaves, but the interweaving branches that made up the roof of the bower were sparse and bare. It probably gave the illusion of privacy to those inside, but from up here she could see through fairly clearly. She remembered the unexpected moment after midnight when she had watched Rob take Elsie aside. The chill she had felt then stole through her body once more. She held her breath as she watched them, standing so close together, talking so earnestly. What on earth could they be discussing for so long? Why so deliberately secretive? Stella stood at the window, her fingertips touching the cold glass, her heart beating quickly but her veins like ice. And then as she watched, her husband reached out and took the woman she thought was her friend, the glamorous heiress Elsie Mackay, into his arms. He held her close for a very long time, his face pressed against her head.

Stella's baby moved. Her stomach churned. Liquid trickled slowly down the inside of her leg.

Her world was falling apart.

Chapter Twenty-Seven

Glenapp Castle

Corran and Arthur stood side by side at the drawing room window. 'Too wet for that walk,' she said. 'I might investigate the library. I've been longing to have a proper browse.'

'Good idea.'

The library lay at the far end of a long corridor and looked out to the front of the house. Although the room was empty, the fire was lit and lamps glowed, and Corran breathed in the familiar scent of musty leather bindings, running her finger along the spines. There was an eclectic mix, from the traditional classics and poetry found in every grand home to books that reflected the tastes of the Inchcapes: volumes on India and on Empire, on commerce, trade and shipping. 'Karl Marx!' said Arthur. 'Not what I would have expected.'

'I imagine Lord Inchcape falls into the "know thine enemy" camp.' Corran pulled out a slim volume. 'I wonder if it's the lord or lady of the house who is the admirer of T. S. Eliot? Or perhaps Elsie. He might be more to her taste.' As she flicked through it, something beyond caught her eye and she moved nearer the window. 'Whoever can be outside in weather like this? Look, it's

Elsie and Rob. They must have gone for a walk and got caught in the rain. They're drenched.' She watched them hurry past the window towards the main entrance. Just as she was turning away she noticed someone coming in the other direction, approaching the main gates from the servants' entrance. A delivery man perhaps. A gust of wind caught his hat and whipped it from his head. He turned around to retrieve it, and for a fleeting moment looked right in at her through the window.

Corran frowned as something tugged at her memory. She was sure she had seen that man before somewhere. But it wouldn't come, and she returned to the books. For a few minutes she and Arthur sat in comfortable silence, until the door opened and Nancy the maid appeared.

'Mr Callaghan, this was handed in for you. And Lady Inchcape would like to inform you that there is tea in the drawing room.'

'Thank you, Nancy.' When the maid had gone, Corran turned towards Arthur, who was seated in a high-backed leather chair with a heavy tome on his knee. 'Whoever is handing a letter in for you on New Year's Day?'

Arthur glanced at it and slipped it unopened inside his jacket pocket. 'It's work. It can wait.'

She stared at him. The man she had noticed had surely brought the letter, but where had she seen him before? Or was she mistaken? After all, his features had been distorted by rain streaming down the glass. There was something here she didn't understand, which Arthur clearly didn't want to discuss. Belatedly she processed the second part of Nancy's message. 'Do you think the mention of tea is a summons? I really don't need another cup of tea. We've not long finished breakfast!'

'These people never stop eating and drinking. It's almost as bad as parliament. And how did they know we were in here? Doesn't it make you uncomfortable, the way they watch us constantly?'

Corran replaced the T. S. Eliot. 'We can come back in half an hour or so, but we should go and keep Lady Inchcape company. She is our hostess after all.'

They made their way along the softly carpeted corridor, past the foot of the staircase that led to their bedrooms, and on into the drawing room where tea, crumpets and Lady Inchcape awaited them with greetings for the new year. The lady of the house seemed brighter today, and was keen to hear about Corran's forthcoming book. 'It should be published by the end of this month,' Corran replied, trying to keep her attention on the conversation but finding herself distracted and uneasy about Arthur's behaviour earlier.

'We shall be on our way to Egypt by then,' said Lady Inchcape. 'We take the P&O express train to Marseilles next week, and there we join the *Razmak* for the voyage. I shall leave word for your book to be sent on to me just as soon as it is published, my dear. It will be the perfect read for my time in Egypt.'

'I do hope you enjoy it.'

'And how is your dear sister this morning? Such a difficult stage, the last few weeks of a confinement.'

'I haven't seen Stella today.' Suddenly keen to have some space to order her thoughts, Corran laid down her cup. 'Actually, I might go up and see her. See if she needs anything. Would you excuse me?'

'Of course, my dear. Arthur and I will finish our tea and he can tell me all about his little boy. How old is he now?'

The usual stab of pain barely penetrated. She was conscious of Arthur's eyes on her as she left the room. Instead of climbing the stairs to see Stella, who would simply be enjoying a well-deserved long lie-in, Corran made her way back towards the empty library, where she returned to the window.

It made no sense, but she was convinced now that the man who had looked in at her this morning, the man who had brought a letter for Arthur, was the same man who had been so interested in the Egyptian relics in Kelvingrove last week, and had walked past Arthur and her in the gardens later.

But how could that possibly be?

She turned and paced across the room. There on a desk in the corner was a telephone. She remembered what Arthur had said last night; that despite all their precautions, someone from the Labour Party had known where he was and had called him.

On Hogmanay.

She had forgotten about it almost immediately, as their stolen lovemaking before dinner had taken over all her thoughts. Now the separate incidents lined up one beside the other like a row of coconuts to be knocked down at the funfair.

The man in the Egyptian galleries at precisely the time she had arranged to meet Arthur.

The phone call last night.

The same man appearing at the house this morning.

Were they being followed? Or more precisely – given that she was an Oxford don with nothing interesting about her whatsoever – was Arthur being followed?

Or was the man a friend of his? A colleague? But if so, why had he not spoken in Kelvingrove?

She had to know.

She turned back towards the door, ready to find an excuse to extricate him from Lady Inchcape's clutches, but as she began to walk along the corridor she heard the sound of running feet above. Corran looked up the staircase to see Nancy scurrying down. 'Miss Rutherford, would you come?'

'Whatever's the matter?'

'It's Mrs Campbell. She's not well. Please come.'

Corran sprinted up the stairs and along to Stella's room. Nancy took a step back and she entered. Her sister was sitting in a chair still wearing her nightclothes. She was pale but looked calm enough. 'Stella? Are you ill?'

'She's bleeding, ma'am,' came the whisper from behind.

For a moment Corran stared, uncomprehending, then she realised what Nancy meant and dropped to her knees, pushing the nightdress upwards. She caught her breath. There was a smear of blood down her sister's leg and she could see that Stella had pushed a towel between her legs, a towel that was stained shocking red.

'It's nothing,' Stella said. 'I'm sure it's nothing. I've had no pains. I felt the liquid and thought my waters had broken, but I seem to be bleeding a little. But it's stopped, I think.'

'Where's Rob?' Corran turned to the girl. 'Go and find Dr Campbell and—'

'No!' Stella made to stand and then dropped back down into her chair. 'I don't want you to tell Rob. It's stopped, can't you see? I'm just sitting here to make sure. Taking it slowly.'

'Stella, don't be absurd. Of course Rob must be told.' She scrambled to her feet and turned back to the maid. 'Nancy, please find Dr Campbell and bring him at once.'

Stella covered her face with her hands and Corran touched her shoulder. 'Rob will come and he will know what to do. If it really has stopped then maybe it's just a scare. Did this happen with the other two?'

Stella shook her head. 'Nothing like this. Pain first.'

Corran stood beside her, cradling her head. 'I'm sure it will all be fine.'

'I wish Mother were here.'

'I know. But Rob will know what to do.' Corran stared at the door, willing him to come through. What was taking him so long? 'Where is he anyway?'

'I don't know.'

'I saw him earlier,' Corran said, remembering. So much had happened since that it had gone out of her head. 'With Elsie. I don't know where they went.' She felt her sister give a sob. 'Hush, Stella dear. It will all be fine, I'm sure. And if it is the baby coming then how thrilling that is! I wonder if it will be another boy or a little girl this time? Duncan and Jacky will be so excited.' She knew she was babbling, saying anything to fill the minutes. At last she heard the sound of feet charging up the stairs two at a time, and Rob threw open the door.

'Stella!'

Corran withdrew to the window, giving him space and privacy to examine his wife. By the time she turned, Stella was lying on the bed, white and still, her eyes frightened. Corran moved back beside her and took her hand.

'Can you help her?'

'I don't know. She shouldn't be bleeding like this. When did it start, Stella?'

Stella turned away and didn't answer, and Rob looked towards Corran helplessly. She shrugged. 'I don't know. Where have you been anyway?'

He hesitated. 'I climbed the tower after breakfast to look at the view.'

Corran frowned. How could that be? Stella gave a sob and she turned her attention back to her sister. 'I wish we were in Glasgow,' Rob went on. 'I have a good friend who is a gynaecologist, and I'd like him to examine Stella. Just to be sure.'

'Phone him up,' Elsie said immediately from the doorway. Corran glanced up quickly. She hadn't realised Elsie was there.

'May I? That would be marvellous, thank you.'

Rob and Elsie hurried away, and Corran saw how Stella's gaze followed them. She pulled a chair close to the side of the bed and sat holding her sister's hand. 'Rob will get advice from his friend and everything will be fine. Isn't it fortunate that Elsie has a telephone?'

Silent tears leaked from Stella's eyes and Corran watched her, feeling helpless. 'Do you want anything? A cup of tea?' she asked desperately.

'I want Mother.'

Corran swallowed. 'I know. We'll get you home just as soon as possible,' she said, wondering as she spoke how on earth they would manage tomorrow's train journey.

Once more Rob seemed to take an age. Getting the connection was always slow, and perhaps his friend wouldn't be available immediately. It was Ne'er Day, after all. But eventually he returned, followed this time not only by Elsie but by Lady Inchcape. 'How are you feeling, Stella?' Elsie whispered, but Stella turned stonily away. When Rob walked over to the bed and took his wife's hand, she pulled it free. Corran watched and wondered.

'I've spoken to Douglas. He would like to take a look at you, just to be on the safe side. Elsie has offered to drive us up to Glasgow today rather than waiting for tomorrow. What do you say, Stella? Do you feel strong enough for the journey?'

Stella didn't answer. Rob looked across at Corran, and his anxious grey eyes urged her silently to help. Corran leant over her sister. 'It's the best thing, Stella, for you and the baby. You'll see Mother sooner too.'

There was a pause, and then Stella nodded, tears still running down the sides of her face. Lady Inchcape stepped forward and unexpectedly took command. 'The rest of you leave this room. Elsie, get your motor car ready at once. I will help Stella to prepare for the journey. Nancy, bring me some cloths.' She slipped her arm around Stella's shoulders and eased her into a sitting position. 'You can do this, my dear. You've done it twice before, and the baby comes a little bit more easily every time. Why, by the time I had Elsie's youngest sister, Effie, it was over in no time! Hopefully all will be well and baby will sit tight for a few weeks, but if not, you can do this. I haven't the slightest doubt.'

Chapter Twenty-Eight

Glenapp Castle

Elsie stopped only to grab a coat, then ran up the hill to the garage, her feet slithering in the mud. One of the first things her father had done when he bought Glenapp during the war was to convert part of the old stable block into a suitable home for their precious motor vehicles. The gates between two old stone pillars opened onto a cobbled courtyard, which now smelt more of petrol than manure, and a grand steel and glass roof had been erected over it to protect the cars from the elements. Lochrie, their chauffeur, lived in the cottage behind the garage and she hammered on the door.

'Miss Elsie!' His eyes were bleary and a smell of whisky clung to him. Last night had been Hogmanay and he would not have expected to be called upon this morning.

'Lochrie, I must go to Glasgow right away. Could you start up my Rolls and bring her down to the front entrance? Make sure she has plenty of petrol for the journey. I'll see you there in ten minutes.' She stopped. 'Oh, and if you could put in a few warm travelling rugs too, that would be grand.'

'Do you need me to drive, Miss Elsie?' he asked, making a valiant effort to shake off the residue of the night before.

'Thank you, no. I will drive. Just get her ready, would you?' She flashed him the smile that generally persuaded people to fall in with her plans, and turned to slither down the hill again. Into the house and up to her room, she threw some clothes into a bag then sprinted back downstairs, planning to go to the kitchen and beg some food for a hamper. But at the foot of the stairs she met her mother, who drew her to one side.

'Get her to Glasgow as quickly and smoothly as you can, Elsie. Her pains have started and I believe this baby will make an appearance fairly soon.'

'Is there time?'

'No one can tell, but you will have Rob in the car with you and he is a doctor. You needn't be afraid.'

'I'm not afraid,' Elsie protested. 'I was on my way to the kitchen for some food.'

'It's already done,' Lady Inchcape said calmly. Elsie stared at her mother. She was used to Lady Inchcape taking a back seat, relying on her husband and daughter to make all the decisions. But today Lord Inchcape was nowhere to be seen, while his wife had assumed an unaccustomed authority.

'How can you be so sure what to do?'

At that, Lady Inchcape laughed. 'Tell me, Elsie, who else among us here has ever given birth to a child?'

Get her to Glasgow as quickly and smoothly as you can.

Her mother's words echoed through her mind as she drove carefully out of Glenapp estate and onto the road that would take them north through Ballantrae and Girvan towards Glasgow. She had tried to hug Stella as she helped her into the car, but her friend had pushed her off roughly. *Understandable with all she's going through*, Elsie thought, trying not to feel hurt. Now Stella was huddled in the back seat wrapped in travelling rugs, with Rob at her side. Elsie tried her best to drive carefully, but the roads here were terribly rough and the car bounced and shook over every bump, occasionally drawing a cry of pain from Stella.

For long stretches the road ran along beside the coast. The scenery was spectacular if anyone had cared to admire it, with Ailsa Craig barely visible, and wild grey waves piling in towards the shore, foaming white as they broke against the sea wall to their left. But no one was interested in the scenery. Elsie's gaze was fixed on the road ahead as rain streamed down her windshield, and her hands gripped the steering wheel tightly. Stella lay on the back seat, cradled by Rob, moaning constantly now, while every now and then her body went rigid and she shrieked in pain. 'I'm glad I take my doctor's bag everywhere I go,' Rob had said grimly to Elsie as they set off. 'At least I can cut the cord safely if it comes to it. But let's hope we get to Glasgow in time.'

I'll do my best, Elsie thought, battling to steer the car as the rain and wind pummelled it. Then they came to a halt so suddenly that Rob swore and Stella nearly fell onto the floor. 'What the hell?'

Elsie twisted round, her face white. 'The road's blocked.'

'What? It can't be. Let me see.' He opened the car door and stepped out into a gale that nearly knocked him off his feet. Elsie followed, and together they took in the scene, hunched against the wind. The power of the waves had shattered the sea wall, hurling huge lumps of stone, pebbles and sand across the narrow road along with a cascade of water. At the far side of the blockage two men with spades were trying to clear the debris, but it was slow work. One shouted across to them but his words were tossed away on the wind. Elsie looked round. There was no one at all to help on this side of the obstruction, with no cottages nearby. Even as they stood there another wave crashed over, soaking them both. 'It's no use!' bellowed Elsie. 'We can't get through!'

Did she hear a noise from behind? She turned and ran back to the car. Stella had pushed the door open and was leaning out into the full force of the gale. She screamed something that Elsie couldn't make out. Elsie reached her and shoved her back into the car, then climbed into the front and looked round, trembling. Stella was huddled on the floor sobbing as the car rocked with the power of the wind. A dark pool of liquid crept out beneath her.

Rob jumped in and slammed the door. For a moment none of them spoke, made speechless by the power of the storm and the enormity of their situation. Then Elsie took control.

'I can't turn here but thank God there is nothing behind us. I'll reverse until the road gets wider, at the corner there. Pray God I can get turned without landing us in the ditch. We'll go back to Glenapp. It's our only option.' She looked at her friend. 'Stella, can you hold on?'

'You can't *hold on* to a bloody baby!' Stella spat. 'Rob, I'm scared. It's too soon. I don't want it to die.'

'I know, my love.' He eased her up gently onto the seat, even as Elsie began to reverse.

The remainder of the drive was a hell that Elsie would prefer never to look back on. She drove almost blind at times as the thick cloud obscured what little daylight remained, and water streamed down the windshield. She navigated the roads as carefully as she could, glad only that there was next to no traffic on the road on this foul Ne'er Day, and doing her best to shut out what was going on in the seat behind. That was easier said than done, with Stella screaming in pain and the smell of vomit pervading the car. But at last she was there, speeding up the drive as fast as she could and screeching to a halt right outside the castle entrance. She tumbled out of the car. 'Shall we carry her inside?'

'No time. The baby's almost here.'

Terrified, Elsie turned to see her mother hurrying out of the castle. 'The road was blocked. The baby's coming.'

'So I see,' Lady Inchcape said, pushing her aside. 'Fetch hot water and some clean dry blankets.' She opened the car door and stepped inside, closing it behind her. Utterly drained, Elsie felt unsteady on her feet and leant against the wall for a moment, marvelling again at her mother's poise amid the confusion. She could scarcely believe that Stella's baby was about to be born in her Rolls-Royce, right outside the castle entrance.

Would it even take a breath?

Chapter Twenty-Nine

Glenapp Castle

Corran tiptoed into Stella's bedroom. Her sister was fast asleep. Lady Inchcape, who hadn't left her side since the car had hurtled back into the courtyard, sat close by the bed, tenderly stroking her hair. Rob sat in the other chair beside a cradle. 'We are in the midst of the grandchildren years, so the cradle is always ready,' Lady Inchcape said quietly. 'My daughter Effie in Copenhagen is expecting her third child any day now.'

Corran barely heard her. She looked down into the cradle at her new niece. All swaddled in blankets, only her white little face and dark hair were visible. The tiniest face she had ever seen. She looked across at Rob, whose features bore the ravages of the day. 'Will she be all right?'

'She's breathing steadily and has fed, so I hope so. She is very wee, though.' His voice wavered. Corran leant over and kissed him.

'Congratulations on your new daughter, and very well done. That must have been a real ordeal.'

Rob nodded and glanced across at the bed. 'As long as Stella and the baby recover, that's all that matters.'

Corran reached out and touched the tiny cheek as gently as she could. 'I won't disturb her. There will be plenty of time for cuddles later and she looks so very fragile. But I wanted to see her before I cable Mother. I'll do that now.'

Lady Inchcape looked across from the bed. 'Please tell your mother to come and stay for as long as she likes. Poor Stella won't be going anywhere in a hurry. Lord Inchcape and I may have to leave for Egypt before she is strong enough to go home but she and your mother are welcome to stay on. The servants will look after them.'

'Thank you,' Corran said. 'What do you think, Rob? What about Duncan and Jacky?'

'I don't know – I can't think. Not yet.'

'When you cable your mother, ask her to telephone us. Is there a telephone she can use somewhere?'

'There's one in my consulting room,' Rob said. 'Alison never answers it, but she can use it to make a call.'

'She will be anxious,' Lady Inchcape said. 'I shall speak to her myself, and we will arrange matters between us.'

With a kiss on her sleeping sister's forehead, Corran left the room and almost walked straight into Arthur, who was hovering anxiously just outside.

'How are they?'

'Sleeping. Everyone's sleeping. But – it's early days, mind you – it seems that all might be well.'

'That's splendid news!' He pulled her into his arms. 'You must be all in, Corran. What a day it's been.'

She closed her eyes briefly, her head resting against his chest, then moved away. 'I'm not finished yet. I need to find Lord Inchcape and ask him to have a cable sent to Mother about the baby, telling her to ring up this evening. Lady Inchcape has suggested that Mother should come down and stay tomorrow, and I know that's what Stella will want.'

'Does the baby have a name?'

'Not as far as I know. I don't believe anyone has had time to think about it.' She paused and looked up at him. So much had happened since this morning, but as she looked into his green eyes she remembered her earlier confusion. 'This has been the most awful day, but hours ago there was something I meant to ask you.'

'Well, why don't I come with you to send your cable and then we can talk? I need to discuss something with you too, as it happens.'

Her mouth was suddenly dry as she pictured him slipping that letter into his jacket pocket. But Stella's needs mattered most. They hurried to find Lord Inchcape, and then retreated to the library to be alone. The fire still glowed with a faint heat but the room was much chillier than earlier. Corran sank into a leather chair. Now that she had sent the message to her mother, she realised just how drained and exhausted she felt. Arthur knelt in front of her and took her hands.

'What's all this about then?'

She took a deep breath. 'Did you see the man who brought that letter for you this morning?'

He looked genuinely confused. 'No. Did you?'

'I saw him outside earlier in the downpour and I think he was in Kelvingrove at the same time as us. What's going on, Arthur? I know it sounds ridiculous, but could someone be following you?'

He let go of her hands and stood up. She watched as he moved to stand in front of the fire and folded his arms, seemingly struggling for words.

'It's something to do with the phone call last night, isn't it?'

'In a way.'

'*In a way?*' Sudden fury bubbled up. 'Arthur, I'm exhausted. My sister has just had an emergency birth and we're all on edge. Just tell me what's going on.'

'Very well.' He pulled a footstool near to her chair and sat down. 'I wanted more time to get my head round things, but I can't see any other way. I think we're going to have to stop seeing each other for a while.'

She stared at him. 'Why?'

'I've been – informed – that our relationship has become known.'

'By whom? The government? The Tories?'

He shook his head. 'My own side.' Then he sighed. 'Look, you know I have a lot of enemies within the party. People who think I rock the boat too much. People who are more concerned with power than with justice. The phone call I had last night – it was by way of a warning.'

'A warning?'

'Yes. Maxton, Cook and I, we are working on a new manifesto for a socialist revival. There are people who would rather it never saw the light of day. They will use any kind of bad publicity to bring it down.'

Corran tried to control the panic rising within her. This was the worst possible timing. She had always known that if her affair with a married politician became public, she would lose her job at Oxford. Now she had her publisher to consider too. What would they say if their new authoress was part of a scandal splashed across the newspapers? They would drop her at once and her precious novel would sink beneath the waves before it was even published.

'And so you think we should stop seeing each other?'

'Just for a while.'

'We've tried that before,' she reminded him. *And you were the one who came running back.*

'I know. But it's different this time. There's too much to lose — *you* have too much to lose.' He leant over and took her hand. 'I won't let that happen because of me.'

They sat in silence for a while. She knew he was right, but it was hard to accept. 'Not even the cottage?'

'Not for a while. Let's say three months to begin with. Then if anyone is watching they will think they are mistaken and give up. In the meantime I will get this manifesto prepared and you will publish your book.'

Three months, thought Corran. *A lot can happen in three months.* She thought of the moments yesterday evening when they had lain together on his bed, their finery discarded, her legs coiled around him, pulling him deeper into her and kissing his salty skin. Unplanned and uninhibited. Was it the last time?

'I'll never stop loving you, Corran. I wouldn't have missed these few days for the world.'

She pulled her hand away gently. 'Three months. To complete your manifesto, to publish my book, to make them think they're wrong. It makes sense. Then we meet again?'

'I hope so.'

She nodded and stood up, straightening her skirt. 'Very well. We start tonight.' She smiled, a brittle, contained smile that did nothing to calm the turmoil she felt within. 'Let's go for dinner.'

PART FOUR
Flight

January to June 1928

*If I take the wings of the morning, and dwell in the utter-
most parts of the sea;
Even there shall thy hand lead me, and thy right hand shall
hold me.*

Psalm 139:9

Chapter Thirty

Helensburgh

The day for Alison's long-awaited trip to Helensburgh arrived. It was nearly the end of January, and heavy skies had finally given way to weak sunshine over the last day or two. 'A perfect day for our excursion,' Matthew said as they boarded the railway carriage. The mid-morning train was quiet and as they settled down in an empty compartment, Alison breathed out slowly. Before leaving the house, she had glanced around the kitchen – at Duncan and Jacky squabbling; at an entire laundry's worth of Juliet's nappies hanging from the pulley while the next load soaked in the pail; at Stella gazing listlessly through the window – and had wondered whether she really could abandon them for an entire day? But now, as she smiled across at Matthew, she was so very glad she had. With all that had happened in the last few weeks, her cruise felt like a lifetime ago.

His silvery hair was shorter than last time, freshly cut for the return to sea, she guessed. He planned to travel south to London tomorrow, and would be gone for many weeks. 'Tell me about your house in Helensburgh.'

'Eleanor and I bought it when Sarah and William were children. We didn't want them growing up in the city. I was away at sea a good deal, but they were happy years.' He paused. 'I tried going back after the war, but Eleanor and William were dead, and Sarah was married and living in the south. The house held nothing for me. I cleared our personal possessions and rented it out. The most recent tenants moved out a few months ago.'

'Are you looking for new tenants?'

'I'm not sure,' he said, watching tall tenements and chimneys flash past the window. 'I'll be sixty-six this year, and the sea is a younger man's game. Time was I couldn't wait to get back on board after a period of shore leave, but recently I've found myself thinking more and more about a fireplace, a glass of whisky, a dog at my feet. Only, if I am to retire I can't possibly live with Sarah. I love my daughter but we would drive each other crazy! She has been very good to put up with me all these years. I'd like to look at the house and decide whether to remain there or move somewhere else.'

The railway line was leaving Glasgow behind now and cutting through a string of small towns and villages separated by brown winter fields, with the river sometimes visible beyond. At Clydebank, Alison caught glimpses of the towering cranes of John Brown's shipyard. As the railway line curved down nearer the river beyond Dumbarton and Cardross she luxuriated in the breadth of sky and shore, and thought about what Matthew had said. She could understand completely the need to close the door on the family home; very similar circumstances had led her to walk away from Thurso. Since then she had led a nomadic existence. Firstly a few years in Aberdeen with her sister and then coming to Glasgow to help Stella with the children. Stella. A cloud cast its shadow on the carefree day, and Matthew noticed. 'Something wrong?'

'I'm just thinking about my daughter. Stella.'

'The one who's recently had a baby?'

'It was a very difficult birth. Stella and some of the others spent Hogmanay at Glenapp Castle with Elsie and the Inchcapes. The baby wasn't due for a few weeks, but Stella went into labour. They had a terrible time trying to get her back to Glasgow, and in the end wee Juliet was born in the motor car right outside the castle.'

Matthew reached across and took her hand. 'My dear, how worrying for you.'

'Oh, I was in blissful ignorance until it was all over. I travelled down to Glenapp the next day to be with her. The Inchcapes were most awfully kind and looked after us until Stella and Juliet were well enough to come home. Such luxury, Matthew! Lord and Lady Inchcape left for Egypt in the middle of January but we stayed on for a while longer. Elsie came up from London but Stella wasn't ready to see her. Luisa and Rob looked after the boys in Glasgow until Stella and I returned last week.'

'But they are fine now?'

Alison hesitated. 'I don't know,' she said. 'Juliet is thriving, and the boys are besotted with her. Stella has recovered well physically, but I'm worried about her. She's been dreadfully low since the birth and she's barely civil to Rob.'

'Common enough after a baby is born, surely. I remember Eleanor struggled for a long time after we had Sarah.'

'I know, but I feel there's something more at the root of it.' She looked out of the window at the river speeding by. 'It's hard for women of her generation. Sometimes I envy my daughters, they have had opportunities that were never open to me. I should have loved to go to university and work for a degree. But then I look at Stella and wonder if I did her any favours by encouraging her to spread her wings. She was a typist at the peace conference, you know, and stayed on in Paris to work for the British Embassy afterwards. Then she married Rob and gave it all up.'

'That's a long time ago.'

'I know but I think it created a conflict within Stella that has never really gone away. She loves Rob and the children but part of her still hankers after the life she had before. Perhaps the birth of another baby has brought those feelings to the fore? It's all I can imagine.' She turned back to Matthew and his sympathetic blue gaze. 'There was a woman living near us in Thurso who never failed to tell me a university education would make my daughters discontented with their role in life. Maybe she was right all along.'

'You don't mean that.'

'No, I don't. I'm glad my girls received the best education we could give them. The problem is that the rest of society hasn't caught up with the new training and education possibilities for women, and a married woman is still not permitted to work in most professions. I have one daughter who can work but not marry and another who can marry but not work. Where's the sense in that?' She glared at him and he held up his hands.

'Don't shoot! I agree with you.'

She laughed. 'I'm sorry, Matthew. I'm anxious about Stella, that's all.'

'I understand,' he said. 'We never stop worrying about our children, do we, even when they're grown adults? Your daughters should be grateful for all you've done for them. They're fortunate to have such a wonderful woman as their mother.'

Alison laughed. 'I doubt they would see it like that!' The train was easing into a station. 'Anyway, I'm determined to forget my cares, just for today.'

He leant forward and she thought he was going to say something more, but then he turned aside. 'We're almost there. Come, let me show you Helensburgh.'

* * *

They emerged from the station and Matthew led her round a corner and down towards the shore. They passed the pier where passengers were lining up to board a steamer, and walked along the esplanade, the water on their left and a ribbon of shops and houses on their right. 'The house is just along here.'

She glanced at him. There was colour in his cheeks and a lightness in his step, and she thought that coming back to Helensburgh was good for him. Looking about her, she could see why. There was a gentle air of elegance about the town, and although quiet in winter she could well believe that this narrow stretch of beach and newly laid putting green were, as he said, busy with holidaymakers and day-trippers in summer. The air was soft, this was not the open sea but the widening of the Clyde, where the great ships all passed on their way out to the Atlantic Ocean. Directly opposite she could make out the familiar industrial activity of shipyards, but it was the tantalising glimpse of the hills of Argyll to the north that made her heart lift. She had expected Helensburgh to remind her of her own life by the sea in Thurso, but instead this landscape stirred echoes of her childhood by Loch Linnhe.

They left the shops behind and came to a row of solid, substantial stone houses looking directly over the water, with narrow front gardens. Matthew stopped outside one of these and fished in his pocket for a key. The curtains were closed and that small front garden was overgrown. He frowned. 'The previous tenants kept it in hand, but it doesn't take long for things to become neglected,' he said. 'I'll have to do something about that. Can't abide untidiness.'

'You like everything shipshape, in fact!' she laughed.

'Precisely.' He inserted the key in the lock and turned, pushed open the door and led her into the hallway. She recognised that stale, slightly damp smell of a house that has not been lived in for a few months, but when he led her through to the sitting room with its large picture window overlooking the water, she cried out in delight. 'How beautiful.'

'It is rather, isn't it? I love to sit here and watch as everything from liners and cargo ships to fishing boats and little pleasure craft sails in and out of that channel. It's a splendid view.' He paused. 'Sarah and William spent much of their childhood playing on the shore down there.'

She leant her head against his shoulder and he put his arm around her. This town and this view might be very different to the exposed open seas that she had known in Thurso, but the rhythm of the tides was the same and she too had watched her children splash in the water and dig among the shells and sand in those fleeting years. Children who had long since grown up – except Jack and William, who had barely become men before their futures were snatched from them.

'I'll light the fire,' Matthew said, moving away. 'Get some heat back into this room. Then I'll show you round.'

The tiled grate was full of ash and he removed his coat to keep it clean then crouched down to lift some coal from the scuttle beside the fireplace. Soon he had the fire going. 'Let me show you the house.'

On the other side of the hallway was a dining room, which enjoyed the same view, and the kitchen was bright and adequately equipped. The kitchen window looked out over a long narrow strip of overgrown garden, which drew Alison's appreciative eye. But what struck her as he led her from room to room was the absence of any suggestion of the family that once lived here. Furnishings were simple and utilitarian, and beyond a few seascapes on the walls there was little ornamentation. 'We only kept what seemed suitable for renting out,' he explained as they climbed the stairs. He opened the door to William's room, but there was nothing of the dead boy in there. Even the room Matthew had shared with Eleanor was plain, containing no hint of their past together, and Alison began to wonder if he had kept anything at all. Where were the photographs, the letters, the knick-knacks? But then he stopped with a little smile and pointed to a hatch in the ceiling. 'Fortunately the house has a large loft. It's crammed full of our personal possessions. At the time I couldn't bear to look at them. I suppose that will occupy me in my retirement. I shouldn't leave it all for Sarah to do when I'm gone.'

They descended the stairs and returned to the sitting room, where the fire was beginning to overcome the chill. 'I disposed of most things when I left Thurso,' Alison said. 'But there are a few boxes under my bed of treasures I couldn't bear to be parted from.' Then she turned to him. 'Are you hungry, Matthew? I think we passed a baker as we walked along here. Shall I go and see what they have?'

'That's a grand idea. I'll light the range and get the kettle on. I'm sure there will be some tea somewhere.'

Before long they were enjoying a makeshift picnic, which they ate in the sitting room in front of the fire. Low winter sunlight glinted in through the window and fell in a streak across the dusty wooden floor. Alison breathed in the pleasure of the moment. Before long she would have to return to Glasgow, where Juliet might or might not be sleeping, where Duncan and Jacky would press around her, where the atmosphere between Stella and Rob hung heavily over them all. But for another hour or two she could enjoy this simple bare house with its open views and, even more, the company of this dear friend. She remembered his words on the train about retiring from life at sea, and felt a sense of warm pleasure at the thought of being able to see him more often. 'What do you think?' she asked, balancing her cup and saucer on her knee. 'Could you live here again?'

At first Matthew didn't answer. He looked into the flames, and then turned towards her with something in his expression she didn't quite recognise. His cheeks were flushed, and his deep blue eyes narrowed a little. For no reason she could logically understand her heart beat a little faster.

'I don't know.' He laid down his cup and laced his fingers together, then unclasped them again, restless. 'I have foolish ideas sometimes.'

'Foolish – how?'

'I'm a crusty old sea captain in his sixties. It's surely foolish to imagine there might be anything new and different ahead for me . . . and yet . . .' He looked directly at her. 'Is it foolish, Alison?'

She swallowed. 'Is what foolish?'

He gestured around the sitting room. 'Let me ask you the question you asked me. Could *you* live here? Or is that the fantasy of a deluded old man? Could you live here with me? As my wife?'

Her hands gripped the saucer tightly and she stared at him. The colour on his weathered face was heightened, and now that he had said the words out loud, he didn't know where to look. When she had set out to meet him today this had been the last thing she could have imagined – and yet part of her felt strangely unsurprised. Had the steps first taken on the deck of a Mediterranean cruise liner always been leading here? To marriage?

She might have laughed aloud if he hadn't looked so vulnerable. It was forty years and more since someone had asked her that question, when she had been a young girl with stars in her eyes. Life had happened to her since, and had left not stars but deep scars. As for her body, no one had seen what was hidden by her clothes since her husband died a quarter of a century ago, other than a brief episode in Thurso with a naval officer, which she had successfully put to the very back of her mind. Marriage? The idea was completely ridiculous.

And yet.

What was it he had said – *It's surely foolish to imagine there might be anything new and different ahead for me.* But what if there could be, for her too? What if there was *more* to the remainder of her life, however long she had left, than responsibilities as mother and grandmother occasionally alleviated by holidays with her sister?

What if she chose to live out these years in the company of this dear, wise, kind man?

She laid down her cup, stood up and walked over to the window. A young woman walked by, wrestling with a big pram, buffeted by the rising wind. She thought about Stella, Rob and the children. They needed her, but she wouldn't be far away, and perhaps they would benefit from their own space too. She thought about children playing on the shore, about Jack, about William. She thought about all that she and Matthew had gone through long before they met each other, decades' worth of stories still to be shared.

She turned to face him.

She said yes.

Chapter Thirty-One

Brooklands Aerodrome, Surrey

In February the aeroplane was finally ready.

The first glimmers of dawn were brushed across the Surrey sky when Lochrie drove Elsie to Brooklands Aerodrome and racetrack in her Rolls-Royce. He held the door open as she climbed out of the back – the stains hadn't quite come off the soft leather seats despite the chauffeur's best efforts – and smiled at him. 'Thank you, Lochrie. You know where you're going?'

'Yes, Miss Elsie. I shall see you at Cranwell airfield in Lincolnshire this afternoon.'

'Four o'clock will be fine. I doubt I'll be free before then.' She turned away and strode across the wet grass, dressed in her padded flying suit, her goggles and helmet dangling from one hand. She had been a familiar visitor to Brooklands over the past few weeks. Hinchliffe had been here every day, supervising the assembly of the plane and the necessary adaptations to make it suitable for their proposed flight, and she had come by several times each week to check on progress. They sat together in a draughty shed, charts and diagrams spread out before them, as they planned every detail of their journey. A fortnight ago he had finally declared that the machine was ready, and they began taking short flights in the surrounding area, familiarising themselves with the handling and testing out cruising and altitude speeds, as well as getting used to communicating in a cockpit filled with the engine's roar. One of the most significant factors in planning a long-distance flight was the fuel load. Captain Hinchliffe had calculated that by removing seats and installing additional canisters and fuel pipes, they could carry 480 gallons of fuel. 'That's fifty hours' flying time, or five thousand miles,' he said. 'Easily enough to take us across the Atlantic whatever the weather.'

A heavily laden plane takes much longer to rise into the air, and so a much longer runway than Brooklands was needed. During the war Hinchliffe had for a while been stationed at Cranwell in Lincolnshire, and it was Cranwell he had used in his abortive Atlantic attempt with American Charles Levine last year. 'It's the only place that will work for us.'

He called them up, and hit a major snag. After the appalling behaviour of Levine and his crew – behaviour that had caused Hinchliffe to walk away from a lucrative contract and abandon the attempt – the air authorities had forbidden the use of Cranwell for civilian flights. *Very sorry, old chap, but it's just not on.*

All this Hinchliffe had reported to Elsie last week, his shoulders slumped. 'We could look at Baldonnel in Ireland, I suppose,' he said. 'That's the one Tony's crew used. But Cranwell would be by far the best.'

Elsie listened carefully and lifted her chin. Some petty RAF rule was not going to thwart her now! The only difficulty was how to achieve what she wanted while maintaining absolute discretion. In the end she called the office of Sir Samuel Hoare, the Secretary of State for Air. Would Sir Samuel have time to meet her for lunch? People rarely said no to a luncheon invitation with the Honourable Miss Elsie Mackay.

They met at The Savoy. Sir Samuel was somewhere in his late forties, a neat little man who was, she knew, passionate about the future of air travel. He and his wife had been on the first civilian flight to India last year, and he had published an account entitled *India by Air*, which Elsie had recently skimmed through. This was her ostensible reason for meeting him. She praised the quality of his writing, marvelled at his vivid descriptions and questioned him about his journey, listening wide-eyed to his long-winded answers. 'Such a courageous undertaking,' she said. 'You and Lady Maude have really led the way with pioneering spirit. Where you lead, others will follow. Do you know Captain Hinchliffe?'

'Fine fellow.'

'Indeed, and a fine pilot also. It so happens that I have a small financial stake in a proposed venture by Captain Hinchliffe to attempt a non-stop flight to India. He has been inspired by your book, naturally.'

'Indeed?' asked Sir Samuel, straightening his collar. 'A noble ambition.'

'I knew you would understand,' Elsie said, her gaze never leaving his face. 'The only *tiny* difficulty is, the authorities won't let Captain Hinchliffe use Cranwell airfield because of the dreadful behaviour of that awful American last year. It's quite understandable – but I did wonder, given your interest in India, whether you could ask them to waive their restrictions just this once? Captain Hinchliffe is a war hero after all. One of our own. It would be such a favour to me.'

Hinch roared with laughter when Elsie recounted her conversation with Sir Samuel, but he nodded in appreciation too. She had won them a reprieve. But her agreement with the Air Ministry had one crucial condition. They would be permitted the use of Cranwell's facilities for one week. If at the end of that time Captain Hinchliffe had not taken off for India, the plane must be moved elsewhere.

Hinch's one good eye gleamed when she told him, and in it she caught a glimpse of the fighter pilot climbing into his plane to take on the enemy, defying death time after time. As for herself, she welcomed the deadline even as her heart pounded. After months of planning here was sharp reality. It was earlier in the year than they might have chosen if all things were equal – but all things were very far from equal. The scales of destiny had tipped heavily towards a departure in the coming days. Cranwell was open to them. Lord and Lady Inchcape were safely away in Egypt. Their machine was ready, tuned to perfection. She had followed Rob's diet sheet and physical training plan religiously, and was as fit as she would ever be. They had studied charts, weather reports and fuel calculations until their eyes could no longer focus, and had laid plans for every eventuality they could think of. What's more, there were rumours of a rival east–west attempt that would soon set off from Berlin. It was unthinkable that after all their preparations, another crew might get there ahead of them by a couple of weeks.

Today they would move the plane from Brooklands to Cranwell. After that?

One week.

Hinch and the mechanics had already wheeled the plane out of the wooden shed when Elsie arrived, and she caught her breath at the glorious beauty of her machine shining in the early morning sunlight. Ever the designer, she was determined that the appearance of this aeroplane would be worthy of its performance. Sleek black paintwork for the fuselage, with vibrant wings of gold that reflected her own exultation. Union Jacks adorned either side, declaring to the world that this first east–west crossing of the Atlantic was a British endeavour. And that, Elsie had finally decided, should be the name of their machine.

Endeavour.

They shook hands with the engineers who had worked hard to get the machine ready over the last month, and climbed into the cockpit, cries of 'good luck' with the flight to India following them. If any of those engineers wondered why the preparations had included having the fabric coated in paraffin to prevent ice forming on the wings, they kept the thought to themselves.

As she settled into the cockpit, Elsie slipped her hand into her pocket and fingered the rosary beads without which she never flew, murmuring a prayer. She and Hinch had flown many miles over the countryside of southern England during the past couple of weeks, but somehow, today's flight felt different. It was only a short hop of little more than a hundred miles but it was also the first leg of their mission. Elsie glanced around. Behind her, the space that would ordinarily be filled with passengers and luggage was taken up with their custom-made fuel system. A large additional tank could hold around half their needs, with a stack of specially designed petrol cans containing the rest. All this fuel must be hand-pumped through to the wing tanks during the journey, and in a dark shed with only the light of an electric torch they had each practised crawling through the tight space to the back and opening the tanks largely by feel, filling, refilling and discarding.

She turned back and looked at the control panel before her. Here were the instruments that, when they were out over that endless sea, would be their only means of navigation. Elsie was accustomed to reading the landscape beneath her, looking for landmarks and the shape of the land, and translating that onto the maps and charts that were the aviator's great friend. But what was the use a map over nearly three thousand miles of ocean?

Hinch had shown her how to use the long-range compass that was the same type as the RAF used, and a drift indicator should help them stay on course. They had discussed the pros and cons of taking a wireless and decided against it. There was too much danger of an electrical spark igniting that enormous fuel load. 'Besides, who would we speak to?' he asked. 'Our route takes us north of the main shipping lanes. There will be no one out there but us.'

She glanced to her right where Hinch was running through his pre-flight checks. His eyepatch meant he always sat on the right-hand side of the cockpit. They were seated so close together that they were almost touching. What would that be like for thirty hours and more? Although they would share the flying, they had agreed that he, with his far greater experience, should be responsible for the initial take-off. Once *Endeavour* had been fully loaded with fuel at Cranwell, this would be perhaps the most hazardous moment of the whole enterprise. Elsie had practised all other aspects of the journey, including bringing her into land. 'The only truly predictable fact with a flight of this nature is that something unpredictable will occur. We must both be ready to react whatever the circumstance.'

The propellor in front of them was a blur of movement now. Forwards, forwards, faster, faster, and then the sensation Elsie loved more than any other, when the wheels lost contact with the ground and she soared, the airfield with its sheds and waving mechanics slipping away beneath them, and the open skies embracing them. Up through weak wisps of cloud and soon they were level and cruising, she could see, at just over 100 miles an hour. Elsie looked down on the patchwork of fields and towns below, and on the familiar sight of the shining River Thames winding its way through the countryside to cut right through the city of London to their east. She loved nothing more than to fly north, all the way to Glenapp, rejoicing as the flat, green fields of middle England gave way to the shimmering water and hills of the Lake District and then the western coastline calling her home. When weather permitted, she would circle Ailsa Craig, a rocky dot in the surging ocean, sending gannets flying upwards in panic, before bringing her plane in to land in the field they kept cut specially short at Glenapp. She had flown north a few weeks ago to visit Stella and her baby, but it had been a wasted journey as Stella had refused to see her. 'She's not ready to see anyone,' Alison had said apologetically. A little hurt, Elsie had left a beautiful shawl for the baby along with a loving note. She supposed Stella would have returned to Glasgow by now, but had heard nothing from her.

She pulled her thoughts back to the present. Even a flight like this one – gentle and unremarkable – kindled again that flame within her that had been lit on her very first flight. *This* was where she belonged. Right here, up in the sky, where the air was clear and the cares of the world were insignificant, while conventions and expectations and formalities were left far behind on the ground. Up here among the clouds, seeing the world from a different perspective, and embracing possibilities that the earth-bound people she spoke to day by day would never begin to experience.

This was living, and they knew nothing about it.

Hinch turned to her with a grin, and she knew he felt the same. 'Want to take over and bring her in?' he asked above the drone of the engine. She nodded and collected her thoughts. It might be a straightforward, simple flight on a calm day, but they were still two tiny fragile humans far above the earth, held here only by some scraps of steel, wood, fabric and the wonders of human engineering. It didn't do to become complacent. She adjusted her feet on the rudder pedals and reached for the throttle, feeling again that miraculous connection with her hand. Like the reins of a horse, a twitch and it would obey.

Bring her in.

Concentrating on her descent over Cranwell airfield, Elsie paid little attention to anything other than the angle of the runway, but as they glided down over the sheds, Captain Hinchliffe beside her said loudly, 'Damn and blast.'

She glanced at him but he gestured her concern away. Down, down, and the wheels touched the ground, and there was a jolt as they slowed to a stop. Only when they were stationary and the engine was off did she turn back towards him. His expression was grim. 'What's the problem?' she asked, removing her helmet and preparing to climb out of the plane.

He laid a hand on her arm. 'Be careful. There was a hell of a crowd around the gates watching us descend. If I'm not mistaken there were reporters among them.'

'Reporters?' Elsie stared at him aghast. 'But how?'

He shrugged. 'Someone has talked. Maybe one of the Brooklands engineers? Maybe one of the ground crew here at Cranwell who knew we were arriving today?'

'After all we've done to keep it secret, we can't have it in the newspapers. Not when we're so close!' Elsie heard the panic in her own voice. The adrenalin of the landing was ebbing away and now there was this new crisis to deal with. Reporters – it was the thing she had feared most throughout this whole enterprise. And now, with just a week or so to go!

Hinch removed his own helmet. 'It needn't be a problem. We stick to our story. I'm preparing for a non-stop flight to India. You are my financial backer, and because you have an interest you sometimes accompany me on test flights. No one can prove otherwise.'

'Will they believe us?'

'I think so. I'll give the impression that my planning is still in the fairly early stages and hopefully they won't watch us too closely for an imminent departure.'

Elsie took a deep breath. 'Very well. It's all we can do.' She shook her head in irritation. 'How I wish I were a nobody. It's infuriating, the way the press think they have a right to take an interest in everything I do.'

He gave a wry smile. 'If you were a nobody you would have none of this.' He gestured round the cockpit. 'She flew rather splendidly, don't you think?'

Elsie reached out and laid her hand gently on the control panel. 'Splendidly,' she agreed.

Chapter Thirty-Two

Glasgow

Stella tied Jacky's woollen scarf around his neck and wiped his nose, then ushered him into the close where Juliet was already bundled in the big pram. She glanced at the closed door to Rob's surgery as she left the house. He had a patient with him, Mrs McIvor from the West End, exactly the sort of person she had long urged him to nurture. He had told her at breakfast, and she could hear the hope in his voice that it would please her.

Only she found it terribly hard to get particularly pleased about anything these days.

She pushed the pram down the steps and into the street below, Jacky wandering along beside. Later, if he was tired or dawdling too much – for he was a terrible dawdler, her dreamer boy – she would let him sit on the pram for the ride home, but it was good for him to walk sometimes. They weren't going far, just the daily trip to the butcher and the grocer for the messages. It was a bitterly cold day with a heavy grey sky, but if it stayed dry she would carry on to the park to let him feed the ducks before they came home. The children should have more fresh air, and as they still didn't have their own garden . . . but the complaint in her mind was little more than an echo of something she knew she had once cared about. The picture that had been so vivid in her mind of herself and Rob and their children living happily in one of those new bungalows had faded. She didn't have the energy to dream these days.

She added Juliet's pram to the line of three outside the butcher's and pushed open the door. Jacky waited outside, hanging on to the handle of the pram. He hated the butcher's shop – the carcasses hanging behind the counter, Mr Martin with his bloodstained apron, the vicious mincing machine – and would cry if she tried to bring him in, so it was easier to leave him in charge of his sister. She could trust him not to wander off. She nodded to the other women in the queue.

'How's the wee one sleeping?' Mrs Oliphant from the next tenement asked. 'You're looking weary, lass.'

Stella forced a smile. 'She's not too bad, actually. Better than the boys at her age.' It was not Juliet who caused Stella all these sleepless nights.

'How old is she now?'

'Two months.'

'Two months already?' The older woman shook her head. 'It's a sin. You'll be getting used to life among us ordinary folks again, I'm sure!' She cackled, but her laugh disappeared into a fit of coughing, allowing Stella to avoid a reply. She guessed that the story of Juliet's dramatic birth and her own recuperation among the posh folks had been told and retold in the kitchens and closes round about. Gossip laced with kindness.

A woman closer to her own age turned and gave her a sympathetic smile before drawing close to whisper, 'Have you heard my news?'

Stella shook her head, trying to place her. She thought the

woman lived in the next street and was married to a schoolteacher.

'We've put down a deposit on one of those new bungalows in Bearsden. You know, the ones you and I spoke about. It really is time for people like us to move out of the tenements, don't you think?'

Stella murmured her congratulations, barely remembering the conversation she was supposed to have had. She took her bundle from the butcher. 'Must go – Jacky's waiting outside,' she said, apologetically. Messages safely stowed under the pram, she glanced at her watch. Rob would need his lunch today, but she had time to go to the park first. Jacky could spend hours by the side of the pond watching the ducks and loved to throw bread onto the path, tempting the pigeons to fly in around him. She gave him the little bag of stale crumbs she kept for him and sat on the bench. Juliet was whimpering so she lifted her out of the pram and pulled back the woolly hat that had slipped down over her deep dark eyes. Her daughter was still so small, but those wide eyes searching her face seemed very knowing. Stella rubbed the baby's cheek gently with her thumb, murmuring baby nonsense to her, and was rewarded with a smile. This was a fairly new trick – Rob had exclaimed with delight last night when she smiled at him, and Stella had kept silent and continued her knitting, slightly ashamed not to have mentioned that Juliet had started smiling a week earlier. They had shared every milestone with the boys, but that was a thousand years ago.

She held her baby close, breathing in her milky scent and, despite herself, felt the tears that came so easily these days fill her eyes.

She knew Rob was worried about her, and she had caught snatches of conversation between her husband and her mother when they thought she couldn't hear. They believed she was exhausted after the birth and struggling with the all-encompassing nature of motherhood. *Give it time*, her mother said. *It will get better with time.*

But Stella knew that nothing would get better until she confronted Rob about Elsie – yet she couldn't bring herself to do something so irrevocable. She carried on through the days, focusing on the children, and lay awake at night, tormented by the sight of Elsie in her husband's arms in the garden at Glenapp.

She watched him closely for signs of the affair continuing but found none. No mysterious letters, no unexplained absences. Elsie had written to her, a warm, effusive letter accompanying a beautiful cashmere shawl for Juliet. Stella had burnt the letter and stowed the shawl away. 'It's too good to use just now,' she had said when her mother asked her about it. 'I'll wait until she's bigger and less sickie.'

Maybe their affair had just taken place that one weekend at Glenapp. As if that made a difference! She had asked herself and asked herself if there could be an innocent explanation, but if so why had Rob not told her about his encounter with Elsie in the garden? Why, indeed, had he lied when asked where he had been, saying he had climbed the tower? No, while his wife had been heavy and ugly with pregnancy, he had betrayed her with her beautiful, glamorous friend. If that was what she had seen, what had happened, unseen? Images of the two of them naked together flashed through her mind like an endless obscene cinema picture.

The depth of this hurt was something she couldn't bear to articulate, but she knew she could never forgive him.

Back at the house, Stella sliced some cold tongue and heated the remainder of the soup she had made yesterday. Her mother would not be in for lunch; she was with Luisa discussing her wedding outfit, which Luisa had offered to make. Through the fog of her own misery, Stella was happy for her mother and Matthew, although she couldn't help but feel there was something faintly ridiculous about two people in their sixties choosing to marry. Could they not just have remained friends – after all, it was surely companionship that they were seeking. They couldn't possibly want the intimacy of marital relations at their age. Her mind turned inwards once more. She had turned away from Rob's tentative touch over the last few weeks, using Juliet as her excuse, but this impasse couldn't continue for ever.

Only she was utterly terrified to break it. What then for her marriage? What then for her children?

It was only when she had everything ready for lunch that she remembered the newspaper tucked under the pram and went to retrieve it. She carried it back through to the kitchen, sat down with her cup of tea before her and spread it out. She flicked through the pages, skimming adverts and headlines, and then stopped.

It wasn't a big paragraph, but in the way that often happens her eyes were drawn to a familiar name.

Miss Elsie Mackay.

With what felt like an iceberg at the core of her, she read the brief story. *CAPTAIN HINCHLIFFE'S SECRET FLIGHT* proclaimed the headline. It told how the well-known pilot was making preparations at a heavily guarded Cranwell Aerodrome for a long-distance flight record, believed to be either over land to India or the much-sought-after east–west transatlantic crossing.

It was rumoured yesterday that Miss Elsie Mackay, Lord Inchcape's daughter, would accompany Capt. Hinchliffe, but Miss Mackay said that she had no intention of doing so.

She intends to sail for Egypt to join her parents within the next fortnight. She has a financial stake in the project.

Miss Mackay is interested in flying and has been a passenger on some of Capt. Hinchliffe's test flights. The wartime flying ace has been at Cranwell every day since his arrival, frequently accompanied by Miss Mackay.

He intends to make his flight in a Stinson Detroiter monoplane fitted with a Wright Whirlwind engine, of the type used by Charles Lindbergh. The monoplane is painted black, with gold wings and struts. The name Endeavour *and two Union Jacks are painted on the fuselage.*

Stella read the column two or three times. Something nagged at her. The letter that Elsie had sent with Juliet's gift a couple of weeks ago, the letter she had skimmed with fury and tossed in the fire. What was it? Something she had barely noticed at the time, but which came back to her now.

I have big plans, which, if they go well, you shall hear more of shortly. I hope I may see you before they come to pass, but you will be busy with the little ones so perhaps not.

The door behind her opened. 'It's snowing, have you seen?' Rob asked cheerfully. She raised her eyes to the window. She hadn't even noticed, but thick flakes were drifting down. 'March – it's late in the year for snow,' he said.

Jacky whooped with excitement and abandoned his toy cars to scramble up at the window and watch the snowflakes. Stella rose to her feet more slowly. She swallowed. 'I'll get the soup,' she said, and her voice sounded tense to her own ears. 'You sit down and have a read of the paper.'

It was open at the page. Destiny had gifted her this moment, and the shroud of secrecy was about to be ripped away. There was a story right there about Elsie Mackay, he could hardly miss it. If

Rob read it and said nothing then he was proclaiming his guilt, for the natural thing would be for him to remark upon it and read it out to her with interest. One way or another, his reaction would reveal the truth.

She ladled soup into bowls, hands trembling, then turned to look at him. Rob was staring at the newspaper, his face white with dismay.

Stella needed no further confirmation.

He loves her.

Suddenly unable to bear it, Stella dropped the bowl on the floor and fled from the room with a sob.

There was pandemonium, of course. It's not how a mother is supposed to behave. She stood in the chilly parlour looking out over the street, which was rapidly disappearing under a blanket of snow. Her arms hugged her body tightly and she listened as Rob mopped up the soup, swept away the broken fragments of the bowl, soothed Juliet and distracted Jacky. Then his footsteps crossed the room behind her and his arms came around her. 'Won't you tell me what's wrong?'

She pulled away from him. Why should she be the one to speak the words that would destroy their marriage?

'Is it something I've done?'

She moistened her lips and turned to face him. She could barely get the word out. 'Elsie.'

Strangely she thought she saw relief pass across his face. 'Oh God, Stella, are you upset because of that newspaper article? I wouldn't worry, you know. You know what reporters are like. And if it's true I'm sure Elsie wouldn't take something like this on without proper preparation.'

She stared at him in disbelief. After everything, did he still think he could lie to her? Mounting anger gave her the strength to stalk back through to the kitchen, Rob following. She jabbed her finger at the article. 'Elsie – and you!'

He faltered then and there was most definitely guilt in those grey eyes. 'I don't know what you mean.'

'Yes, you do. Elsie and you at Glenapp. Don't deny it, Rob. I've known all along.'

He stared, and then he sat down at the table, head in his hands. After a moment he looked up at her. 'I'm sorry. I wanted to tell you, I really did. It's been so hard keeping it from you. I don't know what else I could have done.'

'You could have remembered your marriage vows for one thing. Or, if I meant so little to you, you could at least have thought about your children. How could you, Rob?'

His finger traced the article and she had the feeling he wasn't fully listening. 'It looks as if she's really going to do it.' He lifted his head. 'You have to admire her, though, in a way, don't you?'

Stella steadied herself with a hand on the back of the chair. '*Admire* her? Is that all you can say?'

'I am more sorry than I can possibly tell you that I kept her flight plans from you, but she had consulted me as her doctor and I'm bound by patient confidentiality. But yes, I do admire her. Don't you?'

There was a strong smell of burning soup. Juliet was howling. Stella ignored them both as she processed what Rob had just said.

'She consulted you?'

'Yes. I thought you said you knew that.'

'About her flight?'

'Yes.'

'And that's all?'

'What do you mean – all?'

'You didn't . . .' She swallowed. 'You didn't – sleep with her?'

'*Sleep* with her? With Elsie? No!' He got to his feet, pushing

259

the chair so hard that it fell with a crash. 'What the hell makes you ask that?'

Stella was trembling so violently that she had to sit down. He fetched her some water, then picked up his own chair and sat close beside her. His grey eyes – so untrustworthy, she had thought – were full of concern. 'Stella?'

'I saw you,' she said in a flat voice. 'From the window in Glenapp. The day Juliet was born. You were walking in the gardens with Elsie in the morning. And then you kissed her.'

'I did not kiss her!'

'You did.' She thought back. 'At least, you were holding her as if you were kissing her. And then you lied to me about where you'd been.'

He slammed his hand down on the table. 'Shit, shit, shit. That bloody woman. I should never have agreed to keep her secret.' Then he gripped Stella's hand, and she was startled to see tears in his grey eyes. 'Is this what has been wrong? Stella, my dearest, I promise you I did not kiss Elsie. I'm so sorry that I lied to you. Elsie told me her plan that morning, and asked for my help with the medical side. She made me promise not to tell anyone. Yes, I hugged her – it's such a big thing she is taking on – but as a friend. That is all. Then when you were bleeding and we were frightened it was far too complicated to explain, so I panicked and said I'd been up the tower. I'm not proud of it, Stella, and I'm so very sorry for all the pain I've caused you, but I promise that I have never looked at Elsie in that way. There's only you.'

She believed him. After long weeks of fear and loneliness and suspicion, she believed him. The soup was past redemption. Juliet was purple with rage. She let him take her in his arms and leant her face against his shirt, and felt truly warm for the first time in months.

* * *

Rob went out into the snow to make house calls and it was much later before they could speak properly. Alison had returned, and while she need never hear the reason for Stella's torment, her relief at the change in atmosphere was evident. Once the children were sleeping, the three adults sat around the table, the newspaper open before them. Rob had told them everything he knew. 'She's utterly determined to be part of the first flight east to west across the Atlantic, and the first woman to fly the Atlantic in either direction. This India story must be a diversion.'

'Is it not terribly dangerous?' asked Alison.

'Of course, but there's every chance she will manage it. The pilot she has engaged, this Captain Hinchliffe, is vastly experienced. They have made every possible preparation. That's why she came to me: she said some previous attempts had overlooked the physical strain of such a feat of endurance, and she wanted advice on how to counteract it.'

'When does she go?' Stella asked.

'I don't know. Sooner rather than later, if the newspapers have got wind of it, but they can't take off in this weather.'

Stella glanced towards the window, where the shutters were firmly closed against the winter storm outside. According to the wireless, similar blizzard conditions had blanketed much of the country. Beneath her relief that Rob had not been unfaithful she was aware of a new nagging concern. She had turned Elsie away when she came to visit and she had not written to her friend since before Glenapp. Now Elsie was about to set off on a dangerous flight and might never come back. How would she live with herself if that were the case? She got to her feet. 'I'm going to write to her,' she said. 'I never replied to her last letter or thanked her for allowing us to stay on at Glenapp.'

'I did that,' Alison said.

'All the same.' She hurried out of the room and returned with pen and paper, and something else clasped in her hand.

'Be careful what you put in writing,' Rob warned. 'You never know who could read your letter and it's of the utmost importance that Lord Inchcape doesn't find out.'

'It might be a bit late for that,' murmured Alison, glancing again at the newspaper on the table, but Stella nodded. She sat and thought, then wrote quickly for a while.

'Here – how does this sound? '*Rob has told me everything. I want to send you all my very best love and good wishes, and tell you just how thrilled I am for you. I can't wait to tell the children about their auntie Elsie once the time is right. Juliet is thriving and we remain very grateful to you for your help. I enclose a keepsake, which you will recognise – will you carry it with you? You can return it when next we meet, by which time it will have served its purpose.*"

'What's the keepsake?'

Stella opened her hand. 'It's that brooch Elsie gave me – Lindbergh's plane: the *Spirit of St Louis*. She wanted to remind me to hold on to my dreams.' She curled her fingers tightly around it and held it close to her heart for a few seconds. 'Perhaps it will bring her the good fortune of Lucky Lindy as she chases her own dream.'

Chapter Thirty-Three

Grantham

It had been snowing for days but finally today it had stopped.

Now, in the icy darkness of the evening, Elsie placed her gloved hand on the metal ring and opened the church door. She was here to make her confession. She slipped inside, making the sign of the cross, sat down in a pew near the back and bowed her head, her hands clasped tightly together. She had come here yesterday morning for the Sunday service, and had noted the times for confession. But she was not yet ready to go forward.

For a moment or two she simply breathed, taking stillness into her soul, seeking to calm the swirling maelstrom of emotions and thoughts and plans and snatches of conversation that tossed around within her.

It was finally time.

Tomorrow morning she and Captain Hinchliffe would climb into the cockpit of *Endeavour* and set off on their greatest enterprise. She was convinced they would succeed, but she needed to make peace with God first.

The last fortnight almost had been the most frustrating

of her life. They had flown into Cranwell on a sunny breeze of anticipation, scattering titbits of disinformation that the journalists gratefully swallowed. If only they had been able to press on with their plans, surely all would have been well. But then the weather swept in: a great winter storm battering the whole country, blanketing Cranwell in deep snow. Hinchliffe argued for more time from the authorities – after all, take-off was currently impossible, even to return to Brooklands – but all the while press speculation was mounting. Soon, the inevitable happened. Elsie received a visit at their Grantham hotel from her brother, Kenneth, and brother-in-law Alexander, demanding to know the truth of the newspaper stories and pleading with her, for the sake of Lady Inchcape's health, not to take part in any rash long-distance flight.

Elsie was well able to stand up to her relatives, taking war into the enemy camp as if they were children again and pouring scorn on Kenneth for his own timidity, but she was deeply worried. How much longer could she hold out against her father's suspicion and influence? A telegram arrived from the Air Ministry informing Hinchliffe his time at Cranwell had expired. She couldn't help but wonder if her father had something to do with it.

Meanwhile their efforts at subterfuge continued. Hinch enlisted the help of another wartime pilot friend as a decoy. Gordon Sinclair was presented to the press as the man who would share in the purported flight to India. Elsie made a very public display of continuing with her ordinary schedule, travelling down to London to meet Princess Mary and Viscount Lascelles at Victoria station, where they were setting off on the first leg of a journey to Egypt. At Marseilles they would board the *Ranchi*, Captain Kennedy's ship, and they would be met by Lord Inchcape at the other end of their journey. 'Please give my love to my father and mother and tell them I will join them soon,' Elsie said, as the Princess boarded the train. She stood waving as the royal couple departed, and reflected that if all went well, she would cable her parents from New York or Philadelphia with news of her triumph long before Princess Mary could pass on her greetings. A shiver ran through her as she turned to deal with the insistent questions of the reporters.

If only she could be sure her father would understand.

Today there had come a second Air Ministry telegram, far more peremptory this time, insisting that *Endeavour* be moved from Cranwell tomorrow at the latest. They had considered other options, including Baldonnel, but their careful calculations merely confirmed that only Cranwell met their needs. To move their machine to Brooklands or to Baldonnel would be to admit defeat. The rumours were growing, Lord Inchcape was poised to intervene, their German rivals were said to be almost ready to take off, and Cranwell would not allow them a second opportunity.

Then it stopped snowing.

Elsie, Hinchliffe and Sinclair met in the room they had commandeered at the hotel. The table was strewn with papers and maps, overflowing ashtrays and dirty cups, for hotel staff had been forbidden to enter. The curtains remained closed all day long, and Elsie had obtained a gramophone, which played in the background whenever they were in conference, in case any enterprising journalist was listening at the door. She set the needle going and thought how surreal it was to be discussing their plans to a backdrop of Gershwin's 'Rhapsody in Blue'.

Hinch waved a sheet of paper at them triumphantly. 'This is the best weather report I've received in more than two weeks. They want us to move *Endeavour*? I say we move her – all the way to Philadelphia!'

Hope streaked across the room, as if someone had pulled back that curtain and let in the sunlight. But then . . .

'Tomorrow?' asked Sinclair. 'Are you sure that's a good idea? Have you forgotten the date?'

Hinch stared at him for a moment, then turned away, a sudden frown on his face. 'The thirteenth.'

Elsie glanced between them and almost laughed aloud. 'Surely you wouldn't let a superstition prevent us! Not when everything else is in our favour.'

He bit his lip. It was clear he didn't like it. Perhaps clinging to superstition was an inevitable part of stepping into a fragile frame of steel and wood and taking to the skies, especially in those early wartime days. But then he laid down the weather report and picked up his pen. 'You're right. This is a venture of science not of chance. And I have heard that the German affair is progressing quickly.' He bent over the map. 'Let's go over this one more time, for if the weather is still on our side tomorrow, we take to the skies, thirteenth or not.'

Now Elsie glanced round the shadowy walls of the church, absorbing the reassurance of ancient prayers and rituals. Final confirmation must wait for tomorrow's weather reports, but everything was set. She had ordered up sandwiches, coffee and fruit to be ready for them in the early morning, and they had pored over their charts yet again. 'We head slightly north towards the Welsh coast to avoid the mountains. She'll be so heavily laden at the start of our flight that she may struggle to climb and it's not worth the risk. Across the sea to the south coast of Ireland and then on out west. We'll adjust our course every three hours to take account of the drift. Leaving in the morning we will have many hours of daylight flying ahead of us, and during darkness we'll be above the Atlantic where we have to rely only on our instruments anyway. By the time we approach the coast of Newfoundland, dawn will have come and we'll be flying by sight and landmarks again.'

'Do you still plan to continue on to Philadelphia and claim the prize?' Sinclair asked.

'If all is well and our fuel has lasted, but we can land in St

266

John's if we need to and still achieve our main aims. In theory we should be able to continue on through daylight with a far lighter plane, complete the final thousand-mile leg to Philadelphia, and claim the prize money.' He grinned at them both. 'Simple.'

It was far from simple, but their preparations had been so meticulous that she couldn't believe they had missed anything. Here in the little church she sat, head bowed, scarcely aware of the trickle of people coming and going to the confession box. She whispered the Lord's Prayer. Confession? She had lied and lied and lied – to her friends, to her family, to her parents, to the press – but although she felt a certain sadness about that, she did not feel shame. What she was doing was not wrong; rather she had a profound sense that this was the truest calling of her life. She remembered an intense period of spiritual fervour when, as a teenager lost in deep admiration for a young teacher in her convent school, she had wondered if she might be called to be a nun. It had lasted a term at most, and soon afterwards she met Dennis, at which point any religious vocation could not have been further from her mind! But that deep, restless conviction that she was destined for something out of the ordinary remained. It led her through film studios, nightclubs and parties, through newspaper headlines and scandals. It helped her escape the conventions of her society role by driving her silver Rolls-Royce too fast, and by flying her little biplane without fear. It took her on board the great steamships that crossed the seas, translating ideas for elegant saloons and state rooms from her mind to the drawing board to the workshop to the ship.

All the while her father watched, sometimes approving, sometimes not.

That sense of something just out of reach remained, until the night when she stood at her top-floor window in Seamore Place and dreamt of flying west across the Atlantic, and of using that first flight to inspire and transform the world of commercial aviation.

Tomorrow she would do just that. If she had to tell some untruths to fulfil her calling and to protect her parents from worry, surely God would understand?

After all, He had made her the person that she was, and He had led her to this point.

Elsie got to her feet and walked slowly down the aisle. She entered the confession box, and went through the familiar rituals, trying to cleanse her conscience of all that might burden and distract her tomorrow. The priest spoke words of renewal. '*Give thanks to the Lord for He is good,*' he finished.

'*His mercy endures for ever,*' she replied. Such inexpressible comfort. Only one thing might help her more.

'Father – may I ask you something?'

'Go on, my child.'

'I'm going on a journey tomorrow. I will be leaving early. Would it be possible for me to receive Holy Communion before I go?'

In the dark, heavy pause that followed she wondered if he read the newspapers. Then he spoke.

'Of course. Knock on the door to the red-brick building adjoining this one. I'll be expecting you.'

'Even if it's very early?'

'Any time of day or night.'

She thanked him and walked back along the aisle and out of the church into the night. The air was cold, but she could sense no wind at all, and the sky was clear. As she made her way back to the hotel she looked up at the stars.

Tomorrow night she would soar among them.

She went early to bed, determined to get a good night's sleep. Unlike Lindbergh on his solo flight, she and Hinch would get some rest, but they planned on taking only short naps to keep their stamina up. Most of the time this flight would require the concentration of two minds. Despite her best intentions, she snatched only a restless hour or two of vivid dreams on this last night in a comfortable bed before rising in darkness at four thirty. She dressed quickly in her usual flying clothes – thick tweed trousers and woollen jumper – with her flying suit pulled over the top. She would wrap her long fur coat around herself when she left the hotel to deflect any suspicion. She met Hinch and Sinclair in the corridor, and as they gathered supplies amid whispered conversation and suppressed excitement, she found herself incongruously remembering secret midnight feasts in her boarding school days.

Lochrie was waiting for her with the car as agreed. She would like to have told him what she was planning, but the fewer people who knew the better. Still, the early morning departure was bound to raise his suspicion, never mind the destination of their first call. 'Take me to St Mary's Church please.'

The door was opened by the young priest himself. His face was pale with dark shadows under his eyes and she wondered if he had been to bed. He ushered her into a cold house that smelt of damp, and through an adjoining door to the church. The lit candles on the altar had burnt a good way down, adding to her suspicion that he had perhaps been here all night. Praying for her?

It was the most precious sacrament she had ever taken. She received the broken body and the blood, and took in with it the sense of the One who created those starry heights drawing close to her and filling her with His peace and His presence. She knelt in prayer for a moment or two longer, then lifted her head, calm and resolute. Silently the priest led her back through to the house. She thanked him, and suddenly needed to speak her purpose aloud.

'Today I will fly west across the Atlantic.'

Secrecy had become such a habit that the words shocked her, but there was no hint of surprise in his dark eyes. Whether through the *Daily Express* or divine inspiration, it was clear he had already worked it out. He laid a hand of blessing on her head. 'May the Lord bless you and keep you. I shall pray for you every hour.'

'Thank you.'

He nodded and led her to the front door. *'Give thanks to the Lord for He is good.'*

'His mercy endures for ever.'

As she stood with him on the darkness of the doorstep she felt a profound sense of intimacy with this stranger who had brought her comfort and strength. She longed to hug him, to hold him close and feel his arms around her before she stepped out into the momentous morning. Instead she smiled her warmest smile. 'I'll cable from America when we get there!' she called lightly as she turned away and descended the steps to the pavement and the Rolls-Royce waiting below.

Grey glimmers of light had splintered the darkness by the time she arrived at Cranwell Aerodrome. Hinchliffe and Sinclair were ahead of her and had wheeled *Endeavour* onto the snowy field, helped by a couple of RAF ground crew. Her wings of gold lightened the darkness, never failing to bring a surge of joy to Elsie's heart.

There were very few people about. The white covering added a ghostly quality to the morning light, and their quiet conversations had that strange muffled eeriness produced by snow. Hinch was jubilant. 'It's a better forecast than we could have hoped for,' he said. 'No wind here at ground level as you can see, but the reports say we will have a south-easterly once we're in the air, which is perfect – it should give us a good tailwind and blow us halfway over the Atlantic. The gods are finally on our side.'

Elsie slipped her hand into the pocket of her fur coat and touched her rosary once more. She encountered something sharp and hard. Of course! The little Lindbergh souvenir brooch that she'd given to Stella on the terrace at Glenapp, on a far distant summer's afternoon when today was no more than the glimmer of an idea. Stella had asked Elsie to take it over the sea, and she had slipped it into the pocket of her coat in case she forgot in the morning. Once the publicity broke Rob must have found it too hard not to share the secret, and she found she was glad. She would transfer both the rosary and Stella's brooch into the pocket of her flying suit, and leave her fur coat behind. By the time she returned it to Stella it would have travelled thousands of miles across the water, where no one had ever gone. What greater symbol of the boundless possibilities of life!

She turned her attention to the two men and the final preparations. Everything was ready. The three of them spoke loudly about Baldonnel and swapped places in the cockpit two or three times, before Sinclair clasped her hand tightly. 'Best of luck, Miss Mackay. I know you'll succeed and, by Jove, what an achievement. I'm glad to have been a small part of it.'

She squeezed his hand then climbed into the cockpit, this time closing the door behind her. Hinch was already in his seat and she watched, moved, as he kissed a photograph of his wife and two daughters then slipped it inside his flying suit, next to his heart. He glanced at her briefly. 'Ready?'

'Ready.'

He switched the electric starter as the mechanics began to swing the big wooden propellor. The drone of the engine grew louder; the propellor spun faster. Together, they checked through the control panel. Everything was functioning normally. It was just another flight.

It was so much more than just another flight.

Endeavour began to inch forward across the snowy field. Elsie kept her eyes on the speed indicator and the altimeter as she prepared to adjust the trim. But as the plane trundled along – there was no other word for it – she could fully understand the reasoning behind Hinch's insistence that they take off from Cranwell. The runway was perhaps a mile long, and with the enormous weight dragging them down, *Endeavour* needed every inch of it to gather enough speed to have any chance whatsoever of lifting off the ground. As the noise increased and the propellor disappeared into a blur, every nerve within her was taut. Everything relied on their calculations but some questions couldn't be answered in advance. Even if *Endeavour* got off the ground, would her frame be strong enough to bear the additional strain, or would she fracture and come crashing down to earth, bursting into a fiery inferno?

What a dreadful way to die.

On, on, on, the sheds and posts and beacons flashing past them as speed increased, and then the moment when the sensation of speed melted away as she lifted up, up – would she clear the fence, the trees – up, *go on* – yes! They looked at each other as the ground dropped away beneath them and Hinch raised a fist in triumph. Then he brought her round in a circle, dipped his wing to the upturned faces and waving arms below, and set off west above the snowy English fields.

They were off!

Chapter Thirty-Four

Oxford

A hundred miles to the south, Corran was also awake in the early hours of 13th March.

Her sleep had been restless for the last few weeks as she lay in her narrow bed in her college room playing out conversations in her head. Now, after more than two months of silence, it looked as if those conversations would become reality. Arthur had written suggesting that they meet not in the cottage but in a country pub just outside Oxford. She was a little taken aback – the things she needed to say to him would be better said in private – but at least he had got in touch.

And then she had opened the newspaper yesterday morning to see the startling announcement of his resignation as an MP.

A piece of news that changed everything.

It was hard to comprehend – Arthur was so committed to his work – but the more Corran thought about it, she could only see one sensible conclusion. These weeks of separation had finally convinced him that they needed to be together properly, which could only happen if he stepped down from parliament.

Somehow she got through her morning classes, barely aware of what she was teaching, ate a hasty lunch in the college, declined Katherine's suggestion of a cup of tea together and then boarded her bus to join him. He had remembered that she was free on Tuesday afternoons. She looked out over countryside still blanketed with snow after the dreadful weather of the last couple of weeks, and sensed the ground shifting. They had stuck rigidly to their agreement to have no contact, giving her plenty of time to consider what she would say to him about their circumstances. But that was before yesterday's news. He didn't know – couldn't possibly know – and yet by some extraordinary intuition he had made the one decision that could turn her wintry fields into sweet meadowland.

And she hadn't even had to ask.

As she dismounted the bus she thought how much had happened in the short time since they last met. Her novel had been published to good reviews, and her publisher was keen to receive the next one. Given everything, that was just as well. She had received letters of congratulation from many different people, but not a word from Arthur. No matter: he was just doing what they had agreed.

She walked to the little country inn, pushing open the door with a tendril of hope curling inside her. The warm air was smoky and welcoming, and there was no one there but a young barmaid who ignored her, a solitary man reading his newspaper, and Arthur, seated by the fire. He had bought her a half pint of cider, she noticed, and she smiled. After weeks of worry and tension, it was so very good to see him again. This was Arthur, the man who loved her, and it was all going to be all right.

He stood up as she approached and kissed her formally on the cheek. 'Corran. You look well.'

Discreet, that's all.

For a few moments they spoke about their journeys through the snow, but Corran was impatient to reach the purpose of their meeting. 'I was surprised to read of your resignation in the newspaper yesterday. That can't have been an easy decision.'

He took a long time to reply. 'That's why I needed to see you, although our three months aren't quite up.'

There was something in his tone that made her pause. 'Go on.'

He didn't seem keen to talk about himself. 'Your book is doing well! I'm delighted for you. Congratulations.'

She noticed he didn't say he had read it. She sipped her cider, but the warm liquid couldn't reach the chill that was beginning to spread inside her. 'Thank you. I'm working on the next one.'

'Good for you!' His smile was too bright. 'Things have changed, haven't they, Corran? You are moving on now, you're a published authoress, and I . . .' He stopped.

'Yes?'

He lifted his pint glass and drained it. When he set it down he looked across at her. 'I'm moving to New York.'

It was so completely ridiculous that she laughed aloud. 'Hardly! I'm not falling for that one.'

'It's true.'

That was when the world began to feel unsteady. She gripped the edge of the sticky table. New York. The greedy heart of capitalism. He was a Labour MP! He had dedicated his life to the Labour Party and to improving the welfare of his constituents. How in the world could he move to New York? And what about his son?

She stopped.

This could only be about his son.

'Why?'

'Mary came back from New York after Christmas convinced

it's a far better place for Ronald to grow up. She has asked me to come with them, a fresh start. She also says that if I don't I'll never see him again.'

'Surely she can't do that!' Corran protested. 'He's your son. She can't take him from you. The courts would stop her.'

'Ah, but I can't possibly take it to the courts. Mary has gathered proof of my unfaithfulness – of our affair, Corran. If she divorces me, I've as good as lost him anyway. My career will be over and your name will be traduced too.' He looked up at her, and there was such distance in his green eyes that the Atlantic Ocean might already lie between them. 'I think we always knew this day would come now that I am a father, now that I have a son. You tried to say so, I remember, when Ronald was born, and I was the one who said it didn't matter. I was wrong.'

There were too many implications piling in, one on top of the other, for her to begin to comprehend them. She tried to focus on something that didn't pierce her heart quite so painfully. 'What will you do in New York of all places?'

'I used to be a teacher and Mary's brother-in-law is a headmaster. He has offered me work in his school to begin with. Later, we'll see.' He lit a cigarette and offered one to her. She waved it away. 'I know you think I'm abandoning my principles but that's not true. Once I'm in America I will be better placed to make contact with others there who understand the flaws in capitalism.'

I couldn't give a damn about your principles. Her senses were spinning, a malevolent tornado sucking her in, but at the centre of the storm was a still, small space that she knew was the moment of decision. *Tell him, or walk away.*

Tell him, or walk away.

She pushed her chair back and stood up. The man with the newspaper glanced up at her sudden movement but Arthur looked down at the table.

She walked towards the door, head held high, hardly breathing, praying her legs would hold her up.

He didn't come after her.

Outside, Corran walked around the corner and leant against the wall, trembling and breathing deeply. Across the street a newspaper seller was yelling the headlines from the afternoon edition. '*Mystery flight – is the heiress on board? Where is* Endeavour *now?*'

The words didn't even penetrate her mind.

Gradually, she stopped shaking so violently. She slipped her hand inside her coat and laid it on her abdomen. There was no discernible swelling, but soon there would be.

He had made his decision, and now he would never know.

Chapter Thirty-Five

Above the Atlantic Ocean

Where is Endeavour *now?*

Elsie and Hinch had very little idea.

The first part of their journey had gone to plan. They had skirted the north Welsh coast, flying low and steady with their heavy load of fuel until they reached the Irish Sea, where the cloud began to disperse. Elsie glanced northwards. That way lay Scotland, Glenapp, her family – all that was safe and predictable.

By the next time she saw them she would have accomplished something that they and the rest of the world believed impossible.

It was an extraordinary thought, yet now that the flight was underway, in many ways it was just like any other. The same sensations, the same routines, the same checks and observations. She was glad of that. Nothing was more likely to lead them to make a costly mistake than dwelling on the enormity of the challenge.

Hinch was still at the controls of *Endeavour* and she was free to look out of the window and down to the sea below. Flying over water always gave her a thrill. It was that sense of moving *beyond* – beyond the immutable land, beyond the harbours and the houses, beyond the people with their little lives, beyond what could be known and tamed and defined. This stretch of water teemed with life. She could see trawlers and cargo ships on the busy routes to and from Dublin and Liverpool, long dark trails of smoke hanging behind them. Smaller boats clustered together, operating out of the little fishing communities dotted all down the coast. Wherever there were boats there were gulls and gannets gliding and diving just below *Endeavour*, mocking her with their grace and agility. *Your human engineers may have stolen our secret of flight, but can you dive, can you swoop, can you soar?*

Elsie watched it all, knowing that in just a few hours they would reach a world of water where they would see no people, no boats, no gulls. A world where life did not mean breath, where hidden realms existed far beneath the surface, mysterious, dark and unfathomable.

By the time they reached the southern coast of Ireland the weather had worsened again and snow was falling on little towns and villages below them. They were unconcerned. The easterly wind that Hinch had mentioned was picking up, and they were exultant to have made such good time already. Once they were out at sea they could fly below, above or around the worst of the clouds, with plenty of scope to compensate for adjustments to their route. Elsie had the charts spread out on her lap, along with her small logbook in which she made constant calculations. When they had been flying for nearly four hours she drank some of her coffee, ate a sandwich and then signalled to Hinch that she would take over the controls while he had something to eat. On Rob's advice, she had insisted they make a timetable requiring them both to eat, drink and rest whether they felt like it or not. 'We may not feel hungry, but it's important we keep our stamina up and don't wait until tiredness or faintness overtakes us.'

Hinch did as she suggested and then crawled through the tight space from the cockpit into the cabin behind to check on their fuel system before they headed out to sea, beyond the final possibility of a safe landing. Alone in the cockpit, Elsie looked around. She had flown solo for many years now, and it was a very different experience to share this tiny space with someone else, but there was no one she would rather have at her side on this expedition than Captain Hinchliffe. As they had worked together over the past two months, she had come to respect his wisdom and experience, but also to recognise the steely glint in his eye. He hadn't told her much about his wartime flying days, when each expedition had carried with it a far greater likelihood of death than any record attempt he might now make, and he had never mentioned the crash in which he lost his eye, but she knew that every detail he had learnt through those experiences, as well as his subsequent career with Imperial Airways, had been channelled into his preparations for this flight. Although the spark of adventure might still be there, he was no longer the daredevil pilot of ten years earlier.

He adored his wife, Emilie, and little daughters, Joan and Pamela, and would never have undertaken this flight without complete confidence that he would land successfully in America and return to them, their future prosperity secured. Still, she was glad she had arranged life insurance for him; if anything were to happen she couldn't bear to think of those little girls left destitute because of her invitation. As Hinch crawled back through from the petrol tanks and slid into his seat with a thumbs up, she breathed a silent word of gratitude to Tony for introducing them in the first place. She wondered if Tony had heard that their flight was underway. What were people saying back home? Had news leaked out? It was so strange, not knowing. Did the people on the ground who heard the rumble of their engine passing overhead know who they were? Did anyone believe that Gordon Sinclair was the co-pilot?

Had they told her father yet?

She pushed the question from her mind and turned her attention back to the controls and to the landscape beneath her. They were at last approaching the southwestern corner of Ireland, and the air was becoming bumpier as the warm air over land met the cooler air above the sea. She brought *Endeavour* down lower through the drifting clouds and marvelled at the beauty beneath her. Long fingers of jagged rock stretched out into the dark sea, which heaved and crashed in a tumult of white spray. Hinch pointed. On the longest of those fingers they could clearly make out the flat-roofed buildings and foreshortened tower of Mizen Head Lighthouse, and beside it, three tiny figures looking upwards and waving. Hinch turned the handle to wind down the window beside him, letting a blast of cold air into the cockpit, and reached out his arm to wave back. As he wound the window back up again, he grinned at Elsie. 'The next folk we see will be Canadians or Yanks. Our Atlantic crossing begins here!'

They set their course once more, for this was the final landmark. For the next two thousand miles they would be reliant wholly upon their instruments and their instincts to tell them where they were until, if all went well, spotting land somewhere near St John's, Newfoundland. Drift too far north and they could lose themselves in the great ice floes of the northern Atlantic or be forced down in the wastes of Labrador with little hope of rescue. If their course took them too far south, there was every risk they would miss Newfoundland completely and fly on southwards parallel to the eastern seaboard of America, using up their fuel and never reaching land.

From this moment on they must trust their careful preparations while praying that good fortune was on their side. Their eyes met, and they each nodded. To Elsie's surprise, Captain Hinchliffe reached out and caught her right hand, giving it a quick squeeze. They were in this thing together, for better or worse. In theory they could turn back – Tony's friends had done just that – but Elsie and Hinch knew that for them there were no second chances. For reasons they had gone over and over at Cranwell, today was their one and only opportunity, and this flight was not only achievable but had the potential to blaze the trail for commercial air travel between Europe and America. Elsie smiled at Hinch. *Endeavour* would carry them westwards. If they failed there was little doubt they would perish but if, as they both believed, they succeeded, then this would likely be the first of many journeys they would make together across this mighty sea.

They were not quite alone yet, for their initial course followed the steamship route from Europe to America. Hinch's plan was to fly low when he could, conserving fuel, and so they were beneath the clouds and saw occasional ships ploughing through the water. Elsie wondered if any of those on board glanced to the skies and spotted them. She remembered sitting on the Freiburg verandah last year and reading the story of Ruth Elder, who had tried to be the first woman to cross the Atlantic from New York to Paris. Her aircraft, *American Girl*, had miraculously come down near enough to a tanker for Ruth and her crew to be rescued. Well, that good-luck story had been used up and wasn't likely to happen a second time! She looked down on a grand liner and wondered which one it was. Not one of theirs. Her father's gaze was always set east, to warmer climes. She thought she knew why. The only time she had ever previously crossed the Atlantic had been with her parents on board the luxurious *Majestic*, on her maiden White Star Line voyage after her acquisition from Germany as part of war reparations. She remembered standing on deck beside her father one evening and feeling him shiver beside her.

'Are you cold, Father? Shall we go inside?'

Lord Inchcape shook his head. 'I wonder where his ship went down.'

Elsie was confused. 'Whose ship?'

'My father.' He leant over and looked into the icy depths far below. 'His bones lie at the bottom of the Atlantic somewhere. Two of my uncles were lost in the Atlantic too. It's the cruellest of seas. I loathe it.'

Elsie had always known that her grandfather had been lost on an Atlantic crossing when her father was just a boy of twelve, changing his life for ever, but it hadn't entered her mind as she and her mother packed happily for the voyage. The next day, when her father was reading his newspaper in the smoking room, she lifted some fresh flowers from the arrangement in their suite and went back out on deck. Unseen, she dropped them over the side and watched as they floated down to the black surface of the sea, whispering a prayer for the grandfather she had never known.

'Shall I take over? The wind is picking up,' Hinch yelled, and she started out of her daydream and back into the immediate reality of the cockpit. Had she drifted into a doze? No, all was well and she remembered adjusting their altitude just a moment or two before. Flying such a long distance – they had been in the air for more than six hours now, with no landmarks for the past two – it was terribly easy for her actions to become automatic while her mind drifted off elsewhere. The same thing could happen on a long drive, when the road was relatively straight and unremarkable, but the dangers of a loss of concentration were infinitely greater here. If she dipped too low a huge wave might catch them and pull them down into the sea. If she didn't remain focused on the drift indicator she might well lead them off course into disaster. And Hinch was right, the wind was buffeting the little plane more and more, while a mass of dark cloud ahead looked more ominous than anything they had so far encountered.

She had been making corrections mechanically but now felt fully awake and recognised that the conditions they were about to enter needed full focus. She nodded, and indicated the back of the plane. She had a bucket wedged there and it was time to unzip her flying suit and relieve herself. She would toss the contents out to sea along with the next empty aluminium petrol can.

The experience of using the bucket while the plane rocked about was far worse than she had imagined, and she resolved to wait for a calm spell if she needed to go again. As she crawled back through she felt a sudden shift in direction and angle that knocked her sideways. 'This storm is huge,' Hinch yelled. 'I'm going north, see if we can get beyond it. We can adjust back later.'

The next hour was the worst she had ever experienced in the air, and she was grateful for his calm and determined skill. Hail blattered against the windscreen and the wind howled above the roar of the engine, while the darkness of the shifting cloud seemed almost like night. When jagged lightning flashed through the black clouds she prayed it wouldn't hit them, even as she gazed in awe at its splendour. The ocean was long gone, lost beneath that swirling mass of cloud. Elsie gripped the trim lever and bit her lip until it bled, as she felt the strain of poor *Endeavour* trying to battle through the conditions. Would her wooden wings be ripped apart from her metal fuselage? Was that perhaps what had happened to some of those who had gone before – to Princess Anne, to Mrs Grayson?

How could they ever survive this?

And then with breathtaking suddenness the darkness split in two and the light was so blinding that she exclaimed aloud. All around them was brilliant blue sky, and now they flew on with the sun shining into the cockpit, rapidly transforming it into a hothouse. Below the sea, blue too for the first time, a sheet of smooth, reflective azure glass. 'Where are we?'

'I don't know,' Hinch admitted. 'Somewhere much further north than I planned to be. That storm was a beast, wasn't it, and it must have been hundreds of miles across, lying directly in our path. We couldn't possibly have survived it. I had to either get us north of it or south of it. With the wind coming from the south-east I figured north was better – the weather is likely worse to the south.' He wiped sweat from his brow. 'Got any of that coffee?'

'Of course!' She rummaged in the bag, took out some provisions and passed them to him, taking control of *Endeavour* to allow him to eat and to rest. 'What do we do now?'

It was strange, but while the roar of the engine had seemed loud at the start of the journey, now that they had left the screaming winds behind their progress felt almost quiet and peaceful. She supposed her ears had adjusted to it.

'We carry on. *Endeavour* seems to have come through all right – a bit battered I imagine but no lasting damage that I can sense. In a little while we'll track back towards the south, but we've found ourselves some better flying conditions so I'm not keen to abandon them just yet.'

And so Elsie and *Endeavour* flew on while Hinchliffe rested. She unzipped her flying suit and pulled it loose as the sunshine through the glass heated up the cockpit far more powerfully than its little heater had managed earlier. There was nothing other than sky and sea and friendly white clouds that formed themselves into magnificent shapes: a Highland glen; a fortified castle; a golden full-masted sailing ship. She looked again. Was the gold her imagination? No, that golden light was spreading outwards, tinting the clouds as the sun began to set. She remembered their calculations from previous days. They were well off course and had surely lost time battling the storm, but if their estimates were even vaguely correct then by the time the sun set and night arrived they should be close to halfway into the Atlantic portion of their crossing. She glanced at Hinch, but he was dozing in the next seat. No matter: all was well. *Endeavour* was flying like a dream through a world of indescribable light and beauty.

A few minutes later he jolted awake. 'All right?'

'Perfect.'

He looked about, taking in the sun's dying rays. 'We will have night to contend with soon.'

She nodded, and then turned towards him. Suddenly, she needed to say this aloud. 'Whatever happens from this point on – at this moment, this very moment, I am happy. It's worth it. All of it. I've finally realised – it's not really about the records, or proving things to my father, or even the commercial airline we want to develop. All that is good, but *this* is what it's about. This moment, right here, right now. This very sunset, this very sea. It's about being here and being free, where no one in the world knows where I am, and where no one has ever been before me.'

He nodded slowly, gazing out on that world of wonder, and she thought he understood. 'I spoke to a priest yesterday,' she continued. 'Or I suppose it must have been this morning, thought it seems a lifetime ago. I told him I was going after the thing I was born for. Just now as you were sleeping I found it – the thing I've been searching for all my life.' A laugh of pure joy bubbled out of her. 'I believe I am happier at this moment than I have ever been before. And possibly than I ever will be again. *This* moment – this is it. The reason I was born.'

Chapter Thirty-Six

Glasgow

By the time the newspapers were printed on the morning of Wednesday 14th March, everyone had an opinion about the mystery flight.

The first reports had trickled in during the day on Tuesday. Rob heard from one of his West End patients that *Endeavour* had taken off from Cranwell, but no one was quite sure who was on board. 'Baxter at my club got it from one of his London friends,' the whiskered old man wheezed as Rob tried to listen to his chest. 'Says there's a woman behind it. There are far too many of these wealthy women paying our best aviators to risk their lives in pursuit of glory, if you ask me. Who will pay for the search and rescue mission? You and I, Dr Campbell, that's who. It's completely unacceptable.'

Alison, Stella and Rob sat up late into Tuesday night, going over and over the few details they knew. 'Philadelphia seems to be the most likely destination, although they only need to reach Newfoundland to achieve the first successful flight,' Rob said, opening up the big atlas on the kitchen table and tracing his finger across the Atlantic Ocean. 'I imagine their route will be something like this. You have to allow for the curve of the earth. I've been trying to work it out, and I don't think they can hope to arrive in Philadelphia until well into tomorrow afternoon.'

Stella walked over to the window, Juliet in her arms. She opened the shutter and looked out at the patchwork of other people's windows glowing yellow, with one square of dark sky high above the tenements. Rob watched as she craned her neck, almost as if she might see the tiny, brave lights of a plane. He came up behind her and put his arms around her. She had suffered so deeply when Jack was killed. What would it do to Stella if Elsie didn't return?

But by Wednesday morning Stella was dancing round the kitchen with excitement. Rob pulled on his coat and picked up his bowler hat and medical bag, preparing to leave for the shipyard. 'I wonder if her arrival will be in time for the evening newspapers?' she asked. 'I'll keep checking the wireless bulletins. It can't be much longer now.'

'It depends where they land. Philadelphia is another thousand miles down the coast after they've crossed the Atlantic. Still, someone will surely spot them once they're over land.' He kissed her. 'By the time I'm home we should know much more.'

'It will be hard to settle to do anything today!'

'Just as well you have that pile of ironing awaiting you, then,' said Alison crisply, appearing in the hallway. 'There's not a thing we can do to make a difference, so we're as well to keep busy.'

Stella made a face and Rob laughed and left the house. It was wonderful to have his wife returned to him in place of the cold, sullen stranger of the past two months. They had even made love last night, and then lain in each other's arms talking quietly about their friend high up in her tiny plane over the Atlantic somewhere. Stella had complete confidence that Elsie would succeed. Rob, who had made it his business to investigate previous attempts once Elsie asked for his help, was less confident, but he kept his fears to himself. Time enough for that if bad news came. If anyone could succeed Elsie could, and at least he knew how thoroughly she had prepared.

He bought himself a newspaper and stood swaying in the tram, aware of chatter all around him about the flight attempt. How strange it was to have the whole world talking about the secret he had kept for so long! At the ferry point he wasn't surprised to find Alex waiting for him. His brother-in-law brandished his own newspaper. 'I presume you've seen this? Whatever is the woman thinking?'

It was time to come clean. He filled Alex in on his conversation with Elsie at Glenapp and subsequent advice. Alex listened, his expression grim. 'I can't think why you didn't stop her.'

'If you think it's within my ability to stop Elsie Mackay doing anything she wants, you have a rather exalted idea of my influence. Besides . . .' He hesitated. 'It's rather admirable, don't you think? The reports say she's a passenger, but she is flying that plane for herself. She has made every possible preparation.'

'All the preparations in the world stand for nothing against the power of nature,' Alex said, his arms folded. 'God only knows what the weather will be out there. I can't think why she would set out so early in the year. I've sailed that sea in winter and I'll tell you, there are some storms I'm glad I'll never live through again. Elsie is a woman who understands the sea. It's simply beyond me why she didn't wait for better weather.'

They parted at the gates. Rob made his way to the little room he used for consultations, and spread the newspaper on his desk, eager to find out whatever he could. Journalists had been searching for Miss Mackay in Seamore Place, Glenapp Castle and at the P&O offices and had been unable to locate her, but no one had laid eyes on the mysterious Mr Sinclair either, so some doubt still remained about who was with Captain Hinchliffe in the plane. Mrs Hinchliffe denied all knowledge. One thing seemed certain, though: the pilots were not headed to India. A couple of sightings had been made over Ireland of a large monoplane flying low and fast, including one by the lighthouse keeper at Mizen Head on the south-west coast of Ireland. Another possible sighting had come from a steamship a further 170 miles out to sea. But that had been yesterday afternoon and many hours had elapsed since. Where was Elsie now?

He read about the excitement on the other side of the Atlantic, where crowds were scouring the skies for the arrival of the plane in Newfoundland, New York or Philadelphia. The weather in St John's was said to be fine and clear, with a light east wind – ideal conditions for the arrival of the flight, and hopefully indicative of the weather further out over the Atlantic. Beyond that all was speculation. There was nothing to do but wait, and he remembered Alison's advice. Better to keep busy.

He turned the pages of his newspaper with superficial interest. The sports reports briefly caught his attention. This Saturday would be the Calcutta Cup, the big annual rugby match between Scotland and England. Rob had played rugby for Scotland both before and after the war, and his dead brother-in-law Jack's sketch of the Calcutta Cup match in 1914 was his most precious possession, now framed and hanging in his little consulting room at home. He had played a few matches after the war, but newer, younger, fitter boys came along and he happily relinquished his place in the team for a seat in the stands. These lads bore no scars, and young Ian Smith in particular was a marvel. Scotland had enjoyed a period of unprecedented success, even achieving a first-ever Grand Slam. Saturday's match should be a close one.

But it was hard to care about rugby when Elsie was in the air.

He followed Alison's advice through the rest of the morning. At midday the hooter sounded and the men poured out through the yard gates, most of them returning home for their midday meal. It was too far for him to cross the town so Stella always packed him a sandwich. He ate his lunch quickly and decided to wander out for some fresh air. His path took him down between the huge sheds towards the quayside, and the looming shape of Hull 519. He knew that speculation would be particularly intense down here. Elsie was a familiar sight around the shipyard and with 'Miss Elsie's ship' the main focus of all their labours, each man felt he had a stake in the record attempt – or at least the right to an opinion about it. Rob leant on a fence and looked up. The ship was taking shape, and by late summer or early autumn she would be launched and move to Shieldhall Wharf to be fitted out according to Elsie's grand scheme.

He wondered if she would be here to see it.

'Grand, isn't she?'

He turned round. It was a couple of weeks since Danny had joined him for the walk to and from the ferry. 'Hello, Danny. How are you?'

'All right, thank you, sir. Dr Campbell, have you heard about Miss Mackay?'

'No more than was in the morning papers,' said Rob, feeling uncomfortable. For some reason he didn't want his connection with the Inchcapes to be widely known in the yard.

'Isn't it thrilling? I'm sure she'll make it. Auld Pete, he was at sea afore he moved to Glasgow, and he says it's bad luck to let a woman on a fishing boat, and just as bad luck on an aircraft.'

'I doubt auld Pete has ever been on an aircraft.'

'No, he hasnae, of course he hasnae. But it's what the men are saying. Rich folk have mair money than sense, and a rich wifie the worst of all. But I dinnae think that. I think she's like one o' they explorers, Sir Ernest Shackleton or Captain Scott, and every bit as brave.'

Rob began to rebuke him for repeating gossip, but the hooter sounded and Danny gave a gasp and sprinted off in the other direction. Rob glanced at his watch. He had a meeting with Fred Stephen shortly. As the tide of men swept back into the yard he looked up at Elsie's ship one more time.

Where are you now, Elsie? Where are you?

Chapter Thirty-Seven

Oxford

As Wednesday wore on even Corran became aware of the news and speculation about Elsie, but it barely penetrated the turmoil of her mind.

What on earth could she do?

She didn't regret leaving the pub without telling Arthur she was expecting their baby. He had allowed her no part in the choice he had made. For this next stage of her life, she needed him completely or not at all. It seemed it was to be not at all.

As far their relationship was concerned, she felt as if she had accidentally placed her hand on a hot stove. Soon it would hurt terribly, but right now the main feeling was one of shock. Somewhere deep down there was pain waiting for her at Arthur's rejection, but she had far more immediate concerns.

What on earth could she do?

She stood at her window looking down on the tranquil college garden and tried to gather her thoughts. She was going to have a baby. She was going to be a mother. In all these years she had never once imagined what that might be like. Even when Stella had her children. Even when Roland was born. From the outset of her relationship with Arthur she had been the one to take precautions, and she had been as meticulous about that as she was about anything else she undertook.

Until Hogmanay in Glenapp Castle.

Why had it never entered her mind? Was it something to do with the luxurious surroundings, the unreal, detached atmosphere of those few days? Or was it – and she could acknowledge to herself that this might be true – related to the sense of shock, and yes, anger, she had felt that evening as she held the photograph of Arthur looking down at his little boy with such love?

Somewhere deep down and subconscious, had she wanted this to happen? Not for Arthur, but for herself?

Well, it had happened, whatever the reason, and since the end of January multiple scenarios had played out in her mind about what to do next.

Until yesterday these had all involved Arthur.

She leant against the window and looked down. Despite the cold day there were people in the garden. There was her colleague Katherine walking between the budding blossom trees with a man. That was unexpected in itself. Katherine's academic gown was swinging behind her; perhaps she had come straight from teaching. After registering their presence, Corran turned away, her thoughts all for her own situation. She surveyed her little sitting room lined with bookshelves, and the door off to her even smaller bedroom with its narrow iron bedstead. This was all the world she had known since the end of the war. She could hopefully stay here until the summer holidays – she should be able to hide her pregnancy until then. But at that point she knew she would have to leave her employment and her rooms. Where could she go? Not to her mother and Stella – that was unthinkable. Thurso, perhaps? She could continue to earn some money through writing novels – but would her publisher accept the books of an unmarried mother?

At least she had savings. Life in university residence was very cheap. My goodness, she would have to learn to do for herself – and for a child! Her options were very few and yet they spun round and round her head until it hurt. She needed some fresh air. She was just lifting her coat down from its peg when there came a knock on the door.

'Katherine!'

'Ah, Corran. You have your coat on, I see. That's fortunate. I was about to ask if you would mind coming out to the garden with me? There is someone I would like you to meet.'

Perhaps if she were more in control of her thoughts, Corran would have paused at that point, asked who, asked why. Instead she followed Katherine out into the garden, where the snow had all but melted and spring was doing battle with the final vestiges of winter.

'This is my brother, Simon.'

The broad-shouldered man held out his hand. 'I'm pleased to meet you, Miss Rutherford. May we walk?'

Mystified, Corran glanced at Katherine. She had heard of this brother, whom Katherine regularly visited in London, but she didn't remember him ever coming to St Hilda's before. What was this – a matchmaking attempt? Surely not! Katherine smiled reassuringly. They walked three abreast beneath the emerging blossom, and Simon said gently, 'I believe you have something of a . . . situation. Perhaps I may offer a solution?'

'I'm not sure I understand.'

Katherine slipped an arm through Corran's. 'Simon works for the government, Corran. Intelligence.'

Intelligence? For one slow moment, her own intelligence not working well at all, Corran thought Katherine meant academia.

Then understanding broke through. 'Spies?'

'Most of it is far less thrilling than that – although I will admit that some of my work during the war could be classed as spying,' Katherine said.

Corran stopped and pulled her arm away, looking at her colleague in her dusty gown. '*You* were a spy during the war?'

'Intelligence,' Katherine repeated firmly. 'Simon doesn't have long, and has to return to London soon. Perhaps he should explain.'

'Please do.'

They had come to a halt at the end of the garden furthest from the buildings. No one else was in sight. 'Miss Rutherford, I believe you may soon be moving on from your position here in Oxford. I wonder if you would consider coming to work for me? We always need smart girls like you. I gather you have some Italian, which may in time become useful. I have a particular interest in Italy.'

Corran stared at him. This conversation was so unexpected that she vaguely feared she might find herself agreeing to something without the slightest idea what it was. 'Italy?'

'In essence, our country currently faces two significant threats. One is communism, the other fascism. I have a particular interest, as I have said, in Italy and the growth of fascism there and in our own land. Given your previous – ahem – sympathies with the more left-wing elements of politics, and your family's Italian connections, you could be a useful asset. Not to mention your own natural intelligence.' He glanced at his watch. 'Katherine is right, I have a train to catch. I suggest you think it over and give me a call in a day or two. We can arrange a meeting at my office in London and sort the details. In outline, we would settle you in a house where you would be known as an authoress – you would publish more of your charming detective stories – and in time we would be in touch with instructions. Your salary would be paid directly into your bank account. Confidentiality is, of course, paramount.'

There was something enormous that still hadn't been mentioned. 'I'm expecting a baby,' she said, and only realised as she spoke the words that this was the first time she had said it out loud.

Katherine drew closer with a tiny laugh. 'My dear, why on earth do you think I asked Simon to come and speak with you? It's the perfect cover. Although we've had our eye on you for quite some time – as well as on your politician friend. I believe he plans to leave the country so he shouldn't cause us any problems.'

Simon took his leave then, and Corran stared at Katherine, bewildered. 'Katherine, what's going on? How on earth do you know so much about me?'

Katherine smiled. 'Oh my dear, it's really very easy. Those postcards of yours in the pigeonholes for one thing. Not particularly discreet. And then we do share a bathroom, and our rooms are adjacent.' She shrugged. 'I've long known you are exactly the kind of woman we need, but as you will learn the successful use of intelligence is all about timing.' She patted Corran reassuringly on the arm. 'I'll leave you to have a think, shall I?'

Spying! Corran watched her go, unsure whether to laugh or be angry. It was deeply unsettling to know how closely she had been watched. She began to wonder if some of those times when she had sensed Arthur was under scrutiny it had actually – staggeringly – been her? It was outrageous – but she couldn't deny it was slightly flattering too. *I've long known you are exactly the kind of woman we need.*

More to the point, it was a solution – and a solution that came with a side serving of intrigue, which she could feel reeling her in, despite everything. An hour ago she had stood at her window in despair: now she was being offered a home, a job and the chance to continue her writing while bringing up her child. Awaiting instructions.

As for secrecy, it had become second nature over these last years.

Why on earth would she say no?

Chapter Thirty-Eight

Above the Atlantic Ocean

This black night seemed likely to last for all eternity.

Flying through endless darkness, there was no longer any reason to speak. For long hours, the only light came from the faint glow of the instrument panel and the carefully rationed use of the torch to scribble in the logbook, to locate their supplies or to guide Hinchliffe as he topped up the petrol tanks and pumped fuel through to the wing tanks. They flew through cloud, wind and rain, though nothing as fierce as that storm in the afternoon. They flew at a higher altitude than earlier, afraid of coming too close to the waves in that deep darkness. Occasionally the cloud cleared and they flew beneath a myriad of stars, the silvery moonlight reflecting on the water far below them.

But mostly they flew in smothering darkness, with the drone of the engine their constant backdrop. Although Elsie knew in her head that the hours were passing, and with each hour another eighty-mile segment of the journey was behind them, she had no sense of progress whatsoever. She and Hinch and *Endeavour* would be held in this roaring black night for all eternity. Nothing behind them, nothing ahead of them except darkness, and themselves a tiny speck within it.

She was cold. The heater was having little effect and the sunlit cockpit was a distant memory. She drank some more coffee; she zipped her suit up as far as it could go, wishing she had brought her fur coat; she hugged her arms around herself. It made no difference. She was so very cold.

They continued to take turns flying and she preferred the times when she was in control of the machine. It helped to have something to focus on: the altimeter, the drift indicator, the feel of connection as *Endeavour* responded to her touch. When Hinch was in control she was supposed to rest, but she found she could no longer sleep. *We close our eyes for sleep each night in blithe confidence that the world will still be there when we waken,* she thought. To close her eyes in this terrible darkness felt like surrender to the unknown.

Once, when she was at the controls and she thought Hinch was asleep he started awake with a terrible shout. She couldn't see him but she could feel him moving, struggling, just beside her. 'What am I going to do? I'm lost!'

She turned, reached out in the darkness, laid a hand on his trembling leg. 'It's fine. We're on course, we're safe.'

He didn't seem to feel or hear her. He was still thrashing about. 'Hendy, I'm lost! I've got this woman with me and I'm lost!'

She knew hallucinations and nightmares were a hazard of a trip of this nature. She raised her voice. 'Hinch, wake up! Wake up and drink some coffee. We're fine.'

He gave a grunt, and the movements stopped. He was still. 'Bit of a nightmare,' he said at last, his voice shaky.

She smiled in the darkness. 'You called out about having a woman with you. Am I such a burden?'

She could hear him unscrewing the flask, taking a drink. When he spoke he was still trying to control his breathing. 'I said a nightmare but it was clearer than that. So vivid. So real.'

'Tell me. It'll help.'

There was a silence so long that she thought he would refuse, but then he spoke.

'I was on a ship, somewhere out at sea. Somewhere warmer than this. I remember walking along the deck, seeing the life-ring, seeing the name SS *Barrabool*.'

Elsie's attention was fully caught. 'That's one of ours – a P&O ship. How funny!'

'I was looking for someone, searching in all the cabins. I didn't know who I was looking for until I opened one cabin door, and there was my RAF pal Hendy – Colonel Henderson – asleep in bed. I remember being filled with this awful sense of panic. I shook him awake and told him I was lost. God, he looked scared!' He screwed the lid back onto the flask. 'Is it a message? Are we lost, do you think?'

'No more than we were an hour ago. Or two. We'll find our position again with the dawn.'

He seemed to accept that. 'Time I took over,' he said. 'You have a rest. Sorry if I startled you.'

She relinquished control reluctantly. She knew she wouldn't sleep. Instead as they flew on she laced her fingers tightly together, tried to keep herself from shivering, and stared out into black nothingness.

Black.

Black.

Black.

Grey?

A change in the texture of the darkness, that was all it was at first. Almost imperceptible, and so ethereal that when she looked for it, it was no longer there. And so she said nothing. Then Hinch raised his hand and gestured north.

'Dawn.'

His voice was hoarse. It was the first word spoken in the cockpit for a long time, maybe for many hours. Time, which had been the obsessive heart of their pre-flight calculations, had come to mean nothing. But he was right. The weave of grey had become a glimmer of light, coming from behind them.

The most dreadful night of all nights was almost over.

They had made it through to the other side.

As light spread, Elsie watched in wonder. The cloud surrounding them was soon streaked with pink and gold, and the torpor that had gripped her dispersed. It was still bitterly cold – she could see her breath – but she felt a new sense of life and energy steal back into her body. 'Where do you think we are?'

Hinch was climbing. 'I don't know but we need to find out. Let's get higher and see what it's like up there. If we're lucky there will be a break in the cloud somewhere.'

Elsie wasn't sure what he was hoping for. By her calculations they must still be several hundred miles away from the Newfoundland coast – and that was if they had held to their course, which she was quite sure they had not managed to do. He took *Endeavour* up through the cloud, bumping about for a while, and then broke through into the brilliant light above. Now the clouds beneath them looked like vast mountain ranges and she drank in the beauty. Hinch had lifted the field glasses and was gazing intently. He passed them in her direction and gestured.

Elsie looked. Beyond the shimmering cloud, far in the distance – perhaps a hundred miles away – she could see a streak of dirty darkness.

'Thick mist!'

She stared at him, unable to understand the excitement in his voice. What was so good about yet another spell of flying through dense fog, unable to see?

'The Newfoundland coast is notorious for mist. I wonder. I just wonder.'

She looked down at her maps, but they were meaningless really. Could it be? Was this mist possibly the first indication that they were almost within distant sight of their goal?

Or was it just another bank of Atlantic sea fog waiting to swallow them?

They were flying higher than he liked, given the need to preserve fuel, and he began to bring her down through the cloud once more. Elsie was reluctant to descend and leave behind that tiny glimpse of hope, even if it might turn out to be illusory, but she knew he was right. She began to update their logbook with the time at which they had spotted the thick mist that just might mean land was coming close and they were on track.

And then the engine gave a huge shudder and died.

It was utterly shocking in its suddenness. Complete silence replaced the constant roar that had sounded in their ears for the past twenty-four hours. Elsie's tired brain took a moment or two to catch up with what had happened.

They were thousands of feet above the Atlantic Ocean, and they had no power. Their engine had stopped working.

Silence – silence – silence – and then a cough from the engine and it came to life once more. White-faced, she looked at him. 'What just happened?'

'I've no idea. An airlock perhaps. Anyway, we seem to be going again.' He gave a shaky laugh. 'Thought we'd had it for a moment back there.' He flew on, but something was clearly bothering him. 'She's not handling well at all. Can you feel that strain? She's pulling downwards far faster than before.'

Elsie looked out of the window, but there was nothing to be seen but white cloud. She could feel the strain that Hinch had mentioned and she thought she knew what it meant. 'Ice on the wings?'

'I think so.' He gave a grim shake of his head. 'We always knew this was a possibility. We hoped that by the time it occurred, we'd have lightened our load enough by burning off fuel that she could handle it. I think we're about to find out if that's true.'

They were descending gradually, and then it happened again. That same dreadful silence that filled her with a terror beyond anything she had felt so far. A longer gap this time before the engine spluttered back into life. Hinch shook his head. 'This has to be a fuel problem. Take over and I'll go through and check the connections.'

And so she was alone in the cockpit, in charge of a plane that no longer behaved as it should. She could feel the weight tugging them down, and the engine lost power twice more before struggling to life once again. Grey cloud was swirling all around her, and so when at first she saw the brilliant whiteness ahead, she thought it was more cloud.

But something looked different.

Ice! *Endeavour* was flying low over an absolutely enormous sheet of ice. No wonder they had felt so cold! Did this mean they really were much further north than they had planned to be? She turned to call to Hinch but he was back beside her, climbing into his seat. 'Everything is secure so far as I can see, but our wings are coated with ice.'

He took over the controls, and the engine continued to cut out intermittently. The silence lasted longer each time, until eventually it lasted for ever. This time the engine was dead.

'Are we out of fuel?'

Hinch concentrated on gliding downwards as gently as

possible. 'No. My best guess is that something has frozen in the fuel system, or some ice has become wedged there.'

'Then what can we do?'

He looked at her. 'Bring her down to land and hope for the best.'

'To land? But we must be many miles from land.'

He nodded. 'We're going down in the ocean, Elsie. I'm sorry.'

It was the sound he made afterwards – a kind of dry sob – that penetrated more deeply than his words. Until that moment she hadn't realised. She really hadn't realised. *Dear God, he thinks we're going to die.*

She took it in, but everything within her still protested. *While there's life there's hope.* They could land on the sheet of ice and rescuers would find them. Her father would send someone.

Her father had no idea where she was.

Beneath them as they glided silently downwards was no longer ice. It was black, black water, and it would be bitterly cold, and it was racing up to meet them now faster than she could think. There must be ships out here somewhere if they were getting closer to the coastline. They still had supplies and warm clothing. They could last for a day or two surely.

She knew they would be lucky to last a few minutes.

She thrust her hand in her pocket for her rosary but couldn't feel it. Instead her fingers wrapped around something hard. It was the *Spirit of St Louis* brooch that Stella had asked her to take across the Atlantic. Dear Stella.

We nearly made it.

'Going down *now*!' Hinch yelled with terrible urgency. The brooch dropped from her fingers to be lost on the floor of the cockpit somewhere. She heard the awful screech of metal as the undercarriage was sheared off by the force of the impact. The window beside her shattered, showering her with a hailstorm of fragments of glass. But she could still see, she could still breathe. They were on the surface of the water rather than under it.

And then freezing cold water began to flood into the cockpit.

She had known in her head, of course, that this might be the outcome, but none of her assurance had been bravado. She truly had believed deep, deep in the core of her being that they would succeed. From the bewildered glance that Hinch threw her way, she knew he had felt the same.

They had come so far, endured so much, flown for so many long hours, and in the end it had all unravelled too quickly. Just a few moments ago she had been awestruck and breathless in wonder at the beauty of the dawn, and filled with excitement at the sight of that dark mist that just might mean land was not so very far off. Now it was all over, and no one would ever know what had happened to them.

As panic threatened to overwhelm her, Elsie felt his hand fumble for hers in the darkness, and she seized it, knowing that was all that mattered. Not to be alone. She manoeuvred towards him and they wrapped their arms tightly around each other, cheek pressed to cheek. Clinging together. *Just hold me.* Was that his voice in her ear, or her own voice sounding in her head?

Through their padded layers of clothing she fancied their hearts could sense each other still pumping blood around their bodies, and were drawn together, still beating in defiance of what, now, was inevitable.

They held each other close, so close, as the freezing cold dark water flooded in and surrounded them. Numbing them. Claiming them.

Locked in the tightest embrace, they would not die alone.

PART FIVE
Shadows

September 1928 to February 1929

Let Glasgow flourish
Motto of the City of Glasgow

Chapter Thirty-Nine

Glasgow

'Ready?' Rob asked Stella.

She straightened up from her fruitless attempt to smooth down Duncan's unruly hair, and smiled. 'Ready.'

Each holding the hand of an excited boy, they stepped into the cool close. The faint sound of a baby crying came from behind the opposite door. Stella hesitated.

'Leave it. Juliet will be fine with Mrs Macleod for a few hours and you'll only upset her more if you go back in.'

'You're right.' They walked down the close and out into the street. It was one of those perfect autumn mornings that recall the rare glories of a Scottish summer. A cloudless blue sky and not a breath of wind. The ideal day for a ship launch.

They made their way down into the city centre, the boys skipping between them. They planned to catch a tram to Partick where they would meet up with Alex, Luisa and Giovanni and all cross the Clyde together for the great day of celebration, the launch of Hull 519.

Elsie's ship.

Stella had been undecided about coming almost until the last minute, but Rob was glad she was here. It was six months now since Elsie and Captain Hinchliffe had disappeared somewhere over the Atlantic Ocean. Six months since those days of hope, when Rob and Stella scanned the newspaper reports as eagerly as the crowds in St John's, Newfoundland and Philadelphia scanned the skies. But the hours ticked by and the crowds slipped away, and hope did too, as simple calculations made it clear there was no way *Endeavour* could still be in the air.

What happened to Elsie? It was the question that haunted them all. For a while they clung to the faint possibility of a miracle, and Emilie Hinchliffe in particular remained bravely defiant, declaring to the newspapers that her husband would return to her and their little girls. Perhaps they had come down at sea and been picked up by a ship with no radio. Perhaps they had landed in the wilds of Labrador, and were making their way back to human habitation, or even being cared for by the native community. It had happened before.

But as days slipped into weeks, no such miracle took place. Elsie and Captain Hinchliffe had simply vanished into the ocean, like so many others before them. Grief pervaded the Glasgow tenement flat and Rob watched Stella anxiously. Shock and loss carried with them echoes of older, deeper sorrow, and Stella had nearly drowned in the torrent of her brother Jack's death. What would this fresh tragedy do? But in those initial, fragile days, Stella clung to Rob and her children. Jack had been her anchor and losing him had set her soul adrift. This time she had something to hold on to.

One thing he knew tormented Stella beyond all else, and it was this that had caused her to waver over whether she could face the launch festivities. As they sat together swaying on the tram, each with a child on their knee, he looked at her profile and knew she was brooding yet again on her rejection of Elsie after Juliet's birth. She had sent that conciliatory letter along with the little brooch, but she had no way of knowing if Elsie had received it before setting off. Stella was tortured by the thought that Elsie had died believing her friend had spurned her – and the only person to blame for that was Rob. If only he had been honest with Stella on that New Year's morning at Glenapp. If only he had told Elsie that he had to share her secret with his wife, and they had both known about Elsie's plans, what a difference it would have made. It was too late now.

They dismounted the tram and made their way amid thickening crowds towards the ferry crossing point where they were to meet Alex, Luisa and Giovanni. Launch day on the Clyde was always a day of celebration, best clothes donned and festivity in the air. The boys had been beside themselves with excitement to hear that Uncle Alex had obtained tickets for the whole family at the quayside. Luisa and Giovanni would accompany them, while Alex would join the official party. 'God only knows how Lord Inchcape will be,' Alex said as they boarded the ferry, the adults clinging firmly to the little boys for fear of losing them over the side. 'It will be one of his first appearances in public since they came back from Egypt.'

The news had been kept from the Inchcapes for as long as possible, but eventually a telegram reached Elsie's horrified father. He hid the truth from his wife for a few more days while using all his influence to ensure everything possible was being done to find his daughter. No expense spared. But eventually the search and rescue effort had to be called off and there was nothing for the Inchcapes to do except begin their saddest journey back from Cairo. They retreated to Glenapp and had barely been seen since.

Bunting fluttered from the shipyard gates as they passed through among the crowds. Amid the press of people, Rob hoisted Duncan onto his shoulders and signalled to Giovanni to do the same with Jacky. The little boy chuckled as he wrapped his arms around his big cousin's head and Rob reflected how well Gio had settled in now that he was working at the café. He knew Giovanni believed his father was dead, although Luisa still clung to fragile hope. It was a year since he had slipped onto that ship in the warmth of a Mediterranean night; a year since Signor Rossi had walked down the gangway and been swallowed up by darkness. Nothing had been heard of him since. From the chatter among other Italian families who frequented the café – some supporters of Il Duce and others not – it was evident that most opponents of the regime had by now fled or been imprisoned.

At least Niccolo got Giovanni away when he did.

Alex peeled off to join the dignitaries at the red-brick head offices, and Rob led the rest of the family along the main path towards the quayside, nodding to this man or that whom he had encountered in his work here. Someone tapped him on the arm. 'Grand day, eh, Doc?'

It was Danny of course, looking out for him. He had tried to spruce up for the occasion, but nothing could hide the shabbiness of the oversized jacket he must have inherited from his father. Yes, and there was Geordie Aitken too, giving a brusque touch of his cap when Danny proudly pulled him near. Then Rob heard Stella give an exclamation at his side, and watched as she hurried over to the young woman standing a little way behind Danny. This must be Chrissie, Danny's sister, and the burly man at her side was surely her new husband. Rob noted that Chrissie was in the family way, and wondered whether she had ever taken up Stella's invitation to attend Mary Barbour's women's welfare clinic.

They moved on, and found themselves a good position with a view of the large, looming ship and the walkway and platform that would be used by the official party. It would be a long wait.

Stella had slipped back beside him and was standing gazing up at the ship. 'If only she were here to see this,' she said with a catch in her voice.

If only. So many if onlys. Six months might have passed, but barely a week went by without another story about Elsie and Captain Hinchliffe appearing in print.

Those who knew her well found it hard to recognise the manipulative flapper portrayed in the newspapers. Captain Hinchliffe was hailed as a hero, but Elsie was the rich young thing who had lured him to his death chasing fame and fortune and the dream of being the first female passenger to cross the Atlantic. Rob listened as Stella vented her rage at this portrayal of her friend. 'As if she needed either fame or fortune! Why is he the hero and she the irresponsible one? Because she's a woman, pure and simple. Do none of them realise she flew that aeroplane herself?' The tears in her eyes were caused by both fury and sorrow. 'It's bad enough that she's died but so much worse that they should dismiss her like this.'

Every time their wounds began to heal, some new story ripped them open. The records that Elsie had been chasing soon fell, at least proving she had been right to believe the flight was achievable. On 13th April, exactly a month after *Endeavour* had taken off from Cranwell, the German plane *Bremen* came down on tiny Greenly Island, a thousand miles off course, having nevertheless completed the first successful flight over the Atlantic from east to west. As the family in Glasgow read reports of the German achievement, there was no one to tell them that this was the crew Hinch had feared might overtake him, contributing to his decision to set off as soon as possible. Flight fever intensified, and in early June an American woman, Amelia Earhart, was celebrated as the first woman to cross the Atlantic by air, though strictly as a passenger and in the easier direction. 'I was as much use as a sack of potatoes,' she was rumoured to have said.

The most recent stories concerned Emilie Hinchliffe. *WIDOW LEFT DESTITUTE DESPITE MISS MACKAY'S FORTUNE!* screamed the newspapers. It seemed the insurance policy Elsie had arranged for Captain Hinchliffe had been declared invalid and not paid out. Her bank accounts were now frozen and in the hands of her trustee, Lord Inchcape. A desperate Emilie Hinchliffe, after receiving no reply to her letters to Elsie's father, turned to the press. There was an enormous outcry with questions asked in parliament. Meanwhile the Inchcapes remained silent, cloistered with their grief in Glenapp. Eventually in July the very public dispute was resolved. Lord Inchcape donated Elsie's entire substantial wealth to the nation for the purpose of paying off the national debt, reserving £10,000 for those who had suffered as a result of the crash. That £10,000 would of course go to Emilie and her little girls – the exact amount for which Elsie had insured the life of Captain Hinchliffe.

For Elsie's friends, it was all enormously distressing to read – and how much more so for her parents, Rob thought. But the one mercy during these months was that there was so much else going on to distract Stella. There was the wedding of Alison and Matthew for one thing, and all the work to get the house in Helensburgh ready for their return from the *Ranchi*, where Matthew's final voyage was currently doubling as their honeymoon. Even more significant than that was Corran's astounding news. As they waited in the dusty sunshine for today's ceremony to begin, he could hear Luisa and Stella discussing her.

'Any day now,' Stella said. 'She has a nurse living in with her in Pittenweem so she won't be alone. I wanted her to come to Glasgow to stay with me, or even to go to a nursing home in the city, but she wouldn't hear of it. I just wish it was over. Thirty-nine is old to have a first baby and there are lots of risks, Rob says.'

'Has she still not told Arthur?'

'She won't even discuss it.' Stella paused. 'Even now I find it hard to get my head round the idea that she and Arthur were in a relationship for *eight years* without any of us knowing. I visited her in Pittenweem and she really is happy, though. I couldn't understand why she'd chosen north-east Fife when we're all in Glasgow, but she pointed out that after living in England for nearly twenty years, it isn't so far. And she has always loved the sea. At least she didn't go back to Thurso! She has a lovely little house overlooking the shore and she has more or less finished writing her second book.'

'But how will she manage when the baby comes? Her head is full of nothing but books.'

Rob joined in the conversation. 'I imagine she will manage just fine. That tends to be Corran's way, after all, whatever she takes on.'

Luisa shook her head. 'A baby should have a father. What will people think?'

'I asked her that at the beginning, and she told me she is thirty-nine not nineteen, and the last thing she cares about is what people think,' said Stella. 'Good luck to her, I say.'

There was a flurry of activity to their left. Rob and Giovanni hoisted the boys back up on their shoulders so that they could watch as the official party approached between two lines of tape onto the platform beside the huge ship. At the front walked Fred Stephen in his bowler hat, escorting an elegant woman dressed in flowing grey jacket and dress with a striking patterned sash and scarf. Rob knew that this was Lady Dorothy Irwin, wife of the Viceroy of India. Behind them walked a man, shoulders hunched and leaning on a walking stick. It was only as he drew level with them that Rob realised this old, weary-looking man was Lord Inchcape. He hadn't seen him since Hogmanay, and as he looked at his haggard face he saw just how much the loss of his daughter had stripped from him.

Now he was here to witness the launch of her ship.

Behind these three came a stream of other officials, some with their wives. The atmosphere was light-hearted as they looked up at the ship, pointing things out to one another. He saw Alex deep in conversation with someone he didn't recognise. Mr Stephen stepped forward and made a short speech, thanking Lord Inchcape for his vision in commissioning this, the first all-electric turbo ship in Europe and the largest vessel they had ever built at Linthouse. 'Clyde-built: the greatest mark of quality there is, and in demand the world over.' He spoke about the ship's high-pressure steam and turbo-electric propulsion and the difference this would make to speed, efficiency and comfort. Now she would go to Shieldhall Wharf for fitting out, and he was quite sure the splendid plans for single-berth first-class state rooms, not to mention the exceptional luxury of the public rooms and of course the legendary swimming pool, would create the most comfortable passenger ship of her size afloat. He cleared his throat. 'The interior, of course, will pay tribute to the marvellous skill and eye for detail of the Honourable Miss Elsie Mackay, who is so sadly missed.'

Rob looked at Lord Inchcape. His left hand, which held his cigar, was trembling, but other than that he remained still, his expression unchanged. Then Lady Irwin stepped forward, and Rob wondered if she guessed she was only here because Elsie lay somewhere at the bottom of the Atlantic Ocean. Lady Irwin smiled brightly and pulled on the lever. The rope swung, smashing the traditional bottle of champagne against the steel. 'I name this ship *Viceroy of India*!'

'They dropped the name *Taj Mahal* for fear it would cause offence in India,' Rob murmured to Stella as cheers and applause rang round the yard, and bunnets and bowler hats waved in the air. Then there came the creaking and clanking of the chains and blocks shifting, leading to the slow, almost imperceptible movement of the ship. She picked up speed and there was a collective intake of breath as she slid down the slipway and into the brown waters of the Clyde for the first time, sending foam and planks of wood tossing around in her wake. Here the tugs would manoeuvre her to the fitting-out dock for the next stage in her construction, and many of the men who lined her deck waving were those who would carry out that interior work. She swayed as she entered the water, turning with remarkable speed for such an enormous beast. Rob knew there was always trepidation among shipyard workers during this final part of the launch. More than forty years ago the *Daphne* had been launched from this same yard and had capsized, taking the lives of over a hundred men in one of Glasgow's most dreadful disasters. But the *Viceroy* had launched successfully, and the atmosphere was jubilant. Most of the workers would now head to the local pubs for a celebratory pint or two, while the official party retired for a formal luncheon and more speeches in the boardroom.

Stella clutched his arm. 'Rob, I think Alex is bringing Lord Inchcape this way.'

He looked round. She was right. Quickly he swung Duncan down onto the ground and straightened up. The crowd fell back as the chairman of P&O approached their little family. 'You remember my sister, sir,' Alex was saying.

'Of course I do.' Close up his face was even more ravaged, the lines deeper, the bleakness in his eyes more evident. He held out a trembling hand and Stella shook it. 'How is the baby who was born in our car?' he asked.

'She's very well, thank you, sir,' Stella said, blushing. 'I didn't bring her today because of the crowds, but the boys are here.

They were excited to watch the launch.' She pushed Duncan and Jacky to the fore, but Lord Inchcape barely looked at them.

'Elsie was very proud of this ship.'

Rob heard the unevenness in Stella's reply. 'She was. She talked about her designs often. I know she would have been delighted with today.'

'Pity she'll never see it completed. Pity . . .' His gaze moved from Stella to Rob, and his brows drew together. 'I believe you were party to her misguided plans? Eh?'

Rob felt a prickle of fear. This man was not someone he wanted as an enemy. He took his time, and was glad his voice was steady when he spoke. 'She consulted me on the medical aspects of such a flight, yes, but I was completely in the dark over when it was to take place, or indeed if it would take place at all.'

His gaze was ice cold. 'As a doctor your responsibility was to stop her doing something so dangerous by any means possible.'

'With respect, sir, it wasn't in my power to stop her.'

'Then you should have told me. It would have been within *my* power.'

'Sir, Miss Mackay was an adult. I have a duty of patient confidentiality. But I am most terribly sorry – we all are – that her brave attempt ended the way it did. She was a dear friend.'

'A friend who is dead because of *your* silence.'

He opened his mouth to argue further then thought better of it. Lord Inchcape glared at him for a moment, and then all at once the fight seemed to leak out of him and his shoulders drooped. He turned back to Stella. 'I know you cared for her, Mrs Campbell,' he said. 'Do all you can to protect her memory, won't you? That dreadful woman is about to start spreading some terrible lies.' Then he turned and shuffled away, leaning on his cane. Alex threw them an apologetic glance and followed on.

'Why was the man angry, Daddy?'

Rob let out a long slow breath. 'He's not really angry, Duncan, he's sad.'

'What does he mean?' Stella asked. 'What woman, and what lies?'

'I've no idea.' He gave a shaky laugh and pulled out his hipflask, taking a long drink. 'I thought I was for it there. Not sure I've been publicly told off like that since I was in school! He's still a formidable old battler, isn't he? No wonder Elsie tried so hard to keep her plans from him.'

The crowds were ebbing away now and they joined the flow back along the road towards the gates where they found Alex waiting. 'Thought you had to join the luncheon party?' Rob asked.

'I managed to get out of it,' Alex said, kissing his wife. 'Can't say I'm sorry; the atmosphere isn't exactly the best.' Then he moved to walk beside Rob. 'Sorry about that. Lord Inchcape asked me to take him to you and Stella; I had no idea he was coming in for the kill. I wonder who told him you knew?'

'I imagine he's made it his business to find out everything about her flight, although it's too late now,' Rob said. 'Poor fellow – you can see what it's taken out of him. He's a shadow of the man he was at New Year.'

They walked along side by side, dropping back behind the women and children. 'It's a relief to see the *Viceroy of India* launched safely,' Alex said. 'Now that the fit-out is underway we can plan for sea trials, hopefully by February.'

Rob nodded. 'I was thinking about Jimmy Blake.'

'Blake? I'm sure I saw him there with some of the other lads.'

'Not wee Jimmy – his father, also Jimmy Blake. You remember – the man who fell to his death inside the hull. I tried to save him.'

Alex looked uncomfortable. 'Ah yes, of course. The company will have provided for his widow.'

'That's hardly the point, is it? Lord Inchcape is eaten up by Elsie's death, but what about those who are scarred or maimed or killed building ships for his empire? What do we hear about them?'

'You've introduced changes.'

'I have, but it scarcely scratches the surface.' He sighed. 'Sorry, Alex. I think today has unsettled me more than I realised. I could do with a drink.'

'It's been that sort of day.' Alex paused. 'I have some pretty big worries of my own today, if I'm honest.'

'Go on.'

'You heard Stephen – "Clyde-built, in demand the world over." That's a lie, unfortunately. It's the greatest irony of launch day – the men come out and celebrate because the work is complete and the ship is launched. But the *Viceroy* has provided a huge amount of work to the yard over the last year, and it's nearly over. The order books are looking pretty thin.'

'Really? Is it something to worry about?'

'I'd say so. We have a couple of smaller orders and believe it or not Lord Inchcape has decided to commission a new yacht to be built here at Stephen's. He might be growing old but he understands the picture perfectly and realises the yard is in trouble. He can't justify another liner so soon after the *Viceroy*, especially with the downturn in shipping, so he's investing some of his personal wealth in a luxury yacht. The rumour is he wants the figurehead to be carved in Elsie's likeness.'

'That must be the project young Danny mentioned. He didn't know the details, but he was overjoyed to tell me he'll be working as an apprentice draughtsman on a brand-new yacht.'

'Good for Danny,' Alex said as they boarded the ferry. 'It will provide work for a while, but it won't last for ever.' He gestured along the river at the docks and the yards on either side. 'Look.

319

One, maybe two ships under construction in most of these. A year or two ago there would have been twice as many. There's still work, but for how long? Hard times are coming for the River Clyde; for the men who wok here and their families too.'

The little boys were worn out by the time they arrived back home, and Stella not much less so. 'You sit down and I'll get Juliet,' Rob said. He knocked on the door across the close. Young Mrs Macleod appeared bearing Juliet in her arms. 'Good as gold,' she said in her soft Hebridean voice, handing her over. 'But wait you there, please, Dr Campbell. I've a telegram for Mrs Campbell.'

'A telegram?' he repeated, hoisting his little daughter up to his shoulder.

'Aye. A laddie brought it to my door this afternoon when you were out. Here you are.'

Rob hurried back across the close and into the kitchen. 'Telegram!'

'Corran?'

'Surely.' He handed her the envelope and she slit it open, pulling out the thin piece of paper. She read it quickly then lifted her head, her eyes shining.

'It's here! It's a boy! Take a look. MAX BORN SAT MORN. ALL WELL.' She called to the boys. 'Duncan, Jacky, you have a baby cousin!' She turned back to Rob and he put his arms around her as she leant into him. 'This has been such a hard day,' she said. 'I still can hardly believe Elsie is gone, but how good to return to this wonderful news. New life, and all seems well. Thank goodness it's over.'

Chapter Forty

Glasgow

'Do all you can to protect her memory, won't you? That dreadful woman is about to start spreading some terrible lies.'

It wasn't long before Stella thought she understood what Lord Inchcape had meant. Within a few weeks the papers were full of the sensational news that Emilie Hinchliffe, widow of the lost pilot, had told a packed hall in London about messages she had received from her husband beyond the grave. Stella looked up at Rob. 'Have you seen this?'

'Unscientific poppycock,' Rob said, going to the sink to wash his hands. 'Tricksters preying on people in their deepest grief.'

'I'm not so sure, Rob,' Stella said, pouring him a cup of tea. 'It says here that the medium knew all sorts of things only Captain Hinchliffe and his wife could possibly have known. And the details of the flight sound plausible. It says they hit a storm so he flew south but the plane had been damaged by the wind and they came down near the Azores. That could make sense.'

Rob sat down beside her and picked up his cup. 'It's no coincidence that spiritualism and séances have taken off since the war. Much of it is unscrupulous people preying on the grief of all the poor mothers and wives and sisters who long to know what happened to their boys. It should be made illegal. No wonder Lord Inchcape was furious when we saw him. As if he hasn't been through enough without seeing these stories all over the newspapers.'

'But what if it's true?'

Rob pushed the newspaper away. 'I know you long to know what happened to Elsie, Stella. We all do. But this is not the way, trust me. I feel sorry for Mrs Hinchliffe. Some fraudster has clearly got hold of her and convinced her. Think about it. So many details of the Hinchliffes' lives have been spread across the newspapers, how hard would it be to uncover something additional that would sound convincing? All one would need to do would be to speak to a neighbour or a workman who has been in their house. The poor woman is grief-stricken. She *wants* to believe her husband is communicating with her from beyond the grave.' He stood up. 'Anyway, I've a patient to see at eleven. Must get on.'

Stella watched him go. She too had a busy day ahead, but all the time she found the story of Emilie Hinchliffe's lecture chasing round her head. Maybe Rob was right and it was all trickery – but how could he be so sure? As she walked along the street, Jacky hanging on to the pram as usual, she thought of the widow left alone with two little girls and her grief.

Stella knew all about grief. After Jack had died, some friends who had also lost brothers and sweethearts had tried to persuade her to join one of the séances that, as Rob had said, became so popular during and after the war. She had refused, not because she didn't long to communicate with her brother again but because she was afraid that the Jack who might appear to her would be the broken, tortured soul he had become by their last meeting.

Besides, she had visited his grave in France. She knew where he lay.

Emilie Hinchliffe and the Inchcapes had no such solace.

She cut the article carefully from the newspaper. She had begun to make a scrapbook of stories about the flight of Elsie and Captain Hinchliffe. Only Duncan was likely to remember her, but as they grew older the children should know just what a remarkable woman Elsie Mackay had been.

Events soon put Emilie Hinchliffe's supernatural communications out of Stella's head, at least for a while. On a grey late November day, Luisa arrived breathless at her door. Stella ushered her into the kitchen and poured her a glass of water. Her sister-in-law thrust a letter into her hands. 'Papa!'

Stella pulled out the thin blue sheet of paper with a sense of foreboding. They had dreaded this day for so long and now it had arrived. Pray God he hadn't suffered too much, or Luisa and Giovanni would never know peace.

The writing was in Italian. 'Is there news of him? What does it say?'

Luisa took a drink and steadied her breathing. When she looked up at Stella, her eyes were shining, and Stella felt the first tentative tremor of excitement. 'The letter is *from* him,' her sister-in-law finally managed to say. 'He lives.' Then she started to cry.

By evening they were all gathered in Alex and Luisa's house, even the little children. Alison and Matthew had come into the city from Helensburgh. Such a sense of celebration! Luisa had spent the afternoon in the kitchen, pouring all her relief into food, and an array of delicacies greeted them. The tattered sheet of paper was handed round as proof that the miracle had really taken place, even though Giovanni was the only other person who could understand it.

'Read it aloud, Gio,' Alex urged him. 'In English!'

The boy took the letter in his hand. He swallowed. "'*My beloved children. I pray you are safe. I write to you from London, England. I have many trials in the last year but I am well. I will tell more when I see you. I receive help from good people. I long now to come to you in Glasgow. I have no papers. Perhaps Miss Mackay will help me as she helped Giovanni? Write to me. Your loving Papa.*'"

Giovanni dashed a hand across his eyes. He had grown taller and filled out in the past year, and it was easy to forget he was still just a lad of sixteen.

'He doesn't know about Elsie,' Stella said.

'No, and he is cautious,' said Alex, taking the letter from Gio and clapping him on the shoulder. 'He doesn't tell us where he is staying, just gives a PO box number. His situation is precarious because he has entered the country illegally.'

'But he has fled for his life!' protested Luisa. 'Do you think Lord Inchcape may help?'

There was silence as those who had been present remembered the frail peer at the launch of the *Viceroy*, lurching unpredictably between fury and sorrow. 'Let me see what I can do,' Matthew said eventually. 'I have met Signor Rossi, and I can vouch for him and for the danger he faced. If I need to approach Lord Inchcape I shall do so, but I'll make enquiries first.' He turned to Alison, sitting beside him. 'Shall we take a trip to London, my dear?'

Chapter Forty-One

London

Luisa wrote to her father care of his PO box while Matthew requested a meeting at the Home Office, and a few days later Alison and he took the train south. Luisa and Giovanni had wanted to come too, but eventually agreed it would be better to wait until Matthew had spoken to the authorities. They checked into a small hotel in Piccadilly where Matthew often stayed and was well known. The next day he set off for Whitehall, prepared to wait for as long as it took. They agreed that Alison should stay at the hotel, just in case Niccolo Rossi called round in response to Luisa's letter telling him where they would be. She would rather have spent the day exploring London, but it would be foolish to come all this way and then miss him. Instead she took up a comfortable position in the hotel lounge with a cup of coffee, a cigarette and the latest Dorothy L. Sayers novel. Was it just maternal bias that made her compare it unfavourably with Corran's book? She knew Corran was well on with the sequel, although the arrival of baby Max had rather interrupted her schedule. Alison had gone to stay with Corran for a few weeks after the birth, full of trepidation at how her scholarly daughter would cope with the demands of parenthood, but Corran had rarely seemed happier. She had a local girl in to help her for a couple of hours three days a week, and was managing for herself otherwise. 'The house may not be particularly tidy, but Max and I will get along just fine together. I have my son and I have my writing. It's everything I need.'

Alison returned her attention to the doings of Lord Peter Wimsey for a while, and was unaware of the maid's entry to the room. 'Mrs Kennedy.'

She read on.

'Excuse me, ma'am, Mrs Kennedy?'

With a start, Alison realised that the maid was addressing her. How strange it was to take another name. She had been Mrs Rutherford for more than forty years; it was little wonder she sometimes failed to respond to her new title. She looked up with a smile. 'I'm sorry, I was lost in my book.'

'Mrs Kennedy, there's a strange-looking foreign person here asking for you. I didn't think Captain Kennedy would want him bothering you when you are alone so I told him to come back later but he won't leave.'

Alison dropped her book onto the table and got to her feet. 'Please don't ever send my guests away without consulting me first! Where is he?'

The maid still seemed doubtful. 'He's in the lobby, ma'am, but I'm really not sure Captain Kennedy . . .'

But Alison was gone. She strode through the lounge and into the reception area, where she found a porter remonstrating near the doorway with a tall thin man who had long, greying straggly hair and was dressed in a shabby greatcoat, which had been soaked in a downpour. 'Signor Rossi!' Alison said in a loud voice.

Her stomach lurched as he turned towards her, at once so familiar and so strange.

Alison addressed the curious hotel staff. 'Signor Rossi is a friend of Captain Kennedy and myself and should be welcomed as such.' She moved towards the lounge, but an elderly couple had appeared in the doorway and were watching the whole scene with unashamed interest. She swung back round to the maid who had first approached her. 'Is there somewhere quieter we can sit?'

'The cocktail bar is empty at this hour, ma'am.'

'That's where we'll go. Please bring us coffee and biscuits.'

The cocktail lounge was gloomy with no fire, and they sat down on either side of a table by the window. Rain streamed down the glass. Alison looked at him, remembering the elegant, cultured man who had welcomed her into his beautiful apartment overlooking the Bay of Naples little more than a year ago. She knew, of course, that he had been through an ordeal, but every day of that ordeal was etched on his gaunt, lined face. He refused to remove his coat – *your London air is damp and cold* – and his shoes were barely holding together, though she didn't think this alone accounted for the limp with which he now walked. But the dark eyes that met hers were as beautiful as they had ever been.

'Mrs Kennedy – that is now your name, yes? – I cannot thank you enough for coming to London to meet me.'

He spoke so quietly she could hardly hear him and she too lowered her voice although there was no one else in the room. 'Please, call me Alison. We were overjoyed to receive your letter, Luisa and Giovanni especially. They are anxious to see you.'

He sat very still, but a tremor ran through him as she spoke the names of his children. His lips were tightly pressed together.

'My husband, Matthew, has gone to the Home Office to plead your case. I'm sure there will be no difficulty. Our country welcomes those who flee from persecution.' As she spoke the words she wondered if they were true.

'I am grateful.' His fingers began to tap a rhythm on the dark varnished wood of the table. 'My Luisa – Giovanni – how are they?'

'They are well. Luisa never gave up hope. She prayed for you every single day. Giovanni has settled well in Glasgow. He works in a café that is run by an Italian family, and he is happy.'

'Every day that I was hiding, every day that I struggled on through the mountains, every day that I lay sick, I gave thanks to God that Captain Kennedy helped Giovanni escape when he did. Now you have come to our rescue again. How can I ever thank you?'

She felt a sharp chill, as his words edged open the door to his experiences a tiny crack, letting in a quick blast of that mountain air. What had he endured? 'Coming home to Luisa and Giovanni will be thanks enough. You are part of our family.' She hesitated. 'Where are you staying?'

'If you forgive me, I will not say. I may put others in danger.' He turned away to cough, a deep hacking sound that shook his whole thin body.

'But you need a legal address if you are to remain here. This hotel is quiet – why don't I enquire about a room?'

Niccolo spread out his hands. 'I have no money.'

'We'll pay, of course. You are Luisa's father. And clothes – you must need clothes? Matthew can help you with that. And a haircut.'

'It is too much.'

'It's nothing at all! Not after all you have been through.'

He broke into another fit of coughing, but once it had eased he nodded. 'I am blessed – so very blessed – to have friends like you.' He stared into the distance, and she noticed that the beating of his fingers had begun once again. 'This evil is spreading, and in truth, it is only those with friends or with money who have any hope of escaping. Any hope at all.'

* * *

Matthew returned later that afternoon with an appointment secured for the following day, and Alison had her wish of a day to explore London. She went to the British Museum, but found it hard to concentrate, wondering all the time how they were getting on. How terrible it would be if, after all he had been through, Niccolo Rossi was not welcome. Not so long ago there had been very few restrictions on people from other countries coming to live in Britain, but in the early years of this century a disturbing new sense of hostility particularly towards Jewish settlers from the Baltic had led to the passing of the Alien Act. Additional security measures introduced during the war years had only added to suspicion of incomers, while many of those from across the Empire who had answered the call to fight for the Mother Country found themselves unwanted within her borders once peace was declared. The newspapers seized on and stoked local tensions, and notions of citizenship and right to live and work were mired in layers of paperwork and documentation. It was this documentation that Lord Inchcape had so blithely secured for young Giovanni, and which Niccolo would need if he were to be permitted to stay.

With a retired P&O captain as his guarantor, and a tale of persecution at the hands of Mussolini's fascists, he had a better case than many, but still Matthew returned to the hotel alone, his expression grim. 'Where is he?' Alison demanded.

'Prison.'

'*Prison?* Matthew, no!'

Matthew took her hand. 'It's all right, my dear, or at least it will be. They have agreed he may remain as an alien, but because he entered the country illegally and has no papers, they insist that he cannot be at liberty until everything is in order. I argued that he will be with us, but it made no difference. In the end it was better to accept rather than to annoy them further and risk his application being rejected outright.'

Alison had tears in her eyes. 'But prison! After everything he's been through. How can I possibly tell Luisa and Gio?'

'At the moment there's no need to tell them anything. I'm hopeful it will just be a few days.'

In the end it was a full two weeks before Niccolo was permitted to travel north to Glasgow with Matthew and Alison as escorts, his certificate of registration as an alien tucked carefully in the inside pocket of his crisp new suit. He brushed off his short stay in prison as just another in the long series of unpleasant experiences that had overtaken him in these last years. 'But now I am free, and I can see my children again.'

The emotional reunion with Luisa and Giovanni took place in full view of interested spectators on the platform, but they quickly made their way to Luisa and Alex's home where a feast of magnificent proportions awaited. Matthew had undertaken to the authorities that Niccolo would reside with him, which Luisa reluctantly accepted, and they planned to continue on to Helensburgh later. Meantime there was much to celebrate and there was, at last, Niccolo's story to hear, interrupted intermittently by that deep, bone-shuddering cough that made Alison shiver every time she heard it.

'After Giovanni left, I knew I had very little time. Perhaps I should have fled that evening, but there were people I needed to warn, important papers to pass on and others to destroy. That took me two or three days, and then it was too late. They arrived at the apartment and turned it upside down, but at least there was nothing to be found. I thought they would arrest me then, but those thugs had just been sent to seize my papers. They took their anger out on me and left.'

Luisa was sitting beside him gripping his hand tightly, her eyes very bright. Giovanni shifted uncomfortably. 'It's my fault, then.'

Niccolo reached out towards his son and the gentleness in his expression brought tears to Alison's eyes. 'It was never your fault, *caro mio*. If it was anyone's fault it was mine, for not getting you out much sooner than I did. Thank God you were gone before they came for me. They did not hurt me badly that night, but I knew they would be back. I had to leave that very evening or be sent indefinitely to the penal colony on Ustica. Or worse.'

'How did you get away?' Alex asked.

'There is a network that has existed for some years to smuggle people across the mountains into France or Switzerland. I had been part of it. Now I needed to make use of it.'

He made it sound so simple. 'Why didn't you contact us sooner?' asked Luisa.

'I left early in October. Travelling through the mountain passes in winter is not good but I had no choice. After many weeks of walking, sometimes with a guide, sometimes alone, I fell and broke my leg. I was alone, and I lay many hours. That day I should have died. I thought my body would be taken by the animals, and no one would ever know what had happened to me. But God had mercy. He heard your prayers, Luisa. When I did not arrive at the expected time, one of our people came to find me. I spent months in a mountain hut under the care of a local woman. I was very unwell: I don't remember much of that time. I had to wait until the mountain snows melted in the spring, and then my friends came back for me. After that we had the long, long trek to France. I could not travel far each day before I became exhausted, so it took many months. Eventually we reached Paris, where there is a community of free-thinking Italian exiles. They took me in, and once I was strong enough to travel they provided me with false documents, which I used to get myself to England. Only then was it safe to contact you.'

For a while no one spoke. Niccolo was drained by his travels and his story, and Luisa was weeping. 'We'll get Rob to check you over,' Alison said eventually.

'Thank you. My leg aches at times and this cough does not leave me. But I am here, I am alive and I am safe.'

'Now you must rest and recover,' Luisa said, squeezing his hand.

He smiled at his daughter. 'Yes. And, although it hurts me to leave you, I would like soon to sleep.'

'Stay here tonight, Papa,' Luisa pleaded. 'I can escort you to Matthew and Alison's house tomorrow.'

'You can have my bed,' Gio said.

Niccolo looked at Matthew. 'Do you think that would be permissible? I do so need to sleep, I confess I should find it hard to travel further this evening. And to sleep under the same roof as my children is something I have long dreamt to do.'

With a glance at each other, Matthew and Alison both stood up. 'Of course it's permissible!' he said brusquely. 'We shall see you tomorrow with Luisa. Rest well.'

Chapter Forty-Two

Glasgow

Stella hesitated outside the small hotel and watched as a few women dressed in fur coats climbed the steps from the pavement to the front door. Two months had passed since she first read of Emilie Hinchliffe's supernatural experiences. Now the aviator's widow was here in Glasgow, giving a talk to the local spiritualist society. Should she go in or should she leave well alone?

The past few weeks had only increased her longing to discover more of what had happened to Elsie. In December the first piece of real, tangible evidence surfaced when part of the undercarriage of a plane washed up in County Donegal. The authorities confirmed it came from *Endeavour*. 'It doesn't tell us much,' Alex said. 'Currents are very complex, and it's been in the water for nine months. But what it does prove is that they came down in the sea. We know they didn't crash-land in Labrador and perish there, for example.'

The family gathered in Helensburgh to welcome in 1929, but as they celebrated little Juliet's first birthday on New Year's Day, the shadows of that extraordinary Hogmanay at Glenapp the previous year lingered over them. Stella remembered how Elsie had urged them to stand in a circle and share their hopes for 1928. She looked round her family and wondered if Rob was thinking back on his secret conversations with Elsie, or if Corran was remembering the last weekend she had spent with Arthur, during which baby Max had been conceived. For herself, it was hard not to relive the bewilderment and fear of that nightmare drive through the storm, and her deliberate rejection of Elsie. All this was fresh in her mind when the advert appeared a few days later for the Glasgow date of Emilie Hinchliffe's lecture tour. Rob was disapproving and Stella herself was unsure, but Elsie's last moments still haunted her, as did the question of whether her letter and the brooch had arrived in time. Did Elsie know how sorry she was? 'I've decided to go,' she said to Rob eventually. 'Don't worry, I'm not getting my hopes up, but this woman's husband was with Elsie when she died. I have to hear what she has to say. Mrs Macleod has agreed to look after the children and I'll only be gone a couple of hours.'

Stella took a deep breath and climbed the steps. She was ushered into a dimly lit room and took a seat near the back. The audience was almost entirely made up of women, with just a few men dotted here and there. Stella listened to two women beside her discussing a séance they had recently attended. She shifted uncomfortably in her seat. Had it been a mistake to come?

Soon Emilie Hinchliffe got to her feet at the front of the room and the chatter and hubbub died away. Stella leant forward, fingers tightly interwoven. The woman was tall and soberly dressed, with long dark hair pulled back at either side from a centre parting. In an understated voice, her fluent English accented by her native Dutch tongue, she proceeded to tell her tale. Stella listened intently, but soon sat back. There was nothing new here: this was the same story she had already read in the newspapers. Emilie spoke of messages received beyond the grave from her husband telling of storm damage to his plane, an attempt to fly south to the safety of the Azores, and his eventual drowning as he tried to swim for safety.

As for Elsie, she was not mentioned once. She might not have been part of the flight.

Her flight.

Mrs Hinchliffe finished her narrative and invited questions. Annoyed with herself for having thought it was a good idea to come, Stella stood up to slip out of the room. As she laid a hand on the doorknob, a voice from the front asked, 'What about Miss Mackay? What happened to her?'

Mrs Hincliffe cleared her throat. 'I have no information whatsoever relating to my husband's companion.'

Behind Stella, a woman gave a snort. 'That's because Lord Inchcape's lawyers have got onto her, told her they'll sue if she so much as mentions her name.'

Suddenly desperate to be gone, Stella slipped out of the room and hurried through the hallway onto the top step leading down to the pavement. She stopped and gulped the fresh afternoon air gratefully. What a strange, sad, suffocating experience! She thought about the comment she had heard at the end from the audience member and found she was glad. Elsie's broken-hearted parents – Lord Inchcape, bent and haggard at the ship launch, and Lady Inchcape, who had been so kind when Juliet was born – deserved to be left to grieve in peace.

On the street outside she paused. She ought to hurry straight back home to collect the children from Mrs Macleod, but she needed to clear her head. The hotel was close to the river, so she walked down and onto the bridge that led across to the south side. She stood, her arms leaning on the stone balustrade, as traffic passed behind her, barely noticing the keen wind that wrapped itself around her. A barge emerged from beneath the bridge, laden with goods, heading downstream towards the great shipyards. It would soon reach Shieldhall Wharf, where Elsie's ship the *Viceroy of India* was being fitted out for its luxurious travels. Stella breathed deeply, trying to order the turmoil of her thoughts as she looked down at the barge slipping through the Clyde in the direction of the open sea. Was Elsie right that goods would soon be transported by plane, and people would jump on an international flight, completing their journey in a matter of hours rather than days? Would regular air travel transform this world for her children, drawing nations closer, improving relations and even ending war?

Or did Elsie's death prove that it was an unachievable dream?

She began to walk slowly in the direction of home. Did Emilie Hinchliffe really believe that her husband was communicating with her from beyond the grave? Stella rather thought she did. As for her account of the last moments of the flight, they might be true or they might not, but they brought no certainty or peace. It was a relief to know that Elsie's name would not be tainted by inclusion in Mrs Hinchliffe's grief-driven lecture tour.

No, as she turned in to their own street, Stella realised she was back in the place she had been before, with just a few sparse facts for company. She knew when Elsie had taken off, she knew when *Endeavour* was last sighted, and she knew about the piece of undercarriage washed up on the shore.

If only she could be sure that Elsie knew how much Stella loved her.

She entered the close and decided to pop into their own house first to use the bathroom before knocking on Mrs Macleod's door. She opened the door. A letter lay on the mat. Stooping to pick it up, Stella felt as though a trickle of icy water was sliding down her back. Heart thudding, she lifted the creamy envelope with that familiar coat of arms embossed on the rear.

Elsie?

She stood for a moment in the dimly lit hall, just holding the letter, terrified to move, terrified to open it. Then the sound of a child's cry from across the hallway pierced her numbness. She must do this while she was alone. She hurried through to the kitchen, opened the envelope and pulled out the contents.

Two pieces of paper. One she immediately recognised as the final letter she had scribbled to Elsie here at this table, and with it a short note signed by dear Lady Inchcape.

This was returned to us among Elsie's possessions from the hotel in Grantham. I thought you might like to have it back.

Stella pulled the envelope as wide as it would go, shaking it upside down although it was clearly fruitless.

Nothing. No brooch.

She sat down heavily, her mind racing. Here at last was proof that Elsie had received her final letter and the brooch. What's more, the brooch had not been returned so Elsie had taken it with her on her doomed flight.

The connection Stella feared broken had remained until the very end.

For a moment she gave way to unexpected tears, sobbing out nine months of guilt and fear, her own letter clasped close in her hand. Then she pulled out her hanky, dabbed her eyes and blew her nose. The extraordinary coincidence that this confirmation had come *today*, from a completely different source than she had imagined, filled her with warmth, and Elsie felt very close, not through any séance but right here in her kitchen.

In the immediate aftermath of the flight, Stella had told her little boys that Elsie had been very brave and was in heaven now, all the while wondering whether she believed her own words. That no longer seemed to matter. Elsie, with her strong faith, had certainly believed in eternal life, and all at once Stella was glad to grasp hold of that.

Perhaps one day the sea would give up more secrets.

Until it did, Elsie and she could both know peace, on either side of the watery divide.

Chapter Forty-Three

Helensburgh

That afternoon Alison sat with Matthew and Niccolo on a bench much further downstream, where the river widens at Helensburgh, and watched the same barge head out to the open sea. It was the first time Niccolo had left the house in weeks. Soon after coming to stay with them, he had collapsed with a high fever and that dreadful cough. The fever had finally abated but had left him weak, and he was still prone to long fits of coughing. 'His lungs will always be damaged,' Rob had said, examining him. 'I suspect he had severe pneumonia in the mountains last year and was lucky to pull through. But good food and plenty of rest will help him regain his strength.'

Rain or shine, Alison and Matthew strolled arm in arm along the foreshore each afternoon. Matthew always carried his field glasses to examine the ships sailing in and out of Glasgow in the deep channel nearer the far shore. This afternoon as Alison reached into the cupboard to pull out their coats, Niccolo came up behind her. 'May I accompany you?'

She hesitated and looked at him, so gaunt, so fragile. But the sun was shining and the fresh air would do him good. 'We won't walk far,' she said. And so now, after a brief stroll, they sat down on a bench. Matthew lit his pipe, sitting downwind so that the smoke wouldn't catch Niccolo's throat and set him coughing. 'Grand day today.'

'It is very cold.'

Alison glanced at him. Niccolo was well wrapped up in woollen jumper, thick overcoat and warm scarf and hat. 'We'll not be long,' she said. 'At least it's a dry air, not damp.'

They sat for a while in companionable silence, then Niccolo said, 'I received a letter today.'

'Oh yes?'

'It had taken a long time to reach me but it was from a former colleague in Naples. He also managed to escape to Paris. He wrote cautiously, but I understand that our other two colleagues are exiled in Ustica. Meanwhile he intends to restart our news-sheet, working from Paris. He writes to ask me to join him.'

Matthew took a long puff on his pipe. 'Will you?'

'No. I have only just found my children again. I do not wish to lose them. The thought of travel fills me with horror. Besides, I know I am not strong enough. You are very good to me, and I hope in time to earn some money and repay you. I had money in Italy, but it is stolen.'

Matthew clapped him on the shoulder. 'Don't you be worrying about money. There's plenty of time for that.'

Niccolo gazed across the river. 'You are kind. But I have been idle too long. It is time for me to speak up for my country.'

'What do you mean?' Alison asked.

'I am a journalist and I am free. I can write articles from my room here in Scotland about the evil that has taken hold in Italy. My friend in Paris will publish them and perhaps the newspapers here will publish them too.'

'Many of the newspapers here applaud Mussolini.'

'Only because they do not know the truth. I shall tell them. I am safe but many others are not. I must act.'

His voice was quiet but determined. Alison turned to her husband. 'Matthew, was there not an old typewriter in the loft when we were sorting things out? Could we bring it down, set Niccolo up with a desk and a writing space?'

'Grand idea.'

'Thank you. And please, do not fear, I shall reveal nothing that might endanger you or my children.'

Alison laughed. 'I think we're quite safe here. This is Helensburgh not Naples!'

'Mussolini's reach is great.'

She looked around the promenade, quiet in the wintry sunshine with just the odd dogwalker out for a stroll. How over-dramatic Niccolo was being! It was unthinkable that any danger could reach him here. His fear was simply the result of his traumatic experiences. She felt his thin body give a shiver and remembered how ill he had been. 'Let's go home and I'll put the kettle on.'

They stood up and began their gradual stroll back along the front. Looming clouds had drifted across the sun, and without that weak warmth the icy air was unforgiving. It was time to get Niccolo inside. But Matthew had stopped and raised his field glasses to look at a large ship that had come into view sailing towards Glasgow. 'Isn't she a beauty.'

'I suppose you can tell me what ship it is?'

The family regularly laughed at Matthew's encyclopaedic maritime knowledge. He scoured the shipping columns in the newspaper each day so always knew what was coming out and in, and interrogated Alex regularly about the schedules of the shipyards.

'That's a Blue Star liner, the *Arandora*. I hoped we would see her today. She's been running a freight and passenger service to South America, but she's on her way for a refit at Fairfield. She'll become a passenger cruise ship, just like my P&O ships. The only money these days is in the luxury cruise market and even that is slowing up. I know Alex is concerned.'

'There will always be work for someone of his expertise, no?' asked Niccolo.

'If there are no new ships then there are no safety tests, no sea trials. The future looks grim for shipbuilding. People are struggling already: that's why that Hunger March is setting off from Glasgow to London next week. What will happen if the yards close I hate to think.' He handed his glasses to Niccolo. 'Take a look. Isn't she splendid?'

Niccolo obliged but with little interest, and soon handed the glasses back to Matthew. 'Forgive me, but I hope not to set foot on another ship until I can return to an Italy free of Mussolini and his Blackshirts. Until that day comes, I remain here.' He gestured along the long, grey line of houses looking out across the water. 'For now, Scotland and Helensburgh are my home.'

Chapter Forty-Four

Pittenweem

Corran glanced through the small sitting-room window and wrapped her thick college scarf around her neck. It was dry, but heavy clouds were scudding quickly across that pewter February sky, and she knew the bitter north wind would slice through her the moment she stepped outside her cosy little cottage. She popped her head round the kitchen door where Pearl, the local girl who came in to help, was at work. 'That's Max down for his nap. I'll just be half an hour or so.'

'Right you are, Mrs Rutherford.'

She picked up her canvas shopping bag and opened the door. Bracing. Her house faced directly onto the shore, and she loved the life she had created here over the past eight months. She loved her terraced cottage with its wooden beams and simple furnishings, and the little book-lined study overlooking the sea in which she wrote her novels and practised her Italian. She loved the mornings she spent with Max, seeing to household tasks and shopping, and the afternoons when she worked while Pearl looked after him. She loved the people she had met, friendly enough but slightly in awe of her status as an authoress and content to let her keep herself to herself. Most of all, she loved the feel of the wind and the sea in all weathers, as she walked round the harbour watching the fishing boats or strode out on the pier, Max wrapped tight in a shawl and tucked inside her coat.

It was hard to believe that none of it had been her own idea.

Since those bewildering weeks last spring when she had agreed to work for Katherine's brother, everything had progressed remarkably smoothly. They had set her up in this house in Pittenweem —'there are some people nearby we will want you to get to know, in time'— and requested that she brush up on her Italian. A publishing contract for two more books arrived, and an adequate salary was paid monthly into her bank account. Every few weeks she met a man named Lewis on the pier for a handover of documents – the reports and letters she had translated from Italian, none of them appearing particularly interesting. She couldn't quite understand it – surely there were plenty of people in London with better Italian than her. Why on earth did they have to engage in this subterfuge? She suspected they were testing her out. But most of the time her life was pleasant and simple, and to her surprise she hardly missed Oxford or Arthur at all.

She strolled at a leisurely pace along the side of the harbour, busy with fishing boats, before turning down to the pier that stretched out, a long curved finger pointing out to the North Sea and all that lay beyond. She glanced at her watch. Still a few minutes early, but he was always here first.

Glad of the shelter offered by the high wall on one side of the pier, she walked out to join him. The further out she ventured, the higher the waves crashed, throwing up spray that she did her best to avoid. She could see a figure standing by the lighthouse right at the end, too far away to make out his features but she knew it was him. Their interactions were always brief, and today would be no different. She reached into the canvas bag and pulled out an envelope, exchanging it for the one he offered to her. It was thicker than usual.

'All fine?'

'Yes.'

She expected him to leave, but instead he took out two cigarettes, stepped into the lee of the wall and lit them both at once, offering one to her. They stood watching the white crests whipping up out to sea until he said, 'We're ready to move to the next stage.'

'The next stage?'

'Yes. The local community has accepted you now. There is someone we want you to befriend: a lady living just outside St Andrews who has links to the fascist movement. All the information is in the envelope I have just given you.' He had barely begun his cigarette but tossed it away to be hurled out to sea by the wind. 'Familiarise yourself with it, and await further instruction.' He touched his hat, turned and walked away.

Corran finished her own cigarette with a hand that was not quite steady, then stepped out nearer the edge of the pier into the blast of the wind. She watched him retreat towards the town. When Katherine Jones had first introduced her brother in the garden of St Hilda's, she had expected something like this to happen straight away, but so much time had passed she had almost come to believe that all they wanted from her was to improve her Italian and translate a few mundane reports.

It looked as if that was about to change.

As she turned slowly and made her way back along the pier, she heard the low throbbing sound of an aeroplane and looked up to watch it hug the coastline. There was an airfield at nearby Leuchars: it had probably come from there. Every time she saw an aeroplane she thought about Elsie, and suddenly she wished she could have told adventure-loving Elsie about the conversation she had just had. How intrigued she would have been, and how enthusiastic! But even if Elsie had been alive Corran couldn't have breathed a word. Not even her family knew why she was now based here in east Fife, or the true reason she was working hard to improve her Italian. She had told Luisa she wanted a new hobby.

Thought of Luisa led her to Niccolo, and his passionate conviction that fascism was the next great threat their world must fight. Was Corran herself going to be drawn into that fight?

She thrust her hands deep into her coat pockets and breathed in the salty air. Whatever came next, she was ready.

Author's Note

I've always known about Elsie Mackay and her attempt to fly the Atlantic. I heard about her from my father, whose first ever car journey as a tiny baby in January 1928 took place in her silver Rolls-Royce. 'It's the only time I was ever in a Rolls-Royce,' he told me aged eighty, when I recorded many of his stories.

His parents Donald John (DJ) and Pat Morrison lived in Ballantrae, the little town beside Glenapp, where DJ was the local doctor. Complications with my father's birth meant he was born in Edinburgh (not in the Rolls-Royce!) under the care of an expert gynaecologist friend of DJ's. Elsie later sent her car and chauffeur to bring them home.

Ten weeks to the day after my father was born – and Elsie surely held him in her arms during those ten weeks – she set off on her final flight. My grandfather was doctor to the Glenapp family and was one of the very few people who knew the secret, as Elsie had consulted him about the medical aspects of the flight. When everything finally came to light, Lord Inchcape was furious with DJ for not having informed him of his daughter's plans, but DJ was adamant he couldn't tell one patient another patient's business. Nor did he reveal the secret to his wife.

Rob and Stella are most definitely not my grandparents DJ and Pat, but as ever I owe gratitude to the real people who provide the starting point for the fiction – and most of all to my father, Peter Morrison, for telling me about Elsie in the first place. How I wish he could read this book.

The known facts about Elsie Mackay and Captain Hinchliffe's flight end with the final sighting of their plane 170 miles out to sea, and the piece of undercarriage washed up in County Donegal nine months later. Everything in this novel directly relating to the flight up until that final sighting is based on fact. Beyond that, I had to decide what might have happened. I have chosen to believe that they nearly made it. In researching the flight, I relied heavily on the extensive newspaper coverage of the time, particularly *The Times* and *The Scotsman* but also a wide range of regional, national and international titles, and on two books, *A Flight Too Far: The Story of Elsie Mackay of Glenapp* by Jack Hunter (2008) and *West Over The Waves: The Final Flight of Elsie Mackay* by Jayne Baldwin (2017) with its hugely informative appendix 'The Flight' by Quentin Wilson, which includes a particularly intriguing reference to a wrecked plane spotted in the Atlantic 400 miles from Newfoundland in August 1928.

I also drew on the first-hand accounts of other pioneering aviators of the same period, including Charles Lindbergh, Amelia Earhart and Beryl Markham. The ending I suggest for *Endeavour*, with ice eventually causing the failure of the engine, is similar to that which brought down Beryl Markham's *Messenger* in Cape Breton as she became the first person to fly solo east to west in 1936.

Fascination with the story of *Endeavour* continued. Emilie Hinchliffe's book *The Return of Captain W. G. R. Hinchliffe*, published in 1930 by The Psychic Press, offers an alternative fate for the flight and a detailed account of her supernatural communication with her husband. Some American newspapers suggested that the whole thing had been rigged to allow Elsie and Captain Hinchliffe to elope together. A few years later Hinchliffe's friend Colonel Henderson revealed his own story of being on board the SS *Barrabool*, unaware that the flight was underway, and being awoken in the night by an agitated Hinchliffe, as narrated in *The Airmen Who Would Not Die* by John G. Fuller.

While Elsie Mackay and Captain Hinchliffe and their families are real people, the members of the extended Rutherford family are entirely fictional.

Other useful books included *Fascist Voices: An Intimate History of Mussolini's Italy* by Christopher Duggan and George Blake's 1935 novel *The Shipbuilders*, as well as *A Shipbuilding History 1750-1932 (Alexander Stephen and Sons)*. The engine shed from the Alexander Stephen yard at Linthouse has been rebuilt as part of the Scottish Maritime Museum in Irvine and is well worth a visit, as is the Fairfield Heritage museum in Govan. The Tenement House in Glasgow offers a wonderful insight into tenement living in the first half of the twentieth century.

I'm grateful to all those who have supported and helped me as I've brought Elsie's story to the page. Enormous thanks to my marvellous agent, Jenny Brown, and to the whole team at Allison & Busby, particularly editor Lesley Crooks, Susie Dunlop, Josie Rushin, Ffion Hâf, Christina Griffiths and Daniel Scott. Working with you is a real pleasure.

Thank you too to the writing community in Edinburgh, including the Edinburgh Writers' Forum, and to Susan, Jim and Clare for good advice, writerly friendship and chats over food and wine.

Thank you to everyone at Davidson's Mains Parish Church for

your support and encouragement and for helping me this year to have more space for writing. To God be the glory.

Above all, my love and my gratitude go to David, Elizabeth and Alastair, who put up with my random enthusiasms and come along on associated excursions, and who make life so very much richer. Thank you.

Flora Johnston worked for over twenty years in museums and heritage interpretation, including at the National Museums of Scotland, which has greatly influenced the historical fiction she now writes. *The Paris Peacemakers* delved into the lives of characters picking up the pieces in the aftermath of the First World War, and their stories continue in *The Endeavour of Elsie Mackay*. She lives in Edinburgh.

florajohnston.com
@florajowriter